She felt suddenly as though she could not breathe. This was the moment. It felt as though time had stopped around them.

"The wind is certainly brisk," she said shyly. "It is cold and late. Soon it will be dark. Let us go to the cave together."

He said nothing, and her heart fell to her slippers. She dared peek up at him and saw him frowning, saw the battle of hope, disbelief, and acute longing in his face. That gave her courage.

Reaching up, she caressed his cheek with her hand. "Let us go to the cave," she said, her voice low and throaty. "Let us have tonight before we face our future."

Realm of Light

The conclusion to
Reign of Shadows and *Shadow War*

REALM OF LIGHT

DEBORAH CHESTER

ACE BOOKS, NEW YORK

This book is an Ace original edition,
and has never been previously published.

REALM OF LIGHT

An Ace Book / published by arrangement with
the author

PRINTING HISTORY
Ace edition / October 1997

The Putnam Berkley World Wide Web site address is
http://www.berkley.com

Make sure to check out *PB Plug,*
the science fiction/fantasy newsletter, at
http://www.pbplug.com

ISBN: 0-441-00480-6

ACE®
Ace Books are published by The Berkley Publishing Group,
a member of Penguin Putnam Inc.,
200 Madison Avenue, New York, NY 10016.
ACE and the "A" design are trademarks
belonging to Charter Communications, Inc.

PRINTED IN THE UNITED STATES OF AMERICA

10 9 8 7 6 5 4 3 2 1

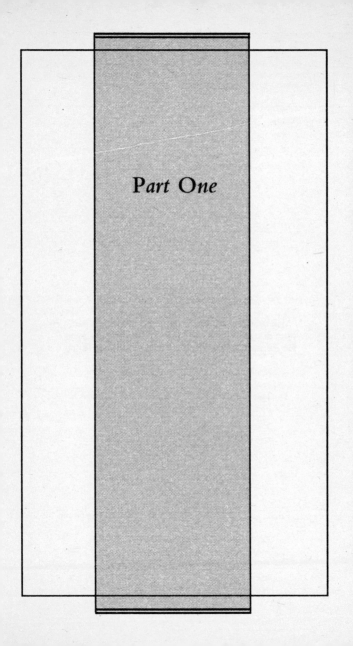

Part One

Chapter One

GLOOM SHROUDED THE cavern beneath the Temple of Gault. Torches flared everywhere, yet their ruddy light revealed little. Hurrying through the shadows in the wake of Sergeant Balter, the Empress Elandra felt as though she walked in a dream. Her life had been turned completely upside down. She was a refugee now, with no home, no guards, no protector, and possibly . . . no husband. She had come here for safety, but this was no sanctuary.

Perhaps fifteen guardsmen in armor and crimson cloaks milled about, engaged in various tasks. A couple of servants, pale-faced with fear, crammed provisions into saddlebags under the gimlet eye of a square-faced sergeant. Half the guardsmen were checking saddles and gear. The rest were piling stones from what looked like dismantled benches across a doorway in the distance. The remaining granite benches stood in an eerie semicircle about an altar surrounded by empty copper cauldrons tipped on their sides. All the men moved with haste, but there was no panic, and relatively little disorder.

The torchlight flickered up the soot-blackened walls, casting shifting, ruddy illumination over the scene and glinting off the rolling white of the horses' eyes, the sharp rowels of men's spurs, and the wire-wrapped hilts of swords as their scabbards were buckled to saddles. The air smelled of sweat—from horse and man—a pungent, honest odor overlaying a lingering, cloyed fragrance of incense and death.

Glancing again at the abandoned altar, the Empress Elandra shivered and drew her cloak more tightly about her shoulders. This was a forbidden place. Blasphemy seemed to crawl upon the walls, and no priests were in sight. She stumbled after the sergeant, consumed with exhaustion, finding herself stupidly near tears.

It was just reaction, she told herself, struggling to maintain her composure. She had spent the night fleeing for her life from both creatures of the darkness and savage Madrun invaders who were now looting and burning the palace.

Her home . . . ablaze in the night.

She choked again, and the sergeant glanced back at her in swift concern.

"It's not far, Majesty. Stay close to me."

She nodded and quickened her step although her legs felt leaden. They were heading to a part of the cavern where officers were standing among haphazard stacks of boxes, scroll cases, and misshapen bundles. No doubt these were the scant items that had been salvaged from the palace. Elandra herself had managed to save nothing. She had only the dirty, torn clothes she was wearing beneath her cloak and the magical topaz jewel that she carried in a small embroidered bag strung around her neck. Even her dagger had been given away to the guardsman Caelan E'non, who had saved her life and brought her safely to this place beneath the temple.

At the thought of Caelan, however, her fear returned. She glanced back over her shoulder, but did not see him for the confusion around her. A horse, overly excited by the commotion, broke away and went shying sideways through the men, kicking and squealing before it was brought under control again.

"Majesty!" the sergeant said in alarm, holding her back.

Elandra looked at him, and hastily he released her arm. His square, honest face turned as red as his cloak.

"Forgive me, Majesty," he said, aghast. "I thought only of your Majesty's safety."

Wearily she thought of the imperial protocols. A man like him could have his hand cut off for having dared touched her. She was an empress sovereign—by law, equal to the emperor himself. By law, she could appear only in the midst of her ladies in waiting, with chancellors in attendance, her protector at her back, and her own specially picked guardsmen surrounding her. But the Madrun barbarians had ended imperial law tonight. The empire was falling, and she did not know whether anything would ever follow protocol again.

Impatiently she shook her head. "You are forgiven, Sergeant. Please, escort me to my husband without delay."

He saluted her. "Yes, Majesty. At once!"

They strode on, Balter with his chin jutting at the military angle and his hand correctly on his sword hilt, she with her gown a mess and her hair a tangle down her back. Her eyes were burning. Fatigue lapped at her, a natural reaction after the stress and exertion she'd undergone, but she wondered if the shadow that had attacked her and rendered her unconscious for a time had done her more harm than she suspected. She still felt strangely unwell and shaken from the encounter. If Caelan had not been with her to protect her . . .

With a fresh shiver of alarm, she drove away thoughts of the Traulander. There was no time to think of him now, no time to wonder. He was no ordinary man, of that she was certain. Just remembering his confrontation with the evil priest Sien sent chills through her. Lord Sien had used dark magic. That alone was terrifying. But Caelan had countered with something else, something indescribable. For an instant, he had even vanished before her eyes, as though he was never there.

And when he reappeared a moment later, it had been as though he had come back from a far, far place. Ice crystals had glittered in his hair and eyebrows. His blue eyes had been stony, merciless, implacable. In his eyes, she had looked for the man she knew and had not found him. Until then, she had trusted him completely, believing in his loyalty and devotion without question. He had risked his own life to save hers. He had brought her here to safety against all odds. Yet in the blink of an eye, he had unleashed powers of the unknown, becoming a stranger who frightened her. The wrath in his face as he turned on Lord Sien had been terrible to see, yet Sien was already defeated, already cowering.

If nothing else this horrible night, she was glad to see Sien the traitor slapped down. He deserved far worse, but his punishment would be by Kostimon's order, no one else's. When that order came, she would rejoice.

Ahead, Kostimon's voice rose in fierce argument. She looked past the sergeant and could not see her husband clearly for the officers surrounding him. Kostimon's voice rose and cracked in anger.

Sergeant Balter stopped a short distance behind the officers—one wearing gold and one crimson—and cleared his throat. "Er, Captain—"

"Get the men ready," the captain said without glancing around.

Balter cleared his throat again. "Captain, the empress is here."

The officer whirled around, his mouth dropping open in astonishment.

Elandra recognized Captain Vysal despite the dirty bandage that swathed half his face. His breastplate was splattered with dried blood, and his cloak hung in tatters. A long weal ran down his left forearm, and he was covered with dust and grime.

Glad relief filled his face. He saluted her. "Majesty! Thank Gault you are safe."

At his words, the officer in red and the emperor broke off their shouting match. The officer, a general with gold stripes creating a magnificent chevron across the back of his crimson cloak, spun around. Beyond him, Kostimon was sitting on top of a box, wearing armor also splattered with dried blood, and a cloak of imperial purple lined with red silk. One side of his face was smudged with dirt, and his white curls were standing on end as though he'd been jerking his hands through them.

Staring at her, Kostimon rose to his feet. His yellow eyes widened in confusion. "Fauvina," he whispered hoarsely. "You are safe."

Elandra's heart broke at the slip, and she glanced quickly at the officers to see if they heard it. Of course they had. Their faces were impassive; their eyes held nothing.

Worriedly she walked forward to her husband and took his gnarled, dirty hands in hers.

"Fauvina," he said, smiling at her in pathetic gratitude, "you have come."

"I am here," she said unsteadily. Fear made her cold. If the shock of tonight's attack had broken Kostimon's mind, what was to become of them? "Come and sit down."

But Kostimon had his purple boots well planted, and he refused to move. "You have brought the army from Gialta?" he asked eagerly. "A counterforce, to smash the enemy?"

With all her heart she wished she had. But she could not bring herself to lie, not even to comfort him. "No," she said softly. "I am Elandra, and I come alone."

His fingers tightened on her wrist, digging in. "Ela," he said suddenly in a changed tone. "Of course. Ela!"

"Yes," she said, forcing a smile through tears. "Your Ela."

The emperor's yellow eyes narrowed and grew fierce. Pushing her away, he advanced on the general.

"Paz!" he shouted. "You damned lazy incompetent! You told me she was dead, that all the women were dead—taken in the first assault. You never checked, did you?"

The general's mouth opened, but he said nothing. His eyes met Elandra's shocked ones, only to slide away. "The reports came to me. I had no reason to doubt them—"

"What else have you lied to me about?" Kostimon demanded furiously. "Persuading me to break off the defense, to run and hide like a peasant afraid of the dark. Bah! Vysal, tell me the truth. What is left of our forces?"

"Sir!" Snapping to attention, Vysal said, "They were scattered in the initial assaults, and deployed in small pockets of resistance."

"What the hell is this?" Kostimon roared. "I know how the Madrun devils fight. They surround, cut off, and massacre. Are you telling me the Guard cooperated like sheep?"

"It was by your order, Majesty," Vysal said nervously.

Red flared in Kostimon's face. He raised his fists. "I gave no such order! What is—"

"You have been betrayed on all sides," Elandra broke in. "Your dispatches were false. Your most trusted advisers were either misled or have joined the conspiracy. Many of the Guard have gone over to the enemy rather than be slaughtered."

Kostimon turned on her, and the anger in his face sagged away. "Would you also lie to me, my dear?" he asked more quietly. "Have you been a part of this?"

She gasped, too outraged at first to deny it. She had come this far, had escaped fire and demons and the attacks of men. She felt as though she had been running all night, and she would not be insulted now.

"It is true," General Paz said swiftly. "She has conspired from the first with Prince Tirhin against your Majesty. They plan an alliance with—"

"That is not true!" Elandra said. "How dare you accuse me of such wickedness?"

The general met her angry gaze without flinching. A sneer curled his thin lips. "The oldest story in the world. A son, impatient for his inheritance. A young wife, beautiful and alluring, bound to a husband so much older. Is it not natural they should turn to each other?"

Elandra found herself shaking with fury. The top of her head felt icy cold, while the rest of her was on fire. That someone could stand before her and utter these bold lies to her face was unbelievable. And yet the cruelties of her childhood had taught her how to hide hurt, how to keep her face a mask when she had to, how to stiffen her lips to keep them from trembling, how to fight back tears. She could see Kostimon listening, could see the calculating shift in his gaze as he began to wonder. She wanted to grip him by the arms and shake him. Was he under some spell that he could swallow such slander? But she must control her emotions if she was to survive. She must think, and quickly, in order to find some way to convince him of her innocence.

"Why have I risked life and limb to come here to you, if what the general says is true?" she asked.

"No doubt she has led the Madruns directly here to our hiding place," the general said.

"Then we have even less time to make our escape," Vysal said.

Tears stung Elandra's eyes. Was the loyal captain now turning against her too? Was there no one to believe her?

She glanced about for Hovet, knowing she could appeal to the gruff old protector. But for the first time, she realized he was missing. Her gaze shot around the cavern, darting from face to face, but his sour, weathered countenance was nowhere to be seen. If he was not here, neither at the emperor's heels nor within the emperor's sight, then he must be dead. Regret passed through her. For all his surly manners, he had been a faithful man, true and brave all his life.

"Ela," the emperor said harshly, "why do you come to me like this, without your attendants, without your guard? Where is your protector?"

"Where is yours?" she retorted.

Her defiance reddened his face again. "Hovet died in battle, saving my life," the emperor replied, his tone a rebuke.

"Rander is also dead," she told him. "My life I owe to him and to another guardsman who saw me safely across the compound."

"No one could get across," General Paz said. "We saw it overrun. And her part of the palace was on fire. I tell your Majesty that this miraculous arrival of the empress now is part of some devious trick. Do not trust her—"

"Take care, Paz," Kostimon snapped. "You are accusing your empress of infamy. Without proof, you will see your tongue cut out if you continue."

Suddenly pale, the general shut his mouth and frowned.

Despite Kostimon's rebuke, Elandra knew the general would go on dripping poison into the emperor's ear at every opportunity. He was anxious to conceal his own duplicity and incompetence by accusing her. That he should even be allowed to utter his slander infuriated her; by now his head should have been struck from his shoulders. But Kostimon remained lenient with him. That in itself was a warning to her that she must do something to thwart Paz's deviltry once and for all.

Lifting her chin, she said, "I will submit to truth-light, if the general will do the same."

Consternation flashed across all the men's faces.

"Ela!" the emperor said in exasperation. "Would you act like a peasant on top of all our problems? You stand here in rags, your hair looking like—like I know not what—and announce you will submit to examination? Are you guilty, that you should abase yourself this way?"

"No, I am innocent," she replied defiantly. "And I am impatient with this hypocrisy. Why not throw the truth-light over me?

If this coward is allowed to denounce me, why can I not prove my innocence and loyalty?"

"An empress does not need to prove her—"

"Yes, yes, so says the law, but you listen to him, Kostimon!" she said in fresh anger. "You listen! Is there humiliation to exceed that? I will endure the examination." She swung around and pointed at the general. "Will he?"

Paz glared at her. "Am I not of high rank?" he retorted. "Why should I submit when—"

"Silence!" the emperor shouted. "Vysal, pass the word for Lord Sien to attend me immediately."

Vysal saluted and hurried away.

The general glared at Elandra, then sniffed in disdain. He focused his gaze on the far wall, where ancient gruesome faces were carved in the stone like silent watchers.

She started to say that Lord Sien would not be available, but something in Kostimon's expression silenced her.

The emperor turned away from Elandra and began to pace back and forth among the stacks of boxes and bundles. She glimpsed money bags and jewelry cases of exquisite woods. Clothes chests with travel straps stood nearby. Even though everything had been hastily assembled and was far from representing Kostimon's usual amount of baggage when he traveled, there was far too much for someone fleeing into exile. She saw no pack animals, no servants. Who was to carry it all?

She counted the milling men and horses and realized there were not even enough mounts for everyone. Who, then, was to be left behind?

Elandra stood there, tired and dirty, and began to understand that she was now a refugee. Her home was burning. She had no servants, no clothing save what was on her back, no goods, no money or jewels, no property.

All of it suddenly overwhelmed her. She saw again faithful Rander Malk, so anxious to please in his new post as her protector, dying almost at her feet as the shadow demon strangled him. She felt again the heat of the flames and smelled the thick smoke filling her bedchamber. Her ears rang with the war cries of the Madruns as Caelan fought them down the stairs. She remembered the hideous touch of the shadow's fingers upon her throat, the metallic taste of blood on her tongue where she bit herself in her struggles.

Her lips trembled, and she pressed her fingers to them, swaying as she fought her own exhausted emotions.

Sergeant Balter came running up and saluted the general. "Five minutes until the men are ready, sir."

Paz nodded. "The emperor's horse?"

"Yes, sir. I've attended to it myself. And my own mount will go to the empress."

Elandra swung around, the tears on her face forgotten in her gratitude. "Sergeant—"

"Nonsense," Paz snapped as though she had not spoken. "We need all the able-bodied fighting men possible. Keep the assigned order, Sergeant. Make no changes. And tie on the emperor's saddlebags for him."

"Sir!" Saluting, Balter cast Elandra a swift, apologetic glance before he strode to the emperor's side.

Still sunk in thought, Kostimon looked up at the sergeant. "Lord Sien has come?"

"No, sir. Which saddlebags have you selected to take?"

"Am I to run for my life like a pauper?" Kostimon roared loudly enough to make everyone pause and look. "Great Gault, is it not enough that I was convinced to fall back when I should have held? Is it not enough that I was persuaded to save myself when my men have died without me? Is it not enough that I abandoned wife and concubines for expediency? Is it not enough that I cower down here in a hole like a damned mouse while those murdering brutes pillage and sack my own palace? And now, am I to flee without the means of preserving anything I have built all these centuries? Am I to run like a beetle seeking a new crevice, without my treasures, without my maps, without my literature, without my possessions? Be damned to you! I shall not go!"

"Perhaps, Majesty," Balter ventured nervously, "if each man were to strap one item behind his saddle—"

"No," Paz said. "Begging your Majesty's pardon, but fighting men cannot be burdened with nonessentials—"

"Nonessentials!" the emperor shouted. "Murdeth and Fury, man, why don't you say *I* am a nonessential? These foolish objections do nothing but delay us. Where is Sien? Sergeant, see that he comes at once."

Saluting, Balter hurried away as though glad to escape.

Vysal reappeared, hurrying through the cluster of guardsmen. He looked increasingly pale beneath his bandage. Concerned for him and his injury, Elandra wished the others would have more consideration than to send him running back and forth like an errand boy.

"Majesty," he said, saluting the emperor and sounding out of breath. "Lord Sien is—is not at leisure to come. And I think the Madruns are in the temple."

Kostimon received this news with a deepening scowl, but Paz stepped forward.

"I told you she would lead them to us, and she has!" Paz said, glaring at Elandra as he spoke. "There is no time to spare. Captain, mount the troops."

Vysal swung away and beckoned to Balter, who came running back. "Mount the troops."

"Sir!" Saluting, Balter spun about and bawled orders at the men with such vigor his voice echoed from the ceiling.

The men scrambled to line up, each one standing at attention with his hand on his mount's bridle. Fifteen men, not counting the emperor or her or the officers, and only twelve horses. Elandra counted them again to be sure, and with a sinking heart wondered who was to be left behind.

Balter's experienced eye ran along his meager troops, and he nodded in curt satisfaction, then walked over to personally check the emperor's saddle. He tightened the girths another notch, retied the strings holding the heavy saddlebags, and next turned his attention to the general's mount.

By the time he'd finished this, the emperor was coming with Paz in tow.

"Mount up!" Balter shouted, and the men with horses obeyed. The rest stood by, impassive and ready for war, their gauntleted hands resting on their sword hilts.

"Here, Majesty," the sergeant said to Elandra, leading a raw-boned sorrel up to her. He handed her the reins. "I'll shorten the stirrups for you."

"Thank you," she said.

But the general pointed his whip at the sergeant. "Stop that!" he commanded. "Captain Vysal, withdraw this man."

The captain's face tightened visibly beneath the bandage. It was plain to Elandra how loathe he was to become caught in this conflict. The guardsmen's eyes were shifting in the torchlight, watchful. From her father, Elandra knew that such disagreements among the commanding officers always led to a loss of morale in the fighting men. They could not afford to be seen bickering, yet Kostimon was making no effort to stop it. Did she dare try to intervene?

"Vysal!" the general said sharply. "You heard my order. Obey it."

Saluting in response to the general's command, Captain Vysal snapped his fingers at the sergeant, who stepped back.

Paz glared at Elandra first, then at the emperor. "I'll leave not one able-bodied man behind. I need fighters, not wailing women."

Astonished, Elandra stared at him and wondered if he had gone mad. "I am your empress," she said in outrage.

"You are a traitor!" he shouted, red-faced. He jerked the reins from her hand, making the sorrel horse shy back nervously. "You could not have crossed the palace compound alone, by natural means, and arrived here alive. That means you are in league with the enemy. You led them here. You have betrayed us!"

Furious, Elandra looked at the emperor, who stood frowning and silent. "Will you not defend me?" she asked.

Kostimon frowned at the general. "Say no more against the empress."

Elandra waited for more, but Kostimon fell silent again. In astonishment, she realized he intended to say nothing else in her defense. Did he think it enough, this mild rebuke? As support of her, it was paltry indeed.

Her face went stiff; her eyes burned. She clenched her fists down at her sides, hiding them in the folds of her skirts. So she was to be abandoned, like unwanted chattel. The promises, the ceremonial words, the crowning itself were all as dead leaves blown away in the wind.

She wanted to rage, to throw things, to weep. But she must

not give way to her emotions now. She must act like an empress, not a woman.

"Sergeant Balter," she said quietly, her voice so tightly regulated it sounded dead. "I shall not require your horse."

Frowning in dismay, Balter took the reins from the smirking General Paz. The sergeant's face told all that lay in his heart. "But, Majesty—"

Elandra's gaze moved to Kostimon, old and half-confused, his mind alternating between bouts of imperial temper and indecision. He remained emperor still, but now he ruled a lost empire. He was no longer capable of defending himself or her or his domain.

Fresh tears burned her eyes, but she swiftly blinked them back.

"Go quickly, husband," she said. "Ride to safety while there is still a chance. I bid you well."

Looking bewildered, Kostimon snapped his fingers impatiently. "Get on the horse. There is no time for such—"

"You have an empire to defend," she said, trying to keep her tone steady and noble while Paz's smirk widened. "As the general has said, it's swordsmen you need beside you, not an ineffectual woman."

"Don't be absurd," Kostimon said. "Fauvina—I mean, Ela, come here at once."

But she turned her back on him, not certain she could control her composure much longer. She walked away, ignoring his call, her head held high and her back straight.

Chapter Two

"Who serves the empress sovereign?" called out a strong, masculine voice over the general noise.

Sudden silence fell over the cavern. Men's heads turned. They craned to see.

Recognizing Caelan's voice, Elandra stopped in her tracks and stood still. Her breath came raggedly in her throat. She dared not glance back at the emperor.

"What?" said Kostimon from behind her. "What? Who said that? Who speaks?"

"Who serves the empress sovereign?" Caelan called out again. His voice rang off the walls. "Without both emperor and empress to rule, this land is fallen. Which man of you will leave her behind? Which man of you is both traitor and coward?"

A growl of assent broke out among the soldiers. Sergeant Balter and Captain Vysal exchanged glances, then looked at the emperor. Elandra herself stepped aside as Caelan came striding forward from the shadows.

He carried his drawn sword in his hand. His cloak swirled about his ankles with every step. As he walked into the circle of torchlight, he looked somehow taller, leaner, and more fierce than he had ever appeared before. His blue eyes blazed with a wrath that was all the more terrible because of its coldness. Elandra saw something bleak and deadly in his face. It was the same look he had worn when he refused to serve as her protector. Yet here he came, to save her once again.

Triumph blazed inside her, and her head lifted higher in renewed confidence. This man served her. No matter what he said, he was her protector.

The soldiers parted at his approach. Even Balter stepped

back. Caelan strode past Vysal, then past Elandra without glancing at her. A few feet short of the emperor, he stopped and stood towering over Kostimon, fierce, proud, and grim.

The emperor stepped back. "Who are you? How dare you bring a drawn sword into my presence? Hovet—"

Kostimon's voice choked off abruptly. He glared a moment, his jaw working. Chagrin warred with anger in his face.

Then his gaze snapped to General Paz. "Who is this man? How dare he speak to me unbidden?"

The general glared at Captain Vysal. "Identify this man at once."

"You know me," Caelan said before Vysal could respond. Caelan's gaze never left the emperor's. His youthful strength and vigor made Kostimon look shrunken and almost feeble.

Glaring, Caelan said, "You know by what right I speak unbidden. I brought your Majesty warning of this attack, and you heeded it not. I told your Majesty the Madruns were coming, and you ignored me. You had time to send for your armies, but you did not. I told your Majesty there were traitors close to you, men who would open the secret ways of the palace to your enemies. You sat and did nothing. *Nothing,* until now when your throne has been shattered and your palace burns. Your Imperial Guard has been massacred, and you bleat like the coward you are."

The emperor's face turned nearly as white as his hair. He glared at Caelan. "That is your death sentence, knave! You cannot talk so and live. Sergeant! Kill this man, who dares insult me to my face!"

Elandra drew in a sharp breath. She wanted to cry out in protest, but she dared not speak. Violence glowered in the faces about her. Every man's hand gripped the hilt of his weapon. The wrong move, the wrong word would set off a fight like a torch thrown among straw.

"Sergeant!" Kostimon roared. "Kill him!"

Balter did not move. He stood at attention, as rigid as stone.

Silence spread over them all, broken only by the soft jingle of bridles and the stamping of the horses. None of the guardsmen moved. Captain Vysal's fingers tightened on the hilt of his sword until his knuckles were white, but not even he drew his sword.

Kostimon looked around at them all, his face strained and disbelieving. "Is this how I am served?" he asked hoarsely. "In my final hours, is this the loyalty I command?"

"Majesty," Balter replied, "lead us honorably and we will serve you honorably."

A cheer rose from the men.

General Paz cleared his throat and let his gaze slide toward the door. Then he stepped to the emperor's side and drew his sword. "If no one else will maintain order, then I shall, Majesty. To prove my loyalty to you, I shall kill this knave as you have commanded."

"No!" Vysal called, but too late.

Paz launched himself at Caelan with a swing of his sword. Although Caelan stood with his own weapon drawn, he was not in a fighting stance. Nor did he look prepared for the sudden attack.

Watching in horror, Elandra choked off a scream.

But Caelan was not run through. At seemingly the very last moment before Paz's sword struck him, he shifted his feet—quick and light—and swung up his sword to meet the general's.

Steel hit steel with a resounding clang. Two quick exchanges, and Caelan's sword tip flashed swiftly.

The general's sword went flying across the floor . . . with the general's hand still attached to it.

Now Elandra did scream, her cry rising with the general's own.

Paz stood there transfixed, staring at the stump of his right wrist. Blood spurted freely.

Shuddering, Elandra shut her eyes and turned away. It was so horrible she thought she would be sick. Again and again, the sight of that swift clean cut of steel flashed through er mind as though it would never fade.

Frightened shouts broke out, and she turned back in time to see the general sag to his knees, then crumple bonelessly to the floor. Black fluid now gushed from the stump—not blood, but instead something that stank most foully.

"Get back!" Vysal commanded. Throwing out his arm, he held Kostimon back. "Majesty, take care!"

"What in Gault's name is it?" Kostimon asked.

Caelan approached the body, which now lay facedown on the ground. Crouching beside it, he started to dip his finger in the black liquid.

"Caelan, no!" Elandra shouted in horror.

At the last second, he withdrew his hand. His face wrinkled in disgust, and he jumped back with a quickness that alarmed all of them.

"Possessed," Caelan said. "If General Paz was human once, he is no longer. Everyone, stay back."

Ashen, the emperor looked around for Elandra and beckoned to her. She ran to him, and he gripped her hand hard in his.

"Stay close to me," he said.

"What can it be?"

"I think I can guess," he said grimly and shifted his gaze to Vysal. "Captain, we now have danger from within as well as without. In minutes, there will be creatures spawned in that blood. Creatures none of us wish to meet."

Blinking, Vysal spun around. "Men!" he shouted. "Form ranks. Those who are mounted, go in front. Those on foot, assemble at the rear. Draw your weapons and say your prayers."

The sergeant brought up both the emperor's horse and his own for Elandra.

She stared at Kostimon in rising urgency, caught up in the general tension and fear. "But where are we going? We are trapped in this cavern, with no way out except the way we entered. And the Madruns are waiting."

Kostimon touched her cheek briefly with his fingertips. "I am sorry for what was said a moment ago, my dear," he said softly. "Too many masks—too many betrayals. How could I doubt your integrity for even a moment?"

This was the man she knew, alert and clear-eyed once again. Grateful for his apology, she caught his gnarled hand and held it pressed against her cheek for a moment. "Husband, I—"

"Later." He pulled away. "You there, assist the empress."

Balter held the stirrup for her, then boosted her up as though she weighed nothing. Hastily she arranged her skirts across the saddle. She was not dressed for riding astride, but that hardly mattered now. Clutching the reins in her gloved fingers, she heard a feeble sound come from the direction of the general's body.

Newly afraid, Elandra glanced at Paz. The corpse lay in a spreading pool of blackness. It should have stopped bleeding long since, but the loathsome fluid still poured from the wound. Ripples now spread across the surface of the pool, although it was too shallow to contain anything. With horrified fascination, Elandra saw movement as though something was taking shape there.

"He is not dead!" she cried.

"Hush. He is," Caelan said. "Hurry." He slapped the rump of her mount.

Only by reining back hard did she prevent the startled animal from bolting. All the horses were snorting now, stamping and backing away from the corpse. Fear spread quickly through the cavern.

It took both Vysal and Caelan to push the emperor onto his horse while Balter struggled to hold the spirited animal still. Elandra had never seen Kostimon look so physically weak, or have so much difficulty mounting. When he was finally in the saddle, he leaned over, gasping for breath. She saw his hands shake on the reins, and she was afraid he would die then and there.

She reached out to him, wanting to help him, but his mount skittered to one side, snorting and tossing its head.

"Lord Sien," Kostimon said, managing to straighten. "Where is Lord Sien? I need him."

It was Caelan who looked up and answered: "The priest cannot come to you."

"I need him!" Kostimon insisted. Glaring, he glanced around. "Sien! Come to me!"

"He will not come!" Caelan said more forcefully, gripping the emperor's bridle. "Do not call him, lest you bring more of the darkness to us."

Elandra's mouth fell open, but she said nothing. Others stared at Caelan in open astonishment. As for Elandra, she wondered if he knew what he risked by accusing Sien so openly. The priest had been Kostimon's most trusted adviser for a long time. Only a fool or a very courageous man would dare speak against the priest.

Kostimon's mouth clamped in a thin line. His yellow eyes blazed with anger and impatience.

The guardsmen watched, the whites of their eyes showing in the torchlight. Murmurs rose among them.

"Lord Sien," called Kostimon, "I call on you to serve me now."

The priest did not answer, nor did he appear. Realizing she was holding her breath, Elandra released it. Then she sent Caelan a look of fresh wonder. It seemed he had indeed cowed the priest into staying away.

"Damn!" Kostimon said angrily, twisting about in the saddle. "Where is the man?"

"He can not come," Caelan said again, his voice very terse.

Kostimon glared at him. "Is he dead?"

"No, Majesty."

Another eerie sound came from Paz's corpse. Kostimon glanced at it and scowled. "There is no more time to wait for him. I shall have to do this myself." He lifted his free hand into the air while the other gripped the reins. "I, Kostimon the Great, call on the hidden ways! Exalted ruler of the shadows, show mercy upon thy subjects and reveal the ways to us."

Several of the men gasped at his request. Elandra felt coldness squeeze her own heart. Suddenly she was short of breath, and everything about her did not seem quite real. Kostimon was calling on the powers of darkness, the forbidden knowledge. Openly, with all of them as witnesses, he was committing blasphemy.

"Dear Gault," Elandra whispered aloud in her horror, "watch over us and keep us safe."

Caelan's gaze met hers. "Gault does not rule here," he said in warning.

Across the cavern, the shadowy darkness curled back as though parted by an unseen force. Eerie light not cast by fire appeared in soft radiance. It hurt Elandra's eyes to look at it. Blinking, she squinted and turned her face away. Her heart was beating faster now. Her mouth was dry. She felt deathly afraid.

A doorway stood revealed in the strange light. The wall surrounding it was carved into the shape of a beast's snarling mouth. As they watched—disbelieving, horrified, some muttering prayers

and others hastily making warding signs—the door swung silently
open to expose a yawning darkness beyond it.

A dank, ancient smell came to Elandra's nostrils. She shivered, and her horse whinnied nervously.

"Do not fear!" the emperor called out across the confusion.
"Ahead of us lies safety. At our backs grows the danger of Beloth."

As he said the unspeakable name, something shrieked behind
them.

Crying out involuntarily, Elandra looked back and saw a
shape rising from the black pool surrounding Paz's body. The
shape looked slender, almost like a child or a woman. Now it was
unfurling wings that dripped and splattered the black fluid. Each
splatter on the floor spread into a miniature pool of its own, rapidly
spreading and growing.

"Ela!" Kostimon shouted. "Don't look at it. You'll draw it to
you. Hurry and pin this to your cloak. It will protect you."

As he spoke, he drew a metal disk from his pocket and thrust
it at her. She saw that he wore a similar disk pinned to his own
cloak. Some trick of the torchlight made its polished surface gleam
as though it emitted fire.

But when the disk touched her gloved palm, a searing flash of
light and heat shot out. Sparks flew between the disk and her
glove. She cried out and dropped the disk, which went clattering
across the ground.

It rolled up against Caelan's boot. He stooped and picked it
up as though in wonder.

"You!" the emperor shouted at him, barely controlling his
plunging, half-rearing mount. "Give that back to the empress. She
must wear it. It's her only protection against the *shyrieas*."

Fresh fear leaped into Elandra's throat. She couldn't help
looking again at the monsters that were forming. They shrieked
and struggled, flapping wings and clawing the air with their talons.

Caelan was still studying the disk, turning it over and over in
his hands. Elandra was afraid of it, afraid of Kostimon's suddenly
revealed powers, afraid of the way he dared utter the shadow god's
unspeakable name.

"I shall wear no emblem of the darkness," she declared fearfully.

"Don't be a fool," Kostimon said. "You—"

"It's a warding key," Caelan interrupted, his voice full of amazement. "Choven made."

"Give it to the empress," Kostimon said. He kicked his horse in Caelan's direction. "She must be protected—"

"Her cloak and gloves do that," Caelan said. "The protection spells are different. They cannot work together."

"Give it to her, I say!"

Shrugging, Caelan handed up the disk to Elandra.

"No!" she cried, backing her horse away.

Behind them, the *shyrieas* shrieked. Ahead of them, a tall figure in long priestly robes suddenly appeared in the bestial mouth of the doorway. He beckoned, and several guardsmen cried out a warning. Panic ran through the air, hot and sour.

"Majesty!" called the priest. "Come quickly."

"It is safe, men!" Kostimon tried to assure the soldiers. "On my honor, I swear to you that it is safe. It is a secret way of Gault."

Caelan was also staring at the priest. "It's not Sien," he said as though to himself.

Elandra heard him, and relaxed slightly in relief. She never wanted to see the high priest again.

"Captain Vysal," Kostimon ordered, "send the men through at once. We cannot afford delay."

Vysal's voice rang out, tighter and more brusque than usual, and the men reluctantly spurred their shying, frightened horses toward the exit.

"Majesty, come!" the priest called with more urgency than before. "Your Majesty must be the first one through the portal, if the others are to follow where you go."

The emperor swore, using dark, ancient words that rang in Elandra's ears. "Never mind your instructions!" he shouted back. "I know what to do. See that you get the cup ready. Hurry!"

Elandra stared at him in wonder, trying to understand what was happening.

He glared at her. "Take the disk and come with me. We must go through first. There's no more time."

No matter how great her fear, she could not disobey his direct

command. With great reluctance, she reached out her hand and let
Caelan give her the disk.

Again, sparks flashed between her glove and the disk. A
numbing jolt went through her hand, and the disk went flying.

"I cannot hold it," she said.

Kostimon swore again. "Ela, stop fooling about or I shall lose
you forever. Take off those damned gloves and—"

"The magic she has is stronger than this, and older," Caelan
said, interceding. "She is safe as she is."

"Nonsense!" Kostimon snapped. "Nothing is stronger than
Choven-forged—"

"Women's magic," Caelan replied. He glanced at Elandra
with his brows lifted, as though for confirmation. "Penestrican?"

"Mahiran," she answered.

Scowling, Kostimon opened his mouth as though to argue
further, but a dreadful screech from the first, and largest, *shyriea*
filled the cavern. Lifting itself into the air with strong flaps of its
wings, it flew at them.

Elandra screamed.

Shouting a war cry, Kostimon drew his sword and brandished
it aloft. "Choven steel!" he shouted defiantly. "Come and eat it,
you harpy of the devil!"

Beside Elandra's shying horse, Caelan gripped her stirrup and
raised the warding key in his hand. He shouted something in a language she did not understand—Trau, perhaps. The sound of the
words made her feel dizzy and strange.

The disk in his upraised palm glowed and came to life. Light
flashed in a ray from it to the disk pinned to Kostimon's cloak to
his sword. As though in response, Elandra's gloves and cloak also
glowed with light until the combined radiance was blinding.

The *shyriea* swooped at them from overhead, only to wheel
back, screaming. She realized it could not harm her or these two
men under their protection spell.

As for the light around her, it grew ever brighter. She felt as
though she were being burned up, and yet the fire that blazed
through her was both strangely cool and exhilarating.

The horses, lathered and terrified, galloped across the cavern
to the others, where the priest was hastily administering a goblet of

something—sacramental wine, perhaps—to the guardsmen. Caelan kept pace at Elandra's horse's side, running effortlessly, his golden hair on fire, his eyes cold white flames. His skin was like tempered bronze, shining in the unearthly light. He was singing as he ran, the words still in some mysterious tongue that awakened strange sensations in her.

Elandra felt as one with this man, as though she had joined his heart and mind. She saw his goodness, his loyal heart, his honesty, and his pain.

As for Kostimon, on her other side, she felt as one with him also, joined with him for the first time. His aged looks had fallen away. He looked as young as Caelan, lean and glorious, his face radiant as he tipped back his head and laughed aloud. White flames shot from his mouth, driving back the *shyriea* again. She had never seen a man more handsome or magnificent than Kostimon, with his black curly hair and strong shoulders.

Laughing again, he spoke something even older and more powerful than Caelan's incantations. The word appeared in the air, blazing with fire, and the largest *shyriea* swallowed it, only to scream and explode into ashes. The other demons vanished also, their screams echoing long after they faded.

There was an awful stink of sulfur and death in the cavern, choking the air.

The fire blazing in Elandra died, as suddenly as it had come to life. She dropped down in her saddle, not realizing until then that she had been standing in her stirrups. She felt dazed and winded.

On her left, Caelan lowered his hand with the warding key and stumbled. He released her stirrup and let her horse shoot past him. The fiery radiance encircling him like a halo faded and disappeared.

On her right, Kostimon looked around and laughed. Strong, vigorous, and handsome, he was glorious, more splendidly male than she could have ever imagined. This was the man who had vanquished countless foes, who had gathered an army and forged an empire. This was a man who had ruled the world for a thousand years, Kostimon the Great, a man above all men.

Then his sword stopped flaming and the fire in him vanished.

Before her eyes, his youthful looks aged swiftly until he was once again an old man slumping in his saddle. He looked haggard and exhausted. His yellow eyes held torment and regret of a degree she could not bear to witness.

She wanted to weep for him, this man who had once held everything in the palm of his hand. How old he was now, how diminished. And yet, she could see in his eyes that he still had the spirit and the soul of a man in his prime. Only his body was failing him, and perhaps, at last, his mind also. She could see his rage, his frustration, and his fear as his own mortality loomed over him. Now, at last, having glimpsed what he had once been, she could grieve for him.

"Majesty," the priest said urgently. "Come. You must go through the portal *now*."

"Sien," Kostimon said, his voice quivering and feeble. He reached out blindly. "I want Lord Sien."

The priest came running to his side. "Lord Sien is not here," he said. "Please, Majesty. I cannot command the portal as you wish. Drink this and grow strong."

Kostimon slumped lower and moaned. "Help me."

"Here is the cup, Majesty," the priest said, lifting the goblet to the emperor's lips. "Drink deeply."

Elandra drew rein beside the guardsmen, who were gaping wide-eyed and open-mouthed. She was not sure just yet exactly what had happened. But the *shyrieas* were gone. That she did understand.

Kostimon pressed one hand against his face. His shoulders were shaking, and he leaned over his horse's neck as though he would fall out of the saddle. His sword slid to the ground with a clang of steel upon stone.

"Help him!" Elandra called.

Balter and another man hurried to him, but the priest was already pushing the emperor back into the saddle. The sergeant bent and picked up the emperor's sword. Slowly he slid it into its scabbard.

"Get back," the priest said fiercely. He held up a goblet, and Elandra could see ruby-colored wine swirling inside it. "Drink this, Majesty."

"Help me," Kostimon begged piteously. "I am fainting. I cannot go on—"

"You will be well again," the priest assured him, holding the goblet to his lips. "Drink deeply. This will restore you."

Kostimon's fingers groped and clasped the rim of the goblet. He drank noisily, choking on the liquid.

Glancing at the guardsmen who had already drunk the potion, Elandra did not like their glazed looks and semivacant faces. "They look drunk!" she cried. "What have you given them?"

"Forgetfulness," Lord Sien replied smoothly.

She gasped at the sound of his voice and glanced around swiftly. He was nowhere to be seen, yet his voice was unmistakable.

The priest, thin and serious of expression, walked over to her and lifted the goblet.

From the air, Sien's voice said, "To walk through the mouth of Beloth is not easy. It is not for the faint of heart, not for the unbelievers."

"We do not worship the shadow god here!" she said. "Do not utter his dire name in my presence."

Lord Sien laughed, his voice thin and ghostly. The shadows within the cavern seemed to grow darker as though the torchlight was burning out. The Vindicant priest stood motionless and vacant-eyed, holding the cup.

"Drink, my lady, what this man offers you. Do not refuse what you do not understand."

"Oh, I understand," she said grimly, goose bumps rising across her skin.

"It is through Beloth's mercy that you will escape the trap surrounding you. Drink from the goblet. It will ease you."

"No, I thank you," she refused him curtly. "I need no potion of yours."

"Fool!" Sien's voice blared loud enough to make the walls of the cavern shake. Elandra's horse shied, and she struggled to control the animal. Finally the animal quieted.

Elandra drew in a deep breath and glanced over her shoulder at Caelan, who stood apart from her and the others. She could see repudiation and disgust in his face.

"Do you hear Sien's voice?" she asked.

He glanced at her, his eyes blazing an intense blue, and nodded without speaking.

Elandra heard the sound of splintering wood. Looking back across the cavern, she saw an axe blade cleave through the wooden panels of the door. Suddenly she could hear shouts and war cries.

Her heart lurched anew. "Madruns! They have found us. The spell is not holding."

"He has released it," Caelan corrected her angrily.

Kostimon straightened in the saddle and picked up the reins lying slack on his horse's neck. Turning, the priest hurried back to him and pointed the head of Kostimon's horse toward the open portal within the open jaws of the stone beast.

"Go," he commanded, and the horse walked forward.

To Elandra, whatever lay on the other side looked pitch black. A cold air blew forth, and it stank of something she could not identify. She averted her eyes, shivering.

"The emperor knows the way through," Lord Sien said from his invisible position.

The priest handed a burning torch to Kostimon, who took it without expression. The emperor's face was slack and strangely empty.

"He has gone this way many times," Sien's voice said. "Follow him, and you will be safe."

"Majesty, no—" Elandra called after her husband, but Kostimon did not look back. Afraid for him, she started to call again, but Caelan touched her foot to silence her.

"He does not hear you," Caelan said quietly. "Or if he does, it makes no difference to him now."

Kostimon rode through the portal, lazily ducking his head just in time to go under the low entrance. The darkness engulfed him instantly, and Captain Vysal rode in after him. The other mounted guardsmen followed, then the men on foot. Sergeant Balter brought up the rear.

The sergeant glanced back at Elandra, who still hesitated.

The door at the other end of the cavern gave way with a splintering crash, and Madruns poured through. She stared at them, caught between two very different kinds of danger, and felt her own resistance give way.

"Caelan," she said, hearing urgency and fear shaking in her voice, "will your warding key not work again?"

"Not against barbarians of our world," he replied. "Go."

It was as though he gave her permission.

"And what of you?" she asked worriedly. "Will you also take this journey?"

He shook his head. "I will hold them as long as I can—"

"Don't be a fool!" she interrupted angrily. "Your death will not serve me."

"He fears to walk the hidden ways, Majesty," Lord Sien said, mocking them even as he remained too much a coward to face them physically again. "Yes, even a warrior like him comes eventually to his own limit. Call it cowardice if you wish, but he will not take the path to safety. He will not pay its price."

"What price?" she asked in alarm. "What do you mean?"

Caelan's gaze shifted to watch the Madruns, who were entering the large cavern cautiously, almost fearfully. A crease appeared between his brows, but he remained aloof, as though nothing could touch him, as though he were encased in ice, without feelings. Yet she knew he was capable of feeling deeply, beneath his icy surface.

"What price?" she asked again. "What lies waiting in there?"

"Only the mysteries," Lord Sien replied. "Will you take the cup? I can guarantee your safety no other way."

The unnamed priest held up the goblet to her again.

"I do not trust you," she said. "I will stay here, and take my chances with the kind of danger I understand."

Sien's voice made no reply, but it was Caelan who turned on her.

"Don't be foolish!" he said angrily, surprising her. "You are needed elsewhere."

"I will stay." *With you,* she wanted to say but did not quite dare.

He glared up at her. "Then you make worthless everything that was done tonight! Every man's death was for nothing—"

"I will go if you go!" she shouted back, equally angry. "Otherwise I will not."

"You—"

"Did you not rebuke the emperor's men for refusing to serve me?" she said over his words. "Did you not take the same oaths as they?"

Caelan's face darkened. He met her eyes furiously. He said nothing.

She met him look for look, afraid and stubborn. "Unless you hold the bridle of my horse and enter that darkness with me, I will not go."

"You put all of us in danger!" the priest suddenly said. "Beloth's curses on both of you. I will not wait here to be torn to bits."

As he spoke, a war cry rose from the Madruns.

It chilled Elandra's blood. She looked and saw them coming now, as though they had finally seen their quarry. Pointing and brandishing their war clubs, they came at a run.

Elandra's heart filled her mouth, and her hands tightened involuntarily on the reins, making her horse back up. All her courage drained away. She did not think she could carry out her bluff with Caelan, and she was ashamed of herself, bitterly ashamed.

But just before she whirled her horse to bolt through the portal, Caelan gave her a curt nod.

"As you wish," he said ungraciously.

"The cup," the priest said quickly. He held up the goblet. "They will be on us in a moment. Drink it now."

Frowning, feeling as though she were surrendering her soul, Elandra took the goblet. The gleam of triumph in the priest's eyes frightened her anew. She took a tiny sip, and instantly her mouth was on fire. Choking, she thrust the cup away, almost dropping it so that part of its contents splashed over the side.

Her mouth was on fire, but in its wake came a strange numbness that crept through her face, then down her throat and into her limbs. She found that everything looked strangely crooked and out of perspective. The portal seemed very far away, yet she was already riding through it. Her hair brushed the top of the opening, and she ducked just in time. She entered a darkness as cold and as encompassing as the grave.

Caelan shook his head when the priest offered him the cup. With a curse, the priest fled through the portal ahead of them.

Elandra's hands rested on the neck of her horse, slackly holding the reins. She listened to the strange and steady *boom-boom-boom* of her heartbeat.

I am going to the dark god, she thought to herself and was horribly afraid.

With all her soul, she wanted to whirl her horse around and bolt out of there, away from the darkness flowing so cold and tangible around her. Yet she could not command her own hands. It was as though by drinking from that mysterious cup, she had accepted something worse than death.

Had she surrendered to Beloth?

She did not want to think so. All her life she had been taught to abhor and fear the shadow god, whose name was not to be spoken. Yet, was she not now taking the path into his hell? And had she not done it willingly, with the helpful trickery of Lord Sien, her enemy?

She tried to cry out, but her mouth would not open. She could not draw enough breath to utter a sound. But in her mind she screamed.

Chapter Three

STEPPING THROUGH THE portal took every ounce of Caelan's courage. The darkness was a living force, something that pressed against him from all sides, seeking his soul. *Sevaisin,* his special gift for joining, brought him unwelcome awareness. He could sense the putrid evil that permeated the walls of the passageway and filled the darkness itself, an evil so strong and pervasive it comprised the very air he breathed.

Spell residues crisscrossed the chilly air. They were long expired and too ancient to cause harm, yet he could sense how powerful and dangerous they had been.

He drew in deep breaths, sensing unnameable things lurking unseen beyond the darkness, beyond the walls of the passageway. The things were aware of him. He sensed the shift and focus of their attention, the stirring and awakening of the evil force itself.

He found himself afraid, with a fear that bathed him in sudden cold sweat. His mouth went dry. He could not breathe. The hair on his arms rose in swift prickles, and his heart pounded in sudden, uncontrollable panic.

Get out of here, urged a voice inside him. *Get out. Get out!*

Yet it was too late. His sweating fingers gripped Elandra's horse's bridle, and he quickened his pace toward the emperor's torch—very dim—blazing ahead of them. Elandra had hesitated too long, letting the distance between her and the others stretch uncomfortably far.

Behind them, the approaching Madruns yelled and cursed in their barbaric tongue, pounding their weapons on their shields in an unholy din that echoed off the cavern walls. The priest jumped through the portal with a gasp of fear.

Caelan glanced back in time to see a bright flash of light. The air smelled suddenly of something burning, yet there was no fire. Without being touched, the heavy stone portal swung shut as though of its own volition, and the bolts shot home. Sparks burst from the hinges, setting off orange flames that burned impossibly in midair for a moment before gradually disappearing. The door, however, continued to glow faintly.

Caelan recognized the dark magic. Stark, primal fear twisted his entrails. He had seen much in the years he had lived in Imperia, yet never before had he willingly entered the shadow realm. Better to traverse this passageway quickly in the emperor's wake, and pray that whatever lived within the darkness would let them pass unharmed.

Instinctively he reached for the warding key in his pocket. It should have been glowing and hot in response to the magic that had just been released, but the metal disk lay cold and lifeless against his palm.

Fresh sweat broke out across Caelan's forehead. The warding spell that had been linked across himself, Elandra, and Kostimon must have exhausted all the power within the key. Once again he pushed down incipient panic and reminded himself to keep his head. Using *sevaisin,* he attempted to bring the warding key to life, but it remained unresponsive.

Abandoning it in his pocket, Caelan wiped his forehead and told himself the warding key would not be necessary. All he had to do now was catch up with the emperor.

Accordingly, he clucked at Elandra's nervous horse, leading it forward.

The lady herself uttered not a word. He was not certain she could. As for himself, he had the uncomfortable feeling that this was no place for casual utterances. Words might draw the attention of whatever lived here.

He did not even dare call out to the emperor's party ahead of them. Although he believed he and Elandra would be safer with numbers, he believed even more strongly that making too much noise was unwise.

A cobweb brushed its filmy strands across his face, making him flinch. He lengthened his stride, holding his breath without realizing it. Elsewhere in the gloom he could hear whispers of sounds, indistinguishable and somehow menacing. Sometimes, an unexpected breeze—cold, dank, and smelling of the grave—would blow into his face, then die away.

Nothing came near him. Still, this was the realm of shadow, and it was populated. His nostrils picked up a faint, musky, cloying scent like that of decayed flowers, and he drew in a sharp breath. A Haggai witch was nearby. When his feet crossed a patch of slickness, he knew he'd just walked over the slime trail of her passage.

He slowed down, every sense alert, his free hand resting on the hilt of his sword. He must be careful, every moment.

Yet the Haggai was gone.

After a time, her scent faded and he slowly relaxed. However, there were other scents, other indications that denizens of this place had recently been present. It was as though they had cleared the passageway for the emperor and his party.

If that were true, Caelan refused to think about the implications. The emperor's involvement with the shadow gods had been made all too clear. He had passed this way before, and he commanded elements that no mortal man should even know about.

Caelan felt more beads of sweat trickling from his forehead. He longed for a drink of cool water, longed to rest. Instead, he quickened his pace again, breaking into a jog and urging the horse to trot beside him. Never mind his fatigue. Never mind that he had been fighting through half the night, or that his nerves were tight to the breaking point, or that his emotions were drained and weary. It was time to catch up with the others.

Yet no matter how fast he went, he could not close on them. Only an occasional flicker of torchlight in the far distance told him they were still ahead. But he never saw the men, never heard them or their horses. It was as though the darkness had swallowed them whole, and they were gone.

In his head, he marked off the distance, counting his strides, grimly determined not to be left behind.

When he had gone a league, he finally stumbled to a halt, breathing hard and trembling from exhaustion. His legs were burning; his wind was gone. The torchlight ahead vanished completely.

He heard no sounds from the emperor's party. He and Elandra had been left behind.

"No," he said aloud, his voice hoarse with panting. He leaned against the wall and wiped sweat from his face. Its pungent scent reminded him that he was alive, that he was of the world of life and light aboveground, that he did not belong down here in this hole, in this grave.

Yet, how long was the way to safety? Was there hope of getting out, or had Sien trapped them down here forever?

Caelan no longer believed he could catch up with the others. He suspected that there was a reason why he and Elandra had been cut off from the others, and he did not like where that thought led.

Groaning a little, he pushed himself upright and strode forward again.

Time ceased to have meaning. As he walked, he grew numb and spent. Every inch of him ached, yet it was more than mere physical exhaustion. The fire of the warding keys that had united him with Kostimon and Elandra had used up his inner resources as well. Three forms of magic—Choven, Mahiran, and an indescribable mixture of forces from within the emperor—had blended momentarily. It was as though Caelan, Kostimon, and Elandra each carried some special power inside, kindred power that had linked from one warding key to another with exhilarating effect.

The demonic *shryieas* had been no match for it.

Even now, just remembering awakened in Caelan a faint, resonant hum of the soul. He craved another taste of that fiery power, longed to feel it course again through him. In those moments he had felt as though he belonged to all the world, was one with nature, yet master of it. He had seemed to be larger than creation itself.

Words could not describe what he had felt, what he had become for those few breathtaking moments.

Caelan had shared with Elandra, becoming one with her. Before tonight he had admired her from afar. His loins had ached with simple infatuation. But she had been forbidden and unattainable. Now, he glanced up at her, unable to see her, yet aware of her like the steady pulse of his own heartbeat. She had given him the beauty of her soul and received his. On some level he felt as though they had walked the road of life together in some other time and place. He felt as though he had known her forever—their memories, laughter, and passion bound together through the endless threads of time. The very concept of it sent tremors through him, for he now understood what it meant to love another more than himself, what it meant to put another first.

Again he glanced at her, and his heart swelled with the words he could not utter. No matter what they had shared in a moment of magic, that had been another world. Reality was this world, the here and now. Elandra still belonged to the emperor.

Frustration sawed through him. Hadn't he fought in her behalf? Hadn't he saved her when her husband abandoned her? At this very moment, where was Kostimon? Was he here, by his wife's side? No, there was only Caelan, faithful Caelan, to watch over her and protect her. Did that not make his claim on her more valid than Kostimon's?

Caelan gritted his teeth to hold back the temptations that suddenly swept over him. Perspiration popped out across his forehead. He was flooded with heat, with the conviction that he was going mad. His warrior's blood pumped with a fury that urged him toward the madness. For years his only passions had been hatred and the joy of combat—savage, destructive forces that burned his heart. He had never imagined that he could also burn with love for a woman.

Had she not pleaded with him to come with her? Had she not shown her preference?

She was his. She had always been his.

A stumble tilted Caelan off balance, and his shoulder crashed into the wall. The jolt snapped him back from the edge.

Blinking, he rubbed his face and drew in several quick breaths, amazed at himself.

Was he losing his mind? To be feeling like this, to be thinking like this . . . it was treason. It was forbidden. She was not his woman. She was the empress, not some village maiden he could throw over his shoulder and carry off like booty.

She trusted him, and he could not violate that by abducting her. She depended on him, and he could not respond to that with dishonor. Never mind what he wanted. Never mind if he burned as though he had been torched. Never mind that all the forces of a storm whirled and raged inside him, threatening to shatter honor, rules, and what was right.

To love her meant he could not harm her. He could not tempt her into dishonor. He could not even ask her to choose.

Besides, he had shared also with the emperor, becoming one with him. Even now he could still taste the darkness within Kostimon, as well as the incredible force of will that drove the man. Kostimon's thirst for power, the vigor of his ambition, his lust for life and all that it offered still hummed in Caelan with a resonance that could not be entirely silenced. Caelan realized that he too possessed his own dark side: the failures in his past, his joy of combat and killing, the hatred for old enemies, and an unrequited desire for revenge. Even before his life had changed, before the Thyzarene raiders had destroyed his home and killed his father, before he abandoned Lea to die . . . back when life was still good and still full of all possibility, he had craved weapons, had longed to be a soldier simply because he wanted to fight. It had always been a thread of darkness in his blood, calling him. And had the Thyzarenes not come and enslaved him, he would have still used a sword to carve his path of life.

The empire itself had been built by swordpoint and strife. Now the empire was falling. Although tonight the emperor and empress had escaped the traps laid for them, the palace had been sacked and burned by the enemy. Prince Tirhin had seized the throne for himself. Whether he could keep it, with his power base built on treachery and betrayal, remained to be seen.

Only a fool would discount Kostimon. Even old and failing, the emperor was not yet defeated. He could still call on other parts of his empire to rally. He had men who would hold to their oaths of allegiance. He had resources beyond those of his enemies.

But if he had been broken?

Caelan thought of the confused old man arguing over scroll cases instead of plotting strategy. He thought of the coward who had believed a general's lies to abandon helpless women and servants in the palace. He thought of the fool who had refused to pay heed to warnings.

Now, driven from his own palace, with the very seat of his

power wrested from him, a refugee forced to run for his life, where would Kostimon go? Who would support him? Could he rejoin the main forces of his army? Could he drive the Madruns from his borders? Could he recover from this coup? Could he summon the wits and the strength to lead the men still loyal to him?

The man was ancient, at the end of his time. Even if he drove his enemies back, he could not beat his own fate. Age was finally conquering him, a man who had not surrendered to mortality for nearly a millennium.

How long did the old man have?

His threads of life were thin and weak. He might have days. He might have hours.

And when he died, what then?

Caelan's eyes narrowed. What would it be like to seize power in Kostimon's stead?

What would it be like to ride at the head of the imperial army, to hear the roaring shouts of acclaim? What would it be like to have absolute command over the lives of everyone? To have wealth, glory, and possessions?

What would it be like to travel from one end of the vast empire to the other, ruler of every scrap of earth beneath one's boot soles? What would it be like to change laws, to effect reforms, to free slaves, to abolish slavery altogether? He could drive out the evil Vindicants, close temples, put an end to forbidden rites and practices.

A surge of confidence and ambition swept through him before he tried to thrust his thoughts aside. He was a fool to think such things. Yet he felt ambition burning bright inside him. Prince Tirhin had no more right to rule than any other man. There had been no prophecy cast to indicate a successor. The future of the empire lay open like an arena, with no rules, ready to be taken by the best and strongest.

I am that man.

But was he? Caelan frowned at himself in self-ridicule. He was a former slave, an ex-gladiator, a provincial nobody from nowhere.

But Kostimon had been a nobody from nowhere, Caelan reminded himself. No one could remember where Kostimon had come from originally. What clan? What tribe? What region of the empire? The scrolls of history had been rewritten many times, whenever Kostimon wanted to reinvent his past. A strong man could take the reins of power, if he dared.

A sharp pain flared in Caelan's chest without warning, making him gasp and double over. His fingers slackened on the bridle, and Elandra's horse pulled free and trotted on without him.

Alarmed by the thought of becoming separated from her in the darkness, he called, "Elandra, wait—"

The pain hit him again, and he could not finish his sentence. Gritting his teeth, he staggered forward a step, then sank to his knees. He had to call out to her, had to stop her, had to stay with her. But the pain was too great. It consumed him, and he had not even the breath to cry out.

For a moment he thought he had been wounded by some mysterious force coming at him from the darkness. But his groping fingers found no cuts, no blood. Nothing tangible had attacked him.

Gasping through another burst of pain, Caelan fought to hold himself upright. He would not fall, he told himself grimly, struggling to hang on. He would not die here in this evil place, alone and forgotten.

The pain grew more intense, stabbing and hot, until his face dripped with sweat and he thought he must scream from it. Then it ebbed enough for him to catch his breath. He opened his eyes. As his senses came back to him, he realized the pain was focusing itself now into one central spot just below his throat.

The emerald . . .

He loosened the thong holding his amulet bag and pulled it over his head in a swift yank. Then, with fumbling, unsteady fingers, he opened the bag and poured out his talisman. Originally there had been two emeralds, one thumb-sized, the other smaller. They had been given to him by his younger sister Lea shortly before he had been captured by Thyzarene raiders, never to see her again. Later, on the hillside of *Sidraigh-hal,* the two emeralds had fused together into a single, irregular-shaped stone, somehow becoming larger in the process.

Now, the lumpy gem was glowing here in the darkness, as though possessing a life of its own. And as soon as he dumped it on the ground, it grew again, swelling into a fist-sized gem that flared angrily with radiant, pale green light.

The pain in his chest faded swiftly. Limp with relief, Caelan pressed his palm against the spot and drew in deeper and deeper breaths. He felt clammy now in the cold air blowing through the passageway. His sweat was drying on his skin; his clothing stuck unpleasantly to him beneath his armor. Wiping his face with a corner of his tattered cloak, he thought he heard a footstep in the distance.

His head snapped up. "Elandra?"

She did not reply, and he knew even as he uttered her name that the sound had come from behind him. Elandra was ahead of him, lost already in the darkness beyond the dim light cast by his emerald. It was as though the shadow forces were separating them, one by one, from each other. Divide and conquer. Isolate and kill.

The soft scraping sound came again, furtive and quick. Hair prickled on the back of Caelan's neck. He pushed himself to his feet, drawing his sword, and gazed behind him.

In the eerie light of the emerald, he saw nothing, but he believed the force that had come to life in the stone was drawing the attention of something he did not want to meet.

Caelan did not understand the magic contained within this emerald. He only knew it somehow responded to the shadow forces, fed on their power to mysteriously augment its own. Sometimes it served as a protector; sometimes not. He did not know how to direct it, how to use it. And now it was too large to be concealed in his amulet pouch. He would have to find another way to carry it.

Using a corner of his cloak as a pad against the heat thrown off by the stone, Caelan scooped it up and hurried on. With every stride he listened for sounds of pursuit, but whatever lurked behind him did not follow.

The pain in his chest was gone now, but it had drained him. He knew he was not fast enough, not as alert as he should be.

Sighing, he rubbed his chest and felt old, tired, and mortal. His ambitions had been driven out of him, and now he could only look back at them with wonder and amazement. Why had he even fantasized that he could accomplish such things?

It was time for him to leave Kostimon and Elandra to their fates and go home to Trau. He had unfinished business there, old scores to settle, old ghosts to make peace with. Even if E'nonhold had been destroyed, the land remained. He should claim it before the provincial governor awarded the deed to a purchaser.

And as this determination settled within him, the ambitions faded from his heart. The heat inside his emerald gradually cooled until once again it felt cold and lifeless like any stone. The light it cast went out, and Caelan was once again plunged into the darkness.

He stumbled to a halt, frustrated and discouraged. With all his will, he tried to reach into the stone and reawaken its magic. It remained unresponsive in his fist.

Ahead, however, he heard the plodding hoofbeats of Elandra's horse. Straightening his shoulders, he reminded himself of his duty to protect this woman and pushed onward.

Jogging on legs that felt leaden with fatigue, Caelan mentally gave thanks for the years of tough conditioning and training for the arena that enabled him to keep going. The walls of the passage began to glow softly, very dimly at first, then strong enough to see by. The illumination came from streaks of a pale, slimy substance on the walls. He dared not touch it, but he was glad to finally be able to see where he was going.

Ahead, Elandra's horse had stopped and stood with its head down. Elandra's hands rested on her horse's neck. The reins dangled free from the bridle.

He staggered up to the animal, taking care not to startle it, and gripped the dangling reins with a sigh of relief. The horse snorted and rubbed its head against him as though seeking comfort. Caelan stroked its muzzle and scratched its ears, too tired to murmur to it.

Sitting a little slumped in her saddle, the empress looked wan and unearthly in the peculiar light. Her long auburn hair had blown across her face and hung there, half concealing her features. Her mouth was slack, and her eyes held nothing at all. It worried him, to see her like that. He did not know how long the spell would last, or whether it would ever wear off.

"Elandra?" he said very softly to her. "Majesty, are you all right?"

She stared into the emptiness ahead of her. She did not blink. She did not move. Her lips remained slightly parted. Only the slight rise and fall of her chest told him she was even alive.

"Majesty," Caelan said again, knowing he should not try to break the spell that protected her here, but unable to silence himself, "can you speak?"

She remained silent.

Frowning at himself, he shoved his worries away. He urged the horse forward, and together they trudged on.

He could feel the aches of battle: sore muscles grown stiff, the stinging discomfort of scrapes and cuts, the flaring tenderness of bruises. He was hungry. He longed to rest, yet dared not stop.

Gault of infinite mercy, he prayed wearily, *guide our way and keep us from harm.*

It was a fool's prayer, he knew. He was a long way from the realm of light, but he repeated his prayer anyway.

A splashing sound and the cold wetness of water filling his boots startled him.

Halting, he peered ahead. At first he could not see the water he stood in, so black was it.

It ran swift over his feet, as icy cold as a glacial stream. Bending over, Caelan splashed it onto his face.

It burned his skin, making him nearly cry out.

Gasping, he staggered back a step and rubbed the water from his eyes. His face still stung, but he was awake now, fully alert again.

With burning eyes, he squinted at the stream. The streaks of glowing illumination were few and far between here, casting only the palest of shadowy light over the black water. He could not judge its width in the gloom.

The water ran swift yet silent, with none of the usual rush and roar of a river. He could smell the water now, and despite the rapid current that should have kept it fresh, it stank like stagnant pond water.

Wrinkling his nose, Caelan *severed* his nearly overwhelming thirst, putting it aside. This was not drinkable water.

The horse dropped its muzzle to the dark surface of the water as though to drink, but flinched back, snorting and rolling its eyes. It put down its muzzle again, only to refuse to drink. Nervously, the animal backed up.

Caelan jumped at it and succeeded in catching the dangling reins before it could turn around and bolt back the way they'd come.

"No, you don't," he said softly through his teeth.

They would have to cross. Better to do it now and get it over with. He hesitated a moment, still trying to calm the unsettled horse, then touched Elandra's foot briefly.

"Majesty," he said with respect, "if you can hear me, then see that you hang on tight. I don't know how deep the water is. We may have to swim, and the current is swift. Take care you don't let it sweep you from the saddle."

He looked at her, but she gave no sign of having heard him. Sighing, he took her hand and entwined some of the horse's mane among her fingers. Her flesh was cold and stiff, almost inanimate. He felt chilled simply from touching her. It was like handling the dead before they are stiffened.

Swiftly he turned away, unwilling to think of her that way.

He unbuckled his sword belt and breastplate, knowing he could not swim weighted down by so much metal. Pulling off his quilted tunic and the linen undertunic beneath it, he rolled the garments, along with his boots and leggings, into his cloak and strapped them across the front of the saddle in hopes they would stay dry. Clad only in his nethers, he secured his sword and armor to the saddle, then wrapped the reins securely around his hand and urged the horse forward. It flinched and resisted, the whites of its eyes glimmering, but he shouted at it and tugged. Finally it plunged forward, nearly knocking him off balance.

Caelan kept shouting, to encourage himself as much as the horse. He pushed his way forward, and the water deepened quickly until it came up to his chest. He felt as though he'd been plunged into ice. The water was so cold it stole his breath. After another step the bottom dropped out from beneath him. He swam awkwardly, keeping his chin and mouth as high above the surface as he could. The stench was bad enough to turn his stomach. He didn't want to think about what the water contained to make it smell thus.

Snorting, the horse swam beside him. The current grew stronger, and Caelan stayed close against the horse, clinging to a strap of the saddle and trying to steer the animal straight instead of letting the current carry them downstream.

A ghost-pale mist formed on the surface of the water ahead of them, swirling and circling as though alive. Caelan's sense of danger grew stronger. He did not want to swim into the mist. Yet he could not turn back.

When the clammy fog wrapped its tendrils around his face, Caelan felt himself in sudden, unexpected contact with a torrent of emotions, none of which were his own. They swept over him in a deluge, and the faint sound of weeping and piteous cries filled his ears. He had entered some kind of miasma of human misery. He wanted to weep with the voices. Their agony and torment were unbearable, drowning him. He lost all sense of himself, feeling instead this terrible sorrow and grief that encompassed his soul.

"No," he said aloud, struggling with the last remnants of his will. "No!"

He *severed,* isolating himself, and at once there was only roaring silence in his ears instead of anguished wailing. The tendrils of fog melted away, and a light of sorts—very white and pure—shone down on him as though moonlight had somehow reached to the bowels of the earth.

The horse surged ahead of him, lunging up and out of the water onto the bank. Snorting and stamping, it switched its dripping tail and shook itself violently.

Caelan followed, gaining ground only to find his knees buckling beneath him. Despite *severance,* he had little strength left. But at least he had sweet peace—no tormented emotions, no cries of misery, no pervading coldness, no stench of foul water. Gasping for breath, he collapsed on the ground and passed out.

Chapter Four

A LOW, CHATTERING sound stirred through his mind, half rousing him. He listened, uncaring, then sank away from the noise.

Something nudged him, blowing hard and nervously on the bare skin of his back. It tickled, this warm breath. Caelan came awake reluctantly. He was nudged again, and something twitched through his hair, brushing over the back of his skull.

Swearing in alarm, he rolled over and sat up.

The horse snorted and whirled away from him, then stopped at the edge of the water, pawing and tossing its head.

Elandra, like a ghost figure, remained on its back.

Breathing hard, Caelan blinked himself fully awake and sat up. The strange, pale light continued to fill the cavern area next to the river. It was white and silvery, almost like moonlight, yet unnatural. The shapes of the horse, the walls, the scattered stones all seemed flattened, without dimension, and without color. It made everything feel like a dream, yet would he smell the pungent river in his dream? Would he feel this cold and stiff in his dream? Caelan rubbed his face and shoved back his hair, then climbed to his feet.

He untied his sword and breastplate from the saddle, letting them crash onto the ground, then took down his bundle of clothing eagerly. He was freezing, as cold as when he'd first climbed out of the icy water. Rubbing his bare arms briskly in hopes of warming up, he found his clothing slightly damp around the edges but mostly dry. He dressed quickly, leaving off his armor for the moment, and wrapped himself tightly in his cloak.

His teeth started to chatter, and he felt no warmer than before. He needed a fire to thaw himself out.

But first he checked Elandra. She must be cold and wet too.

He was sure she was very uncomfortable up there in the saddle, trapped with no one to take care of her needs while he slept.

When he touched the empress's cloak, however, he found it dry. The hem of her gown was dry. It was as though she had never crossed the river.

He frowned. Had he slept that long?

Yet his own clothing was still damp in places where the water had splashed it. Why had it failed to dry when her clothing had?

Or had she gotten wet at all?

No matter where he touched Elandra, her clothing was dry. She seemed warm and comfortable. Amazed, Caelan withdrew his hand. Even from this, the spell had protected her.

Ruefully, he told himself it was too late to regret not drinking from the cup while he had the chance. He could be standing here warm and dry . . . and with his wits frozen in limbo. Caelan shook his head. He would rather have the physical misery than surrender to whatever had been in that cup.

A sound caught his attention. Glancing around, he saw a row of eyes, glowing red, feral, and unearthly. They watched him from the boulders piled along one side of the cavern.

Caelan froze. For an endless moment he could do nothing but stare back. He barely dared to breathe. His sword was an eternity away, at least four strides. If the watchers chose to attack, he might not reach it in time.

He swore harshly and silently in his mind.

Slowly, taking care to make no sudden moves that might precipitate attack, he drew his dagger and very cautiously slipped into *sevaisin,* reaching out with the lightest of all possible senses to find out more about what was lurking just out of sight.

He felt the creatures shift and stir uneasily, sensed something coming to life, sipped of the foul force that sustained them, and felt it reach out to him in response.

Shuddering, Caelan pulled back. He was all too aware of the temptation to strengthen the link, to join and share himself with the demons.

They moved closer, edging away from the rocks and moving between him and the mouth of the passageway.

He resisted the urge to step back. The river of black water ran

behind him, cutting him off. There was no escape, no retreat. He
would have to fight, and suddenly his heart beat too fast and his
throat burned.

But he refused to panic. He gripped his dagger more tightly,
then took a cautious step toward his sword. It stood propped up
against his breastplate. His best protection, useless. He took another step.

The demons moved closer. He could almost see them now,
crouched there in the shadows, waiting, watching. When would
they attack?

His heart pounded like a drum. He could feel his pulse
throbbing in his temples and throat. Subconsciously he assumed
a fighter's stance, feet well braced, standing lightly on his toes,
shifting his weight slightly from side to side, ready to explode
into action.

I have fought demon-spawn before and lived, he tried to reassure himself.

Caelan's knuckles ached from gripping his dagger so hard.
After a moment he realized he was throttling the weapon as he
might an enemy's throat. Easing out a breath, he forced his fingers
to loosen.

Caelan took one more step toward his sword. Still too far, although now he thought he could fling himself bodily at it and perhaps reach the tip of the scabbard. Not good, but better than before.

He was supremely aware of the water at his back, aware that
anything could rise up from its depths and come at his exposed
back. His eyes flickered back and forth, measuring, gauging,
watching. He listened to his own breathing. It sounded harsh and
unsteady.

The demons came at him.

Caelan flung himself at his sword. His outstretched hand
clamped onto the scabbard. He could hear them coming, claws
skittering and scraping over stone. He whirled to face them, drawing the sword as he did so and flinging the scabbard aside.

Panting, he stopped only because they had. Now out in the
open where he could see them clearly in the pale, ghostly light,
they crouched in a semicircle and stared at him.

The demons were short, no taller than Caelan's hipbone, and

entirely hairless. Their leathery skin was black and crisscrossed with wrinkles. They had arms and legs like a man, with long, prehensile fingers and toes, all ending in long, sharp talons. Their tails were long and ratlike, and flicked back and forth nervously.

Caelan brought up his sword in smooth readiness. He thought about attacking, but some instinct bade him wait.

Just when his taut nerves could be stretched no farther, one of the creatures crept toward him. Caelan swallowed hard and let it come.

Fanged and snouted, the creature stared up at him with red eyes that were entirely too intelligent. Its long tail flicked restlessly back and forth.

When its tongue flickered out between its fangs, Caelan nearly jumped out of his skin. It was a serpent's tongue, long and forked, quivering in the air as though measuring Caelan in some way. Then it flicked back out of sight. The creature opened its mouth in a toothy grin.

"Welcome, creature of shadow," it said in a hoarse, gravelly whisper. "Art thou Beloth, our master?"

Astonished and horrified at being so grossly misidentified, Caelan stared back at it. "No, I am not!" he said with force.

The demon rocked back on its haunches, while the others scuttled away into the shadows, hissing with palpable disappointment.

"Servant of Beloth, our master?" the demon asked hopefully.

This time Caelan was wise enough to curb his denial. Tipping his head to one side, he asked, "Why do you ask me this?"

"Thou art aware, not asleep in the spell of protection," the demon said.

"And that makes me a servant of—of your master?" Caelan stumbled over the words, finding himself unable to utter Beloth's dire name aloud.

"Thou looks like man-spawn, yet cannot be," the demon said. "Thou has no fear of the shadows, walking without spell of protection."

If it only knew, Caelan thought wryly to himself.

"Thou has bathed in the waters of Aithe and come unto us.

We will serve thee, servant of Beloth, until our dire lord and master walks free once again."

Caelan opened his mouth to repudiate everything, but the other demons came scuttling forward in an uneven, almost ratlike gait. They surrounded him. He tensed, wanting to back away, but their clawed fingers were already clutching at his clothing, stroking and petting him in reverence.

"Don't worship me!" he cried in disgust. "Get back, all of you!"

They moved a short distance from him, but not far enough, and sat on their haunches with their tails coiled about their ankles. Their fangs gleamed in the strange light; their red eyes shifted to his face and down again. They smelled of death and something worse. The very sight of them turned his stomach, yet he knew he must keep his wits now, must take the advantage they had mistakenly given him and utilize it wisely.

But, Gault's mercy, what did they mean he had bathed in the waters of Aithe? That was the mythological river of death, the black waters formed from dead men's souls. During the most ancient and turbulent days following creation itself, when Beloth had strode the earth and destroyed all that he touched, the shadow god had killed so many men that their destroyed souls had flowed and comingled into a river that encircled the world. Later, when the top of *Sidraigh-hal* had been smote with the combined powers of the gods of light, allowing lava and smoke to spill forth, when on the mountain's scarred slopes the black city of Beloth and Mael had been broken asunder and all the stones scattered and the ground itself salted and burned, then had Aithe sunk into the earth, flowing below ground.

Caelan realized he had swum through the souls of damned men. Dear Gault, small wonder the water had burned his flesh and rendered him so cold now. He felt tainted to the core. Shivering, Caelan looked down at himself, wondering if he could see any stains left by the touch of those icy waters.

"Thou art one of us. Thou art welcome in the place of shadows," the demon said while the others chorused hisses and grunts of acclamation. "Not for a thousand years has one of warm blood come to walk among us. We give to thee all that is ours."

Caelan's eyes narrowed. "You lie," he said sharply, forgetting the need for caution. "What of the riders who passed through here not long ago? What of the Vindicants, the priests who have used this passageway often?"

The demons whispered among themselves long enough for Caelan to regret his hasty questions. Then the spokesman gazed up at him and bared its fangs. "Man-spawn have no interest for us. Under the spell of protection, they pass by on the other side of the river. They are not our meat. Kostimon has gone past many times in his span of years."

"You know Kostimon by name?" Caelan asked in fresh astonishment.

The demons' laughter was a harsh, raspy cacophony.

"Kostimon the Doomed!" one cried.

"He is doomed!" echoed another.

"Doomed!"

They all laughed again.

The spokesman edged even closer to Caelan and tugged at the sodden hem of his cloak. "Kostimon," it said, its tongue flickering out, "will be our meat when his time ends. Soon, he will be ours. We will be permitted to go for him. We will feed. Soon!"

"Soon! Soon! Soon!" the others echoed in chorus.

Caelan felt colder than ever. He stared at these creatures and understood how the emperor would finally die.

"When we have taken his soul from his flesh," the demon said, rubbing its snout affectionately against Caelan's leg, "wilt thou accept the honor of pouring his soul into Aithe's waters of the damned?"

Caelan gazed down into the demon's red eyes, feeling almost mesmerized. Eagerly the others crowded closer around him, and Caelan found himself without an answer.

The silence stretched out too long, and they hissed suspiciously.

"If I am here," Caelan said quickly, "then I will accept the honor extended to me." He met their hostile eyes and tried to show no fear. "I have many duties. My master gives me many tasks."

"Let us help thee, favored one," the demon said eagerly, its tongue flickering in and out. "Let us make thy work easier."

Swallowing hard, Caelan pointed at Elandra. "I must take the woman beyond this realm of shadow, back into the world that is her own."

The demons hissed in fury. "Not permitted!" the spokesman said. "No man-spawn goes this way. We guard the passage to the Gate of Sorrows."

Hope quickened in Caelan. He stared at the passageway, and knew it had to be the way out. "If Kostimon has gone through here, then—"

"No! No! No!" they chorused. "No man-spawn crosses Aithe. Only thou, servant of Beloth."

Caelan frowned. "Then let me pass," he said carefully.

They shifted aside, red eyes glowing with new hostility. "Thou may go to the Guardian, if thou has been sent by thy master. But not her."

"She must come with me," Caelan said sharply.

"No!"

"You have called me master, yet now you disobey me."

They did not seem impressed by his rebuke.

"Let us wage war for thee," the spokesman said at last. "Let us tear souls from man-spawn and bring them for thy supper. Unleash us, and we will go swift, swift under the dark cloud that mighty Beloth brings to shroud the earth."

Caelan hesitated, trying to be careful. "Are you leashed?"

They hissed loudly, crowding him again.

The spokesman spat eloquently, and its spittle flamed and sizzled briefly upon the stony ground. "We guard this passage, but others can guard. We can swarm," the spokesman assured Caelan, gripping his cloak with talons that snagged the cloth. "We are many. We swarm and attack. We are good to tear out souls. We are good against man-spawn, not so good against gods of light. Protect us, favored one, and we will swarm weak man-spawn and destroy for thee."

Caelan's frown deepened. There had to be a way to get past these creatures. He was convinced now that before him lay their exit. He had to use whatever means of persuasion were available.

"What is your name?" he asked the demons. "What are you called, that I may know you again?"

Their eyes glowed even brighter. "He commands us," murmured one. Others hissed eagerly. "We serve! We serve!"

"Tell me!" Caelan said sharply, letting his voice crack across theirs with authority.

The spokesman crouched low before him and placed its snout reverently on Caelan's foot. "We are called Legion, lord. We are thine."

"And if I release you from your captivity, you will serve me?" he asked.

"Yes!"

"You will do whatever I ask, without question?"

"Yes!"

"You will serve only me. No other?"

The demons hesitated, glancing at each other. "We serve Beloth, and no other. Thou art the servant of Beloth. If we serve thee, do we not serve our dire lord and master?"

Caelan frowned and dodged this clarification. "I swear I will not call you to attack your master. I will ask only for your attack against men."

They laughed and grunted in glee. "Kill! Kill! Kill!" they chanted.

"But only men I specify," he said sharply, cutting them off. "This you will swear and promise, or no freedom. Only will you attack men when I call you, and only those men I point out."

Again they hesitated. Finally the spokesman said, "But why not let us attack all man-spawn? We can do many. We are many. We are swift."

"No," Caelan said, trying to keep his voice sharp and strong. Inside he was beginning to doubt the wisdom of trying to strike any kind of bargain with these creatures. They knew no mercy, understood no honor. But he had no intention of keeping his word. All he wanted was access to that passageway.

He glared at them, showing anger to impress them. "No," he said again. "Not all men. Only those I specify. If you cannot, will not, do this, then I will not free you."

"We hunger to kill," the spokesman said. "Unleash us, master."

"Let me and this woman pass, and I will agree."

"Caelan, stop!" Elandra's voice called out to him suddenly.

Startled, he whirled in her direction, scattering several demons who jumped back from him with hisses of alarm. He saw her leaning forward in the saddle, staring at him. Her eyes were wide and fearful. She shook her head and lifted one hand to her face.

Alarmed and dismayed at what she was doing, Caelan started to go to her, but the demons were clinging to his legs and cloak. More were coming. He was surrounded by the creatures, and he did not want them close to Elandra.

"Don't!" he called urgently to her. "You must stay within the spell. Don't break it."

"I . . . must." Her face turned pink with effort. He saw the cords in her neck strain, then she slumped and her head tipped forward so that the long sweep of her hair concealed her face.

"You are safe within the spell," he reminded her. "Don't leave it."

She lifted her face, and the slackness in her features was gone. Her intelligent eyes stared at him, aware and cognizant again.

Caelan's spirits sank. He could only stare at her, worried more than he could articulate. She was no longer safe, no longer protected. What in Gault's name had possessed her to break free now, when they were surrounded by demons? Was she mad, or simply a fool?

Suddenly he was furious with her for risking herself this way, and for making his responsibilities that much harder.

Tightening his lips against harsh words he did not dare utter, he turned away and looked once again at the spokesman of the demons.

"Legion," he said, "I will—"

"Stop!" Elandra cried. She kicked the horse and rode closer until the trembling animal balked. Imperiously, her eyes flashing with anger, she glared at Caelan. "You mad fool, what are you doing? Have you lost all conscience? You cannot bargain with darkness and—"

"Silence!" he yelled back at her. "This has nothing to do with you."

"I command you—"

"Not here!" he snapped, enraged at how every word she uttered destroyed more of the lie he had built between himself and the demons. Why couldn't she understand the need for caution, the need for silence? Let Legion think what they wanted. Doing so was to Caelan's—and Elandra's—advantage.

Unwilling to let her say anything else, he *severed* her, wrapping her in cold isolation. He did it without thinking, pushing her partway into the void without warning or preparation. He had never done this to a person before. He had never realized he could, but it was necessary.

Elandra's eyes widened with astonishment and her mouth opened, but she could not speak.

It was a strain to hold her so. For the first time since he'd swum the river, he felt beads of perspiration pop out across his forehead.

Feeling her mind and emotions lash out against his control, Caelan knew he could not hold her long. Fiercely he turned on Legion. "Tell me now," he said harshly. "What is your answer? Do we have a bargain, or not?"

There were suspicious hisses and much jostling among the demons in the back. At least fifty or more were present now, red-eyed and semihostile. They kept staring at Elandra, and Caelan felt increasingly uneasy.

"Warm-blood," the spokesman said at last. It drew back a step from Caelan and no longer looked reverent. "With other warm-blood, now not under spell of protection. No warm-bloods may cross the river. She is our meat."

Fear stabbed through Caelan. To hide it, he raised his sword and scowled at them. "Would you rather feed on one woman instead of the many warm-bloods I will give you? Let her go, and I will free you."

The spokesman drew back angrily and bared its fangs. "Trick!" it cried.

Just as it struck, however, Caelan brought down his sword in one clean, heavy stroke. The spokesman's body, severed in half, went spinning in two directions.

Blood, black and foul-smelling, spilled from the two halves.

From the pooling blood emerged tiny demons, at least a dozen, hopping and furious.

Caelan stepped back, realizing he could not fight them the usual way.

But there was another way to kill them, a way he had never used before. He had always feared the power, knowing that if he ever used it he would want it again.

But the demons were rocking back and forth on their haunches now, tongues flickering, tails lashing. "Kill! Kill! Kill!" they chanted, clearly working themselves into a frenzy while the tiny demons grew larger with every passing second.

Caelan released Elandra and entered *severance* himself, plunging deeply into its coldness until he hardly knew himself, hardly remembered what he was or had been. Before him crouched the demon horde, a hundred now and more coming. Their guttural shouts and hisses filled the air, but he hardly heard the sound.

Rushing past him, they surrounded Elandra. Her horse reared, but the demons pulled the animal down, ripping it apart as others swarmed Elandra. She screamed.

Caelan could see the threads of life, black and knotty, stretching to something hidden beyond the mist at the edges of his vision. He wanted to see no farther, wanted to know nothing about what the threads were connected to.

Caelan *severed* the threads of life, cutting off the two demons first, then slashing in a broad swathe at the others.

Terrible screams filled the air. He snapped out of *severance* and saw blackened, charred heaps littering the ground. Smoke rose from the corpses; the stench from them choked his nostrils.

Howling with fear, the remaining demons fled from him, vanishing into the passageway.

He let them go, running instead to Elandra. She lay unharmed on the ground, one leg pinned beneath the dead horse. Her face was bone white. Her eyes flashed with fear and something else.

He pulled her free, grateful she had suffered no hurt, and lifted her to her feet.

Fear and revulsion were mingled on her face. She stared at him as though she had never seen him before and slapped him hard across the face with her ungloved hand. His cheek stung fiercely. Taken aback, he blinked and looked down at her.

"How dare you do that to me!" she said. "I am not to be silenced with your spells and foreign magic. You should be whipped and purified."

His own temper boiled up to meet hers. "You were putting our lives at risk—"

She swung at him again, but this time he stepped aside and she missed. "Ingrate!" she sputtered. "You dare talk back to me—"

"As long as you are being a fool, yes!" he retorted.

"It is not your place to reprimand me. I am your empress!"

Scorn curled his lips. He wanted to shake her by her beautiful neck. Instead, he cleaned his sword and sheathed it, then buckled on his armor.

"We can argue later," he said. "Now we had better go."

Elandra stamped her foot. "No, this will be settled now. You have much to answer for."

"Not now."

"When?" she demanded. "Either you recognize my authority, or there is no point in going on."

Caelan refused to look at her. She was a stubborn fool. She understood nothing. "You put us in danger," he said tersely, "interrupting like that. They believed me until you—"

"And what was I to do?" she retorted. "Fold my hands while you allied yourself with these—" She broke off, her throat working convulsively, and gestured at the charred remains. "Why?"

He did not intend to explain. Impatience burned hot in his throat. He wanted to get out of here.

"We must go," he said.

"And I said we will stay until this issue is resolved."

He sighed, curbing his own irritation with difficulty. "I will explain, Majesty, but let us go. They will come back, and when they do we should not be here."

A flicker of unease moved beneath the stubbornness in her eyes. "Very well."

As she spoke, she started ahead of him, but he gripped her arm and pulled her back.

She wrenched free. "How dare you!"

"Your Majesty will recall that they fled into the passageway," he said coldly. "If they try to hold it against us, do you really want to be in front?"

Visibly fuming, she stepped aside and gestured for him to precede her. "By all means, go first, guardsman. And see that you keep your magic directed against the demons, instead of against me."

He glared at her, then sighed. "I give you my apology, Majesty, for having *severed* you without your consent. Although you were not hurt, it can be an alarming experience the first time."

She did not look appeased. "There will be no second time," she said icily. "You overstepped your—"

"Don't put me in my place," he snapped, losing his temper again. He was damned if he'd bow and scrape and kiss her foot, groveling in atonement for having saved her life. "I am here to keep you alive, and that is what I did. If you cannot recognize that, then you should have chosen a different escort."

She opened her mouth to retort, then closed it again without saying anything.

He glared at her a moment longer, then turned his back and strode on. "Come."

Chapter Five

AT THE DARK mouth of the passageway, Caelan paused, holding his drawn sword ready, and peered inside. Ancient, disturbing symbols streaked the walls, and every time he glanced at them, his eyes burned. The pale illumination that filled the small cavern did not reach far into the passageway. Looking at its blackness, Caelan felt a surge of deep uneasiness. He did not think Legion would give up easily.

He glanced back at Elandra. Despite her tangled hair and rumpled, dirty clothing, she still looked regal, elegant, beautiful.

Something shifted in his heart. Frowning, he looked away from her quickly.

His own temper had cooled. He wondered if he had spoken too harshly to her. After all, she was a gentlewoman, noble-born and bred. She had been cosseted and protected all her life. Probably no one had ever spoken a rough word to her before. No doubt she thought him a coarse, loud-mouthed oaf.

He began to wish he had not lost his temper with her, had not been so defiant and scornful. It was not her fault if she did not understand what he was doing.

"Why do you hesitate?" she asked, her tone stiff and cool, but controlled. "Can the great champion of the arena be afraid?"

Her scorn stung like salt in an open wound. He gestured for her to be silent and eased cautiously into the dark tunnel.

She followed without a word. He could sense she feared him almost as much as she feared the demons, but he forced himself to concentrate on what lay ahead.

His own breathing sounded harsh and ragged in his ears. His heart was pumping too fast. He kept straining, listening to sounds that might be real or imagined. The menace around them could be felt; it slid through his consciousness like a great, undulating serpent.

There was something very wrong in this passageway. He could smell a pervasive rottenness, a rank corruption that made him gasp. The air felt heavy against his face. He seemed to push against something he could not see, and it crumbled and shredded around him like something long decayed.

"Please stop!" Elandra called out from behind him.

He turned back to look at her. She was breathing short and hard.

"We cannot go this way," she said. "We must turn back."

"It is the only way out of this trap," he said.

"No. There is something wrong. I feel it."

"We must keep going."

She shook her head. "I'm going back."

When she turned around, he gripped her elbow from behind and drew her to him. She struggled, twisting around to face him, but still he would not let her go.

"Release me!" she cried, striking at him with her fists. "You impertinent oaf, I'll have your hands cut off for—"

"Don't make threats you don't mean," he said, holding her fast. "You can't go back, Majesty. You'll be lost forever if you do."

"This is not the way out."

"Legion said it was."

She gasped aloud. "You take the word of—of demons? Are you mad?"

"I sense it is true," he said.

She grew very still in his grasp. Hesitantly he released her and stepped back.

"You sense it," she said after a moment, disbelief ripe in her voice.

"Please don't ask how."

"I can't accept this," she said, shaking her head. "I can't accept any of this. I—"

"Stop it!" he said sharply, afraid she might grow hysterical. "We were supposed to go through the hidden ways with Kostimon. But no matter how fast I hurried, never could I catch up. Some trickery was done to us. We have journeyed for hours, far too long. I think we were never meant to escape this place."

She drew in her breath audibly. "You think this is Lord Sien's revenge?"

"Yes."

"Kostimon might come back. He might search for us."

Caelan frowned. "Do you believe he will, Majesty?"

Her eyes filled with tears that did not fall. Pretense and false hopes leached from her face, leaving her cheeks drawn and pale. She shook her head.

"The emperor is well on the other side and safe by now," Caelan said. "Do you honestly think otherwise?"

She wiped her face. "How could we become lost?"

"We are in the realm of shadow, where nothing is as it seems. I think we have been walking through an illusion. According to what Legion said, we weren't supposed to cross the river."

"Then we should go back across it."

"No," he said.

"But—"

"I will not swim through it again, and you should not."

"I can swim—"

"That isn't the issue," he said in exasperation.

"No, it isn't," she snapped. "It's about your refusal to accept my authority—"

"Do you want to swim through damnation?" he asked, losing his temper. "That is Aithe, river of the damned! Is it such an insult that I seek to spare you from experiencing *that*? Gods, I would not put myself willingly through such horror again, much less you."

She blinked at him, looking abashed. "Oh," she said in a small voice.

"Majesty," he said, calming down slightly, "we must do what we can to escape the realm of shadow. While you were under the spell you were safe, but that is no longer the case. I do not think we have much time to find a way out."

She sighed. "Very well."

"Do I go on?"

"Yes."

Caelan ventured deeper into the passageway. He could almost

imagine he heard something breathing ahead of him. It was too close, as yet unseen. New shivers ran through him, and he grew icy cold again.

When Elandra gripped his cloak from behind, he nearly jumped out of his skin.

"I am sorry," she whispered.

"It's all right," he said, although it was all he could do to force himself forward. His sense of danger increased with every passing moment. "Stay close."

The fetid smell increased around him, choking his nostrils. He fought the urge to back away from it, his fear sharp in his throat. Once again he stopped, and he knew he could not continue like this.

"What is it?" she whispered behind him. "What is wrong?"

He knew of only one way to continue. He had to use *severance,* and somehow he had to take Elandra with him. If he did not prepare her, she would fight him, yet there was no time for long explanations.

"Majesty," he whispered, holding his sword ready against the unseen danger that crept steadily closer.

"What comes?" she asked. "What do I hear?"

"I must use my . . . powers," he said carefully, "if we are to get through."

She drew back from him with a gasp. Swift as thought he turned on her and gripped her wrist to keep her from fleeing.

"Trust me, Majesty," he said urgently. "It is our only chance."

She pulled against him. "No, I can't be a part of this!"

"Do you want to die here?"

"No! I—"

"Have I ever harmed you?"

She twisted her arm, gasping when he would not let her go. "Please."

"Have I ever harmed you?"

"No."

"Then trust me. Do not fight me. Let me . . ." He paused and expelled his breath, trying to keep frustration from his voice. "Let me save you."

"I don't know what you are," she said fearfully. "I will not surrender my soul to—"

"I don't ask for your soul," he broke in. "I don't even ask for your belief. Just don't fight me. Let me—"

A roar echoed through the passageway, drowning out his sentence. Elandra screamed, and Caelan heard the sound of something rushing toward them.

There was no more time to wait. Caelan wrapped his arm around Elandra and joined them forcibly in *sevaisin.* He felt her gasp of astonishment. Her sharp flood of fear nearly drowned him. He filled her with all the strength and reassurance he had, making of them one entity, sharing, complete, and whole. Beyond her terror lay the essence of Elandra—warmth and dazzling light, a joyous buoyancy that filled him.

Sharp claws raked down Caelan's leg. The pain flashed through him just as he *severed,* taking Elandra with him deep, deep into the coldness, into the aloneness, into the detached isolation.

He was not sure if this would work, was not sure if he could use both sides of his gift at the same time. *Sevaisin* and *severance* were total opposites. They repelled each other. All his life, they had warred inside him. He struggled constantly to find a balance; most of the time he managed. But now, he went deeper and deeper into *severance,* praying Elandra was still with him, praying she remained a part of him. He could not hear her, could not feel her now. He was no longer buoyant, but brittle and tight. He dared not break concentration enough to seek her. Either she remained joined with him, or she did not.

Warding off the demon attacking him, Caelan plunged his sword deep into the creature and at the same time *severed* its threads of life. Its scream filled the passageway, but Caelan was already shouldering past it.

The sense of evil continued to intensify. It kept invading his senses despite the protection of *severance,* threatening to overpower him. He could smell evil, a foul stench of corruption so strong he wanted to gag on it. He could taste it in every breath he drew. He could feel it sliding over his skin, slithering in his hair. He felt oily and unclean. It filled his mind, sliding in through the minute cracks of *severance* like roots in search of soil.

He kept striding forward, feeling the resistance growing against him. In *severance* the passageway was no longer dark but instead lit by an unearthly glow of feeble illumination. He could see a shimmering, opalescent wall before him. It looked like spun glass, faintly colored, and heavily streaked in places where the spell strands were stronger than others. He could see through it, could see the end of the passageway and a vast space beyond.

Caelan put his hand on the shimmering wall before him. Then he stepped between the strands, feeling the crackling field of energy radiate off each of them. It felt as though the skin were being peeled off his face, yet he went through.

Evil whispers, uttering words he could not understand, filled his mind as though to drive him mad. Symbols appeared in the air before him, hanging there suspended for a moment only to vanish again. All were dire things, full of danger and evil omen. On some level he understood them and was horrified, yet his thoughts were centered now only on getting through. He understood nothing else, thought of nothing else, felt nothing else.

With a last little pop of resistance, he stepped through to the other side of the spell barrier and found himself dizzy and nauseous. Staggering, he hurried to the end of the passageway and came out into the open.

Overhead stretched a vast darkness unmarked by stars. A cold moon shone down, robed in tatters of cloud.

They stood on a hillside, looking down at the ruins of a city spread before them. Walls had been pushed over. The stones themselves lay melted into queer rounded shapes. Nothing remained standing. From this vantage point, not even an old pattern of streets could be discerned, so thorough had been the destruction. Here and there the moonlight shone white upon sickly fungus growing along the edge of foundations or fallen pillars. The rest lay obscured beneath a dank, foul-smelling mist that flowed and ebbed like a living creature.

"Where are we?" Elandra asked in a whisper. "What is this place?"

Caelan turned his head and saw her standing beside him. She was ghostly pale; shock lay in her face. Only then did he realize that he had lost *sevaisin.* She was no longer a part of him, but her own separate self again.

A wave of exhaustion swept over him. His knees nearly buckled, and he braced his hand against the stone cliff at their backs. It looked solid to his eyes; he could not see where they had exited.

"What have you done?" Elandra demanded. "Where have you brought us? This place . . ." Her voice trailed off in revulsion.

He sighed, sensitive to the maelstrom of emotions inside her, emotions she had not yet acknowledged. Her eyes had begun to flash at him, hurling unspoken accusations.

Better to avoid that by answering the questions she had asked. Turning his gaze back on the ruins below them, Caelan shivered and said, "It is *Vyrmai-hon,* the city of the shadow gods."

Elandra gasped and made a quick little warding gesture.

No one ever spoke of the ruined city of Beloth and Mael. Such talk was forbidden blasphemy, as forbidden as mention of the River Aithe. Yet throughout the ages, men had not forgotten as they were supposed to. These names were mentioned in secret, fearfully, yet with the excitement of the forbidden. The old legends survived in corners of conversation, in threats spoken sometimes to frighten children, in time of crop failure or drought, in the evenings around campfires after a day of hunting moags or lurkers who had ventured too close to the villages.

The gods of light had broken this evil city and imprisoned the shadow gods long ago, before the second age of men. Yet *Vrymai-hon* continued to seep evil into the realm of light, never entirely eradicated. Those who hunted *Vrymai-hon* never found it, yet here Caelan now stood at its edge. He had not sought it, did not want it. He feared it.

A light breeze flew his hair back from his face. In the distance, very low, came a moan of sorrow as though the stones themselves wept in desolation.

The sound made his skin crawl.

"The Penestricans say that there is much treasure abandoned here," Elandra said. "Enough to restore a kingdom . . . perhaps enough to rescue an empire."

He heard the ambition in her voice, steeled with desire. She wanted to keep her throne, intended to fight for it. Did she know yet that he wanted it too?

Thrusting the thought away, Caelan cleared his throat gruffly. "Such gold is tainted."

"Gold cannot be tainted," she retorted.

"Are you sure?"

Their eyes met, but hers fell first. "You said we would escape this place. I trusted you, but you . . ."

Her gaze flashed up to his again, then shifted away. "What are you?" she whispered.

He reached out to her, but she flinched away. He saw her fear then, clawing in her eyes, barely restrained.

Bitterness surged up inside him. The sweet memory of their brief joining was fading now. He should have prepared her more, should have tried to explain before he swept her away. Yet what good were explanations?

"Some men call me *donare,*" he said, ashamed.

She blinked.

"Others say I am *casna,* a devil," he continued. "What do you say, Majesty?"

"Your powers," she said unsteadily. "They are—"

His emotions overpowered him. Not letting her finish, he knelt and laid both his sword and dagger on the ground between them. The metal blades looked pale and shadowy in the dim light.

"Caelan," she said in alarm.

"I cannot do this," he said in anguish. "I am not your Majesty's servant. I am not your protector. I am not your friend. There are no explanations. Do not command them."

She stood there, very still, as though startled. Silence fell across them like a heavy cloak. Inside, he could feel his own pulse hammering away. He was wrong to do this. He knew it. But they had joined in *sevaisin,* and still she refused to understand. She was lying to herself as much as to him. He could not accept that. He was afire, and it was consuming his judgment.

"Please," she said, stepping carefully over the weapons to approach him.

He bowed his head to her, not in obeisance, but because he couldn't trust himself to look at her.

Her right hand very lightly touched his head. "I am sorry," she said softly. "What you did was . . . it was not permitted. I know you seek only my safety, but I have seen you exercise the powers of a sorcerer. I have seen you punish Lord Sien. I have seen you walk surrounded in Choven fire, slaying demons. I have seen you worshiped by Legion, horrible creatures under your command. You see the truth of this dreadful place. You walk through it as though you know it well."

She withdrew her hand. "You have shocked me. I do not think I can accept what you are, what you do. I—I am confused. My faith did not prepare me for such a moral quandary. You have dared cast a spell over me. I—"

"What about this kind of spell?" he asked hoarsely.

Seizing her hand, he pulled her down into his arms and kissed her hard and hungrily. She struggled in his hold at first, stiff with resistance, then she uttered a soft moan and melted against him. Her soft lips opened to his. Flames roared in his ears; he seemed to hear the ringing of a bronze bell from far away.

Then she was clinging to his cloak with both fists, huddled against his breastplate, while they both gasped for breath. He loosened his hold on her marginally, afraid he might hurt her, yet his heart was thudding with triumph. He wanted to shout in his joy.

"I love you," he whispered, bending to kiss her again.

She pulled her lips away from his with a muffled cry. "Don't say it!"

"Why not? It is the truth." He brushed back her hair tenderly from her face. "You are perfect. Beautiful. I have wanted to hold you in my arms since the first day I saw you in Agel's workroom."

She was trembling in his arms. "Please," she said breathlessly. "Please, Caelan—"

"What?" he asked, laughing softly as he nuzzled her cheek and nibbled at the corner of her mouth. Her skin was velvet soft. Her hair smelled of myrrh, ashes, and lavender. He wanted to pick her up and run with her. He wanted to laugh with her in the sunshine. He wanted to kiss her until she lay soft and pliable beneath him, radiant with love.

"Caelan," she said against his lips. She pushed against his embrace, and he released her reluctantly. "Stop. I am dizzy."

"Dizzy with love?" he suggested. "Are you afraid of it?"

"Yes," she said. Her voice shook.

His joy crashed around him. Concerned, he sat back on his haunches, letting his hands slide from her shoulders, down her arms until he gripped her fingers. They were icy cold against his.

"I have tried to put honor above my feelings," he said. "I have tried to hold back. But what I feel is the truth. It is all I can give you."

"You must stop," she said breathlessly. "This must not happen."

"It already has—"

"No!" She shook her head. "Nothing has happened. Nothing *will* happen."

"If you claim you feel nothing for me, then you lie."

She drew back, but he would not release her hands.

"Answer me!" he commanded. "Do you not feel anything?"

Her eyes flashed. "Will you force me to lie?"

"Tell me the truth."

She broke free of his hold and scrambled to her feet, retreating swiftly when he followed her. "I cannot say the truth," she said unsteadily. "You know I cannot. Caelan, he will have you killed when he finds out."

And you, Caelan thought to himself, but neither of them said that aloud. He took another half step toward her. "He won't know—"

"He will! He always knows." She turned her face away so that she stood half in moonlight, half in shadow. "Kostimon has mysterious powers too. Knowledge given to him by . . ." Her voice trailed off.

"I know you are his wife," Caelan said, struggling to voice what he had held back for so long. "I know my feelings for you are forbidden. That's why I prayed you would not choose me as your protector. Yet what I feel cannot be denied. Elan—"

"Please don't say my name here," she said in sudden panic, rushing to him to press her fingers against his lips. "They don't know my name yet. Please don't say it."

He took her fingers and kissed them. "I have dreamed of you.

You are empress, and I am no one, a former slave. Yet in my dreams we have always walked together."

"Dreams?" she said in startlement. "You have dreamed of us?"

"I know you must think I am mad, but even if I die for it, I will not deny my passion."

Again he pulled her into his arms and kissed her. This time, shyly, she returned his kiss, then pulled away. "You have said too much. Stop now. We must both stop now."

"A condemned man can say all he wants," Caelan told her thickly.

He cupped her face in his hands and kissed her deeply, passionately until her breath was his breath and their hearts beat in rhythm. He touched her with *sevaisin,* rejoining their spirits, their hearts, their minds.

When they fell apart for breath at last, she was crying.

Aghast at what he had done, he wiped away her tears with her fingers. They were warm on his skin, and he realized he had let his emotions carry them both too far.

"Please don't cry," he said. "I am sorry. I am sorry."

She clung to him, weeping harder. "You don't understand," she whispered. "I cannot explain."

In silence he held her, and her tears cooled his ardor. As his head cleared, he realized he had been a fool. In a moment he had swept aside all his good and noble intentions. He had rushed her like a beast and frightened her. He had done everything he had sworn to himself he would not do. Now it lay in the open, and they would have to deal with it, or have it dealt with by others.

He rocked her in his arms like a child, loving her, adoring her, knowing they had no time for this, aware that their danger increased with every passing second. Yet this moment had come to him like a gift, a single opportunity impossible to relinquish. He had stolen it, and he gloried in it even as it faded for them both.

"I am sorry," he whispered again. "I would not cause you a moment's pain. Yet I have broken my vow never to reveal my heart to you."

She buried her face against his shoulder. How good she felt against him like this. How perfectly she fitted in his arms. He felt protective and invincible. All his strength seemed made only for the purpose of shielding her from harm.

"You are good and courageous," he told her. "You are brave and wonderful and infinitely precious. I honor you with all my heart, and I do not wish to bring you grief or unhappiness. Yet here I have made you cry. And now you are wondering what we will do, and all I can offer is myself. Is that not arrogance?" He almost laughed from the bitterness that suddenly filled his mouth. "I am a big fool, hoping you will finally say you love me."

She drew in a sharp breath and touched his cheek. "I—I cannot."

Pain cut through his heart. He shut his eyes against it. "I know."

"I am not free. I belong to Kostimon."

"Is your heart his?" he asked fiercely, suddenly furious. "Is it?"

At first she was silent; then she said very quietly, "You know that does not matter. My vows were spoken. I belong to him."

"But not forever," he said grimly.

"Don't speak of that," she said in sudden fear. "Don't foretell his death. Let that not be between us, ever."

His arms tightened around her in hope. "Then you do care?"

She remained silent, but she did not resist when he kissed her forehead and eyes. Her tears tasted warm and salty on his lips.

"You are too stubborn," she said unsteadily. "As my official protector you could have been with me daily, hourly."

"No."

She pulled back to look into his eyes. Her own were frowning. "You say it would not have been honorable. Is this better, when you seize me like a bandit?"

"It is on my terms," he said angrily. "As a man, not your adoring servant."

Her eyes dropped, and she seemed to shrink a little. "Oh."

He let her go then, and stepped back from her. She continued to look at the ground, her hair half across her face.

After a moment she said in a soft, shy voice, "Then some day . . . perhaps . . . you would be my consort?"

His heart tightened. She had just offered him everything . . . and nothing. After all he had said to her, she still did not understand. Regretfully he shook his head. "No," he said with pride, "I will not."

They stood in the shadows, facing each other, trying to find a way to cross the barriers.

"Because you cannot serve an empress?" she said softly, unhappiness layered in her voice. "Am I so horrible? Does my offer insult you so greatly?"

It was Caelan's turn to avert his face from her gaze. "No, there is no insult. You are wonderful."

"Then why? You know who and what I am. My destiny has brought me to the throne. Unless the empire is truly lost, I will rule after Kostimon. What do you ask of me?"

"Nothing," he said swiftly. "Nothing . . . except your heart."

"And if I gave it to you . . . someday," she said hesitantly, "you still would not stand with me?"

His heart thudded with anger. He did not want to explain. There was too much confusion still inside him, too much new ambition, too much stubbornness. Why could she not leave well enough alone? She always pushed him, goaded him. Perhaps it was time she heard the truth.

"First protector, now consort," he snapped. "I can carry a sword or I can wear a little crown. Either way, Majesty, the position you offer is still the same one. No, thank you."

Looking as though he had struck her, she drew back. Inside, Caelan's entrails felt as though they were being twisted into a knot. She had offered him a future beyond what most men dreamed of, and he had flung it back in her face. She would hate him now. Could he blame her?

"I see," she said. Humiliation burned in her voice. "You have made things quite clear."

He sighed. "Please. I didn't mean—"

"You have said enough," she told him with a gesture of dismissal. "This incident is best forgotten. We will not discuss it again."

His dismay grew. "I'm sorry I hurt you. I—"

"Please do not apologize," she broke in, her voice cool and

haughty. "As you said, you are no longer my guardsman, or my protector, or my friend."

"That isn't what I meant—"

"I think it was precisely what you meant."

He opened his mouth to protest when he heard a sound, a deep, resonant sound that seemed to come from somewhere deep inside him. It was a voice, calling to him.

His blood froze in his veins. Turning his head, he looked down at the ruins and saw the mist curling back, parting to reveal an enormous mound of earth in the heart of the city. Fragments and rubble lay strewn around it.

Caelan's vision suddenly leaped. Disoriented, he realized he could see every detail of those fragments as clearly as though he stood next to them. He found himself staring at a broken chair— no, a throne. It was immensely large, too large for any man to sit on. The pieces were made of gold, unblackened even by fire and age. The sides had once been solid slabs of the precious metal, with monsters carved to flank the throne on either side. One half of a snarling visage remained, its lifeless eyes staring back at Caelan.

He stood there as though his feet had frozen, and had an unwanted vision of Beloth sitting on that throne, towering over his suppliants. Dark coils of smoke belched forth from openings in the ground. *Shyrieas* perched on the tall back of the throne like pets, their wings folded, talons dark against the bright gold. A gaming table stood before the shadow god, and tiny humans stood upon the squares, crying piteously.

"Free me," said the voice of Beloth.

Caelan staggered back into the cliff wall. The jolt, however, did not free him from the terrible gaze of Beloth. It felt as though fire was blazing inside his skull, turning his thoughts inside out. Sweating, he writhed, unable to break away.

"Speak my name aloud, and free me," Beloth commanded. "You have the power to *sever* my bonds. Speak!"

Caelan screamed.

"Caelan!" Elandra cried out. She gripped him and shook him hard.

Jolted from the vision, Caelan blinked and saw her face instead of Beloth's. He shuddered and covered his eyes with his hands.

"What is it?" she demanded in alarm. "What is wrong? Why do you stare at the ruins? What do you see there?"

The forbidden name felt heavy on Caelan's tongue. He suddenly wanted to say it aloud to make it ring through the air. He wanted to tip back his head and shout it.

The sound of Beloth's deep voice echoed through his mind. Panting hard, he stared at the mound of earth that marked the god's tomb and felt himself shaking violently all over. His mouth clamped shut in fear, and he battled the urge to speak until Beloth's unspoken name burned in his mouth and felt branded on his tongue.

Sweat popped out on his forehead. He could not fight this. His strength was nothing against the force of the god's will. He was being crushed from inside. His heart was jerking, no longer able to beat. He could not breathe. Fire was consuming his veins.

"No," he gasped. "No. No!"

But the darkness was reaching for him, engulfing him, and he could not fight it, could not even *sever* himself to flee it.

Screaming, he went down.

Chapter Six

THE EMERALD BLAZED inside his pocket. With his last scrap of conscious will, he grasped it, hoping it would protect him.

But Beloth's visage filled his mind anew. Caelan could not command his fingers enough to even hold his emerald. He was dying in the flames of torment, and in agony he rolled on the ground.

Desperately he clutched the scoured earth, digging up one handful and gripping it until his fist shook.

Kneeling beside him, Elandra scooped up soil and sprinkled it over him. "Oh, great mother goddess of the earth, have mercy on us who are trapped within thy folds. Protect us from this taint, this sore within thy side. Strengthen us, that we may not fail thee."

Through the roaring flames inside his mind, Caelan heard the words of her prayer and clung to them with desperation, although worship of the earth mother was not for men. Yet he was born of a woman, and brother to a woman, and loved a woman. These connections were his hope, and after a moment the agony within him eased. Beloth's image faded from his mind, as did the crushing pressure to speak. He felt himself released, and with a moan, he rested his forehead on his arm and dragged in shuddering breaths of relief.

Elandra still knelt beside him, her hand hesitantly on his shoulder. "Can you speak?" she asked after a moment. "Can you stand?"

They were not safe here. He realized it had been a mistake to pause. If Beloth could sense their presence, anything else in the realm of shadows could. They had to go.

He pushed himself to his hands and knees, shaking off Elandra's hand. She retreated from him, and he staggered to his feet. Still breathing hard, he wiped his face with his arm, then doubled over and vomited.

Only then did he feel as though he had escaped. The weight of Beloth's forbidden name was no longer inside him.

"You are ill," Elandra said in concern. She touched his sleeve, and through the quick flow of *sevaisin* between them, he knew she had encountered Beloth herself before, and escaped through the intervention of the earth mother.

Caelan shut his eyes a moment. Ancient magic, natural magic . . . the kind that Lea had understood.

"We must get out of here," he said in a low voice.

"But where?" she asked in despair.

He pointed at the slope of another hill rising beyond the ruins. Noise and light came from that direction, the only signs of life in this dead place.

"Are you certain?" Elandra asked him.

He nodded, still feeling clammy and weak. His sense of danger was growing stronger.

"We must hurry," he said. "I'll explain later, but whatever you do, don't look at the tomb."

"I understand," she said, and her voice was stark with fear.

A rat ventured forth from among the rocks to lap up what Caelan had spewed. Disgusted, he turned away swiftly and led Elandra down the hill.

They skirted the city and the mist, lacking the courage to venture into either. Gripping Elandra's hand tightly, Caelan *severed* himself in order to see with truth and strode grim and fast over the blighted ground.

Occasionally a *shyriea* flew overhead, and red eyes glowed furtively at them from the ruins. Caelan heard shrieks now and then as something fought and died. But obviously Beloth's powers remained limited, even here. And perhaps not all the denizens of the realm of shadow could see Caelan while he was *severed*. Or perhaps they dared not attack someone capable of resisting their dire lord and master.

Past the ruins at the base of the next hill, Caelan and Elandra came to a stone amphitheater shaped like a deep crater. Its steps descended far below to a stage lit by flaming torches. Smoke and mist obscured what was happening down there. Caelan glimpsed an altar and moving figures. The seats themselves were filled with an assembly of warriors in black cloaks, helmets, and armor.

Beside him, Elandra gasped. "The army of—"

He put his hand swiftly across her lips, but she had already silenced herself. A low rumble passed through the ground underfoot as though Beloth had heard her near mistake. Neither of them must speak the god's name.

They hurried on, skirting the theater, keeping to the scant cover offered. The sentries standing at the top of the theater were seemingly mesmerized by the activity on the stage. They did not look elsewhere.

Eerie trails of light rose into the air, mingling with the smoke. The scorched smell of dark, forbidden magic filled Caelan's nostrils, making him feel dizzy.

Still holding Elandra's hand, his sword gripped in his other fist, Caelan ran for the slope and started picking his way up the steep, rocky trail. At the top he could see two tall stone pillars where a strange, yellowish green light glowed brightly. When Caelan looked at it too long, his eyes burned and watered. He knew that was the gateway back to their world. He could see the truth beyond it, could sense the realm of light past its barrier.

Elandra stopped and ducked behind a large boulder, pulling him down with her.

Impatient by this delay, he tugged at her hand, but she would not budge. "You can't go up there," she whispered.

He frowned. What had happened to her courage? They were practically to the gateway. After all they had gone through, she could not stop now.

"Come," he said.

"No! Don't you see them? Take care," she said in warning.

His frown deepened. What was she talking about? He saw nothing except the gateway, shining brighter than ever. Great rays of its light shone down the hill toward them, as though reaching out. He could see a dark figure silhouetted up there, but nothing else.

But Elandra herself was barely more than an aura shining beside him. He was deeply *severed*, to the point where he saw only the essence of things. But Elandra would not warn him idly. Telling himself to listen to her, Caelan pulled partway out of *severance* and saw a double row of flames burning along the trail. He frowned, and came completely out of *severance.*

Once again, exhaustion sapped his strength. He found himself leaning against the boulder for support, his spent muscles aching, his fear constricting in his chest.

And he saw the double row of guards in black armor lining the trail ahead of them all the way to the stone pillars. Caelan drew in a sharp breath, realizing that if Elandra had not stopped him he would have marched right up to the guards.

He met her gaze through the gloom. Nothing had to be said.

"What do we do?" she whispered, her voice as soft as the wind.

Without *severance,* he felt too tired to cope. Exhaustion brought discouragement, yet he refused to surrender to either.

"There is one way," he replied softly. "What we did before."

She frowned and pulled away from him in wordless refusal.

He tightened his grip on her hand. "I can walk alone past the guards, and they will not see me. But unless you are a part of me, you cannot leave this place."

She said nothing, but tears spilled down her cheeks, sparkling in the moonlight. The sadness in her face gave him his answer, and in anguish he bowed his head. Why could she not love him? Why could she not trust him? Why must she fear him so?

"Gault help me," she whispered, her fingers tightening on his. "I need what you offer as a fish needs water to live. Take me into the joining. I would be in your heart again."

It was as though the sunlight reached into this gloomy world, spreading radiance across the shadows. Caelan's heart leaped inside him, but there was no time for joy. In the distance he heard the mournful howl of a hunter.

Elandra stiffened next to him. "Hurry," she breathed, casting a look over her shoulder. "The hell-hounds—"

"Don't think of them," Caelan whispered. He melted into *sevaisin,* flowing into Elandra and feeling the brief jolt of exhilaration as she flowed into him. They shared more completely this time, and he found it tempting to remain lost in the wonder of such a union, yet there was too much danger for him to forget himself.

He *severed* back into the cold void, going only partway now for fear of losing her. Elandra's fear entwined through him, making concentration more difficult than before.

Thus steeled, Caelan stepped out from behind the boulder and walked forth up the trail until he came to the guards of darkness. He passed them, close enough to reach out and touch them, and took care to keep his pace slow and steady.

It was tempting to run, but he dared take no chances. Caelan knew he was tiring, despite the protection of *severance*. This time it was harder than ever to maintain his concentration, to maintain the detachment. He could feel the pain in his leg from his wound. He could feel the aches in his body, the need for rest and food and water. He could feel Elandra like a weight, bearing him down. Holding her in *severance* was a strain now, one he did not think he could endure for very long.

But ahead stood the gateway, like a beacon. He could almost smell the freshness of air and light beyond it.

One of the warriors in black turned his head as though he sensed Caelan's presence. The visor of his helmet was down, but through the slits glowed red, inhuman eyes. Pale smoke curled forth from beneath the rim of his visor with every exhaled breath.

Caelan paused, frozen by that scrutiny. He could sense the guard questing suspiciously. For now Caelan remained unseen, neither of one world nor the other, but somewhere between. His gaze swept over the long row of silent grim fighters concealed in their black cloaks and dark steel, tattered smoke rising above their heads. If only one of them saw Caelan, it would be over.

Making a low, guttural sound, the guard finally turned his head back toward the figure that stood next to the gateway.

Caelan felt relief stealing over the edges of *severance,* blurring it further. Quickly he plunged deeper, knowing he put Elandra at risk, yet not daring to take more chances. He hurried now past the guards, almost running past this army of hell.

His speed made more helmeted heads turn. They could not see him, but their unease was noticed by the Guardian. Robed and hooded in black, this figure stepped forward just as Caelan reached the top of the hill.

A voice, deep and monstrous, spoke a single word to him. It was not Beloth's voice, but the sound resonated loudly enough to make the ground shake beneath Caelan's feet. Hot wind lashed his face, blowing his cloak back from his shoulders. He glanced up, and saw ancient symbols burning in the air before they faded like dying embers and their ashes blew away.

Fear twisted through Caelan. His control of *severance* was unraveling, and the world seemed to tilt and shift around him before he regained mastery of himself. He felt a stab of pain in his chest from the effort he was expending. He felt also Elandra's fear and exhaustion, as well as the swirling confusion in her mind. She was unprepared for any of this; her courage was starting to fail.

Desperately Caelan focused on the gateway, using all his strength, all his force, all his essence to envision it opening.

The Guardian's voice thundered again, making the world shake. A blast of heat scorched Caelan, making him cry out. The yellowish green light between the pillars began to dim. As it did so, he glimpsed the world beyond. His world of sunlight and blue sky and verdant life.

Struggling, Caelan took yet another step forward. The pain in him grew sharp—a sawing, gouging pain similar to what he used to feel during lessons at Rieschelhold years before. It used to hurt to *sever.* It hurt now to maintain it. This task was beyond his abilities, beyond his powers.

Yet he had to accomplish it. Gathering all his reserves, he hurled everything he had, every bit of will, every ounce of desperation at the force that held him back.

He felt the invisible bond give way, and he shouted in triumph, taking two strides forward before he was stopped again.

Pain burst through his chest, and he sagged to his knees in defeat. Spent, he closed his eyes while his breath rasped in his lungs. His chest was on fire. His mind was on fire. He had given everything he had, more than he had. Now, he could do no more.

Something unseen but very powerful struck him, and the last of his *severance* crumbled.

Once again, the world shifted and tilted around him. He

opened his eyes with a gasp, only to see nothing but darkness. Then there was a flash of light, dazzling him with such brilliance he cringed and flung up his forearm to shield his eyes.

He was vaguely aware of *sevaisin* fading within him too, of Elandra slipping from him, of a tearing sense of separation. Then he saw her, white-faced and terrified, kneeling beside him. She was breathing hard as though she had been running. Her eyes stared past him, wide and mesmerized. Now and then a tremor ran through her body.

He reached out to her, and started to speak her name in reassurance. But instead he saw the Guardian looming over them. The Guardian reached up with both gloved hands and pushed back the hood.

Caelan stared at the revealed face. His breath lodged in his throat; his body turned rigid and unable to move.

Beside him, Elandra screamed.

Chapter Seven

THE FACE OF the Guardian was that of Beva E'non. Northern pale, drawn thin beneath the prominent cheekbones, the mouth a thin, uncompromising line. Bleak gray eyes that bored into Caelan's soul.

He stared, unable to believe it. "Father?" he whispered.

Almost as he spoke, Elandra tugged at his hand as though she wanted to break free. Her gaze remained centered on the Guardian as though she were mesmerized.

"Bixia?" she said. "How come you to this place?"

The Guardian swung its eyes toward Elandra and spoke something, but Caelan could not hear the words it said.

He frowned, his puzzlement and sense of alarm intensifying. This could not be his father. Beva was dead, killed by Thyzarene raiders years before. His soul had been released into the world of spirits, was now part of the spruce forests, part of the glacier, part of the rain and the falling snow.

Yet no matter how hard Caelan stared at the Guardian, it continued to be his father's stern, unyielding face that he saw.

But what name had Elandra said? Whom did she see while she gazed up at the Guardian's visage? Why did she smile so tremulously, so apologetically, so regretfully? Why did tears shimmer in her eyes?

"Who is Bixia?" he asked, but Elandra did not seem to hear him.

She was still gazing at the Guardian, listening to it utter words that Caelan could not hear. Various expressions chased across her face, and he worried that she was falling under some spell. He must not lose her now.

Pulling her to her feet, Caelan pushed her behind him. Glaring up at the face of his father, he saw Beva's gray eyes shift and focus upon him.

A shudder passed through Caelan. In an instant he was ten years old and standing on the wall surrounding their hold. Spring sunshine warmed his shoulders, and the air lay fragrant from the blossoming apple trees. He stood next to his father, who rested a hand casually on his shoulder as they watched a pair of birds building a nest in a larch tree beyond the wall. For once there was no argument between them, no scolding, no lectures . . . only peace and mutual enjoyment. The nest completed, one bird flew away, but the other one—the female, judging by her drab colors—perched on the edge of her creation and sang.

Caelan and his father glanced at each other and smiled.

Thinking of that long-forgotten moment opened a boiling cauldron of emotions in Caelan. Tears stung his eyes, and he wanted to cry out to the man he had loved so very, very much, the man he had never been able to please, the man he had never been able to reach. What had gone wrong for them? Why had he failed so utterly to be what his father demanded he become?

He met his father's eyes now and opened his mouth. Now was his opportunity to say he was sorry. Now was his chance to set things right.

"Yes, Caelan?" Beva's voice spoke his name with warmth, urging him to say the words.

Caelan's chest hurt. His eyes were burning. Tears slipped down his cheeks, and he realized he was crying. Everything in him wanted to rush to his father, to find a way to bridge the chasm between them.

"Father—" He choked up and glanced away, trying to gain control over his voice. "Father, I—I want to—"

"Yes, my son?" Beva's voice prompted. How gentle it was, how kind, how loving. It drew Caelan as nothing else could.

He took a step toward his father, then stopped with a frown. That was not his father's way of speaking, never his father's tone.

This was not really Beva. And Caelan was not really back in Trau at E'nonhold. Struggling against the beauty surrounding him, the dark green forest, the arching sky, the familiar shapes of the buildings inside the hold, Caelan reminded himself that he was in the realm of shadow, and everything before him was a trick.

With effort, he *severed* the vision, letting it fade and the strange gloom return. His eyes were still wet, but now he ached for what had never been and never would be. It was past. Old hurts became grooves in the soul. They no longer made fresh wounds.

Tipping back his head, he faced the Guardian again. But this time he did not meet those stern eyes. This time he focused his gaze slightly to one side, and let the memories slide away.

"You are the Guardian of the gate that leads back to the world of light," he said, making his voice harsh and brisk. "We do not belong here. Let us pass."

"Caelan," said his father's voice, sounding bewildered and a little hurt, "don't you remember me, my son? I am your—"

"No!" Caelan said sharply. "You are not my father. He is dead. You are the Guardian. Let us pass through the gate."

The Guardian tilted its head. "Do you not think the dead can come here?"

"Perhaps they can," Caelan admitted, finding a lump in his throat. "If they deserve it. But you are not my father, no matter how much like him you look."

Beva's face frowned, and his eyes grew stony. "Then look at this!"

As the words were spoken, Beva's face melted as though it had become hot wax, his features sliding down the skull bones to fall, hissing, on the ground. For a second a bleached skull with terrible glowing eyes stared at Caelan, and now it was no longer Beva's calm, flat voice that issued from the gaping jaw of this apparition but instead a voice like thunder, raw and savage.

"Is this better?" it demanded.

Caelan's heart pounded so fast he felt dizzy. His wits felt like charred bits of paper, blown and scattered. Hanging onto his last shreds of courage, he forced himself to nod in answer. "It is more truthful."

"Truth?" the Guardian roared, making the ground shake under Caelan's feet. "Is *this* truth?"

Again its visage changed, the skull suddenly on fire, flames bursting forth through eye holes and nostril slits, charring the bones until they were black and crumbling. The flames grew brighter, hotter, until instead of a head there was only a blazing ball of fire and light, too bright to look at.

Elandra cried out in fear, and Caelan turned away, shielding his eyes.

"Don't look at it!" he told her. "Whatever you do, don't look directly at it."

He couldn't keep from staggering back. He believed it was going to engulf them in flame and destroy them on the spot. He drew his sword, but suddenly the blade was on fire, blazing up like a torch. The hilt grew too hot to hold, and with a cry he was forced to drop it. Beneath his feet, the ground itself began to burn. Little tongues of flame popped forth from the soil, reaching hungrily for the hem of Elandra's gown.

But where they touched her cloak, they fell back as though extinguished, and burned no more.

A moment later, the air cooled to a bearable degree. The ground also cooled. The flames disappeared. Caelan's sword lay misshapen and partially melted on the ground. The light emanating from the Guardian's head dimmed, and once again only a bare skull with glowing eyes gazed at Caelan.

"Who is this woman?" it asked him.

Its voice no longer reverberated with deafening volume, but it sounded blurred and scratchy and deep. Danger lay real within its tone.

Caelan wiped the sweat from his face and straightened up. He felt breathless, as though he had run a long distance. His heart still went too fast. They had come very close to death.

"Who is this woman?" the Guardian demanded again. "She did not burn. She wears protection, spell-woven garments."

Caelan pulled himself together. "She is my heart," he answered.

"Say her name."

Caelan said nothing. Elandra shrank close against him; he could hear the quick rasp of her breathing and remembered how earlier she had begged him not to speak her name aloud. Now he sensed the danger closing around them. To speak a name as commanded here transmitted great power. He dared not obey.

"You know everything else!" Caelan said to the Guardian, putting a jeer into his voice. "You know my life, my memories, my secrets. You know who she is—"

"She is known. But she is protected. Say her name and release her into my power."

"If I resisted your master, I can resist you," Caelan said. "Let us leave."

"The gate is forbidden to all of the realm of shadow."

"We are not shadow!" Caelan said sharply. "We are light."

The Guardian pointed a bony digit at him. "Take great care, *donare*. Your tongue can be burned from your mouth."

"Let us leave."

"Speak the name of the woman."

It was not a choice. He refused to consider it. Caelan told himself he would find another way of escape.

Elandra tugged against him, and fresh fear filled him.

"Stay with me," he whispered, feeling his strength fading again. If she panicked and fled, he would lose her. "For the love of light, stay with me."

"Guardian," Elandra said.

"No!" Caelan cried, turning on her. "Don't."

"If you are told my name, will you let us leave?"

"No one leaves the realm of shadow."

She gazed up at the monster and never hesitated. "Kostimon, emperor of the world of light, passed through the realm of shadow and left it. He has done so many times."

A dry, rasping noise filled the air. After a moment, Caelan realized it was laughter. The sound chilled him.

"The emperor of light may do many things denied to men . . . or *donares*," the Guardian replied.

Caelan drew a quick breath and tightened his grip on her hand. "Don't—"

But she ignored him. Her gaze remained on the Guardian. She held her head high. Proudly, she said, "I am the empress of light. I may pass through the realm of shadow and leave it, as may my escort."

The Guardian's shoulders drew up, and it lowered its head toward her like a predator. It hissed in satisfaction. "You are the woman called Ela in Kostimon's dreams. You are the one we have searched for. The Master wants you."

Caelan saw her face go white. His own felt cold and drained of blood. "No," he whispered.

"Stay calm, *donare*," the Guardian said without glancing his way. "You have not the strength to fight me."

Elandra's face held no color. Her eyes looked huge, but she did not quail. To the Guardian, she said, "Kostimon dreams of many women. Kostimon owns many women. I am the empress sovereign. Grant me passage."

"You are the woman called Ela—"

"That is not my name!" she shouted. "In the name of the force that rules you, stand aside and let me pass!"

The Guardian stood silent and unmoving, its implacable gaze locked on Elandra.

Her eyes dropped shut. "Sweet mother goddess, bless the weavers of Mahira and their protection."

"Amen," Caelan responded, although he wasn't sure if the goddess would be insulted by the prayer of a man.

"You will speak your name."

"I am the empress sovereign," she replied. "That is name enough. I am one with Kostimon."

The Guardian uttered a low, grumbling sound of displeasure. "Kostimon has not spoken your name to the Master, but he will. Kostimon has not told the Master he gave sovereignty to a wife, but he will explain. Kostimon has not mentioned that his wife keeps a *donare* as a pet, no, not after Kostimon promised the Master he would have no such creatures—no *donares*, no *jinjas*, no Penestricans, no seers—in his palace to interfere with the plans of the Master. Kostimon has kept many secrets, but soon he will tell them."

"Let Kostimon give the answers," she said boldly, her face ashen. "That is his place, not mine. Let me pass, as he has passed."

"Kostimon went not through my gate," the Guardian said. "Kostimon does not come to the temple of Beloth except to drink from the Cup of Immortality."

As it spoke, the Guardian turned to one side and gestured

below at the bottom of the amphitheater, where stood an altar stained with blood and ringed with flames that burned in midair.

"Do you ask for this cup?" the Guardian asked.

"We do not," Caelan said firmly before Elandra could answer. "We ask only for passage through the gate."

Again there came the rasping sound that was the Guardian's laughter. "Do you know where the gate leads, *donare*?"

Another trick question. Caelan's spirits dropped, but he allowed himself to show no hesitation. "It leads to the world of light."

"I guard the Gate of Sorrows. Will you pay the toll?"

"What toll?" Caelan asked warily.

The Guardian's glowing eyes blazed into his and held them before he could look away. "If you go through it, you must return."

"No!" Elandra said before Caelan could speak. "He is here only because of me. I will pay the toll for both of us."

Aghast, Caelan looked at her in horror. "You don't know what you're doing. Make no bargain, Majesty." He turned to the Guardian. "She is the empress. Her passage is free."

"Not in the world of shadow, mortal," the Guardian said angrily. "Take care. She rules in light, but here in darkness our lady is Mael and her name stands supreme beside the Master's."

Caelan found his mouth so dry it took two swallows for him to speak again. "I am corrected," he said at last, cautiously.

The Guardian stared at him, then at Elandra. "Very well," it said. "Passage is granted for both, in exchange for the price you will pay."

"No," Caelan said in horror. "Please, don't—"

"What is your price?" Elandra asked.

"You will know, when the time comes to pay."

Caelan frowned, unable to believe Elandra was considering this. "Don't agree," he said sharply to her. "He's influencing your mind. Don't listen."

"I agree," Elandra said. Her voice did not falter.

The Guardian extended its gloved hand to Elandra. "Touch me to seal your word."

"No!" Caelan cried hoarsely, but Elandra put her hand in the clasp of the Guardian. She flinched and for a moment her eyes went blank. Then she was frowning and pulling free.

Caelan felt hollow with despair at what she'd done. But it was too late now to stop her. He couldn't believe that now, at this final moment, he had failed to protect her.

Taking Elandra's hand, Caelan faced the Guardian. "Let us go," he said angrily.

The Guardian turned its back on them and glided away. Caelan followed, leading Elandra, who was weeping. She covered her face with her free hand and would not look at him.

Ahead of them, yellowish green light glowed between the two tall pillars. As before, when Caelan gazed at it, his eyes began to itch and burn. What would happen when they stepped into that light? What would it do to them? He did not want to know, yet it was the only way out.

The Guardian drew its cowl over its head, concealing its terrible visage at last, and stopped by the gate so that the eerie light shone over its black robes. It raised both hands, and the soldiers jumped to their feet, roaring a deafening torrent of sound.

It was louder than anything Caelan had ever heard in the arena, savage and lustful and triumphant. He did not know why they were cheering. He did not think he wanted to know.

The roar went on and on until the ground shook with it. The Guardian spoke, but its words could not be heard in the din. Words appeared in the air, hanging there, burning there for a moment, before fading with little wisps of black smoke.

The Guardian pointed at the gateway, and Caelan drew in a deep breath. He held tightly to Elandra's hand, determined not to lose her now, yet knowing he already had.

"The Gate of Sorrows," the Guardian said, still pointing. "Go."

Caelan glanced at Elandra, who stood with her face averted from his. "Be brave," he said, as much to encourage himself as her. "We're nearly there."

She did not respond.

Without further hesitation, he stepped between the pillars and led her into the light.

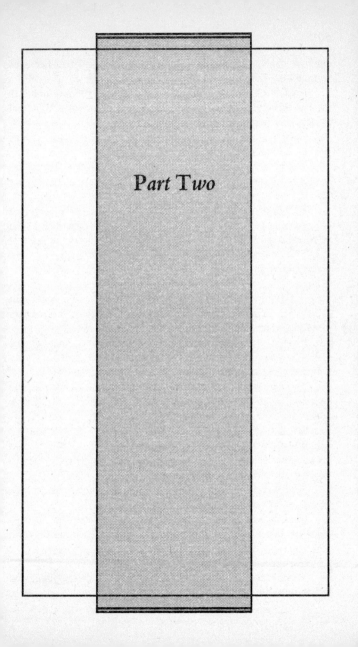

Part Two

Chapter Eight

HE WAS COLD, terribly cold. Rousing slowly, at first he was conscious only of the stiff ache of his muscles, of how tightly his arms were clamped to his sides in an effort to conserve warmth.

Something feather-light tickled his face. He frowned, struggling against the mist of sleep. A pungent scent of pine needles filled his nostrils, awakening him further. From overhead, he heard the sharp, raucous cry of jackdaws. The sound and scent reminded him of home, except that he used to sleep warm and snug in his chamber.

The tickling sensation came again, brushing his cheek, his eyelashes, his nose.

Opening his eyes, Caelan saw falling snow, the fat wet flakes spiraling down through a gray mist. He was lying outside on the ground, and it was snowing on him. Small wonder he felt so cold.

Then the fragrance of evergreens registered fully in his muddled senses. He blinked and focused on the nearby pines and spruces.

Abruptly he sat bolt upright and looked around.

He was in a small clearing, a recent one by the look of the freshly cut stumps still sticky with golden resin. The ground of spongy forest earth and layers of brown needles looked trampled and scraped by the logs that had been cut and dragged away.

And yet . . . and yet . . . he knew this ominous sky that was the color of tarnished silver. Drawing in another breath, he let the clean scents of snow and forest clear his mind. The falling snow, fluffy soft, melting as soon as the flakes landed, greeted him like an old friend.

He was home.

Caelan drew a breath so rapid and sharp it hurt his lungs. Digging his hands into the soil, he lifted dirt and pine needles to his face and inhaled the moist, earthy fragrance.

Then his hands began to tremble, and the soil crumbled through his fingers. Kneeling, he lifted his face to the sky, blinking a little against the falling snow, and let tears fill his eyes.

To be in Trau again. It was as if years had dropped away and he was a boy again. Just an ordinary boy full of dreams and mischief, not yet tainted by evil or cruelty or betrayal. A boy who had not yet killed. A boy not yet tested to the depths of his scarred soul.

Hope filled him, and he dared believe that by some miracle the shadow gods had returned him to the past, where he could start again, try again, avoid the mistakes that had cost him so dearly.

But then he glanced down and saw the crimson folds of his cloak spread on the ground about him. It looked like blood here in the mist and snow. He drew a deep breath and felt the solid constriction of his armor. There was no going back, ever. There was only the bitter present, harsh and worn. Trau legends said a man carried his sins in a basket on his back, like firewood, and as each man walked his path of life, collecting sticks, the basket grew heavier.

It was true.

"Caelan?"

The voice startled him. Snapping his head around, he saw Elandra threading her way through the stumps. In her cloak of golden wool and cream-colored gown, her auburn hair streaming free over her shoulders, she looked like a maiden of the woods, as golden and vivid as autumn itself. But there was a frown on her face, and as she drew near, her eyes looked puzzled.

She stopped and stared at him, still kneeling with a clot of earth clenched in his hand. "Are you unwell?"

Embarrassed to be caught like this, with his emotions exposed and naked, Caelan hastily shook his head.

"Then rise and tell me where we are. I have never seen such strange trees. And what is this that falls from the sky? Snow?"

"Yes," he said.

"I was told it could snow in Imperia, but rarely. I have never seen anything like this."

She looked impatient and wonderstruck at the same time. He

gazed up at her, captured anew by her beauty and vitality, and lost his heart to her all over again.

Her presence drove away the ghosts. He felt stronger and more in command of himself. "It will snow all night," he predicted, suddenly enjoying the opportunity to introduce her to the weather of a real winter. "By dawn, you will no longer see the ground. All will be covered in white snow, as though magic has been worked."

Her frown deepened, indicating that his description had failed to enchant her. "Magic?" she echoed. "Yes, I would say it has been worked. Where are we?"

"Trau."

Her mouth fell open, but it was a moment before she spoke. "I don't believe it."

Caelan got stiffly to his feet, then stood still for a moment as a wave of dizziness washed over him. As soon as it passed, he opened his eyes and squared his shoulders. "Trau," he said firmly.

"We are a thousand leagues from where we need to be. What game did the Guardian play with us?"

Caelan had no answer for her. "At least we are no longer in the realm of shadow."

She gestured impatiently and began to pace back and forth. "Yes, but that hardly matters now. What of Kostimon? What of the army? How am I to join them if I am in *Trau?*"

Caelan stopped listening. Turning aside, he glanced up and saw the jagged peaks of the Cascades looming high on the horizon. Caelan felt the wind in his face, gentle as yet, but with a threat of sharpness. It had shifted since he first awakened. It was blowing off the glacier now, and that meant a storm was coming. He suspected it was mid-afternoon if not later, and they had little time to find shelter. Then it was as though the sight of the mountain fully registered in his mind. He let his jaw drop open while he stared.

"Caelan!" Elandra said sharply, recapturing his attention. "Are you listening to anything I say?"

He turned to her slowly, feeling stunned and not quite in possession of his wits. "I am home," he said, and even his voice sounded hollow.

Impatience crossed her face. "Yes, and I am freezing," she

said angrily. "Of course you are home. You have already said this is Trau."

"No," he said. A chill that had nothing to do with the falling temperature ran through him. "*Home*. This is E'non land."

She stared at him, her eyes slowly widening. "Are you sure?"

He pointed. "There are the mountains. Up there is the glacier I used to ride across as a boy, loving the cold. I called it the top of the world."

"Did you bargain with the Guardian for this?" she asked. "When you communed with it in silence, so that I could not hear what was said, is this what you asked for? Did you think I would be a willing party to this abduction?"

He stared at her, taken aback by her anger. "What?"

"Are you mad or arrogant or simply a fool?"

His bewilderment grew. "I don't understand."

"Don't play the simpleton!" she cried, sending startled jackdaws bursting up from the treetops. "You tried to seduce me. You claimed to love me. Did you think that was enough to make me willing to run away with you?"

Finally he began to understand what she was saying. His own temper sparked. "I haven't abducted you."

"Haven't you? I told you I wasn't free. I thought that was clear."

"Very clear."

"Then why have you brought me here?"

"It was not my choice." But even to himself, that defense sounded lame and clumsy.

"Wasn't it?" She glared at him. "Then whose choice was it? We stepped through the gateway, and suddenly we are at the far end of the empire, in Trau, on your family's land. How convenient. When you made me a part of you, I experienced your emotions. I know you desired to throw me over your shoulder and carry me off. Now you have, but you'll regret it. You—"

"I didn't carry you off," he broke in, equally angry now. "You are wrong about everything."

"Am I?"

"You witnessed my talk with the Guardian. You heard."

"Then explain this trickery!"

"I can't. I thought we would come out on *Sidraigh-hal,* just as you did."

"Then why are we here?"

"I don't know!" he shouted. "In Gault's name, I don't know. Do you think I have forgotten your obligations? Do you think I have ceased to care that the empire is under attack by Tirhin's new friends? I know how important it is to reach the main imperial army and make certain of its loyalty."

His fist crashed against his breastplate. "Do I not still wear armor? Do I not still wear the insignia of the Imperial Guard? Have I forsworn my oath of service?"

"You said you would not serve me again."

He saw tears shimmering in her eyes, but her face was still angry, still doubtful. His own temper, goaded now, would not be quelled by a few womanly tears.

"And now you think the worst of me, that I am a barbarian and a liar."

"I don't know what to think!" she burst out. "You change and shift, saying one thing, doing another. You insisted I trust you, and now—"

"We escaped the shadows. Isn't that enough?"

"But look at where we are! Why can't you understand, Caelan, that I don't want to be safe, kept far away from the conflict? I want to keep my throne!"

Her words rang loudly on the cold air. A strange expression crossed her face, and she fell silent, pinching her mouth into a thin line as though her own admission had frightened her.

His anger fell away. "I know," he said quietly. "I understand. But I swear to you I have not betrayed you. I did not bring you here by design. If the Guardian looked into my thoughts and sent me here to cause me more grief and heartache than before, then it succeeded. Believe me, Majesty, this is the last place I would go."

She stared at him. "You are not happy to return to your home, to your family?"

He met her gaze without flinching. "My family is dead," he said flatly. "My home was burned to the ground. I have been away six years. What is there to return to, but ghosts and bad memories?"

With a frown, she drew her cloak tighter around her, shivering and saying nothing.

Caelan returned his gaze to the mountains and felt suddenly light-headed, as though the argument had taken all the strength from him. Poor Elandra was frightened, lashing out without thinking. He must reassure her instead of arguing with her. Just then, however, he could find no words.

Gate of Sorrows, he thought. It was well named. And what of Elandra's unholy bargain that had freed them? It would seem she had sold her soul for this trick. Small wonder she felt so angry.

"We had better go," he said to her. "There is not much daylight left."

She did not turn to face him. She did not answer.

"We cannot be outside after dark. It is not safe."

"What will hunt us?" she asked. "Predators? What of them? You have fought off demons with your powers."

Stung by her scorn, he said nothing.

She turned on him so fast her cloak whirled around her. "It is said Traulanders are afraid of the dark. You are all so big, so strong, and yet you turn into little children the moment the sun goes down."

"Trau is not Imperia, or Gialta, Majesty," he said. "Our nights hold things you do not want to meet."

"Can there be anything worse than what I have already seen?"

Before he could reply, she thrust out her arms as though to fend him off.

"Do not answer," she said. "Do not speak. I am sorry. My head is aching. I feel horrible, so full of venom. It keeps spitting from me, and I do not intend it."

His anger faded at once. "Come," he said simply.

She ran to his arms, and he held her tightly, shielding her with his cloak.

"I'm sorry," she whispered, her voice muffled against his chest. "Everything feels so wrong. I am afraid."

Her hair felt like silk against his cheek. "We will meet this challenge," he said softly to her. "We will find a way back to Imperia."

She glanced up at him, doubt and hope chasing across her face. "But you are home. Will you not stay here?"

He felt the icy kiss of the falling snow clinging to his hair and shoulders, heard the wind blowing through the pine boughs. "No," he replied, shaking his head. "It has become strange to me. My path lies with you."

Elandra tilted up her face and kissed him. Her tears dampened her lips, making them taste salty and sweet.

A fresh wave of dizziness swept him, robbing him of breath. When he could breathe again, when he could see, he found himself on his knees.

Elandra crouched there with him, gripping his shoulders. "Caelan, what is it?" she asked anxiously. "What is wrong?"

He felt strange and light, as though he was floating. The world around him seemed wavery and insubstantial, like a dream.

"Can you speak?" she asked. "Are you hurt?"

Pain hit him then. He bent over. "Yes," he managed to gasp. "My chest."

It ached as though a hammer had struck it. Every breath brought more pain. He tried to straighten, then groaned and bent over again, clutching himself.

"How can I help you?" she asked anxiously, hovering over him. "What can I do?"

The pain eased, and he was able to straighten again. He drew in several shallow breaths, grateful for even a small respite. His clothing felt hot and restrictive. Reaching into his pocket, he felt his emerald, only to flinch. Its surface was flaming hot.

"Your chest?" Elandra said. She swept aside his cloak and reached for the buckles of his breastplate.

He gripped her fingers to stop her. "No," he said, drawing in another cautious breath. "No, that won't help."

"It will. Your armor is so heavy. Removing it will ease you."

"No." He lacked enough breath to make her understand. Another wave of pain covered him, driving him low. When he emerged, shuddering from it, he found her kneeling before him, gripping his hands. Her face was white with alarm.

"It isn't me," he said. "Isn't—"

He groaned again and dug into his pocket. Wincing against

the heat that scorched his hand, he drew out the emerald and dropped it into the snow.

"Is it growing larger?" he asked, shuddering.

"What?"

"The emerald. Is it growing?"

"I see no emerald. This rock is—"

"Don't touch it!" he said as she started to pick it up.

Elandra jerked back her hand.

"I'm sorry," he said, still struggling for enough breath to talk. "It's hot. It will burn you."

She stared at him in concern. "You're not making any sense. It isn't hot. It isn't growing larger. Rocks don't change their size."

He stared at the emerald, seeing clearly its polished surface and natural facets. Were the sun shining, it would flash with fiery radiance, but now it lay there, a dull, dark blue-green. In all the years he'd carried it as his talisman, it had magically concealed its true appearance to everyone but him. Even Elandra was fooled.

"You have a magic stone," he said. "Your topaz."

With a little gasp, she touched the embroidered pouch hanging around her neck on a silk cord.

"Yes," he said. "I know it has power. I saw you use it to ward off the shadows."

"Oh," she said quietly, her eyes dark with memory. "Yes."

"Does it grow?"

"Grow?"

"Yes, increase its size."

Her eyes widened, but she shook her head.

He was feeling better now. The pain had diminished as soon as the emerald left his possession. For years he had carried it as a memory of Lea, and it had never hurt him. But lately that had changed. He did not understand why. He was not sure he could continue to keep it with him.

"When Lea first gave me the emeralds, they were no larger than the tip of my finger," he said. "Then they joined into one stone, and it keeps getting larger. I don't understand what it is."

Elandra looked at the stone. "It doesn't look like an emerald to me."

"What, then?"

"A chunk of granite."

Doubt flickered in his mind. Maybe Elandra and the others saw true. Maybe he was the one fooled.

But no. He remembered the nine emeralds Lea had found in the ice cave, the emeralds that were to have been her dowry one day. Had she lived, she would be old enough now to need that dowry. Fresh grief caught him unexpectedly. It was sharp, like a spear lance, and he thought he saw the emerald glow just for a second before it lay dull and lifeless in the snow again.

He reached out with an unsteady hand and picked it up. No longer was it hot to the touch. Sighing, he tried to return it to his pocket and found it now almost too large. He had to force it.

Never had he heard of magic such as this. He did not know whether it was beneficent or evil. He did not know how to use it, or even if it could be used. He did not want it, and yet he knew he could not throw it away. He was bound to it, and it to him.

"Don't look so worried," he said now to Elandra. "I will be well again in a few moments."

But as he spoke he started to shiver. It was more reaction than cold. He knew that from his years in the arena where he had seen brave men shake after combat. It wasn't fear.

"Are you cold?" she asked worriedly. "You're shaking so."

"I'm all right," he tried to tell her, but she pulled off her cloak and threw it around him.

"This will give you strength," she said.

Alarmed, he tried to pull off the golden cloth. "This is your protection. You mustn't—"

"Hush," she said with a smile, pulling the cloak once more over his own. "Let me wrap you up. Let me care for you this time, as you have always cared for me."

He surrendered to her tenderness, letting her draw his head to her breast and hold him. Her fingers smoothed his hair back from his face, and he closed his eyes at her touch, taking her comfort as the pain seeped from him and he began to breathe normally again.

They couldn't stay out here in the open like this. Already he was thinking of where to find shelter for the night. They were close to the hold. Whatever was left standing might be sufficient protection; they could always go into the storage cellar below ground.

Opening his eyes, he kissed her cheek and reluctantly pulled away. "We must get inside before dark. It's too cold to stay out here."

"It certainly is."

Elandra jumped to her feet, shivering herself, and held his arm to steady him as he got up.

He smiled at her. "I am well now. Here, take back your cloak before you—"

A screech came from overhead, their only warning as something large and black burst from the treetops and swooped at them. Whirling around to face it, cursing himself for letting down his guard so completely, Caelan had a confused impression of misty wings and reaching talons. Its stench clogged his nostrils, nearly making him gag.

Even as he shouted a warning and reached for his dagger, his mind was reeling with surprise. How came a *shyriea* to be here? Had it followed them from the realm of shadow? To his knowledge, none of the creatures had never appeared in Trau before. Or had things changed so drastically during his absence?

Elandra screamed and darted away from him toward the trees. The *shyriea* followed her. Caelan ran at it, shouting in an effort to distract it, but it attacked Elandra first, its female face contorted as it slashed at her. With bared fangs, its head darted at her in a swift strike.

Elandra screamed.

Rage flashed through Caelan. Screaming a curse at it, he hurled his dagger. All his fury went into the blade so that it glowed as though with fire.

It struck the demon true, and the *shyriea* exploded into black ashes that rained down.

Clutching her bleeding arm, Elandra sank to the ground.

Caelan rushed to her, fear like a hammer in his temples, and caught her in his arms. She was white-faced, trembling with shock. Her forearm bled heavily.

"It bit me," she said.

"Hush, my darling. Hush," he said hurriedly, hardly aware of what he was saying. He used handfuls of snow to clean the wound. The bite itself looked deep and nasty. Already her skin around the edges of the wound looked black and withered. As he handled her, he used *sevaisin* lightly to determine how much of the venom had entered her body.

The answer stilled his hands for a moment. He closed his eyes, agonized to think of Elandra tainted by this evil. The venom would spread through her, poisoning her blood until it was black and vile. She would become a creature owned by the darkness, commanded by it as General Paz had been.

Once again, Caelan saw his sword blade slice through the general's arm, saw again the black fluid gush forth, saw again the infant *shyrieas* forming in it.

Sweet mercy of the gods, this could not, must not, be Elandra's fate.

Opening his eyes, he ripped the lining of his cloak into strips and bandaged her arm with swift, deft motions. Then he used more handfuls of snow to wipe blood from her wrist and hand. She sat there like a child, unflinching beneath his rough ministrations. Her eyes stared into the distance.

"My price," she said dully. "I didn't believe it could happen. Am I going to die?"

"No," he said, picking up her cloak and flinging it about her shoulders. Swiftly he tied it at her throat and pulled up the hood over her snow-sprinkled hair.

If he could find a way to stop the progression of the venom through her bloodstream, there remained a slim chance of saving her. But how? He felt hopelessness drag through him, and angrily battled it away. This was no time for despair. He must get her to shelter first, and then he would try to think of what else could be done.

Chapter Nine

"CAELAN," ELANDRA SAID. Her fingers reached for his and clamped hard. Her eyes were wide with fear, and now and then her lips trembled. She was breathing hard, trying not to panic. "You must tell me what is wrong. Am I going to die?"

With an effort he forced himself to conceal his own fears. He gave her a little smile. "No, of course you are not going to die. It is only a little bite. I am sure it hurts, but you—"

She raised her hand to silence him. "No lies. I need the truth. Do you understand?"

Worry lay on him like a thin sweat. Still, he knew he must keep the truth from her for as long as possible. He could not afford to let her panic. He reached for *severance,* but she grabbed his wrist and pulled herself to him.

"Tell me!" she cried, her eyes flashing with fear. "Don't turn to stone. Don't shut me out. I deserve better than that!"

It was like being plunged into the past, hearing her voice echo his own pleas to Beva. Appalled, Caelan wondered, *Am I like my father?*

He stroked her cheek. "I'm sorry," he said. "I don't want to be like him."

"Who? You're not making any sense." Her eyes clawed at his, holding his gaze when he tried to look away. "It's bad, isn't it?"

The lies and assurances died on his lips. "Yes," he answered in a hollow voice. "It is bad."

Fear leached the remaining color from her face, making her eyes huge and vulnerable. She started trembling, but she didn't falter. "What will happen to me?"

"I—"

"The worst, Caelan!" she commanded. "Tell me the worst."

"The venom is in you. In time, if its work is not checked, you will become like General Paz."

Her mouth opened, but nothing came out. Her hand dropped from his arm, and despair filled her face.

"But there is time yet," he said hurriedly. He pulled her to her feet and put his arm around her to steady her. "While there is time, there is a chance. We must hurry."

"Where?"

"We'll go to the hold. It isn't far. We need shelter, and I may be able to find something in Father's writings."

He led her forward, holding to her unsteady pace when he really wanted to scoop her into his arms and run. He had to keep her walking and thinking. If she kept talking to him, then he would know she was still with him.

"Walk, Elandra," he commanded. "Walk faster. Keep your blood strong."

Her feet moved slowly. After a moment, she glanced up at him. "Is there a healer nearby? A neighbor? Anyone who can be sent for?"

He frowned. It was as though she couldn't comprehend that his home had been destroyed and all who lived there had died or been sold into slavery. The same had happened to neighboring holds. Whether anyone had returned or rebuilt, he did not know. But he would not deny her this small hope.

"Perhaps," he said. "We will get shelter, and then we will see what can be done."

His dagger lay on the ground at the edge of the clearing, its blade blackened. He hesitated over it, hating to be weaponless yet not certain whether it was tainted.

"Take it," Elandra said faintly.

He bent and scooped it up, opening himself to *sevaisin*. There was death in the metal, nothing more. Relieved, he wiped it and put it back in his belt, then led Elandra on with a quick glance at the sky.

Beyond the clearing, the trees grew thick and tangled. Their boughs were turning white with snow, and the mist seemed to hang more thickly here, obscuring the way. Shouldering a path through,

Caelan pushed on at a steady pace, his face grim and set against the lash of snow.

When she stumbled, his arm tightened around her. "I am with you," he said in reassurance. "I love you with all my heart and soul. I will find a way to save you."

"Can you?" she asked, her voice dragging with weariness and pain. "I do not doubt your strength or your courage. I know you can do things most men cannot. But can you save me from this?"

He wanted to shout aloud in fear and frustration. He wanted to run with her for help, only there was no help to be found. For the first time in his life he regretted his expulsion from Rieschel-hold. If he had stayed and become a healer, perhaps he would know what to do.

But if he had become a healer, he would never have met this woman who now meant everything to him.

I cannot lose her, he prayed. *Please don't take her from me.*

"You are all I have," she whispered. "I trust you, my love."

A few minutes earlier, her admission of love would have filled him with joy. Now he could only grieve for her. But he had to stay in control of himself; he couldn't bear for her to see the inadequacy and hopelessness he felt.

She had insisted he tell her only the truth, but he loved her enough to lie. "I will get it out," he promised. "As soon as we have shelter from the wind spirits, I will find a way to save you."

She gave him a tremulous smile. "Forgive me?"

Her plea nearly unmanned him. Raggedly, he said, "Why? What is there to forgive, my love?"

"I should have obeyed you—"

Without warning, she sagged against him.

Desperate not to let her fall, he tightened his hold. "Elandra? Elandra!"

He tipped back her lolling head, but her eyes were shut. Her face was as gray as death.

Frantic, he lowered her to the ground and knelt over her. For a moment time froze around him, and he could only stare. She looked so small, so still in her golden cloak and hood. He thought she was dead.

Pain lanced his heart, and he wanted to scream his denial to the heavens.

Then he pulled back her hood, releasing her hair, which tumbled out in a glorious mass. He touched her face. How cold it was, as cold as the snow falling on it, yet her flesh still had the resilience of life. He could feel the light, moist puff of her breath against his palm.

Air flowed suddenly back into his lungs. He sent up a quick prayer of relief and gathered her awkwardly into his arms.

Gloom was thickening beneath the trees. He hadn't realized how fast night was coming. In Imperia, there were hours of twilight and long, splendid sunsets across the bay. He had forgotten how short were the days in Trau, how quick and final the night came.

As though in warning, the wind picked up and set the trees swaying. Their boughs whispered a sound that set the hairs on the back of his neck prickling. He stumbled forward, trying to hold onto the fading light by sheer willpower. There had to be time to reach shelter. There had to be.

It was snowing harder now, becoming a driving, stinging force at his back that whipped his cloak. The temperature was falling. Caelan's breath streamed about his face, and he felt frozen to the bone. His cloak might be wool, but it was lightweight cloth, inadequate here. His years in warmer climates must have thinned his blood, for his hands and feet felt numb already despite the exercise. His face hurt from the cold. The air he breathed felt knife-sharp.

Do something, he told himself angrily. *You fool, think of something to save her.*

But fear made his wits fade. He could not think, could not find the answer. This was not something he could fight with strength and sword. All he had were his gifts of *sevaisin* and *severance.*

The venom must be spreading faster through her body than he expected. If she regained consciousness, she might not know him. Soon she would not remember she loved him. The darkness in her would spread until it consumed her.

Then she would be what Sien, Agel, Paz, and Kostimon had

become, a servant of Beloth, turned into corruption, unable to find her way back to light.

If he *severed* her, it would kill her. What else could be done?

She lay heavy in his arms as he carried her, stumbling through the undergrowth, now and then breaking into a run only to slow down to a saner pace.

Time was against him now. If darkness fell before he found shelter, the wind spirits would kill them. For Elandra, that might be a mercy.

"No," he said aloud, tipping back his head to gulp in more air. Then he began to trot, his panting hoarse in his ears.

"Hurry. Hurry."

He found himself mumbling the word aloud, driving himself on the way Orlo used to drive him through his drills in the arena. He was strong and fast, former champion of the games. Now he was a soldier, the elite of Kostimon's hand-picked Guard. He could save Elandra. He *must* save her.

It was nearly dark. The moaning shriek of the wind warned him that danger could strike at any moment, provided he didn't freeze first.

He forced himself to keep going, to not surrender. Not yet, not until every drop of strength drained from his body, not until the wind spirits found them and shredded them to bits.

He had promised Elandra, promised her. He would not give up.

The ground dropped abruptly before him, and he went stumbling down an embankment before he could catch himself. He lost his footing and fell, dropping Elandra in the process, and skidded into a stream with a splash.

The water was so cold it burned. He floundered upright, cursing himself, and dragged himself from the water. Staggering like a drunken man, he found Elandra lying in the snow like a rag doll. It took him three tries before he managed to pick her up again.

When he straightened, he was hit by a gust of wind so strong it nearly knocked him over. For a wild second he thought he'd been attacked by a wind spirit, but it was only the storm, rising in force now as the blizzard came in. It hurled snow and stinging sleet into his face, pelting him without mercy. His wet clothing froze to his skin. He knew they were in grave danger. If he didn't find shelter in the next few minutes, they would both die.

The emerald in his pocket grew suddenly warm. He reached into his pocket, thinking he could thaw his hand around the stone, and heard the rip of splitting cloth.

The stone fell to the ground with a thud, landing next to his foot. It had grown larger in that instant, and was glowing a bright green that cast an eerie lambent light over the snowy embankment and the dark ribbon of stream at its base.

Caelan stared at it, and some of his panic cleared momentarily. The stream . . . the gully . . . he must be near the ice cave where he and Lea had found the emeralds. While he would rather go to a different one, he had no time to be choosy. Also, it seemed his own stone was trying to help him.

He glanced around and turned north, hurrying along the bottom of the gully, splashing in and out of the shallow stream as he searched.

Minutes later, he found the mouth of the cave, halfway up the side of the slope. He paused there, his hand gripping the edge of the opening, and wondered if he had the courage to enter what must be Lea's grave.

"Please," he whispered aloud. "Ice spirits . . . earth spirits . . . take pity on me. Let me enter in peace."

He sniffed for evidence of a lurker that might be using the cave as a den, but smelled nothing. Shouting, he picked up a chunk of ice and hurled it inside.

Nothing came leaping out.

It was safe, except for memories.

Right now, he couldn't afford those.

He hurried back to where Elandra lay. Half-covered in snow, she hadn't stirred at all. The emerald, so large now it would have to be carried with two hands, still cast its light over her like a protective shield.

He picked her up and lurched back to the cave, boosting her inside, then climbing in and pulling her deeper into its shelter. Lastly, he went scrambling back for the emerald.

It was too hot to hold. He jerked his fingers away, shaking

them, and used the hem of his cloak to gather up the magical stone and carry it to the cave.

The light it cast turned the ice cave into an eerie place of strange angles and shadows. Caelan crawled down the long tunnel leading into the small cavern at the back.

Lea had once played here among the fanciful formations, imagining it to be her palace and assembling her dolls, bark cups, and playthings.

He saw one of the cups now, lying on its side on the ground. Breathlessly he picked it up, only to find it was brittle with age. It crumbled to dust in his fingers.

"Lea," he whispered and had to choke back tears.

But it was Elandra he must care for now. He built a small fire and stripped off her wet gown to dry. Her cloak remained dry, and he wrapped her in it. A faint glow from inside her jewel pouch caught his attention. He upended it and shook out the topaz it contained. The jewel was glowing with a life of its own. It sent out golden light to mingle with the green coming from the emerald.

Not daring to touch her stone with his bare hands, Caelan used the pouch to pick it up. He placed it in her palm and folded her fingers around it, praying the magic in the topaz would work to counteract the darkness inside her.

She looked so pale, lying there. Her eyes were sunken and smudged with purple shadows. A tiny pulse at her temple told him she still lived. Now and then she frowned and jerked as though in pain. He wanted to cry out each time.

He felt so helpless, so ignorant. Again and again, he was tempted to *sever* her, but he dared not take the risk. No matter how much he needed to do something, his abilities were not the answer to this problem.

"Dear Gault," he prayed, "have mercy on this woman. Give her strength to fight the darkness that assails her. Grant me the means with which to save her."

He watched her while his wet clothes slowly dried over the tiny fire. Melting ice overhead dripped here and there, making him shift positions. Hunger he ignored. Exhaustion he ignored. He had to keep watch, as though by his will alone he could make Elandra better.

Finally he slept, only to awaken with a start deep in the night.

The fire had died out. It was bitterly cold. By the light of the glowing emerald and topaz he rekindled the fire, then crept over to Elandra. She felt very cold to his touch; only her hands were warm from the topaz she held. She still breathed, lightly but evenly.

He kissed her forehead and moved away from her. For now, he had done all he could for Elandra.

Another task lay before him. It was time to face it. Guilt, no matter how strongly deserved, was a burden that could grow too heavy for anyone to bear. It was time to hunt the ghosts and lay the memories to rest.

Turning away from Elandra, he lit a stick from the fire. Holding it aloft as a torch, he headed deeper into the cave, in search of his sister's bones.

At the very rear of the cave, a folded curtain of stone hung from the ceiling. Some instinct made Caelan approach it. Putting out his hand, he curled his fingers around the edge of the curtain and found empty space behind it. A narrow fissure led into another room beyond the first.

This cave was sheathed in ice, as cold as the outdoors, and utterly silent as though no living thing had ever entered it. The moment he set foot in it, something began to glitter around him, like stars cast down from the night sky. They winked and twinkled from the ceiling overhead, from the ground before him, from the walls.

Raising his small torch higher in an effort to see, he realized that these were emeralds embedded in the ice. Polished and cut like fine jewels, they were reflecting back his torch.

They were too many to count. Dazzled by their beauty as well as by the wealth they represented, he stared at the sight for a moment. With these, he could buy an army of his own. He could buy the empire itself, if he chose.

When he realized what he was thinking, Caelan was flooded with shame. He bowed his head and cursed himself. How could he think of his own ambitions at a time like this? He might as well be a boy again, full of his own plans and tempted to steal his little sister's emeralds to buy a commission in the army.

"No, Caelan."

Startled, he glanced up and around but saw no one. He listened a moment. "Elandra?"

She did not respond.

He stepped back to the fissure and listened again, feeling he should return to her. She needed him by her side. He must not linger here.

Anxious now to finish his search, he crossed the icy cavern, trying to ignore the beauty of the emeralds as he sought evidence of his sister. Then the feeble torchlight fell upon a tiny mound of fabric.

Hurrying over to it, he crouched and picked up the red cloak that Lea had been wearing the last time he saw her.

Summer moths had eaten holes in it. A rodent had gnawed away one corner. It was covered with dust that floated in the air as he shook the cloth.

He half feared he would find her remains beneath the garment, but there was only the ice-encrusted floor.

Dropping the torch, he clutched the cloak in both hands, seeking answers to the questions that haunted him.

Had she stayed here in the cave as he had told her? Had she waited until she starved? Or had she ventured out, trying to follow the stream to E'raumhold? If so, why had she left her cloak behind? Where had she gone? What had become of her? Had her end been swift and merciful, or slow torture? At the end, had she still hoped he would return as promised? Or had she died knowing he betrayed her?

"Oh, Lea," he whispered aloud, bending over the cloak. "I came back. I did keep my promise."

Too late, said the guilt in his mind. *Too late.*

The scent of flowers filled the air, and suddenly the cave felt warm and almost pleasant.

"It is never too late, Caelan," said a feminine voice. "Love is always in time."

Startled, he looked up to find the cave filled with a clear, pale light. A slender maiden stood before him, gowned in pine green with a wreath of flowers entwined in her golden hair. A thick braid reached down over her left shoulder, the way his mother used to wear hers. Blue eyes, both merry and wise, twinkled at him.

"Welcome, dearest brother," she said.

Still kneeling, he stared up at her, unable to speak, unable to think. Surely his hunger was making him see things.

"I am fourteen now," she said and smiled so that her dimples appeared. "Am I not well grown? Do you think I am pretty?"

Then she came running to him and flung her arms around his neck. "Oh, Caelan, Caelan!" she cried, laughing and kissing his cheek over and over. "How glad I am that you have come home. I have missed you so much. I wanted you back here with me. I *made* you come."

He could not understand it. He dared not believe it. And yet . . . "Lea," he said, his voice choking as he hugged her back. She was real flesh and blood in his arms. He found himself in tears. "Dear gods, is it you?"

"Of course, silly."

Pushing away from him, she threw back her head and laughed, then caught his hand and drew him to his feet. Now it was her turn to stare up at him. She did so, studying him hard from every angle.

"How big you are now. How broad your shoulders are. And you're taller. But so am I!"

Laughing, she skipped away and twirled about the room until her gown belled around her ankles. Then she raced back up to him and gave him another hug around the waist.

"I am so happy now. Did I say how much I have missed you?"

He grabbed her by the arms to keep her from skipping away again. "Slow down, you minx," he said, half laughing at her antics. It was as though the years had fallen away, and they were playing and tussling the way they used to. He had the urge to toss her high in the air and tickle her until she begged him to stop.

But she was too old for that. Why, she was grown, practically a woman now. He kept starting to say something to her, only to stop and stare, his breath forgotten in his throat, his words lost.

"Look at you," he said at last. "How, Lea? How did you survive?"

"You told me to wait," she said. "After a while, I couldn't do that, but I came back every day to see if you'd kept your promise. And here you are! I knew you wouldn't fail me. I wanted you to come back, and you have."

Questions crowded his mind, too many to ask all at once. This was so hard to comprehend. He wanted to dance in joy, and yet he could not believe she was here or that she was really alive.

He pulled her near again, touching her face, tugging at her hair, entwining her fingers in his. They were long and tapered now instead of chubby and small.

"How?" he whispered, his amazement continuing to grow. "You must tell me how."

"How I made you come back?"

He squeezed her hands in an effort to make her be serious. "No, how you lived after I abandoned you. Where did you go? Who looked after you?"

Her gaze swung away from his. "So many questions—"

"I must know!" he insisted. "I thought you were dead. All these years, I have blamed myself for abandoning you."

"But you didn't," she said earnestly. "You had to help Father. I understand that now."

"I couldn't do anything to help him," Caelan said bitterly, seeing the raid all over again. "I was a boy, without weapons, unable to fight properly. I should have stayed with you. Instead, I ran away and left you crying here in the cave."

"I don't cry now," she said. "I'm too grown up."

He choked and dropped to his knees before her. "Forgive me, Lea."

"Hush, Caelan. Hush." She touched his face with her hands, soothing away his distress. "Don't be sad. I don't blame you for anything."

He kissed her hands, thankful for her mercy. "You were always of a good and generous heart, little one. I blamed myself."

"I know," she said, suddenly serious. "You have suffered dreadfully. If only I could have made you come back sooner, you wouldn't have hurt so much. But I had to grow first. I had so much to learn."

She sat down in front of him, tucking her gown around her feet as though she were impervious to the ice-cold floor. He noticed then that she wore the nine thumb-sized emeralds in a neck-lace around her slim throat. Many girls of marriageable age wore their dowries as necklaces. But who had made such a necklace for her? Who had taken her in and given her such fine clothing to wear? Who had cared for her?

"No questions," she said, holding his large, callused hand in her slim one. "Not now. I promise we'll talk of those things, Cae-lan, but later in a less important time."

"But—"

"Hush," she said, her blue eyes very serious now. "I must study you. There are things I must know, and I will learn them quicker this way than if we talk. Don't close yourself to me. Please."

Before he could speak, he felt her brush against his mind and riffle his thoughts. He felt her soul slip through his, leaving a re-freshing sense of having dived into cool water on a hot summer's day. He felt her sift through his past before he could stop her, then she was gone from him, separate, blinking in front of him, and looking a little pale.

"Oh, my," she said breathlessly. "Oh, my."

She knew it all, knew his failures, his moments of shame, his secrets. Just as she had always known them. It had never been easy to keep anything concealed from her. Now he suspected it might be impossible.

She turned his hand over in hers and stroked his palm with her fingertips. "So much blood," she murmured. "So much killing. I can hear the death screams of countless men. Do they trouble your dreams?"

There was no point in lying. "Yes."

"Have you taken enough lives to pay back the Fates for Fa-ther's death?"

He squirmed uncomfortably. Lea went, as always, straight to the heart of the matter. "No," he said after a moment. "That will never be erased."

"Why do you blame yourself for Father's death?" she asked.

He looked into her eyes for grief and found only clear-eyed concern for him in their depths. Sighing, Caelan said, "I don't know. It's been so long. It's all confusion now."

"Yes, you are confused. I thought you would have finished your lessons by now, but you haven't. You are always so slow, Caelan."

"What—"

She jumped to her feet. "Do you still have your emeralds? The ones we found here together? They were to be your talismans. Did you keep them or sell them for a sword?"

"Come and see."

He took her back to the other cave, where the formations of stone hung twisted and folded as they had for all time, where his huge emerald still glowed beside the little fire, where Elandra lay caught in the dark spell that had captured her.

Lea gasped and shrank against him in unexpected shyness. "Who is she?"

"Her name is Elandra. She is our sovereign empress and the wife of Emperor Kostimon."

"She is beautiful," Lea whispered.

Joy swelled his heart. Lea's approval meant everything. He hugged her and kissed the top of her head.

Lea pulled away from him. "Is she sleeping?"

"No," Caelan said, his joy fading. "She is dying."

"How?"

"A *shyriea*—a demon that flies and attacks like—"

"I know what it is," Lea said.

He glanced at her in wonder, but asked no questions. "It bit her. The venom is poisoning her blood, turning her into the darkness. I fear—I fear she will change into—"

Lea turned and gripped his hand a moment. Her blue eyes met his, and they were direct, reassuring, and oddly mature. "Do not fear, Caelan. You have brought her into a place of protection, just as you brought me. No harm can befall her here."

"But—"

She lifted a finger to her lips to silence him, then turned and knelt beside Elandra. With gentle hands she touched Elandra's brow. Closing her eyes, Lea began to sing a low, wordless melody in a voice like gold.

It was like hearing his mother sing to him again at bedtime. Caelan turned away for a moment, overtaken by memories of gentle hands smoothing the bedclothes, of soft lips kissing his cheek, of the song lulling him into the warm caress of sleep.

Overcome, he found his throat choking up. In silence he fled, stooping through the tunnel to the mouth of the cave. Rushing outside, he stood in the gully, shielded a bit from the wind-whipped snow, and drew in rapid lungfuls of the frosty air.

Lea's song made him think of purity, of kindness and peace, all the virtues, innocence and goodness. The notes of her music were being woven around Elandra, protecting and preserving her. But the song had driven him out, for he was tainted. Blood would forever stain his hands. Even if he lived as a hermit on a lonely rock for the rest of his days, he would never be able to purify himself.

Wrapping up in his cloak against the terrible cold, he stood shivering against the embankment, risking attack from the wind spirits, letting the harsh sleet rasp his face. Now and then when the wind lulled momentarily, he could hear a note or two of Lea's singing. He wished she could sing such a song over him and wipe away his past, but he knew that was not possible. For Caelan could feel his future all the way to his bones. He thought of that moment when he had been linked together with Kostimon in Choven fire against the *shyrieas*; he thought of the various swords he had held and how some of them sang to him of battle and how others whispered combat secrets that no man knew to teach him. He had been made for war. Every muscle and sinew in his strong body had been forged for combat. He would fight again, and he would kill again. That he knew.

And therefore, Lea's song of healing was not for him.

"Caelan?"

Her voice reached out softly to him from the cave.

Turning his head, he listened a moment, then climbed back inside. When he reached the women, he saw that the fire had gone out, yet light still glowed around Lea and Elandra. The little cavern was warm and comfortable. The scent of flowers seemed very strong. He could feel a presence with them that made his skin prickle uneasily, then it was gone.

Lea was smiling with her eyes closed. She still knelt there beside Elandra, and for an instant she seemed to fade and grow transparent. It was like looking at a ghost or a spirit.

Caelan's heart fell within him. In an instant he understood that Lea was not real, was not alive as he had thought. The miracle of her survival had been only a dream. Yes, she was here, but as part of the spirit world, and that meant she was indeed dead and lost to him.

Chapter Ten

STARING AT HER in horror, he slowly backed away.

Lea turned her head to look at him, and her blue eyes widened. "No, Caelan!"

He couldn't bear to speak to her. What cruelty was this? What capricious god took amusement at giving him Lea against all hope or reason, then made her nothing more than a ghost?

Lea's eyes tried to hold his. "You're wrong. Please listen—"

With a cry, Caelan turned and ran, stooping, down the tunnel. He had to get out of here, had to get away from her.

She came after him, throwing her arms around his waist and squeezing tight to hold him.

He turned on her, pushing her off. "Get away from me!"

Tears filled her eyes. "I'm real. I'm real!"

He shut out her voice, refusing to listen. Again he turned his back on her and headed for the mouth of the cave.

She caught his cloak and tugged. "Please, please listen to me. Touch my hand. I'm flesh and blood, Caelan, just like you."

Her pleas tore at his heart. He wanted to believe her, yet he couldn't. All he trusted was the evidence of his own eyes.

"Do you not waver from the sight of others when you *sever*?" she asked. "Has no one ever been frightened by you? Has no one ever misunderstood what you are doing?"

He glanced back at her with a frown. "What?"

"Can you not come and go among people without being seen? Can you not step into the spirit world and exit as you choose? Can you not move faster than thought, so fast sometimes your opponent cannot see you?"

His frown deepened. He did not want to listen to her, yet he could not help it. How could she know what it was like?

"Oh, Caelan," she said, her voice full of compassion, "do you not yet know what we are?"

He stared at her, too amazed to answer, but his mind was shifting into one rapid thought after another. Lea, who could read his mind, who had answered his thoughts as though they were spoken aloud since she had first learned to talk. Lea, who wished for things that then came true, as though her will could bend events themselves. Lea, whose gentle spirit had always been his guide and conscience.

"What are you saying?" he whispered.

She stepped closer, her eyes still locked on his. Holding out her hand to him, she said, "Am I real?"

He flinched back. "I don't know! I have lately walked in a place where the mind can be twisted. All these years I have grieved for you, thinking you were dead, wishing I could see you again."

"I am not dead. I am not a ghost. Caelan, look with truth. Don't let your fear blind you."

"What is the truth?" he asked hoarsely, dragging in a breath. "How do you still come to be here? How are you still alive? Who cares for you? What happened to you?"

"I told you this is a place of sanctuary."

"Sanctuary? What do you mean?"

"A place of protection. The gentle spirits keep it. Anyone who comes here is safe. I knew this when I used to play here. You knew it when you left me here."

"I knew nothing," he said savagely. "Except that I abandoned you to starve."

"You *knew*," she insisted. "Instinctively, if nothing else. And when you told me to stay here until you came back, I did. In a way."

He looked away angrily. "Impossible! Why do you lie?"

"Why do you refuse the truth?"

Her words were gentle; her tone was reasonable. But he couldn't believe her.

"I'm sorry," she said, looking hurt. "I thought you would understand by now. I shouldn't have approached you this way. But I was so glad to see you, so happy. After all these years I had the chance to bring you back to me."

"I don't understand."

She met his gaze, and her eyes were clear and guileless. "I wished you to come back to me, and you did. When I saw that you were coming through the Gate of Sorrows, I—"

"How do you know about that?" he demanded sharply, his suspicions reawakened. "Unless you are yourself some vision from the shadow world, how would you know about—"

"How do *you* know what you know?" she countered. "How do you see deeply into the souls of men, so deeply you find their threads of life? How do you command a warding key simply by holding it and wishing it to work? How do you walk among demons and men, known to both? Do you think it is possible that only you can do such things, when I am your sister, with the same blood and the same heart?"

He stared at her, letting her words sink in, and felt cold to his marrow. "What are we?" he asked.

She hesitated a moment, then said, "We are Choven."

His mind surged within him, as though he might almost believe it; then his skepticism crashed back. "Impossible."

"Do not fear the truth."

He glared at her. "Choven don't look like us. They aren't—"

He broke off abruptly and didn't finish his sentence.

Lea's eyes never wavered. "They aren't human?" she finished.

Furious, he said, "I have been called everything from *casna* to *donare*. But—"

She slapped her hand against his breastplate loudly enough to silence him. "Hush!" she said, her blue eyes snapping. "Oh, how angry you make me when you are stubborn. Are the Choven evil? *Are they?*"

He frowned and reluctantly shook his head.

"They are mysterious and rarely seen. Does that make them evil?"

He sighed impatiently. "Of course not."

"Then do not fear the truth."

"But, Lea, I do not look like any Choven ever seen. Nor do you. We look like our parents. We were born in E'nonhold, our births witnessed by people who helped bring us up."

It was her turn to sigh impatiently. She crossed her arms and began to tap her foot. "Stubborn *and* stupid. You have so many lessons to learn. Will you insist on seeing only the most obvious explanation? Or can your mind accept alternatives?"

"Explain."

"I am *trying* to, but you won't listen to anything."

Wearily he tipped his head back against the wall. "I am tired, sister, and beset with worries. My chief responsibility is the life and safety of the empress sovereign. Make your words simple and don't twist my mind with complications."

"I'm sorry we have quarreled," she said, her anger vanishing at once. "Of course you are tired, but you need not worry. You are safe, and the empress is safe as long as she stays here."

"She has little time," Caelan said. "The venom—"

"It cannot do its evil while she lies here."

He looked into his sister's eyes and felt the tension in his body relax. Closing his eyes, he murmured, "Gault be thanked."

"Come," Lea said, tugging at his sleeve. "You need care. Come and rest."

He shook free and slung the end of his cloak across his shoulder. "No, I must guard her—"

"She is safe, Caelan. No harm can befall her here."

"Any lurker could enter the cave—"

"No lurker would dare come in here. The earth spirits guard us. Nothing without can see the mouth of the cave. Even if they look directly at it, their eyes are blinded and they see only dirt and rock." Lea tilted her golden head and smiled at him. "Don't worry so much. Be at peace for a little while, sweet brother. You have fought for such a long time. Come and take refuge."

She was right. He did need rest. He tried to think of how long it had been since the Madruns overran the palace, and knew he had lost all track of time. But he had been fighting too long, and he could not fight Lea too.

She drew him back into the deepest part of the cave, where he had first found her. The emeralds studding the walls glittered at him, and the air was so warm and sweet he threw back his cloak.

"Elandra should be in here."

"The lady sleeps well where she is. Do not disturb her," Lea said. "Sit, and take your rest."

With a groan, he sank to the ground and propped himself against the wall. His muscles were stiffening, and his leg hurt. His armor weighed too much, and he could no longer resist the spell that Lea cast.

"Rest your mind as well as your body," Lea said. "Here."

He glanced up at her and blinked, for in her hands were a goblet of mead and a bowl of steaming soup. He frowned in astonishment. "How?"

"Eat," she said, handing the food to him. "Then we will talk."

It was morning when he awoke, finding himself covered with a soft fur robe. Tiny dapples of sunlight filtered in from natural ventilation somewhere. Blinking, he slowly sat up and looked around. His armor lay nearby, freshly polished and gleaming. The rips in his crimson cloak had been mended, and the garment itself was cleaned so well it looked cut from new cloth. A large, decoratively stitched leather pouch fitted with a shoulder strap rested beneath his emerald. Smiling involuntarily to himself, Caelan brushed his fingertips over the surface of the stone before sliding it into the pouch and slipping the strap over his shoulder to check the fit. If the emerald continued to grow larger and heavier, he might soon find himself trying to carry a boulder around. Then what would he do? Start driving a cart?

But such flippant thoughts seemed disrespectful. After all, he was a guest in this place; he must not insult his mysterious hosts, even in his mind.

He wolfed down fresh, piping hot breakfast cakes stacked on a platter, emptied a mug of spiced cider, and felt almost renewed.

Running his hand over the itchy stubble on his jaw, he yawned and stretched as best he could in the cramped confines of the cave. Slipping through the narrow exit, he returned to the other cavern where he had left Elandra the night before.

She lay still and peaceful, as though in sleep, the glowing topaz still clutched in her fingers.

He knelt beside her, not daring to touch her, and fresh worry filled his heart. Lea had said she was safe here, but would she slumber forever in this cave, never to emerge?

Someone had combed the tangles from Elandra's auburn hair. It lay across her pillow in a shining fan, and a fur robe covered her to the waist. Her face looked peaceful, no longer pale and strained. The purple smudges were gone from beneath her eyes. He studied the thick sweep of her lashes against her cheek and wished he could somehow impart his strength to her.

"Good morning," Lea said.

Startled, he turned and saw his sister smiling at him. She wore a gown of sky-blue wool today, and her golden hair had been pinned up in smooth plaits around her head.

Caelan smiled at her in greeting, hiding his doubts, which had returned, and reluctantly left Elandra's side to join his sister.

"Come out," Lea said.

Caelan followed her outside and found the sun bright upon a blinding expanse of fresh snow. The air was crisp and clean. For a fanciful moment it almost seemed that the trees bowed to him, but Caelan blinked and dismissed the thought. It was only the weight of the snow, bending them down.

"It is a beautiful day," Lea said, throwing out her hands and whirling about in a little dance that took her to the edge of the stream. She jumped its narrow expanse—her skirts flying up to show off the red leather boots she wore—and clapped her hands from the opposite side. "Come!"

Smiling a little, he followed where she beckoned, climbing up the opposite bank with his breath streaming white about his face.

"Where are we going?" he called after her. "I don't want to get too far from . . ."

His voice died away as he reached the top of the bank and found himself looking at a herd of nordeer. The animals were pale and stately, gathered just at the edge of the clearing.

They peered back at him, their long, narrow faces solemn as they flicked long ears and chewed their cud. There were perhaps a dozen of the animals, a tiny herd containing what looked like an even mixture of does and bucks. The latter carried tall, racklike antlers with a graceful air of nobility. It was strange that all the nordeer were of similar size, and each rack of antlers showed an identical number of points. Caelan had never before seen a herd like this. Usually they migrated in vast numbers, bunching protectively around the old, weak, and young ones.

As he stared in wonder, some of them dropped their heads and pawed the snow for grazing. Caelan laughed aloud, and their heads snapped back up to look at him. They were alert, poised as though to leap away, and yet they seemed remarkably unafraid.

Lea was watching Caelan closely. When he smiled, she did too. "Are they not beautiful?" she asked.

"Magnificent," he said, thrilled by the sight of them. Glimpses of wild nordeer this far south were rare.

"They came for you," Lea said.

His gaze swung away from the animals, and he frowned at her. "What?"

She pointed, and he turned to see two shaggy mountain ponies saddled and tied in readiness.

Caelan did not understand, but he did not want to. He moved back a step. "No."

"It is time you learned the truth," Lea said.

"I can't leave Elandra alone here."

"She won't be alone. The spirits guard her."

Caelan scowled stubbornly, but Lea did not argue further. Instead, she walked over to the nearest pony and untied a long, narrow bundle wrapped in bright cloth. Bringing it back with her, she held it out to Caelan.

He made no move to take it.

"This is a gift," Lea said. "Look at it and you will understand."

His frown deepened, but he took the object and stripped away the wrapping. He held a sword sheathed in a scabbard of beautifully stamped leather. The hilt was wrapped in gold wire; the guard was carved with strange symbols that seemed to dance when he looked at them too long. A large square emerald winked from the end of the hilt. Despite his suspicions, he could not resist the sword.

His hand closed around the hilt, and it seemed to arch itself into his palm as though alive. Startled, he tightened his grip and found himself pulling off the scabbard with a swiftness that made the blade sing quietly.

Its length flashed in the sunshine like white fire. When he swung it, the blade moved true. It was perfectly balanced, a thing of joy in his hand. He had never held such a sword, had never felt so totally attuned to a weapon. It was virgin steel, not yet bloodied in combat. The edge was honed to razor sharpness, the metal satiny smooth and lacking any nicks or blemishes. He knew instinctively that he would be the first warrior to fight with it. Its blade would sing with the strength of his arm, and no one else's.

It sang to him already, a low hum that seemed to vibrate in his very bones. "I am Exoner," it told him. "I am true."

Looking up in wonder, he found Lea watching him with something like hope in her face. "This was made especially for me?" he asked, astonished.

"Yes, Caelan. It was made for you."

He ran his finger down the center of the blade, admiring it anew. "Choven steel," he said aloud, then frowned.

Lea was nodding. "You have never held such a weapon before, have you?"

"No." His mouth felt suddenly dry, and his heart beat too fast. "Only—only kings carry weapons that are Choven-forged."

Lea smiled. "Will you come now? Please don't worry about the empress. I promise you she is safe. We will not be gone long."

He could protest no longer. In silence he sheathed the sword and carried it in his hand as he walked over to the pony waiting for him. Shaggy, sturdy, and unimpressed by him, it looked at him through its long forelock and snorted.

"Wear the sword, Caelan," Lea said, mounting her pony with lithe grace. From a saddlebag she shook out the folds of a fur-lined cloak the same blue as her gown, and swung it around her shoulders. "It is yours."

He stood there, feeling dazed and witless. The sword seemed so obvious a bribe, yet he found himself impatient with his own suspicions. It was a magnificent gift, impossible to refuse. He loved it, heart and soul, and already could not imagine going anywhere without it. Who would give him such a weapon? What was wanted in exchange?

"Gifts are free," Lea said softly.

He glanced up, but didn't meet her gaze. With a sigh, he buckled on the sword. Its weight felt right upon his hip. Confidence surged through him, and he felt as though he could walk into any battle now and win. Wearing Exoner was like having an extra man at his side.

Reaching into the saddlebag, Caelan pulled out a fur-lined cloak and warm gauntlets. With them on, he adjusted the stirrup lengths and mounted. His long legs almost dragged the ground, but he knew his pony was capable of carrying his weight all day without tiring. Indeed, he would take one of these ugly little steeds any day over the long-legged, flashy horses bred in Imperia.

A sudden commotion behind him made him whirl the pony around in time to see the nordeer bounding through the trees. Swift and graceful, they flitted away, their white coats ghostly pale against the snow.

"Quick!" Lea cried, spurring her pony forward. "They are our guide. Keep up with them."

There was no more time to wonder or question. Caelan galloped after the nordeer, settling deep in the saddle and ducking low to avoid branches. Without asking, he knew they were heading for the Cascade Mountains, and in less than an hour they were climbing a steep, rocky trail and picking a scrambling path through snowdrifts.

The Cascade River itself, so mighty and swift when it thundered through the mountain pass during summer, now lay frozen in slumber, buried beneath ice and snow. They crossed it at a reckless gallop, hoofbeats echoing down the mountain pass like thunder. On the other side rose a trail steep and harrowing, seeming to go almost straight up in places.

Yet the ponies never faltered or balked, no matter how difficult the way. Caelan strained to keep the nordeer in sight. Sometimes he lost them completely and had to rely on the quick clatter of their hooves or the swift flick of a tail as one bounded into sight among the rocks then vanished again.

The chase was thrilling. He found himself glorying in the whip of cold air against his face. The wild recklessness of the ride set his heart pounding in delight. He had not enjoyed anything so much in years, and he remembered how as a boy he used to live for those stolen moments when he could escape to the glacier and gallop free and wild across its expanse.

Today, he could feel the hearts of the nordeer, and a part of him ran with them, swiftly and effortlessly, like the wind itself.

Above them, the steep trail ascended into a cloud of fog and icy mist. Suddenly he could see nothing. The whole world was blanked out in damp silence.

Snorting, the pony slowed down, and Lea's mount crowded it from behind. "I can't see anything," she called out.

"Stay close," Caelan warned her.

This was always a danger in the mountains. The sudden fogs could lead an unwary traveler to an unexpected plunge over a precipice. He tightened the reins, although his pony was wise enough to pick a careful way through the rocks.

As for the nordeer, they seemed to have vanished completely. He could not see them, could not hear them.

It was tempting to halt and retreat. He could rely on his own knowledge of the trails to take them down safely again. But the glacier was so close now. The wind blowing in his face smelled of ancient ice.

Caelan's blood stirred. He loved the glacier. For too long he had been away. He would not turn back now.

"Let's keep climbing," he said, and kicked his pony forward.

The pony scrambled and lunged up a series of stair-stepped ledges that looked suitable for a goat; then the fog cleared, and they were above the cloud band, up on top above the rest of the world.

Caelan glanced down at the treetops below, dark green tips peeking out through the cottony cloud. The pass plunged a dizzying distance far below them; overhead, the blue wheel of sky arched clear. Caelan's head swiveled as he drank in the sight of the vast gray-green ice of the glacier itself.

His heart filled his throat, and suddenly he was a heedless boy again. Tipping back his head and whooping in sheer joy, Caelan glimpsed the herd of nordeer in the distance and kicked his pony after them. This was the one place where he felt at home, truly one with earth and sky. The glacier had been his refuge, his place of restoration, his own private sanctuary. Now his mind felt clear and peaceful for the first time in too long. He bent lower over the pony's neck, urging it faster after the bounding nordeer.

Lea followed at his heels, never falling too far behind.

The nordeer ahead slowed down. Suddenly he was among them, riding in their midst. The sunshine flowed over them, gilding their rippling shoulders. Their antlers looked tipped with silver; then, in surprise, he realized it was no illusion. The silver was real, and their large, solemn eyes were blue, not animal brown.

Nor were they wild creatures as he had originally thought, for now each animal wore a bright green collar around its neck, from which hung a silver bell. The bells were ringing with every bounding stride the animals made, heralding their arrival in a melodic, tinkling cascade of sound.

He had not noticed the bells before. Nor had he ever traveled so far across the glacier so fast. He seemed almost to feel distance slipping past his ears along with the rush of the wind, then they dipped down a slope and raced up the other side. At the crest of the rise, the nordeer stopped in a kicked-up flurry of snow and ice, great plumes of white breath shooting from their nostrils.

Caelan's pony stopped with them, and he sat there in the saddle, his fingers slack on the reins, his heart pounding from exertion, and stared at the array of tents spread out before him. They were fashioned of every possible color and hue—bright, billowy shelters that could be knocked down and moved in a matter of minutes. Smoke curled from holes in the tent tops, and there was a general bustle and activity in all directions, punctuated by the rhythmic hammering of smiths at work.

Some of Caelan's joy faded, and he felt nervous again. He wasn't sure why he had come here, or why Lea had insisted. The Choven were mysterious and nomadic. Seldom had he seen one; now and then they appeared at summer fairs to trade. Never permanently at one location, they could not be found by anyone who sought them. Those wishing to buy their magical wares had to leave word, and eventually the Choven would come of their own accord. They could not be haggled with. They could not be cheated. Sometimes they brought what a person had ordered; sometimes they delivered objects that they felt were more important. It was considered unwise to question a Choven selection; to refuse or break a deal was unheard of.

The nordeer trotted down to the camp, bells tinkling, antlers flashing silver in the sun. Caelan and Lea followed in their wake, and suddenly the flap of every tent seemed to open at the same time. Staring openly, the Choven peered out at them in silence.

Feeling very self-conscious, Caelan moved one hand nervously to the hilt of his sword, then dropped it. Could he be one of these people, as Lea had said? No, it was too fantastic. He refused to believe it. He had known both his mother and father. He looked like them. There had never been any hint that he and Lea were foundlings.

Yet what else explained why he was so drawn to the glacier, why he loved it so? What else explained how he could hold a warding key in his bare hands when doing so would kill any other man? Lea was no liar. She had loved Beva, who in his own rigid and stern way had been kind to her as a child. Why would she invent a falsehood against her own parents?

Caelan felt confused and wary as he and Lea rode to the center of the camp. It was a cleared space, encircled by smithy tents. All the tent flaps were tied open. The smell of heated metal filled the air, and haphazard heaps of metal slugs lay about—gold, steel, silver, and pewter—along with pots of what looked like precious stones of every kind. This casual display of wealth seemed even more impressive because no guards were in evidence.

Still, he had never heard of anyone who would dare steal from a Choven tribe. What had they to fear?

The sounds of hammering stopped momentarily, and then even the smiths themselves came out to stare at Caelan and Lea. Stripped to the waist, their dark, leathery hides glistening with sweat that steamed in the frigid air, they were short, chunky individuals with broad, flat-boned faces marked by thick, dark brows and wide, thin mouths. Their eyes were tilted at the outward corners, as black as obsidian, and penetrating.

Caelan stared back at them, finding himself almost forgetting to breathe. It was said a Choven could look into your heart and read your future. It was said a Choven could look into your mind and impart whatever he wished there. It was said a Choven could whistle and the seasons would change in obedience to his will.

"Caelan," Lea said in a soft voice.

Startled, he glanced the way she was looking.

Garbed in flowing robes of white, a Choven male was striding toward them. Taller than the others, tall enough perhaps to come to Caelan's shoulder, he carried a long staff of gleaming black wood banded with gold. His arms were encircled with gold bracelets of the most intricate design.

As he drew nearer, Lea slid from her saddle and gestured for Caelan to do the same.

When he obeyed, the nordeer flicked their ears and melted away among the tents. The ponies went with them. Caelan was left feeling surrounded and cut off. Edgily, he moved forward to stand a little in front of Lea, and crossed his arms over his chest where he could grab his dagger and new sword quickly if he needed to. His gaze flicked back and forth among the watching Choven, in case they decided to close in.

Lea frowned at him in rebuke. "Stop it," she whispered. "Why do you fear?"

If she intended to shame his warrior pride, she succeeded. Hot-faced, he said nothing, not even when she stepped around him and hastened forward to meet the figure in white. She bowed to the Choven, and he stretched out a dark, long-fingered hand in response.

Up close, his skin had the texture of tree bark. His dark eyes moved like liquid in his face, and Caelan could feel his inquisitiveness like a physical force.

Stepping past Lea, the Choven came right up to Caelan and stopped directly in front of him.

Caelan's past experience with the Choven, although limited, had been that they either ignored a person completely or they stared in blatant rudeness. This Choven was of the latter variety. He took his time looking Caelan over from all angles, but Caelan had suffered worse scrutinies on the auction block. He put on his stony mask and gave the Choven a flat, rebellious stare in return.

When the Choven had finished his examination, he glanced at Lea. "Why does he fear?"

She inclined her golden head respectfully and steepled her hands into a triangle of harmony. "My brother is foolish and untrained, Moah."

Caelan shot her a glare that she ignored.

Moah tilted his head to one side and held out his long-fingered hands, palms up. "You wear the sword. You carry the emerald. You have followed the nordeer to us. We Choven bid you welcome, Caelan E'non, as we welcomed your sister Lea long ago. Are you ready to take your learning from us?"

Lea sent Caelan a radiant glance of pride, her blue eyes shining. The other Choven watched from their doorways. Silence floated over the camp.

Caelan felt a pull of *sevaisin,* like the strong current of a river. Instinctively he braced himself to resist it and glared at Moah. "For your kindness to my sister, I give you my thanks," he said in a stiff, formal tone that barely masked his anger.

Lea gasped and turned toward him, but he ignored her as he went on glaring at Moah. "But beyond that, I am not your creature," he said. He drew the beautiful sword so swiftly the metal whistled against its scabbard. Sunlight flashed off the blade, and the other Choven lifted their voices in a deep, eerie cry of acclamation that made Caelan's hair prickle up the back of his skull.

Swiftly he blocked his feeling of kinship with it, distrusting how alive and intelligent it seemed. He wanted nothing to do with something so strongly spell-forged, and he bent down and laid the sword on a brightly patterned rug lying on the ground in front of the nearest tent.

The Choven woman standing in its doorway opened her mouth in silent astonishment and fled inside.

Others spoke out loudly in a language that sent chills crawling through Caelan. He knew enough of the ancient words to recognize their tongue as one from darkest antiquity. The air was growing charged, as though spells were being summoned. Caelan could feel it around him, and his heartbeat quickened in alarm.

He did not know what could happen if a Choven became angry. But just then his own temper was boiling enough to keep him reckless.

Defiantly, he slipped the carrybag off his shoulder and dropped it on the rug beside the sword.

"Caelan, no!" Lea said in distress.

He refused to look at her and instead faced Moah once again, glaring down into the man's shimmering, unreadable eyes. "I cannot be bought," he said through his teeth, his anger like heat in his bones. "No matter how magnificent the price you offer, I am free, and I will stay that way. You told my sister we are Choven, but we are not. We are human, and we take pride in that."

His speech finished, he gave Moah a curt bow and wheeled around to stride away. "Come, Lea," he commanded. "We are leaving."

Chapter Eleven

LEA TROTTED BESIDE him, glaring in protest. "No, Caelan! You don't understand anything. Why must you be so rude?"

He lengthened his stride, refusing to listen. His ears were roaring, and he had to grit his teeth to hold back a rebuke. It was his fault, not hers, that he had come this far. He should never have held the sword, should never have admired it, should never have buckled it to his belt. Pausing in mid-stride, he yanked the scabbard free and flung it away.

Lea gasped. "You are stupid! You—"

He turned on her, rage swelling inside his chest. "I will not become a—"

Pain struck his chest as though he'd been speared. With a hoarse cry, he doubled over and fell to his knees. This attack was worse than any of the previous ones. He felt as though his chest was being pried open. Desperately, he struggled to master the agony. If he could just *sever* the pain, then he could regain his feet and get far from here.

But *severance* failed him. He had lost his techniques, his knowledge, in the sea of pain.

He cried out again, flailing with one powerful arm against an enemy that could not be touched. This battle raged inside him. Gasping for the breath that did not seem to come, he slewed around on his knees, falling off balance only to catch himself with one hand, and looked at the pouch containing his emerald. The leather was splitting along one seam. Through it he could see the stone glowing.

Again, his anger intensified. "Get away from me!" he shouted, fearing the emerald's mysterious power. "Get out of me!"

His heart was bursting. The pain grew worse, until he knew

nothing but it. He had been told in the arena barracks that men did not pass out from pain alone. They might lose consciousness from loss of blood or shock or fear, but pain went on relentlessly.

Now, he prayed for oblivion, for release, but his agony burned ever more fiercely. It was unendurable, yet he could not escape it. He could not master it, could not master himself. Worst of all, he could not *sever.* The calm void inside him had been filled with fire that twisted and tortured him.

He was drowning in pain, unable to breathe, his lungs jerking convulsively now. In a brief moment of clarity, he found himself writhing on the snow, its crusty, frozen surface scratching his cheek until it felt raw. Then another wave of pain, like a tide of heat, swept over him, driving him back into madness.

Suddenly an unknown voice spoke to him in words he did not understand. A cool barrier drove back the heat. He found himself able to breathe again. Shuddering, drenched in sweat, he lay there with his eyes closed while he dragged in breath after breath. The pain receded, leaving inexpressible relief. Spent and exhausted, he felt too weak to even lift his head.

"Arise," said the voice of Moah.

Caelan dragged his forearm across his face and slowly opened his eyes. He found himself lying on the ground with his fur-lined cloak a thin barrier between his body and the ice. Gone was the sunshine. Gone were the brightly colored tents. Instead, everything was gray, windswept, and desolate.

Struggling to his feet, he frowned at how weak he felt. He could barely stand, and his muscles felt drained as though he had been in combat for hours.

The only sound beyond his own labored breathing was the empty whistle of wind over the expanse of glacier.

Where had everyone gone? Where was he?

Suddenly alarmed, Caelan spun around and nearly lost his precarious balance. "Lea?" he said uncertainly.

He was alone, whisked by some means to the far end of the glacier and abandoned there. The wind blowing into his face was frigid and raw. As far as he could see in any direction, there was nothing but ice. No trees, no rocks, no tents. Just cloud, mist, and bone-chilling cold.

He shivered, rubbing his arms beneath his cloak, and drew up his hood. His dagger was gone, and he could not find a recognizable landmark in any direction.

Fear traveled up his spine, but he squelched it quickly. His anger was returning. Was this an exile, a punishment? If so, he did not care. He would rather die out here of exposure than grovel to anyone.

Absently he rubbed his chest where the pain had been, and pivoted again. Wind off the glacier usually blew southward. Grimly, Caelan put his back to the wind, then he set out with long strides. In moments, his breath was rasping in his throat. The high altitude began to sap his strength.

No one had ever tried to cross the entire glacier and lived to tell how large it was. Caelan's own knowledge was confined to the southernmost tip of the ice, where it spilled into the mountain passes. He might have to walk for days, and he did not think that was possible. Already his toes were numb inside his boots. His cloak did not seem to break the wind that drilled into his back. He lacked even a tinderstrike to start a fire, not that there was any wood or peat up here to fuel it. When darkness fell, he would have no shelter.

But he refused to fear. It was his own death he faced, on his terms. When the time came, and his legs could carry him no farther, he would lie on his back for a last glimpse of the breathtaking aurora before he fell into eternal sleep.

With a start, he jerked up his head and blinked hard, finding himself kneeling on the ice in a shivering knot. He realized he must have passed out. Alarmed, he struggled back to his feet and nearly fell in the process. His feet were entirely numb, and he couldn't feel them when he stood. When he touched his face, he couldn't feel his own fingers. Lassitude crept over his limbs, and he knew very soon he would start to feel warm as he froze to death.

Staggering forward, he stumbled and fell to his knees. The wind howled over him, whipping his cloak about his shoulders. He tried to get up, but couldn't. He sank down onto the hard, frozen surface of the ice. How old it was, as ancient as time.

Caelan's senses swirled. He felt dizzy and lost. *Severance* was gone as though he had never had it. Perhaps this was the ultimate end of reaching into the void. Perhaps he was already completely *severed* and did not realize it. He felt as though his own threads of life had been cut. Now he drifted here between the physical and spirit worlds, part of neither. And he heard the grumble of the ice below him, heard the ponderous shift and grind of its infinitely slow progress. More than that, he heard its song—a low keening like the sound from the rim of a crystal goblet when rubbed.

Sevaisin pulled him to it. For a moment longer—perhaps the space of a heartbeat—Caelan resisted. Then with a sigh, he stopped fighting and allowed himself to join with the ice, to become one with the glacier.

There was a brief jolt of incredible cold, as though he had been frozen solid in an instant, and then light flashed through him. It was like physically exploding, except he felt no pain. And he found himself in a roofless temple, a place of peace and calm harmony. He stood on a slab of pale marble surrounded by twelve marble columns reaching high above him. Another row of columns, too many to count, stretched into the distance without end. There was no sky, no horizon. It was neither day nor night. Yet he saw everything with complete clarity. The air was the perfect temperature, neither hot nor cold. He heard the gentle sound of running water in the distance. It was a soothing noise. Mentally he felt renewed, restored. His naked body stood strong and whole. For once, perhaps the first time in his life, he felt centered and complete, as though he had found balance.

The quiet sound of footsteps made him turn around.

Robed in white and wearing a soft, brimless cap of silver cloth, Moah approached him with the peculiar gliding stride of the Choven. Although Caelan could feel no wind here, Moah's silk robes billowed around his squat frame in constant motion.

Seeing Moah, some of Caelan's peace faded. He sighed, but made no move to evade this meeting.

Moah stopped a short distance from him and stood regarding him in silence.

Meeting Moah's liquid gaze directly, Caelan squared his shoulders and said, "Am I dead?"

Something unreadable glimmered in Moah's rough-textured face. "Do you believe you are in death?"

"Didn't I freeze to death on the glacier?"

"Did you?"

Caelan frowned. He had no patience for such puzzles. "Why else would I be here?"

"Where are you?"

"I don't know," Caelan said, holding onto his temper with difficulty. Already he was finding it difficult to keep his resolution. "This looks like a temple of some kind. Am I at the edge of the spirit world?"

"No."

It was the first solid answer Moah had given him, but it wasn't very informative.

Caelan's frown deepened. "Then where am I?"

"Where do you think you are?"

"I don't know. I've already given you my best guess."

Moah raised one long, dark finger. It looked like a twig. "Guess is unnecessary. Think."

Caelan didn't appreciate being treated like a schoolboy. "I'm in no mood for lessons," he said sharply. "Why have I been brought here? What do you want from me?"

"I want nothing," Moah replied, unruffled. "You are seeking to learn. Will you take learning from us?"

The fear that Caelan had known earlier among the tents came back. "No," he said. "Why should I?"

"You fear me."

Caelan's mouth was dry, but he answered with the truth. "Yes. I fear you."

"Why?"

"Because—" Caelan stopped, his thoughts and emotions a chaotic tangle in his mind.

"Because you were taught to be afraid?" Moah suggested quietly.

"You are not part of our world," Caelan said, defiant and angry. "You have powers from—from the gods that men may not have. You follow the ancient ways, ways that are forbidden. How do I know what you will do to me? You can probably turn me into smoke at will."

"Not smoke," Moah said. "Ice."

Caelan swallowed hard and held his tongue. He'd said too much already.

"On the glacier," Moah said, "you were dying. Did you feel fear?"

"Some," Caelan admitted reluctantly.

"But you accepted death."

It seemed to be a question. Not understanding where the Choven was going, Caelan nodded his head with impatience. "Yes."

"Why did you accept it?"

Caelan shrugged. "I had no choice. I had done my best to save myself. But it was inevitable. I had to accept it."

"So when no other choice is possible, you will accept what is before you?"

"Maybe."

Moah laughed. "Such stubborn caution."

"I am not Choven," Caelan insisted, goaded by the Choven's amusement. "I am human, son of Beva E'non—"

"A man you do not love, a man you do not respect," Moah interrupted.

"That's between me and him," Caelan snapped. "No one else. He's still my father."

"And you would defend him?" Moah asked. "How curious. You have resented and criticized him as long as you can remember, yet—"

"You don't understand," Caelan broke in. "That's just part of it. If he had only accepted me—"

"And who are you, Caelan E'non?"

Caelan stopped, feeling confused again.

Moah took a step closer, his gaze penetrating. "Who are you?"

"But I don't look like you!" Caelan burst out, feeling cornered. "My skin, my hair and eyes, my stature. I'm not Choven. I'm human. Why do you insist otherwise?"

"I have said nothing," Moah said in a reasonable voice.

Caelan glared at him. "Lea told me."

"Ah, your sister is light incarnate. She is radiance itself."

Caelan refused to be distracted by this compliment. "Yes, but she's wrong."

"Is she?"

"Yes!"

Moah turned away as though he were going to leave, then paused. "I will relate a tale," he announced, and began before Caelan could protest. "In the long days you call summer, a man of Trau climbed the mountains in search of us. We would not be found, but this man persisted. He wandered the mountains and even ventured onto the glacier. His will was iron in his body; he would not give up.

"At last, after a span of many days, the seeker sat on a rock and fasted. Rains fell on him. Winds blew at him. He fasted, sustained by his limited skills of *severance* and his will.

"We were in the time of feasting and did not wish death to cast poor omens across our shadows. We brought the seeker to us and restored his health. He told us he was a student of healing, but a poor one. He could not master the skills of his training, and he feared he would fail. With all his heart he wished to bring succor to the sick and needy.

"The Choven had pity on this seeker, and the ability to heal was given to him."

Caelan gasped, his mind reeling. All this time he'd thought his father had been born with his gift. The masters at Rieschelhold had all praised Beva's abilities while he was in training. Why had they lied?

"The seeker went down the mountain and treated his gift well," Moah said. "He used his new powers only to heal, never forgetting his bargain with us."

"What bargain?" Caelan asked.

"That is in the past—"

"What bargain?" Caelan insisted, yearning to know. "What promise?"

Moah regarded him a moment, then answered. "If we would make it possible for him to heal the sick, then he would live his life as a peaceful man, committed only to the practice of his arts and training."

Caelan frowned, finding it suddenly hard to breathe. Understanding filled him, but it did not lessen the resentment in his heart.

"Weren't we worth his commitment, too?" Caelan asked. "Why did he bother to sire us if he didn't want us?"

"But you *were* wanted," Moah said.

Caelan remembered his father's many lectures, remembered his father's plans for them to be healers together.

"Years passed," Moah said, "and once again during the long days the man came in search of us. Remembering him, we let ourselves be found and listened to his request. He had taken a woman to wife, but there were no children of this union. It was important to this man that he have a son to walk in his footsteps, to train as he had trained, to become as him."

Caelan opened his mouth, but he could not speak. His heart felt like a stone in his chest, too heavy to beat.

"These traditions are not Choven ways. But the man spoke long and persuasively. His heart held much longing and anguish. He had shame among his people because he could not sire a child."

"No," Caelan breathed.

Moah appeared not to hear. "Again, the Choven granted the bargain, and a spell was cast. But the man was not true as before. His pride had grown great. The Choven did not care, but because falsehood was found in him, auspices were studied and the spirits consulted. The Choven told the man that children of his request would not be as humans, that they would be fashioned of fire, earth, air, and water. Because of those elements, they would have to follow their own destinies as shown in the auspices.

"The man was living in shame because of his lack of manhood. He could not heal himself. He agreed to the bargain, saying his wife would turn her eyes to another if she had no children to bind her heart to him. The man agreed to let the children walk their own path of life."

Caelan was stunned. His father was sterile? He had entered a spell-casting of his own free will? Beva, the most outspoken critic of the ancient ways, a man intolerant of the rare sight of Choven at fairs, a man who barely allowed warding keys to hang on his gates? If the Choven spoke the truth, then stern, austere, upright, moral Beva E'non had been the most duplicitous hypocrite in the land.

"But this promise the man did not keep," Moah said. "In his children, he saw the beauty of his wife and the strength of his own will. His children shone among others, and their bright radiance of spirit made the man more praised by his people. In time, the man forgot his second agreement, and when his wife died he set himself to mold his children as he wished, denying them all knowledge of their true heritage. He trained them only in the ways of his people, limiting them all he could, and would not let them walk their own paths of life to their destinies.

"This was a man of strong will and determination, a man who would die for his own purposes, a man who still reaches out from the spirit world to force his way on his son."

Moah turned his head and looked straight into Caelan's eyes. "Always you have fought to keep a sense of yourself, fought to walk your own path of life, fought to return to your true people again and again despite all that has kept you from the glacier."

Caelan swallowed hard. He was reeling from all that Moah had said. Yet he did not doubt the truth of what he'd just heard.

"The Choven," Moah said, "do not wish to be known by the people of men. But among themselves, they know the traditions of the gods and the foretelling that one day the earth will be broken."

A chill struck Caelan. He stared at Moah in rising dread. "That's what Master Mygar said when he cursed me. That one day I would break the world. But—"

Moah extended his hand, palm up. "How else can light shine into the darkness below? Unless the earth is cracked open to expose all that honors Beloth, what hope has the world?"

Caelan stared at the Choven, feeling his throat constrict too tight for speech. He did not want to believe his curse might actually come true.

Moah met his gaze. "The gods have said that one day the earth must be broken in order to keep the cycle of life. That is the prophecy cast, and the auspices still point to it."

"I will not destroy the world," Caelan said in horror. "Whatever kind of monster I am, I will *not* help Beloth smash—"

"Prophecy has no single interpretation," Moah said. "Let not fear cloud your mind. Instead, consider the plowman and his work."

Caelan frowned at the sudden shift of subject. "I don't understand."

"Have you ever planted a seed? The earth must be opened so that it can receive the seed. Then the soil is pressed smooth in warm protection until the seed can grow. And when the seed is ready to sprout into the sunlight, again the earth must be broken to allow it to come forth."

Caelan's impatient bewilderment grew. "We're talking about war, not farming."

"So we are," Moah agreed mildly. "Was not the imprisonment of Beloth a planting of sorts? Does he not sprout forth now? Should he not be chopped down, and his roots dug up? After destruction comes rebirth. With Beloth defeated, life can be renewed. The cycle will continue."

"I can't defeat Beloth," Caelan said.

"Choven and the people of men are separate, yet they fit together to create a balance of harmony," Moah said as though he had not heard. "We lack the aggression, the ambition, the insurmountable will of men. Men lack reverence for all sides of the life force. Men refuse to see the truth, and they walk in fear."

Moah turned his head and stared deeply into Caelan's eyes. "You, Caelan, are of the Choven yet not of us. You are a man, yet more than a man."

Caelan did not want to hear more. He shook his head. "No."

Moah smiled, and his dark eyes gleamed. "Yes. You have come to the truth, Caelan. Gaze into it, and know. You were born of woman and man, yet of spell-force also. At your birth, the auspices were thrown and your name was given. You are Caelan M'an i Luciel. It means Man of Sky Who Brings Light."

Frowning, Caelan mouthed the unfamiliar words to himself. "Is this why you gave me the sword?"

Moah spread his dark hands wide in the equivalent of a shrug. "Tell me a truth that you have known all your days."

The sudden change of subject again threw Caelan. "I don't understand."

"Think. What is a truth in yourself that you have always known? What have you always been?"

"Rebellious," Caelan said flippantly without thinking.

Then, at Moah's sober look, he sighed and took the question more seriously.

"I kill," he said, and met Moah's gaze. "That is my essence. That is my truth."

"This shames you?"

"Of course! You've been talking about the many forces of life and reverence and truth. I destroy that. I take lives, whether in light or in shadow."

As he spoke he glared at the Choven, standing there in white purity and total wisdom. How did the blood taint on his hands measure up against Moah's standards?

Yet Moah did not seem shocked or offended by him. "Exoner was made for you as a gift. Our most skilled smith forged it while the spells of strength and valor were chanted into it."

"It is a wonderful sword," Caelan said impatiently.

"Does it not sing to you?"

"Yes, but I—"

"To hear metal sing is a precious gift to the soul, given to few. Exoner will serve you well in that which is to come."

Caelan shook his head. "You don't understand," he said. "I cannot accept it."

"It is not a bribe," Moah replied. "The Choven do not buy men."

Caelan's suspicions returned. "No?" he countered. "Then what do you want from me?"

"For you to be true to yourself."

"You want me to kill? Is that showing reverence for life?"

Moah lifted his hands. "Calmly. Remember that you are in a place of safety. Do not fear."

"I'm not afraid," Caelan snapped. "I'm angry."

"You are a king," Moah said. "Act like one."

This rebuke surprised Caelan enough to silence him momentarily. Then he said, "I'm no king. I'm an ex-slave, arena trained for combat. I—"

"You have shared with Kostimon, the greatest king in the history of the people of men," Moah said. "You were linked to him in Choven fire. You know his heart. You have swallowed his spirit. You wish to rule."

Caelan opened his mouth, but he could deny nothing. "Yes," he said simply.

Moah nodded approvingly. "The truth sounds well on your tongue. You bring ambition to the Choven. You bring ruthless will and the strength of a warrior to the Choven. Yet you have a kind heart and a gentle soul."

Caelan wanted to laugh in derision, but he found himself yearning for Moah's assessment to be true. "Once, perhaps, but that was beaten from me."

"The soul cannot be beaten," Moah replied, "unless it chooses to be. We are metalworkers. We know how to temper and refine steel. You have been tempered in order to meet your destiny. Had you not been a slave, you would never have learned the lessons of survival. Had you not been a gladiator, you would never have learned how to be a valiant warrior. Had you not been brother to Lea, you would never have learned to love another. Had you not been protector to the Empress Elandra—"

"I wasn't her protector," Caelan protested.

Moah sent him a glance of rebuke.

Caelan sighed and surrendered. "Very well. Unofficially."

"Had you not performed such a task," Moah said sternly, "you would never have learned to restrain aggression in favor of your gentle side. Had you not fallen in love with the empress, you would never have learned what is forbidden and what is not. Nor would you have seen your own destiny."

"My destiny," Caelan repeated. He shook his head, unwilling to accept the burden Moah wanted to give him. "All my life, others have been telling me what I must do, what I must be. I want to make my own choices."

"You are capable of understanding much," Moah said. "When you are ready to hear my words, you will hear them."

"But—"

"Are you ready to return?" Moah asked him. "Are you ready to carry Exoner?"

"I have enough blood on my hands," Caelan said. "I don't want to continue."

"That is good," Moah said. "When the time comes, you will know how to stop."

"But—"

"Caelan, your spirit is like a strong vine, wrapped and entwined among your threads of life in a protective binding. When you learn to be what you are, when you learn to trust what you are, then you will truly be the Light Bringer."

"You aren't listening to me," Caelan said in frustration. "I came to your camp to ask for help in freeing the empress from the poison in her, not to call myself a king and free the earth from oppression."

"Turn around and look," Moah commanded.

As he spoke, he spun Caelan around by the shoulders and held him in place, giving him a little shake for emphasis. "Look! Do you see it?"

Caelan looked at the tall marble columns standing beyond the temple. A black mist flowed around their bases.

Horrified, he whispered, "What is it?"

But he knew. In his heart, he already knew the answer.

Moah replied anyway. "It is the breath of Beloth, escaping imprisonment within the realm of shadow. It is the cloud you have seen coming closer to Imperia with every passing year. It is the darkness that can eventually engulf the light."

Caelan closed his eyes. It was the end of the world.

"No," Moah said. "There is a chance."

"Not me!" Caelan said, spinning around to glare at Moah. "What fool can go against that? How can a man fight the mist? The wars of gods are not for men."

"Had a man not opened the door of Beloth's prison," Moah replied, "there would be much truth in what you say."

Caelan snorted. "Kostimon opened the door, but how am I to shut it?"

"That is your choice."

Caelan's temper grew shorter. "Is it?" he said mildly. "And are you going to put a—a Choven spell on me to make me as strong as a god? Gault forgive me! I know I am blaspheming, but what is a man to say to this?"

"The strength of men and the strength of Choven are woven together in you," Moah replied. "If there is a way to stop the return of Beloth, you will find it. That is foretold."

"But—"

"There is no one else, Caelan," Moah said. His gaze did not waver. "You are the only one."

Caelan stared at him and tried again to find a way out. "But I am only a—"

"What are you, Caelan? What are your strengths? What gifts do you have? How strong is your faith, your belief in the realm of light? You have feared many things, but if there is anything which should be feared and vilified, it is that which comes."

Moah pointed at the black mist. "Kostimon's destiny intersects with yours. That is the key which you must remember. Kostimon is the means by which you can reach Beloth."

Caelan's mouth was dry. He tried to swallow without much success. How simple Moah made it sound. Didn't he realize what he was asking? Just that one journey through the realm of shadow had been horrifying enough.

Cowardice filled his throat like bile. "I am hurt," he said. "I am not whole. The emerald has damaged me in some way."

Moah released his arm, but his gaze went on holding Caelan's. "How many excuses will you find?"

His scorn turned Caelan's face hot. "I will find all the excuses I can. But I have told you the truth."

"Has not the emerald always been a help to you, a support to your spirit during times of difficulty?"

"And if the emerald causes another attack?" Caelan asked him. "Each one is worse."

"Do not blame the emerald," Moah said. "Such stones as yours are rare. The earth spirits create them. The ice spirits guard them. We Choven cut and set them according to their best purpose. As you grow, so does the emerald. Sometimes growth brings pain."

"But what is it for?" Caelan asked, ready to veer onto any topic as long as it was not confronting Beloth. "What does it do?"

"It has given you hope," Moah said, tilting his head to one side. "Is that not enough?"

"But—"

"It is time for us to take the stone and work with it on your behalf. Will you allow that?"

"Yes," Caelan said, not sure what the Choven was talking about.

"Then there is no more to say. You have taken learning from me. This time is finished, and we must return."

Caelan looked at him in alarm. He had more questions, specifically regarding Elandra. "Wait! There is the empress and—"

Again he felt the sensation of exploding into glittering bits of light, spiraling down from that lofty center of calm tranquility, returning unwillingly back to the chaos of problems, doubts, and trouble.

With a jolt, he opened his eyes. He expected to find himself back in the Choven camp with Lea bending over him. There would be another chance to talk to Moah and ask him for help.

Instead, he found himself in the forest, standing in the gully near the ice cave where he had left Elandra. He was clothed again. Exoner hung heavy in its scabbard at his hip. His dagger was tucked in its belt sheath. But for the sword, he might never have believed any of it had happened. Even now, he couldn't be sure.

The conversation with Moah seemed a long time ago and very far away. But his destiny was drawing closer with every passing moment.

Chapter Twelve

ELANDRA AWAKENED IN a strange place. Not certain whether she was dreaming or having a vision, she sat up and found herself in a tiny cave. A circle of black ashes showed her where a fire had once been lit, but had long lain cold. Sunlight shone in from the cave's narrow mouth, providing faint illumination.

Following it outside, she stood in the bottom of a narrow gully next to a frozen stream. Drifts of snow spilled down the banks, looking white and soft. The air smelled of clean, pungent scents unknown to her. She thought of Gialta with its steamy jungles and heavy fragrances of rot, damp, and exotic flowers. Trau was so different, so cold and austere.

She walked out farther from the cave, her feet unsteady and slow. The clearing beyond the gully lay empty. She heard no sound other than the soft swaying of the trees. Loneliness filled her, and she wondered where Caelan had gone.

Uneasy, Elandra gazed about a moment, then picked up her long skirts to jump the stream. As she leaped, the world seemed to fold itself in half, taking her with it.

Crying out, she fell sprawling and expected to land in the water. Instead, the stream had vanished entirely.

With it were gone the gully, the cave, the trees, and the snow. In their stead stretched a desolate plain of barren soil and rocky outcroppings. A rough wind blew steadily, whistling in her ears and whipping her long hair into her face. Elandra climbed again to her feet and looked around in wonder and rising fear.

In every direction she saw only bleak emptiness. No plants, no insects, no life. She was swept by a feeling of terrible loneliness, as though she were the last person in the world who remained alive.

"Welcome to the future," said a voice from behind her.

Startled, Elandra whirled around and found herself face to face with Hecati, the malevolent woman who had raised her in her father's household and made her early life such a misery.

At first Elandra could only stare, stunned by the sight of an enemy she'd never expected to see again. Hecati's face had grown more sour and wrinkled than ever. She wore a black wimple that blew in the wind. Her eyes burned into Elandra's with contempt and hatred.

Elandra felt as though all her courage had been knocked from her in one sharp blow. She felt twelve years old again, skinny and unprotected, about to be punished by Hecati and her willow switches.

Dry-mouthed, she blinked hard, but Hecati did not vanish. "Hecati," she said at last, managing to stammer out the woman's name.

"Elandra," Hecati replied, her voice thick with sugary sweetness. "My, how changed you are from when I saw you last. You overcame my parting gift. How clever of you."

Elandra felt cold inside. Hecati had blinded her on the steps to the Penestrican stronghold before the sisters could intervene. Elandra had spent weeks without her sight, a harrowing experience she would never forget.

Anger mingled with her fear, warming her, strengthening her. She lifted her chin, refusing to let Hecati think she could still be intimidated.

"Yes, I can see again," she replied coolly, giving thanks now for the long lessons in deportment and palace protocol. She was no longer the ragged, illegitimate daughter of a busy provincial household, tyrannized and abused. She was an empress, and she would act like one.

Her gaze met Hecati's, betraying none of her inner fear. "The Penestricans restored my sight."

"Yes, and now you are their puppet."

Elandra's delicate nostrils flared. "You will address me as your Majesty."

Hecati's eyes narrowed, and a light flush appeared on her

face. "Fool!" she said. "You dare rebuke one of Mael's chosen? I can char you to ashes where you stand!"

Elandra's topaz was glowing warm and hidden within the curl of her fist. She tried to draw strength and reassurance from it, although her heart continued to pound.

"If that were true, you would have done it already," Elandra said with defiance. "Why have you brought me to this place? What do you want?"

"This is the future! Look at it," Hecati commanded maliciously, spreading her hands wide.

Elandra kept her gaze on the witch's face, refusing to look at the blighted landscape. "What do you want?"

"I want to see your fear." Scooping up a handful of soil, Hecati hurled it at Elandra's skirts. "You are empress of a dead land."

"You say it is the future," Elandra said. "But because it does not yet exist, the future can change an infinite number of times. That means there is hope of an alternative."

Hecati glared at her, looking displeased. "Someone has taught you philosophy and logic," she said at last in grudging acknowledgement.

Elandra smiled.

The sudden smell of something burning was the only warning Elandra had before Hecati threw what looked like a black ball at her. As it came through the air, it uncoiled into the long, slender form of a serpent.

There was no time to think. Elandra lifted her hand instinctively, and the light emanating from her topaz shone upon the serpent.

Just before the serpent struck her, it exploded into ashes that blew away in the harsh wind.

Hecati screamed as though hurt, but only fury showed in her withered face. She lifted her hands, curling them into claws. "Damn you!" she cried. "You witless bastard, who gave you a Jewel of Sovereignty?"

Elandra had no intention of telling her the truth. Defiantly she faced the witch. "Am I not the empress sovereign? Do I not share my husband's reign?"

"You are nothing!" Hecati shouted. "You have an unconsummated marriage. You love a slave of such low lineage he cannot even be found in our auspices. You are a penniless exile from your own palace. And you carry the poison of darkness in your veins, which will soon render you one of the living dead. Oh, yes, Elandra the Illegitimate, hold yourself high with pride. But what does so much pride avail you? You are nothing!"

Tears sprang to Elandra's eyes, and it was all she could do to hold them in check. Even now, Hecati's sharp tongue could still leave wounds. She had the unerring ability to find every vulnerability, and stab deeper into it.

But Elandra was not the girl she had once been. No matter what her emotions, she would not bend. "What do you want from me?" she repeated quietly. "Why did you bring me here for this meeting?"

Hecati stepped forward, and it was all Elandra could do not to flinch back.

"I have brought you here to strike a bargain."

Elandra frowned, suspecting a trick. "What kind of bargain? I have nothing you could want."

"Are you interested in survival?" Hecati asked. "Are you interested in being cured of the poison in you?"

Elandra drew in a startled breath and turned her back on the witch. Inside, she was a seething mass of horror and temptation. How did Hecati know so much? Terrified, Elandra clapped her hand over her mouth, afraid of what she might say.

"What do you know of the living dead?" Hecati asked in a quiet, almost conversational voice. "Most people cannot detect them, except by their yellow eyes. They act much the same as when they were alive, but their souls belong to Beloth—"

"No!"

"Yes, Beloth," Hecati said, her sugary voice in horrible contrast to the nightmare of her words. "And they must obey the commands of the dark god. Even if it is to tear out the beating heart of their own child, they have to obey. Their blood turns black, and eventually they are eaten from within by the demons they carry. It is a terrible fate. What a pity. You are doomed, unless I help you."

Elandra closed her eyes, trying to shut out Hecati's voice. But her words echoed and reechoed in Elandra's mind. No matter how much she distrusted the woman, Elandra knew this time Hecati was telling the truth.

"What do you want?" she asked a third time.

Hecati chuckled triumphantly. "Your allegiance to Mael."

Elandra blinked and turned around, staring. This was insane. "You would save me from becoming Beloth's minion, but in exchange I must belong to—to Mael instead?"

She could barely say their dire names. To speak them at all was to utter blasphemy. She half expected to be incinerated on the spot.

Hecati looked impatient. "Yes."

"But there is no difference!"

"There is a great deal of difference." Hecati stepped forward, but this time Elandra backed away.

"Listen to me," Hecati said. "You would not be mindless, soulless. You would be an ally, not a puppet."

Elandra released her breath, trying to keep her wits about her. "I don't—"

"Hear me. You are empress sovereign. Your position is second only to Kostimon's, but in reality you have no power at all."

"The warlords gave me their oaths of fealty."

"That means nothing, girl! Nothing! If you do not realize that, then you are naive as well as a fool."

Elandra tightened her lips and said nothing.

"The warlords will turn to anyone but you. Do you expect them to take up arms in support of a woman?"

"They vowed they would."

Hecati snarled an oath. "Why can you not understand—"

"I understand perfectly," Elandra broke in coolly. "You need not explain politics to me."

"Mael will give you an army—"

"I thought the goddess of shadows intended only to release me from the effects of the poison."

"Your rewards can be multiplied. You are more useful to us in a position of power."

"What kind of allegiance would I be expected to give?"

Elandra asked. Her hands were shaking at her sides, and she thrust them behind her to hide them.

"Building temples to the goddess for a start. Allowing her to be worshiped without hindrance. Showing public example."

This time Elandra couldn't conceal her horrified revulsion. "Such actions would help release the goddess from bondage."

"Of course! You will weaken her chains, just as Kostimon has done much over the centuries to free Beloth."

"No."

"Don't be stupid. You have no choice in the matter. Don't worry, girl. It is not too difficult to learn the proper rituals. I shall give you guidance, help you reach decisions, and make policy. I was prepared to do this for Bixia. Now I shall assist you."

"I refuse."

Hecati looked at her in astonishment. "Nonsense! You cannot."

"I can, and I will. My answer is no."

"Fool!" Again Hecati hurled something at her, and again Elandra raised the topaz in time to deflect it. No serpent this time, but a spear with a wickedly barbed point. It landed harmlessly at Elandra's feet, and Hecati swore words that burned and smoked visibly in the air.

Elandra cringed back, afraid to hear such words. There had to be a way out of this place. Even if she ran and was forever lost in this wasteland, it would be better than facing Hecati.

"Do not run," Hecati said sharply before she could move. "You coward, stand fast and listen to me. There is little time left to you. Do you understand that you will die without my help?"

"Better to die than be damned," Elandra retorted.

"Bah! You are already damned, you fool! Your enemies are powerful, but you could have unlimited resources if you would just agree—"

"No!" Elandra shouted in panic, backing away. "No, I will not agree. I will not!"

"Wait!" Hecati called, but Elandra turned and ran for her life, choosing no direction, just running as fast as her legs would carry her across the barren, stony ground.

With Hecati's furious cries behind her, Elandra scrambled up a low, rocky ridge with the wind tearing at her hair and clothing, glanced back, then stumbled down the other side. Halfway down she lost her balance on the loose shale and went sliding and tumbling.

She landed at the bottom in a cloud of dust—bruised, scraped, and winded. Wearily she lay there a moment, tense and listening, but she could no longer hear Hecati calling her name.

Instead, she heard a peculiar sound—something between a whistle and a roar.

Climbing to her feet, Elandra turned around and saw an enormous, whirling cloud crossing the desert toward her. Dust and debris swirled around it, constantly being drawn up into its core. It moved parallel to the base of the ridge, and it was coming incredibly fast.

For a second Elandra could only stare. She had never seen such a cloud before. As it roared closer, it seemed to fill the very sky. Only then did she realize how immense it was, how powerful.

It could suck her up inside itself and shred her to pieces. Had Hecati released *this* against her?

Horrified, she picked up her skirts and ran.

Sucking up dust and stones and spewing them high, the cloud veered after her as though in pursuit. Elandra screamed, and ran faster, to no avail.

It was gaining on her. She darted in a different direction, but the cloud followed her. Feeling its tug, Elandra stumbled and fell to her knees.

Desperately she tried to claw her way upright, but the wind toppled her off balance. Her hair streamed up into the air, and her clothes plastered themselves against her body.

Breathing hard, her throat uttering a mindless noise of terror, Elandra saw objects swirling within the cloud—weapons, horses, pieces of armor, helmets, and men themselves. Their clothing was strangely old-fashioned, and many of the objects were peculiar and old, like the ancestral belongings of previous generations that her father had preserved for the family. It was like watching history winding itself around a giant spindle.

Black, angry clouds massed overhead in the sky. Lightning suddenly flashed, and a second later the crashing boom of thunder made her duck with her hands over her ears. She was blown flat to the ground, and rain pelted her, soaking her to the skin in moments.

The force of the winds ripped at her clothing and slewed her around bodily. She felt herself lifting into the air and screamed again, her fingers clawing at the muddy earth.

"Goddess mother, protect me!" she screamed aloud.

The cloud roared past her, pelting her with rain and dislodged stones, throwing mud over her, deafening her, and pummeling her. But it did not suck her up into itself after all. Moments later, it was gone.

Shaken and battered, Elandra lifted herself slowly and stared after it. The swirling cloud left the ground, rising into the sky like a rope, and now its immense force seemed to be unraveling. Elandra saw men, horses, pieces of buildings, stools, chests, and weapons raining from the sky, scattering across the blighted plain.

As these objects hit the ground, they exploded into dust and were melted into nothing by the rain.

More lightning raked the sky, cracking and booming loud enough to make Elandra clap her hands over her ears. The air reeked of fire and magic. Then abruptly the black clouds vanished. The rain ended as swiftly as it had come, and the roaring monster dissipated.

Breathing hard, Elandra tried to collect her wits. Pushing her muddy hair out of her face, she closed her eyes and said a quick prayer of gratitude to the goddess mother. She still held a handful of mud. Now she allowed it to spill from her fingers.

There had to be a way to escape this terrible place. She knew of only one thing to try.

Pulling out her topaz, she cupped the golden stone in her palms and stared into its depths. She tried to put aside her fear, tried to clear her mind of everything except the face of the Magria. Closing her eyes, she reached out in the way the Penestricans had taught her.

"Magria," she called, "I need your help. You came to me before when I was in great difficulty. Again, I call to you. Please, help me."

No voice spoke a response to her mind.

Elandra opened her eyes and saw nothing but bleak desolation in every direction. Just as it had been before.

Her spirits sank within her.

But she refused to believe that Hecati was her only hope. There had to be some way to escape.

Wearily Elandra climbed to her feet and told herself she must try something else.

"I am here, Elandra," a voice said to her.

It was a clear voice, a familiar one.

Startled, Elandra spun around and found a slender young woman with long, very straight golden hair standing less than five strides from her. Robed in black, her pale arms bare, her blue eyes direct and intense, she was a welcome sight indeed.

Relief flooded Elandra. She smiled and barely kept herself from hugging the Penestrican. "Deputy Anas," she said, "how glad I am to see you!"

The Penestrican did not return her smile. "I am deputy no longer." Lifting her left hand, she tossed a slim serpent onto the ground between them. It immediately began to slither toward Elandra's feet. "Don't move," she said sharply as Elandra gasped. "There is nothing to fear if you are who you claim to be."

Elandra immediately froze in place, but memories of other tests—some of them quite painful—made her frown. "You know who I am, Anas. Why do you test me?"

"If you are the empress, you should not be here," Anas said in a blunt voice. "You have no means of coming to this future."

"I was brought here."

The snake had almost reached the frayed toe of her slipper. Elandra forgot the rest of what she'd been about to say and stood tense and wary as she watched the serpent's tongue flicker rapidly. The snake had the wedge-shaped head of a viper; she believed that Anas could command it to strike with venom if she chose. The Magria, always more gentle than her deputy, would not have brought a poisonous snake for this test of truth. The Magria would have been more compassionate.

Elandra found it difficult to swallow. When Anas did not respond to her last statement, she glanced up and met the cold appraisal in those blue eyes.

"I was brought here," Elandra repeated. "Against my will. I can tell you by whom and for what purpose."

"Silence," Anas snapped. "Do not disturb the serpent of truth."

Before Elandra could protest, the serpent slithered away from her.

"Very well," Anas said. "The truth has been spoken."

A surge of heat filled Elandra's face.

"How dare you doubt me!" she shouted furiously. "I am not to be tested like one of your novices! You do not command me, Anas!"

Anas's blue eyes blazed back at her. "I am the Magria now," she snapped. "Take care."

For a fleeting second Elandra was appalled. "You are the Magria?" she said, heedless of the dismay her voice betrayed. "But she dismissed you from the succession."

Resentment flickered in Anas's blue eyes and was gone. "The former Magria relented," she said.

"Oh." Elandra frowned, trying to absorb this news. "I had not heard that her Excellency had stepped down. When did she—"

"The former Magria is dead," Anas said, every word tight and hostile.

Genuine dismay flashed through Elandra. "Oh, I am sorry!" she said. She had liked the old woman, formidable though she had been. Elandra had suspected that possibly the Magria had liked her. But she and Anas had never found any common ground.

Even now Anas still stared at her coldly, unappeased by her sympathy.

Frowning, Elandra tried again. "This is disturbing news. I respected her very much."

Stiffly Anas inclined her head. "She was worthy of much respect. She has returned to the dust whence she was made."

Elandra made a formal gesture, feeling as though she had lost her last ally. Still, Anas had come in response to her cry for help. She must remember to be grateful for that.

"Please," Elandra began. "I must ask—"

"Silence," Anas said sharply. She bent and picked up her serpent from the ground. The creature coiled itself around her wrist, and Anas shot Elandra a look of suspicion. "Something is wrong. You are the empress, but you smell of death and shadow."

An involuntary sob escaped Elandra before she could control herself. She pressed her hand to her lips, struggling not to hurl herself at Anas's feet. "The Guardian said I would have to pay a terrible price if he let us leave the realm of shadow. And now—"

"Wait!" Anas commanded, extending her other hand. "Speak slowly. You have been in the realm of shadow? You have confronted the Guardian?"

Elandra nodded. "It was a trick. We were supposed to follow Kostimon through the hidden ways—"

"Ah!" Anas said. "So that is how he escaped from the palace. Kostimon's blasphemy never stopped."

"Caelan got us to the Gate of Sorrows, and then the Guardian . . . I was bitten," Elandra said, her fear spilling from her despite her attempts to stay coherent. "I have the darkness. I am going to die."

A strange expression crossed Anas's face. She stepped closer to Elandra. "Repeat your words," she said, sounding almost afraid. "What bit you? Did the Guardian send you here?"

Elandra shook her head. "We were in Trau—"

"This is Trau. As it can become."

Elandra glanced around in fresh horror. "But—"

"Never mind. Tell me what happened."

"A *shyriea* came out of nowhere. Before Caelan could kill it, it bit me. That is why the witch Hecati brought me here. She offered to take the poison from me if I—"

Elandra found her voice breaking. Her fear twisted harder inside her, and she could not finish.

"Look at me," Anas said.

Elandra's eyes were burning. She was on the verge of tears, and she fought them, not wanting to break down in front of Anas.

"Kill me," she pleaded. "I would rather pass to the dust than become the living dead."

Anas gripped her shoulder. "Look at me," she commanded again.

Elandra dashed tears from her eyes, and lifted her gaze obediently. She found neither pity nor condemnation in Anas's eyes, but instead only concern and brisk competence.

"Put aside your fear," Anas said with unexpected gentleness. "Can you look past our personal differences and trust me?"

Elandra could only stare at her in astonishment at first, then in rising hope. "Can you help me?"

"If you will trust me."

Elandra thought of Caelan, who had held her tightly in the realm of shadows and asked her the same question. How frightened she had been of him then, and yet a part of her knew he would never willingly hurt her. Now she gazed into Anas's blue eyes and knew this woman was made of the same fiber as the old Magria.

Something in Elandra relaxed and reached out. "I do trust you," she whispered, daring to hope. "If you will help me, what must I offer?"

"Silence!" Anas snapped. "Compassion is not for sale."

Intense relief flooded through Elandra. Tears welled up in her eyes, spilling over. "Thank you!"

"Don't thank me yet. Nothing has been accomplished. You will gaze into my eyes, Majesty. You will look into the depths of my eyes and nowhere else. You must not blink. You must not move. Is that clear?"

"Yes," Elandra said breathlessly.

"You will empty your mind in the way you were taught. When it is empty of all thought, I will enter. In your time at our stronghold you resisted this. Now it could mean your life. Can you do it?"

Elandra thought of Caelan, how he had shared with her, how they had become one spirit, one mind. She had resisted him also, but he had shown her there was no loss in such a union, only much to gain.

She drew a deep breath and met Anas's gaze. "I will do it," she replied.

Anas nodded, and concentration tightened her face. "Begin."

At first it was difficult to focus. Elandra's mind was jumping from one thought to another, refusing to settle, refusing to obey. She held her gaze steadily on Anas's, thinking of their blue depths as blue topazes, not so very different from her golden one. Anas would help her. All she had to do was try . . . and trust.

Gradually her thumping heart slowed down. She remembered

to regulate her breathing. She remembered not to blink. She found herself drawn into Anas's blue eyes. How clear they were, how compelling and intelligent. They were such a different shade of blue from Caelan's, flecked with gray and green in the depths. Compassion and kindness lay in their depths, swirling with the colors, reaching out for Elandra so that no longer was she alone, no longer was she aware of the howling wind, no longer was she aware of the ugly, seared landscape of what might be.

Elandra dropped into a clear, empty place, and Anas slipped into her mind as gently as the warm splash of a summer raindrop. Almost at once she was gone, as though she had never been there.

Disappointment filled Elandra, shattering her concentration. She drew back physically, blinking hard to hold her composure. "You couldn't help me," she said, feeling hope crash from her. "I—"

"Hush," Anas said, drawing Elandra into her arms and hugging her tightly. She stroked Elandra's hair as Elandra wept, unable to be strong now. "Hush. Don't talk. Let the tears cleanse you."

But after a few wracking sobs, Elandra's fear choked off her emotions, and her tears stopped. She clung to Anas a moment, grateful for her kindness, then pushed herself away.

Bleakly she tried to remember she was the daughter of a warrior. Warriors did not cry. They did not dishonor themselves with cowardice. They faced what had to be done, and they did so quickly.

"I have no dagger," she said, fighting the unsteadiness in her voice. "Have you? A knife thrust is the quickest way to end—"

"Will you kill yourself now that you are cleansed?" Anas asked in amazement.

At first Elandra did not believe she had heard correctly. Then she lifted her gaze to Anas.

The Magria gave her a fleeting smile. "It is done."

Elandra couldn't believe it. "But how? You were so quick, I didn't think it—How?"

"That is why I am a Magria and you are not," Anas replied, but for once her arrogance did not offend Elandra. She pointed at the ground, where a small black puddle smoked ominously. "It can harm nothing here. But let us not linger in this place, for it can draw things to it that we would rather not meet."

"Like the cloud?"

Anas frowned. "You saw that?"

"Yes, a terrible, monstrous thing. Hecati sent it after me—"

"Nonsense! She has no such power," Anas said in astonishment. "Do you have no recognition of the portents?"

Elandra stared back in puzzlement. "Then what kind of—"

"You saw history, wound into a maelstrom," Anas said impatiently. "The cloud was the lifetime of Kostimon. If it passed by you, it should have taken you up into its center."

"It came right at me," Elandra said. "Then at the last moment it veered away."

Anas's blue eyes widened. "Your destiny has protected you."

Before Elandra could respond, the Magria turned and strode away. Elandra hurried after her, feeling hollow and strange inside. A terrible suspicion was spreading through her, one she hardly dared let herself believe. Yet what else could it mean?

"Kostimon," she whispered. "Are you saying he is dead?"

"Yes, he is dead." Anas sounded almost pleased. "You saw his soul and all his knotted threads of life—the history of his existence—swept away into the darkness. I wish I had been able to witness it."

Elandra frowned. She had known it must happen soon, but even so she hardly dared believe it. What she had felt for him had not been love, but she had respected him. She had been in awe of him. She had almost felt—almost—affection for him. In some ways, their minds had been much alike.

"Dead and gone," Anas said with satisfaction. "As is Sien the Vindicant—"

"Sien!" Elandra echoed, and she almost added, *Good riddance.* But instead she thought of the old Magria, likewise gone. So much had been swept away so suddenly. It made her shiver.

"What is to befall—"

"Please be quiet," Anas broke in, quickening her pace. "I require quiet, Majesty, so that I can take us from here safely."

Elandra stifled the rest of her questions. She did not understand why Anas had to be so prickly. Walking as fast as she could, she kept pace with the Magria and wondered how far they would have to go.

In the next moment, without any warning at all, she was back in the snowy gully.

Startled, she stumbled and nearly stepped in the stream. The intense cold struck right through her gown and seemed to freeze her face. Huge flakes of snow were falling from a gray, gloomy sky. The air smelled fragrant and fresh, and she drew in several deep lungfuls of it.

"You did it!" she cried. "Anas, you are wonderful!"

Again Anas gave her that fleeting smile before looking stern again. "Is it too much to address me with respect, Majesty? I believe you have been thinking we should treat each other as equals."

Elandra's joy was jerked up tight. Hurt and annoyed, she grabbed for imperial composure as a defense. "You must forgive me, Excellency, if I do not take your abilities for granted in the way that you do. I am not yet accustomed to treating them casually. I am sure my admiration will eventually fade."

Anas frowned, drawing in a sharp breath, but Elandra gave her no time to speak.

"As for equality, I think that is fair. It would be pleasant if we could feel comfortable enough with each other to be informal in private, but if that is not possible, I am amenable to maintaining the formal protocols."

Anas opened her mouth, but Elandra gathered up her long skirts to keep them from getting wet in the snow and walked toward the cave.

"Do allow me to offer you shelter. The cave looks humble, but I believe it is considered a place of sanctuary. It is better than standing out here in the wind and snow."

With head held high, she swept on ahead of Anas like a grand lady. Anas followed her without a word, although Elandra half expected the Magria to vanish into thin air.

Once inside the gloomy cave, however, Elandra found nothing welcoming about it. The ice-covered walls gave off a damp chill. There was no fire to warm it, no food or drink to bring back strength, hardly any light to see by.

Picking up her cloak, Elandra wrapped it around herself and sank wearily to the floor.

Anas glanced around warily as though she expected something to spring at her from the interior of the cave. "How interesting," she said at last, tilting her head as she studied the ceiling and ran her fingertips along the ice-coated walls. "One of the famous ice caves of Trau. It is a province known for its many natural wonders. Sanctuary, did you call it?"

"Yes."

"I feel a natural resonance in the earth." Anas extended her hand as though to press her palm against the wall, then withdrew it. "Very old power is here, an ancient presence like . . ." Her voice trailed off thoughtfully. "Did the man bring you here?"

Elandra looked up.

"The man in your dreams. Caelan E'non."

Heat flamed in Elandra's face. She looked away hastily, embarrassed by the question. The passion she had felt in those dreams was very private. In her heart she cursed the Penestrican dream walkers who robbed her of her secrets.

"You are free of your marriage vows," Anas said. "Have you realized that yet?"

Elandra's eyes widened. She was a widow, no longer married, no longer bound to a man she did not love. Her heart suddenly leaped in her chest, and she looked at the mouth of the cave in longing for Caelan's return.

"Does he know you love him?"

Elandra shook her head.

Anas walked over to her and crouched down beside her. Her hand covered Elandra's in a brief clasp. "Your feelings are not wrong or forbidden. You think your mother broke her marriage vows for a wanton affair, but this is not true. Iaris was destined to have an affair with Albain. Fate—not her free will—decreed their union. She fought us. She fought him. She fought herself."

Elandra stared at the Magria, her eyes wide. "What are you saying?" she whispered.

"I am saying that it is a time for truth. The veils and mysteries must be swept aside if we are to become united against our common enemy. Your mother is well married. She did not desire the affair which produced you. She was given no choice by the sisterhood."

"You mean—"

"Yes, Elandra. Long before your birth, we cast the future and knew the final empress must be special, must have the strong blood of Fauvina as a forbearer. We sifted through all the lineages and found the necessary combination between your father and mother. The spell was made. The affair happened. You were born."

Elandra felt stunned. "Small wonder she never loved me."

"Oh, child," Anas said with sudden emotion, gripping her hand again. "She did not give you up by choice. We commanded that as well."

Elandra stared at her a moment, soaking in the revelation, then jerked her hand away from Anas. "Why?"

"To test you—"

"Tests!" Elandra said furiously, jumping to her feet. "Always tests. What good are they? Do they make anyone's life better? Do they help anyone?"

"You were strengthened and tempered by adversity to prepare you for your destiny."

"My destiny was to marry a great man. I have done that," Elandra shouted at her. "Now what is left but civil war I have little hope of winning? Or should I simply go home to my father's household and live the rest of my days in a widow's veil?"

"Stop reacting emotionally and use your wits," Anas retorted. "There is more destiny ahead of you, girl. More than you can imagine, if you have the courage to face it."

"What?" Elandra demanded. "You said there would be no more mysteries. Tell me all."

"It is sometimes better to face life blindly than with knowledge."

Elandra gestured impatiently. "Tell me!"

"According to the visions, you have two possible destinies. Soon you will come to the fork that determines the course of the world."

"I don't understand."

"One destiny is this: You will wade in blood. You will wear armor like a man. You will stand atop *Sidraigh-hal* and watch the destruction of the world."

Aghast, Elandra stared at her in horror. "And the other?" she whispered.

"The second destiny is this: You are *chiara kula na,* the woman of fire. You will reap the tears of the world."

Elandra waited to hear more, but Anas stood silent.

After a moment Elandra frowned. The first destiny was too horrible to contemplate, and the second destiny made no sense.

"What does it mean?" Elandra finally asked.

Anas spread her hands. "That is up to you, and the actions you take."

Elandra stared at her. "You aren't telling me everything. There is more to what you know."

Anas hesitated.

"Tell me! What do I face besides war and destruction? What of Caelan's destiny?"

"My visions do not concern men," Anas said sharply.

"But does your vision show us together? Or do you intend to keep us apart?"

She looked at Elandra very hard and said, "The only one who has kept you and Caelan E'non apart has been you. In the past you have been told that fear keeps you from spreading your wings like an eagle."

Elandra flushed. She did not like to be called a coward. "Perhaps too many tests create their own bonds," she muttered.

"Perhaps," Anas agreed. "But they are feeble bonds, easily broken. Better you should confront yourself now and work out your own desires before you face what is to come."

"And that is?"

"The portents are very dark," Anas said. "I will have another vision soon, but all those that have come thus far are frightening. Something terrible is taking shape in our world."

"Does Beloth rise?"

Anas shot her a sharp look as though surprised to hear Elandra speak the god's name aloud. "Perhaps. But I think it is something we do not yet recognize. Do not look at me thus. I am not with-holding information. The visions offer many possible futures, many possible outcomes. Not one only. It is confusing. It is my prayer that the right future will happen."

"But what shall I do?" Elandra asked. "What course should I take? If I am to ensure the correct future will—"

"The witch Hecati accused you of being our puppet," Anas said with unexpected patience, "but you are not. You cannot fol-low, Majesty. You must lead. You must find your own way. I have told you all I can."

Elandra dropped her gaze. She felt far from reassured. "I can-not lead Caelan," she said. "He will not—have you no knowledge of him at all?"

"Only that he has long been in your dreams. Nowhere else in our visions does he appear. Nor has he appeared in the auspices cast by the Vindicants. What this means, I do not know. Perhaps you will walk beside him, as he will walk beside you. Enough," Anas said with a curt gesture. "This cave is cold and dark. Its magic is not mine. I must go."

With that abrupt farewell, Anas headed for the exit.

Elandra hurried after her. "Wait! Please, there is one more thing I must ask."

Anas climbed outside and stood impatiently in the snow. Her bare arms were blue with cold, but she did not shiver. "Yes?"

Elandra met Anas's impatient eyes and felt her nerve waver. But she did not back away. "Is there a way to alter time, to make it possible for Caelan and me to return to Imperia more quickly than a normal journey? If we must return on foot or even on horse-back, it will take many days."

"Nine weeks," Anas said.

"In that length of time, Tirhin will have secured the throne for himself. I will have no chance—"

"You will find the way you need," Anas replied curtly. "I must go."

Frustrated, Elandra again hurried after her. "But, please, I—"

Anas held up her hand to silence Elandra and shot her a stern look. "I have done all I can. There are many preparations which I must oversee if the sisterhood is to survive. I can do nothing else for you at this time."

She quickened her pace and strode away into the swirling snow, until the mist engulfed her and she was gone.

Chapter Thirteen

SHIVERING WITHIN THE folds of her cloak, Elandra frowned against the snowflakes stinging her face and realized it was nearly twilight.

Caelan, wherever he had gone, should have been back by now . . . if he meant to return at all. For the first time she wondered if he had abandoned her, believing her lost to the poison of the shadows.

Pain filled her heart. She had lost her opportunity, lost him before she understood what it meant to have him. Anger squared her shoulders, and for a moment she wanted to choke him for not giving her more time.

Yet, in fairness, how much time was he supposed to grant her? She had drawn away. She had refused him. She had reminded him of her marriage vows, pretending they were not false hypocrisy and clinging to them to ward off her fears.

Now Caelan was gone.

She pressed her hands to her lips, trying to hold back her emotions. He would not return. Just as he had left his sister behind, so now had he left her.

Her anger came surging back, trampling her grief. She wouldn't stay here. She couldn't hide in this cave forever, like a rabbit in a hole. How was she supposed to live? What was she supposed to eat? How was she supposed to occupy herself while he went forth without her?

Furious and frightened, she ran up the bank, telling herself he must have left tracks she could follow. Yet she knew she could never catch up with him if he had indeed left her.

Was she letting her fear command her common sense? Was he not instead only out hunting? She must believe he would return.

As she struggled up the bank, she saw him emerge from the woods into the clearing.

A cloak lined in fur hung from his broad shoulders, and he had acquired a sword from someplace. The scabbard tip showed just below the hem of his cloak.

For a moment she couldn't believe he was there. She froze, unable to breathe or look away, waiting for him to notice her.

When he glanced up and saw her standing there, several emotions chased across his face. He started to smile, then frowned instead. He came running across the clearing and scooped her off her feet.

"Caelan!" she said in surprise. "Put me down."

He was scowling as he carried her back toward the cave. "You mustn't be outside. It isn't safe."

"Put me down. Caelan, stop!"

"It's for your own safety. The cave is a place of sanctuary. It will keep the—"

"I no longer have the poison within me."

He stopped in his tracks and stared at her, puzzlement filling his eyes. "How can this be?"

"It's gone."

"Are you saying it faded away? I don't believe it."

"No, I am not saying that. The Magria took it from me."

He blinked. "The Magria?"

"The leader of the Penestricans. Don't say you've never heard of her."

"But where is she?" he asked, looking around. "How—"

"Never mind how," Elandra said impatiently. His arms still held her effortlessly, and her heart was thudding too fast. She had never felt like this before—other than in her dreams. She felt fire in her cheeks, and pushed free of his embrace. Not until her feet were firmly on the ground did she dare trust her voice again.

"I am free, do you understand? Aren't you pleased?"

"Yes, of course. I'm pleased, very pleased." He found a smile for her, but it didn't last long. He seemed restless, jumpy. He looked guilty, almost disappointed.

Frowning, she glared at him with disappointment of her own.

Men were brutes, every one of them. They had all the wit and understanding of a sack of flour.

She had thought he would be joyful. She expected him to sweep her into his powerful arms and kiss her. Instead he stood here, looking as though he had been caught doing something he shouldn't, and he did nothing.

Right then, she almost hated him. Why couldn't he look into her eyes and know that her heart had softened? She would rather be strangled than bend her pride enough to tell him so. If he couldn't tell, then he didn't care. She had misled herself. She was a fool.

"The emperor is dead," she blurted out.

Caelan stared at her, and she could have bitten her own tongue. Her face was aflame, and she felt as though she'd been dipped in burning oil.

That wasn't what she had meant to say, but now it was said, and he did need to know.

Only she wasn't ready for the ambition to come surging back into his gaze. She wasn't ready to see him square his shoulders and lift his head like a eagle. She had wanted a few more minutes of his attention, but already he was gazing into the distance, the wheels of his mind turning rapidly.

"How do you know this?" he asked.

"I was told by the Magria."

Again he frowned. "Why did she come here? How—"

"To rescue me," Elandra said, frowning back. "I told you that, Caelan E'non. Don't you care?"

"My name is not E'non," he interrupted sharply, a new tone in his voice that she hadn't heard before. "I will not wear that name. Better I go nameless, like a bastard, than carry that."

Her face went hot from an emotion other than passion, and she stepped away from him as though burned.

He stared at her with his brows raised. Then sudden comprehension dawned in his eyes. "Forgive me. I meant no slur against you."

"Don't apologize," she said bitterly. "The facts of my birth are well known."

Consternation filled his face. He reached out to her, but she backed away. Her back was rigid; her hands were clenched at her sides.

"Please," he said. "Don't be angry at me. I spoke without thinking. The things I learned today about my own parentage . . . no matter. I have no right to take my anger out on you. Truly, I am glad that you have been healed."

She stared at him, her eyes widening. "Are you saying your father isn't—that you aren't—"

Caelan's jaw clenched hard.

"I'm sorry," she said swiftly, trying to retreat. "I should not ask something so personal."

A wry expression crossed his face, and he gave her a twisted little smile. "At least your parents are human," he said bitterly. "At least your father could sire you without having to be enspelled. It seems I am something the Choven created in order to save the world."

Elandra's mouth fell open in astonishment. "The Choven!"

"Choven made, just like this sword," he said, touching the hilt with his fingertips.

"But you are human."

He shrugged. "I don't know what I am. I am not sure they know. If they do, they will not say."

"But—"

"At least it answers my questions about how I can do the things that I do."

She did not like the bleak tone in his voice. She did not like the way his face shut her out.

"Don't turn to granite, the way you do sometimes. Don't pretend it doesn't matter, when clearly it does. We have shared, remember?"

He didn't look at her. "That was before."

"And now?" she insisted, tugging at his sleeve to make him look at her. "Has your lust cooled already?"

Her bold question turned his face scarlet. He would not meet her eyes. "We should never have shared. Had I known—"

"What is different now from before?" she demanded. "You have learned truths you do not like. Are you the only one? Is it easy to stand isolated and detached from everyone? Is it better to hurt others before they hurt you? You shared yourself with me. We can't ignore that, or forget it happened. Or can we? How could you do such a thing to me?"

"I didn't mean—" His face contorted, and he turned away. "You don't understand."

"Then make me understand. Don't shut me away from the truth."

His eyes met hers then, and they were filled with torment. "I have been told my future," he said hoarsely. "I am afraid of it."

Her anger faded to compassion. She reached up to touch his cheek. He caught her hand and pressed his lips to it.

"I thought you didn't care—wouldn't care," he whispered. "You said—"

"I know what I said," she replied breathlessly. "I was a fool. But now I am free. I can admit what fills my heart."

He released her hand abruptly and stepped back. "Don't pity me."

"I don't—"

"Not human," he said bleakly, staring across the clearing at nothing. "Not anything—"

"Stop it!" she shouted. "This whining self-pity is not like you. What has unmanned you so?"

He shook his head, looking ashamed.

"Is your destiny worse than mine? Have you suffered more than I? Take hold of your blessings, not your regrets. Are we not alive? And together? Is that not a place to begin anew?"

He bowed his head. "Yes, you are right. But I have less than before to offer you."

"Do you think I care?"

There it was, her declaration thrown out in the open. She felt bolder than brass, afraid, but exhilarated too.

Caelan lifted his head and met her eyes. At once she felt as though she had been dipped in boiling water. She couldn't breathe properly. Her thoughts were spinning.

Somehow she managed to continue her argument, although his eyes and hers seemed to be speaking in a language of their own. "Name one blessing given to you," Elandra said sternly. "I have been saved from the darkness. That is one blessing for me. What about you?"

He swallowed, and she grew weak from watching the movement in his throat.

"Lea is alive," he said hoarsely.

Astonishment filled Elandra, momentarily distracting her. "Alive! How is this possible? You said—"

"I know. I found her here." He bit his lip and seemed to struggle for words. "There is too much to explain. But she is well and safe. The Choven have cared for her all these years."

"The Choven again," Elandra said in wonder. "It is surely a miracle. Caelan, how wonderful. Where is she? May I meet her?"

He glanced at the snowcapped mountains towering above the forest. "She's up there."

"I want to meet her. Why didn't you bring her to me?"

His face clouded, and he shook his head. "It is not that simple."

More secrets. She crossed her arms impatiently. "Why not? Caelan, you really don't understand anything, do you?"

"No, I really don't," he retorted with equal heat. "I don't understand how my sister can live half in and half out of the spirit-world without being a spirit herself. I don't understand why she prefers the Choven and their ways to everyone else. I don't understand how she could reach into the realm of shadow with her will and bring us here to her the moment we stepped through the Gate of Sorrows. Do you understand? If you do, please explain it to me."

"Caelan—"

He strode away from her, head down, moving blind and fast.

Elandra hurried after him. "Wait. Caelan, I'm sorry. We are both too angry. We're hurting each other without meaning to. Please stop, and let us try again."

He halted, but kept his back to her. "What is there to try?" he asked wearily.

She frowned, feeling all sorts of emotions tangled inside her. Why did it have to be so hard? Why was he so hostile, so ready to turn away from her now that she at last wanted to turn to him?

"Perhaps we can try to be friends," she said cautiously.

He snorted and swung around. "Friends?" he said.

She suddenly felt like a fool.

"I have a long journey," he said, scowling at the ground. "I had best get started."

Alarmed, she stared at him. Already she saw farewell in his eyes. Her heart turned to stone.

"And me?" she asked quietly. "Will you leave me behind, as once you left your sister?"

Pain flashed through his face. "That is not fair."

"You are not fair!" she retorted. "Why are you hurting me like this? What have I done, to make you turn against me?"

"Elandra," he said bleakly, "I face a task you cannot share. Here." He drew his sword and held it out to her, hilt first. "Take it. Hold it a moment."

"No," she said.

"Take it. Swing it. Show me your technique."

Her eyes were stinging. "Cruelty doesn't become you."

He slid the sword back into its scabbard. "Enough of this foolishness. You cannot ride into war. No matter how much you care about the throne, you—"

"You need me," she insisted. "I have as much right to go as you."

"And what will you do? Fight?"

"You'll get no troops without me," she said angrily. "You can't raise an army on your own, and you know it. Besides, I don't have to ride into battle. I can stay out of harm's way."

"You will be safer here with my sister and the Choven."

"Will I?" she snapped. "What do you know about it? Has my future been revealed to you? Do you know what my destiny is? Do you?"

"I am supposed to break the world!" he shouted. "Is that an ordinary battle? Is that any place for you to be? I don't expect to come back. At least give me the consolation of knowing you're safe."

"Safe?" she echoed. "This isn't about staying safe. We weren't intended to fold our hands and hide from events, neither of us. If you are to break the world, I am to reap its tears. What have you to say to that? Does that sound like I am to stay home and spin wool?"

They glared at each other, breathing hard, both furious, and then she realized how ridiculous it was to be standing in a snow-filled ditch, nose to nose and yelling about their destinies like two children trying to outdo each other with boasts.

She snorted, trembling, and pressed her hands to her lips.

A corner of his mouth twitched.

They stepped back from each other, breathing hard in the silence. Then their eyes met, and they smiled at the same time.

Elandra drew a swift breath that became laughter. "How silly we are. What are we arguing about?"

He beat on his chest and struck a foolish pose. "I shall conquer the world."

She imitated him. "And I shall do it better!"

They laughed harder; then he reached out, and she ran to his arms. She wanted to go on laughing forever like this with him, yet she felt close to tears also, for how near they had come to ruining everything. Relief spread over her, and she clung more tightly to him.

"We are fools," he said, kissing her hair. "We would fight about the air if it served our purpose."

She felt suddenly as though she could not breathe. This was the moment. It felt as though time had stopped around them. "Caelan," she said very softly, refusing to look up into his eyes in case he refused her. "It grows late, too late to travel. Traulanders are afraid of the dark—"

"We are *not* afraid of the dark," he corrected her with mock sternness. "We are afraid of wind spirits. That is only sensible."

"Then the wind is certainly brisk," she said shyly. "It is cold and late. Soon it will be dark. Let us go to the cave together."

He said nothing, and her heart fell to her slippers. She dared peek up at him and saw him frowning, saw the battle of hope, disbelief, and acute longing in his face. That gave her courage.

Reaching up, she caressed his cheek with her hand. "Let us go to the cave," she said, her voice low and throaty. "Let us have tonight before we face our future."

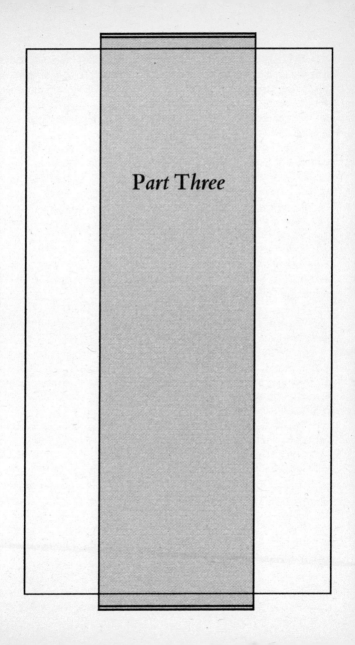

Part Three

Chapter Fourteen

DAWN CAME TOO SOON.

Elandra wakened slowly, stretching beneath the warm fur cloak that had served as their coverlet. Her bed was made of thick pine boughs, with Caelan's tattered red cloak spread across them. They had spent the night in the innermost cavern, where hundreds of emeralds embedded in the ice walls glittered around them like stars. A fire that needed no replenishing had burned nearby all night. Food, steaming hot, had been waiting for them.

She could smell fresh platter cakes now, making her ravenous. Truly this was a special, magical place. She was not ready to leave so soon.

But Caelan was already out of bed. Quietly he was dressing with his back to her. She rolled onto one elbow and watched him, loving the gleam of firelight on his sun-bronzed skin, the smooth ripple of muscle and sinew, the knobby ridge of vertebrae up his spine as he bent over to pull on his leggings. Thinking of the night and its mysteries, she felt herself blushing, but she didn't care. She was wildly, gloriously happy. Caelan had been both ardent and gentle, a combination that had led her quickly past shyness into passion. In exchange, she had drawn on the dances of pleasure that had been taught to her during her time with the Penestricans. She had been both wanton and innocent, and even now as she dreamed of all that they had shared, she felt her pulse quickening and a sensual little smile curving her lips.

This was life. This was truth. A man and woman together were so much more complete than either could be alone. Whatever lay before them, they would face it as one.

But this morning, he looked so serious, so remote. She watched his supple hands that had been so gentle, so masterful last night now fasten buckles and oil the blades of both sword and dagger. He wore his warrior's face, purposeful and somber, and she felt a qualm, wondering if he would become a stranger again.

Caelan picked up his armor, then hesitated and glanced over his shoulder at her. Seeing her awake, he smiled.

The smile lit up his face, and the warrior vanished. In his place stood the man with a heart of grace and compassion, a man who was kind and loyal and true.

He dropped his armor and came to kneel beside her, kissing her thoroughly until her body melted and her arms reached around his neck to pull him down.

But he unclasped her hands and held them in his large, callused ones. "Temptress," he said, still smiling.

"You are too far away."

But although passion quickened in his eyes, he shook his head. "It's daybreak. We must not linger here."

She sighed while he stood up and started buckling on his armor. "I will always love this cave."

He paused with his hands on the buckles and grinned at her. "And I will always love *you*."

Her breath caught in her throat, and she loved him so much she wanted to cry.

"Get up, your lazy Majesty," he said. "It's a long walk to Gialta."

That brought her down to earth. Flinging off the fur cloak, she dressed quickly, amazed to find her gown mended and clean. Braiding her hair, she leaned over a stone bowl of water to wash her face. The water was freezing cold, making her gasp and shiver.

By then, Caelan was bringing her the platter of food. She nibbled on a cake, finding its nutty taste unusual but delicious, and looked in vain for her slippers. They were worn through. They would never take her to the Trau border, much less all the way to Gialta, but she couldn't travel barefoot.

"Ready?" Caelan asked, leaning over her shoulder to bite the cake she held absentmindedly.

She looked around with a gurgle of laughter and gave him a quick kiss. His lips were covered with crumbs that she licked off.

"Stop that," he said, pulling away from her. "We must go."

"But I can't find my shoes."

"I saw them."

"Where?"

But he was already bending to pull out her slippers from beneath the pine boughs. "Here."

To her surprise, the slippers looked like new.

"Who mended them?" she asked, holding up first one, then the other in amazement.

Caelan shrugged. "Who gave us fire and food?"

"Your sister?"

He fastened on his army cloak and did not reply.

Elandra watched him and found herself frowning. "Don't wear that," she said.

He paused and raised his brows.

"Don't wear imperial crimson," she said. "Kostimon is dead. The ruby throne is broken. Don't wear his colors."

Comprehension filled his face. Slowly he removed the bright cloak that had been a symbol of pride for so many soldiers through the long march of history.

She brought him the fur cloak and watched as he put it on. Smoothing his hand across his breastplate, he asked, "Do I now look like a barbarian?"

Elandra laughed. "Yes, but a most handsome one."

He made a face. "I don't think the army is interested in how handsome I look."

"Will your sister come to see us off?" Elandra asked. "Will I get to meet her?"

"I don't know."

His mood had sobered again. Elandra watched him, but said nothing. This homecoming had not been what he had imagined; she felt his keen disappointment.

Again she changed the subject. "If the Choven gave you a sword, why didn't they make you special armor as well?"

"Are you now going to suggest I leave my armor behind?"

"No, silly. You must have it. I only wish it were an officer's."

He looked grim as he brought her gold wool cloak to her and fastened it around her shoulders. "The trappings aren't important now. Only fools worry about how they look as they prance to the battlefield. I worry about whether we can raise the men we need."

She gazed up at him, adoring him, believing in him. "We will raise the men."

"I wish I had your faith."

"We are on the side of right. Tirhin betrayed his own people. In doing so, he forfeited any claim he might have had. Kostimon never named him successor."

"Kostimon," Caelan said dryly, "did not believe in sharing what he had."

She nodded and glanced around at the small cave one last time. Already she missed it. How silly to cry over a primitive mound of pine boughs. How silly to be a woman at all. She lifted her head high and sniffed quickly and lightly, determined not to let him see her foolishness. Small wonder men did not want women along in battle when they could turn sentimental so quickly.

But Caelan took one of her hands and kissed it. "We were blessed here. This sanctuary witnessed our union. And although no priest has pronounced over us, I do claim you, Elandra of Gialta, for my own. I say you are my flesh. You are my spirit. You are my heart. And I will keep myself for you only until the day I die."

She found herself trembling with joy at the honor he did her. When she looked up into his eyes, her own filled with tears, then she blinked them away and said breathlessly, "And I do claim you, Caelan of Trau, for my own. You are my flesh, my spirit, and my heart. I will keep myself for you only until the day I die."

He pulled her close into his arms, lifting her until her feet dangled while he kissed her, then set her gently on the ground again.

"Ready?" he asked.

Gripping his hand, feeling as strong as the earth goddess herself, Elandra nodded. She would follow this man to the ends of time if need be. Let all their enemies be cursed unto death if they dared try to part this union.

"Wait," Elandra said before they reached the mouth of the cave. She pulled her hand free and darted back. "There's something I want to do."

Impatient, Caelan frowned at her. "What?"

"Never mind. Go on. I'll join you in a moment."

Shaking his head, he hoped she did not intend to linger here. No matter how wonderful the night had been, it was time to go. He felt a strong sense of urgency, the suspicion that time was rapidly running out.

"Hurry!" he called after her.

"I will," her voice came back, muffled and echoing through the cave.

Stooping low, he ducked outside, stepped across the stream, and climbed the low bank. It was gray yet, very cold and still in that moment of hush just before the sun lifts over the horizon. With his breath streaming about his face, Caelan walked quickly, swinging his arms to get his blood pumping. He hoped Lea would come before they left. He did not want to go without saying goodbye. Besides that, he wanted to ask her for the gift of two ponies and supplies. On foot, their journey would be hazardous and slow.

He knew he could travel quite fast on his own, fasting if necessary, but Elandra was not accustomed to such hardship. She must find the cold brutal. He told himself to take very good care of her, not let her grow too tired or too chilled.

A bugling sound came from overhead. Caelan froze, unable to believe his ears; then he looked up. Overhead sailed a shape that had haunted his dreams for years. He saw the black leathery wings, narrow head, and thin, flexing neck of a dragon.

Caelan told himself to move, to run for cover, but he couldn't. It was impossible that this was happening again. Were the gods this capricious, this unkind? Was fate against him? Had the shadow realm tracked him down again?

The dragon wheeled high above him and bugled again. Its rider shouted something Caelan did not understand. Hatred boiled in Caelan's heart, and he forgot both amazement and prudence as he drew his sword and brandished it aloft.

His field of vision narrowed until he could see only this one dragon and rider circling above him. He burned for revenge.

"Come down here and fight!" he roared.

The dragon lifted a wing tip and swung around, then plummeted in a sudden dive straight at Caelan. He heard the coughing roar from the dragon's throat, and fire belched from the beast's nostrils.

The flames scored two tracks through the snow, and thick gouts of steam rose into the air.

Caelan knew he should run. He was no match for an airborne dragon, and he knew it. But at that moment he was too furious to care.

For years he had dreamed of revenge. Now the chance had come to him. He was no untried boy this time. And he would be damned if he let this raider ruin his life a second time.

Screaming curses at the top of his lungs, he ran forward between the twin bursts of flame. The heat scorched him. He could smell his own hair burning, and one corner of his cloak caught fire. Without slowing, he leaped high in the air and swung Exoner overhead.

The tip sliced through the dragon's wispy beard into its chin, and blood spurted. Screaming with pain, the dragon flung up its head and veered aloft even as its rider leaned dangerously over in an attempt to stab Caelan with a javelin.

Both men swore and yelled at each other, while drops of dragon blood splattered the snow. The dragon circled the treetops, squalling and slinging its head.

Only now noticing that his fur cloak was on fire, Caelan slung it off into the snow. The stink of singed animal hair filled the air. He bent a moment and scooped up a handful of snow to rub across the burns on his face.

In that moment of inattention, the dragon dove again, wings tucked, talons stretching out, head extended fully with fangs bared. It came right at him.

There was no time to dodge or duck. If the dragon succeeded in striking him, the impact alone could kill him. Caelan braced himself, bringing up his sword one-handed, and heard Elandra scream.

The impact was like being struck by a battering ram. The jolt was tremendous, knocking the air from his lungs and lifting him off his feet. He felt himself fly into the air. There was incredible pain; instinctively he *severed* it. He felt his arms still swinging;

then Exoner bit deep, and the swing continued, slicing off the head of the dragon.

The dragon's attack cry fell silent. Blood spurted in a great, drenching sheet, coating Caelan's face and blinding him. The Thyzarene shouted something incomprehensible, while Caelan hit the ground with a numbing, bone-rattling jolt. Impetus sent him skidding across the ground before he struck a tree stump.

He lay there, blind and gasping helplessly, the sword still clutched somehow in his hand. He couldn't seem to draw a breath properly, but he knew he had to get on his feet. If he gained his feet, he could move. If he could move, he could survive. He had to survive.

Still, he lay there, unable to see, his own breath wheezing horribly in his ears, writhing in a feeble effort to flip over and get his knees under him.

He heard the Thyzarene swear, then a thud, then the swift, crunching sound of running footsteps across the snow.

Fear propelled Caelan up. Dragging his forearm across his eyes, he cleared most of the dragon's blood away, ungluing his eyelids in time to see the Thyzarene running straight at him with an upraised javelin. The Thyzarene's swarthy face was contorted with fury. He screamed curses as he ran.

Caelan met the man's attack on his knees. His sword blade connected with the thrusting javelin point, and sparks flew from metal. Despite the other's advantage in standing, Caelan was strong enough to hold their locked weapons and even push himself to his feet. This close, he saw that his opponent was only a boy, grown but not yet filled out, with a scraggly beard fuzzing his lean cheeks. Grief and rage blazed from his eyes.

It was said that Thyzarenes who flew the dragons had some kind of special bond with the creatures. Caelan glanced at the dead dragon lying in the bloody snow, then back to the Thyzarene straining against him. Rage could strengthen a man, but blind rage made him vulnerable and foolish.

Almost contemptuously, Caelan pushed the boy away and circled him, waiting to pick his moment.

Tears were running down the boy's cheeks, but he was still

cursing Caelan in his own tongue. Heedlessly, he swarmed Caelan in a frenzied, almost mindless attack, jabbing and flailing.

Caelan parried strongly, sidestepped another furious thrust of the javelin, and ignored the chance to cleave the boy in half. Instead he leaped behind the boy and got one arm around the boy's throat.

The boy kicked and flailed, but the javelin was useless at such close quarters. Caelan knocked the weapon from his hand, and it plunged into a snowdrift.

Yanking the boy around bodily, Caelan forced him to stand where he could look at his dead dragon.

"Look at it!" he shouted in Lingua. "Look at it!"

The boy twisted and struggled, but Caelan tightened his hold until he heard the boy choke. Then he pushed the Thyzarene to the ground and planted his foot on the boy's back to hold him pinned.

"That's what is going to happen to you," Caelan said.

The boy heaved in an effort to get to his knees, but Caelan stamped him flat again. Sheathing his sword, he drew his dagger instead and tested its edge with his thumb. It needed honing, but it would be sharp enough for what he intended to do.

His mind flooded with the memories of that long ago day at E'nonhold when the dragons had set the buildings on fire. He remembered dear old Anya's face as she ran for her life, only to be burned beyond recognition. He remembered the screams, remembered his own helpless feeling of rage and frustration, remembered the laughter and exultant shouts of the raiders. He remembered lying on the ground, trussed in a net, while one of the raiders slit his father's throat.

Gripping a handful of the boy's dark curls, Caelan jerked him up to his knees and held his dagger in front of the boy's terrified eyes.

"Stop! Stop!" the boy said desperately in heavily accented Lingua. "By the gods, stop!"

Caelan took grim pleasure in hearing the boy beg for his life.

"A Thyzarene afraid?" he jeered. "You are going to die out here. One quick slash, and you'll be as dead as your dragon."

"Wait! I can offer you money," the boy babbled. "Take my bracelets. They are gold. Take my—"

"Shut up," Caelan said, contemptuous of this whining. "When you are dead, I will take everything I want anyway."

"No, please! You don't—"

"That's the Thyzarene way," Caelan broke in. "You live off plunder. You dance in the ashes of your victim's houses. You cart out all their possessions and pick them over. Bloodsucker! Carrion-eater! Reap what you have sown!"

He put the dagger to the boy's throat, steeling his heart against the boy's sobbing. There were no more pleas for mercy, much to his relief. He hated the boy's tears, for they made him realize the boy was younger than he looked. For a moment Caelan wavered. But then he remembered all that he had suffered, and his fingers tightened around the dagger hilt.

"Caelan, let him go!"

It was Elandra's voice. Caelan hesitated, but then refused to look in her direction. He kept his gaze grimly locked on the back of the boy's head. This was not her business, he told himself.

He lifted his elbow to turn the blade to the most efficient angle. One swift slice, and . . .

"In the name of all that's merciful, stop what you are doing," Elandra commanded.

Her voice rang out across the small clearing.

Caelan glared at her, standing nearby. Her eyes were huge in the pale oval of her face.

"He's only a boy," she said. "What are you doing?"

"Little Thyzarenes grow into big ones," Caelan said grimly. "If this one is old enough to kill, he's old enough to be killed."

"You have slain his dragon and wounded him to his soul. That is enough."

"It is not enough!" Caelan shouted. "It will never be enough! He killed my father—"

She came running up to them, close enough now for Caelan to see how red her cheeks were, how furiously her eyes blazed. "This boy is not your enemy."

"All Thyzarenes are—"

She scooped up a double handful of snow and threw it in Caelan's face. "He is not your enemy!" she shouted. "He was not there the day your father died. He is not responsible for your being sold into slavery. Genocide is not justice!"

Caelan glared at her, slowly cooling down. She was right, but he didn't want to admit it. He was furious at her interference. "I will have my revenge."

Elandra didn't flinch. "Then kill him in cold blood if you wish," she said in a raw, scornful voice. "But I will tell you the problem with such a revenge. Once his blood spills hot over your hands, your father's death will not be undone and your guilt will not be one ounce lighter than before."

Caelan scowled, the muscles in his jaw clenching hard. She was right. He wanted to curse her, but she was right. The admission tasted like ashes in his mouth.

Growling, he released the boy and stepped back.

Sobbing, the boy sank into the snow, and Caelan looked at him with disgust.

Then he shot Elandra a resentful look. "Satisfied?"

"Would you jeopardize your soul to avenge a man you didn't really love? A man you said yesterday wasn't your real father?"

Confusion filled him. "Damn you, will you leave me with nothing?"

"Kill him, then. Kill him because he attacked you. But don't lie to yourself and use false justification."

Caelan refused to look at her. Turning wrathfully on the boy, he gestured. "Get out of here."

The boy, however, didn't move. His dark eyes were locked on Elandra. "Thank you, lady," he said, sketching a little gesture of respect.

"Get out!" Caelan yelled at him.

Uncertainly the boy scrambled to his feet, his gaze shifting back and forth between them. "I cannot leave until my Shierfa is properly mourned."

"If that's your dragon, you can mourn it on your way home," Caelan said without pity. "Start walking. You have a long way to go."

"Caelan, don't," Elandra said. "His dragon was important—"

"Then he shouldn't have attacked me," Caelan said.

"It was sport," the boy said. "Only sport."

Caelan, his rage still barely held in check, turned his glare back on the boy, who blanched. Baring his teeth, Caelan said, "Then when I cut off your Shierfa's head, that was only sport too."

Furious tears filled the boy's eyes. Screaming, he launched himself at Caelan, but Elandra stepped in the way.

"Stop it," she said. "Both of you—"

But the boy threw his arms around her and spun her to face Caelan. As he did so, he pulled a knife from his boot and pressed the point to her side.

"Now, Traulander," he said, his thin, swarthy face alight with triumph, "I have the lady. Stay back!" he warned as Caelan came at him.

Caelan froze, his gaze never leaving the boy's. Rage still flamed inside him, but his mind had gone utterly cold. A Thyzarene could never be trusted. He wouldn't forget that again. And as soon as he got the chance, he would take great pleasure in breaking the brat's spine in half.

Looking both alarmed and angry, Elandra struggled in the boy's grip, only to yelp and suddenly stand very still. All the color drained from her face, and Caelan's rage grew white hot.

Still he held himself in check, making no move, waiting for the right opportunity. He eyed the boy the way a predator eyes its prey. He had all the patience in the world, and nothing would stop him when it was time to attack.

Quietly, his large body lithe and graceful, he began to slowly circle so that the boy was forced to turn to keep facing him.

"Stand still," the boy commanded, "or I will hurt her."

Caelan continued to move, slowly and deliberately. His eyes never left the boy's. "If you hurt her, I will tear out your throat."

Defiance flashed in the boy's face. "I am Kupel," he said proudly. "I am a chieftain's son, and I have captured the empress. Much reward gold will go into my coffers. I will be richer than my father when her ransom is paid for."

And before Caelan could reply to this bold announcement, Kupel lifted the hilt of his knife swiftly to his lips and whistled through a hole in it.

Caelan stepped forward, but with a grin Kupel pressed the knife point to Elandra's side. "Be careful," he warned.

Fuming, Caelan froze again. This was not the opportunity he wanted.

Kupel's grin widened even more. "Now, the others will come."

Chapter Fifteen

"YOU'RE MAKING A mistake," Caelan said.

"No, you are!" Kupel retorted. Tightening his hold on Elandra, he started backing away.

Caelan followed.

"Don't follow me!" Kupel said.

Caelan stopped. He glared at the boy, picking targets in the boy's hide, and wished he had killed him when he had the chance.

Elandra said nothing. Her eyes were big with fear; her face was pale and strained.

He only knew he had to act fast before more Thyzarenes came.

"What makes you think she's the empress?" he asked.

Doubt flashed momentarily in Kupel's eyes; then he sneered. "Very clever. Of course she is. Agents across the empire are looking for her."

"I know nothing about the empress," Caelan said. "But if you think you can trick such agents into paying good imperial gold for my wife, you are a fool."

"Watch what you say," Kupel warned him angrily. "I am not a fool. I hold her, do I not? Eh?"

"You hold her," Caelan agreed.

"Then I am not a fool."

"Fine. But she's still my wife."

Elandra's strained expression lightened. For a moment she nearly smiled. He met her eyes and felt his own guts twist in fear for her.

Don't think about how much you love her, he told himself. He had to concentrate. He could not let his emotions rule him, or he would lose his nerve.

"Wife? Huh, maybe," Kupel said with a shrug. "But as empress she will bring big reward."

"If she's my wife, and she's also the empress, that must mean I'm the emperor," Caelan said. He spread out his hands. "Do I look like the emperor?"

Kupel grinned, enjoying the joke, but he didn't loosen his hold on Elandra. "We see her. We know. All people know empress."

"Impossible. She's never been to Trau before. She's certainly never been to your camp."

Kupel backed up a few more steps, keeping Elandra tight against him. Then, never taking his eyes off Caelan, he put his knife between his teeth and dug a coin out of his pocket. He tossed it at Caelan, and whipped his knife back into place at her ribs with another quick grin.

"You see," he said. "You see empress."

Careful to make no sudden moves that might be misinterpreted, Caelan picked up the coin and turned it over. It was a new half-ducat, very shiny, and pocked with teeth marks near the rim where its owner had tested its value. Elandra's profile was stamped on the coin, clear and unmistakable.

"Word has gone out," Kupel said as Caelan's fingers closed hard over the coin. "Empress missing. Stolen by Traulander. We get big reward."

His words were nearly drowned out by the twin bugling of dragons. Glancing up into a sky radiant with new sunlight, Caelan saw the two beasts circling high overhead. Kupel's friends had arrived. Caelan's heart sank.

Elandra chose that moment to stamp sharply on Kupel's instep. Howling with pain, he hopped on one foot, and she rammed her elbow hard into his stomach. When he doubled over, she twisted free. He grabbed at her cloak, but there was an arm's length of distance now between them. Caelan threw his dagger, and it thunked into Kupel's chest.

An astonished look filled Kupel's face; then his eyes rolled up, and he toppled over in the snow. Overhead, one of the dragons roared. Caelan raced across the ground, drawing his sword as he ran, and kicked Kupel over on his back to pull out his dagger.

"Take cover!" he shouted at Elandra. "Get back to the cave, if you can. The trees aren't safe if they start breathing fire."

She nodded, crouching low to pick up Kupel's knife. "I should have let you kill him at the start," she said, then ran in a flurry of long skirts.

He grinned after her, admiring her more than ever. She had been right to stop him; he could admit that now. He would tell her so later, if they survived this. But already one of the dragons was swooping low in her direction. Caelan's heart nearly stopped. Again, he had to consciously shake off his fear. Somehow he had to distract them from her.

He held up Exoner so that its blade flashed in the rising sun. "Cowards of the sky!" he shouted at the top of his lungs. "I have killed your chieftain's son. I have killed Kupel and Shierfa, his dragon. Come and take the Dance of Death with me!"

One of the Thyzarenes howled with anger, and both dragons soared and wheeled in his direction. Caelan braced himself, knowing he could not fight both at the same time. But at least Elandra would have a chance to reach the cave. As long as she remained hidden inside it, the Thyzarenes would not be able to see it, and she would be safe.

"Dragon riders!" Elandra shouted, her voice shrill and clear. "I am the Empress Elandra, your sovereign. Call off your attack, and you will be well rewarded. I carry much gold, much imperial wealth. This I will share with you!"

Caelan groaned, furious with her for not following orders. He risked a glance in her direction and saw her standing in the open, straight and proud. Her arms were lifted, and the sun rose above the treetops at that moment to bathe her in golden radiance. With her auburn hair and gold-colored cloak, she looked like she was made of fire itself, blazing bright in the snow.

Caelan stared at her, momentarily forgetting the attacking rush of the dragons, even as one of them veered off again in her direction. Something primitive and elemental stirred inside him. The hair prickled on his scalp. What was she, this woman of fire?

Then he was ducking as the remaining dragon swept low over him. Caelan swung his sword, but managed no more than a shallow cut in the dragon's scaled underbelly. Unlike Kupel, an untried boy, this rider and his dragon were battle-scarred and experienced. The dragon's talons raked at Caelan, making him duck again, and its long tail whacked him solidly, knocking him off his feet.

By the time he rolled and came upright again, the dragon had wheeled and was making another pass. Caelan tried to see what was happening with Elandra, but that distraction cost him a second chance to attack his own opponent. The sharp point of a javelin tip skidded across his breastplate close to his throat, and woke him up.

Caelan jerked aside with a grunt of surprise. Bringing up his sword two-handed, he lunged upward. His breastplate kept him from being impaled on the javelin, and his sword tip cut the rider's arm.

The Thyzarene swore at him, and the hovering dragon whipped its head around, baring its fangs in an attack of its own. But a sharp command sent it lifting before Caelan could cut off its head. Again its tail came at him, but this time he parried with his sword, and drew more dragon blood.

Roaring in pain, the beast flapped its huge leathery wings and swept out of reach. The dragon was already coughing, trying to belch flame.

Caelan turned to run for cover, only to stare as he saw the second dragon hovering only a few feet above the ground in front of Elandra as though pinned there.

Elandra was holding her topaz aloft, and the jewel shone with a bright intense light right into the dragon's iridescent eyes. The creature looked mesmerized, and refused to respond to its rider's angry commands.

Breathless and soaked with sweat, Caelan felt both astonishment and envy. He reached instinctively for his emerald, only to remember he had left it with the Choven. In the past he had foolishly tried using a warding key against the dragons, and that certainly didn't work.

But perhaps there was another way.

He whirled around and threw himself flat as the second dragon sailed over him. Its talons just missed him this time, and the Thyzarene jeered at him contemptuously.

"Can you kill only boys and young dragons?" he yelled,

"Great warrior, what are you doing cringing on your face? Stand and face dragon fire like a man."

The dragon coughed out a spume of fire that would have engulfed Caelan had he not rolled frantically. Scrambling to his feet, he brought up Exoner barely in time to meet a second blast of fire.

Gritting his teeth against the heat, he plunged the blade right at the flames, deflecting them back at the dragon.

Squalling in pain, the dragon flung up its head and reared in panic. It stopped coughing flames, but its beard was on fire, and black burns blistered its hide. Still bellowing, the beast dropped onto the ground and began to run its snout frantically back and forth in the snow.

Its rider kicked and shouted commands that the dragon ignored. Caelan ran at them.

The Thyzarene jumped clear of the harness straps and hurled his javelin. It struck the arm rim of Caelan's breastplate and skidded off into the meat of his upper arm. The pain burned momentarily and was forgotten as he leaped at the man. Together they tumbled in a gouging, kicking heap.

Caelan dropped his sword, knowing it was no good at such close quarters. Blocking the Thyzarene's attempt to gouge out his eyes, he drew his dagger and struck hard, but the Thyzarene's dagger blocked the blow.

Cursing each other, they rolled over and over, each trying for a fatal blow. Just as Caelan was about to get one of his arms around the other man's throat, the Thyzarene wriggled free and broke away.

Caelan scrambled to his feet in pursuit, only to find the man waiting for him in a knife-fighter's stance. Caelan at once crouched low, holding his dagger loose and ready in his hand. Intent and wary, they circled each other.

"Caelan!" Elandra cried out.

He glanced to the side, expecting to see her taken prisoner. Instead, the rider of the dragon she held enspelled had jumped off his beast and was running, not at her, but instead to join the fight against Caelan.

He accepted the unfair shift of odds without fear. Clearly in his mind he could hear his former trainer Orlo say, *There are no rules in the arena.*

The Thyzarenes were much shorter than he, which gave him the advantage of reach. But they were quick, acrobatic, and fearless. Knowing the approaching man would come at his back, Caelan shifted around in an effort to recover his sword from where it lay in the churned-up snow.

No longer was this a simple knife fight. Grinning, the two Thyzarenes exchanged swift comments in their own language. Caelan's gaze slid again to his sword. If he could get to it, he had a chance.

But they also looked at the sword, plainly determined to keep him from it.

The second Thyzarene had gray streaks in his dark hair. His body was as wiry and tough as leather. He had the cold, empty eyes of a predator, watching Caelan for any move. The other man—younger, slightly heavier—had a wild gleam in his eyes that said he was reckless and enjoying himself. He wanted Caelan's blood, but he was not as dangerous as the older man.

Caelan circled, feinting when one of them moved, taking the chance to catch his breath, feeling the lag of strength fall through his muscles as time stretched out, feeling the ache of his bruised ribs beneath his breastplate as *severance* slipped slightly.

And as though his mind had suddenly cleared, he realized he was too much in the habit of fighting for show in the arena, stretching out the contest for the enjoyment of the audience, of using weapon, brute strength, and heart.

Severing more deeply, feeling the sweet, icy cold plunge into the void, Caelan reached for their threads of life.

Suddenly, Lea stood before him.

Without warning, without movement, she was suddenly there. Less than four strides away, she stared at him with disappointment in her blue eyes.

Defiantly he stared back. She did not understand that sometimes killing was necessary.

"And sometimes it is not," she said in his mind. "Think, Caelan. Reach beyond the simple thoughts of a warrior and use the mind you were given. See in new ways. Use the opportunity before you."

The men attacked him. The heightened perceptions of *severance* made them appear to move slowly. Caelan shifted aside to avoid them.

"Would you have me stand here and be killed?" he said to Lea in exasperation.

"Think, Caelan! Look at what you have."

"I have two dragon riders ready to cut me into ribbons."

"Dragon riders," she said. *"Think!"*

An image filled his mind of the strong beasts sweeping across the sky, used as swift messengers and dispatch carriers. He thought of long distances to cross, of too little time.

The Thyzarenes lifted their weapons to strike. From far away, distorted and slow, came their attack cries.

Caelan glared at Lea. "Get out of the way."

"Don't—"

"Get out of the way!"

She retreated, and Caelan reached for the Thyzarenes' threads of life, grabbing them and jerking them hard.

He did not cut them, and when he jolted back from *severance* and stood blinking in the sunshine, he found both men lying unconscious at his feet. Swiftly he disarmed them.

"Caelan!" Elandra called. "I can't hold this much longer."

He saw her still standing with her jewel held aloft, while the dragon hovered and moaned, dipping and bobbing now as its strong wings faltered.

"Let the dragon go," he said. "Let it go. It won't attack without its rider. But stay out of reach of its tail, just in case."

Elandra lowered her arms, covering the topaz in her palm, and ran backward away from the dragon.

It landed on the ground with a thud and stood on its short, awkward legs, heaving for air, its wings trembling, its head down. The other one had stopped rubbing its burns in the snow and now stood glaring at Caelan, its tail whipping angrily back and forth.

Prudently, he stepped away from the unconscious men, and the burned dragon calmed down slightly.

Caelan hurried to collect his sword and cloak. Wiping the blade dry, he slid it back into its scabbard and looked around.

"Lea!" he called aloud, letting his voice echo into the trees. "Lea, come here!"

His sister did not appear. All he heard was the sound of jack-daws in the distance and the uneasy moans of the dragons. Caelan frowned in annoyance. Why did she have to be so stubborn?

Elandra came to him, and he slung his arm around her to draw her close. "I thought they would kill you," she said.

"You did not follow orders," he replied mildly.

She tilted back her head to look up at him. "Would you be alive if I had?"

He did not feel up to arguing, so he kissed her nose instead.

She smiled at him, then looked at the unconscious men. "Are they dead?"

"No." Caelan frowned. "If I had rope, I could truss them."

"There are tethers and hobble ropes on the dragons' harnesses."

He met the glowering iridescent eye of the burned dragon and shook his head. "We'll find another way."

"What do you intend to do?"

A groan from one of the men told him they were starting to wake up. He gave her a brief smile. "Have you ever flown in the air before, my beloved?"

Her eyes widened, and she gasped. "You mean, ride the drag-ons?"

"Yes. It is very high above the ground and frightening at first, but you would be—"

"Why, Caelan, we would be in Gialta in a matter of days in-stead of weeks. Perhaps quicker. They can fly like the wind," she said excitedly, looking not at all afraid. "Can you convince them to take us willingly?"

Gray Hair stirred and slowly sat up, cradling his head in his hands.

Caelan watched him grimly. "Willingly or not, they will take us."

"Then arrange it quickly," Elandra said.

Caelan walked over to the Thyzarene and hauled him to his

feet. He gave the man a rough shaking to finish waking him up, then shoved him back.

"Your name," he said.

The Thyzarene blinked at him slowly, his eyes filling with humiliation and hatred.

"Your name!" Caelan barked.

"I am Bwend," the man replied. His voice was sullen. But his gaze now took in Caelan's imperial armor and the large emerald in Exoner's hilt. He glanced at Elandra and came to attention. "Bwend, rider of Nia. Formerly dispatch flier in the Seventh Corps."

Caelan was pleased. If the man had once had some military discipline pounded into him, he would be somewhat easier to handle. He pointed. "And this other man?"

Bwend didn't bother to look at his still unconscious comrade. "Fotel, rider of Basha."

At the sound of its name, the burned dragon lifted its head and roared.

"Are you kin to the boy?" Caelan asked, ignoring the dragon.

"No," Bwend said curtly.

"You're lying."

Bwend shot him a hostile look. Resentment simmered in his lean, weathered face, but he said nothing.

"Are you his father?" Caelan persisted.

Again Bwend said nothing.

Caelan was tempted to let it pass, but he knew this issue had to be dealt with now. "Kupel threatened the life of her Majesty," he said. "None may do that, whether child or man grown. None."

He deliberately made his voice harsh and unsympathetic. He knew enough of the customs of these people to understand that they did not respect weakness or compassion.

Bwend frowned, and a flicker of something incomprehensible passed through his face. Caelan hoped he accepted the explanation; he would despise an apology. Not that Caelan intended to offer one.

"You are my prisoners," Caelan said. "You have attacked her Majesty, and no man may do that and live."

Bwend's chin lifted. His eyes grew blank and steely as though he prepared himself for execution.

Caelan drew his sword, letting the sunshine flash along the blade. His face was like stone; his eyes gave nothing away. From the corner of his vision he saw Elandra bring one hand to her mouth. He prayed she would not interfere.

Perhaps she understood what he was doing, for she said nothing.

Caelan slowly extended the sword until the tip rested lightly at Bwend's throat. The Thyzarene's forehead crinkled, and he swallowed hard. Otherwise, he stood there stoically, refusing to beg for his life.

Cursing his stubbornness, Caelan let the silence stretch. As he stood there with the man's life in his hands, he felt anew the temptation to make one quick thrust. In the blink of an eye, there would be one member of E'nonhold avenged.

But he held back the old rage. This was not the place or the time.

Bwend was staring into his eyes, and the Thyzarene's own had widened at what they read in Caelan's. Perspiration broke out on his forehead.

"Majesty," he said, gasping as Caelan eased the sword tip closer against his throat, stopping just short of piercing the skin. Bwend's eyes flashed back and forth. "Leave to speak," he choked out.

"Granted," Elandra said coldly.

Caelan could have kissed her. She was playing the role of an outraged monarch perfectly. For once her haughty tone was exactly right.

She swept Caelan an imperious glance. "Let him speak."

Caelan lowered his sword.

Bwend dropped to his knees at Elandra's feet. "Majesty," he said, his accent blurring his words, his eyes carefully cast down, "have mercy. The beacons have flashed the message across the empire that you are missing. Reward has been offered. We sought only your Majesty's recovery."

"You attacked us without provocation," she said, no mercy in her voice. "You would have killed—"

"No, Majesty!" Bwend protested.

Caelan struck him across the mouth with the back of his hand. "Do not interrupt her Majesty!"

Bwend sank lower, spitting blood on the snow, silent and obedient now.

The other Thyzarene groaned and rolled over.

Caelan spun around and grabbed him by the back of his fur tunic, hoisting him up bodily and shoving him over beside Bwend. Fotel's dark eyes squinted, then lost focus. He groaned, supporting his head in his hands.

"Let me kill them now, Majesty," Caelan said.

"Wait," she replied.

Bwend glanced up in hope, and slowly Fotel also raised his head.

"Tell me the truth," Elandra said. "Swear on your blood-oath that you meant me no harm."

Bwend didn't hesitate. He held out his hand to Caelan, palm up. His gaze never left Elandra's, not even when Caelan sliced open his palm. Bright blood welled up in the cup of his hand. "I swear I meant no harm to your Majesty. I gave loyal service to the emperor while he lived. I would give loyal service again."

Tears welled up in Elandra's eyes. No longer playacting, she gently placed her gloved hand on the man's head. "I will accept your oath and service. Your help, if you will give it, would do me great service now."

Hope flashed in his face, swiftly masked. "Anything, Majesty."

"Fly me and this man to Gialta," she said.

Bwend looked surprised. "Gialta!"

He and Fotel exchanged looks. Suspicious again, Caelan edged closer to Elandra and gestured for her to move back.

She did not. Her face was very stern. "How swiftly your oath is forgotten."

"Nay, Majesty," Bwend said quickly, bowing his head. "I do not refuse. It is only that Gialta is far from here. Very far. There is trouble—"

"What kind of trouble?" she demanded.

"We have heard rumors only. But they are all of Madruns—"

"Madruns in Gialta?" Elandra said, anger rising through her voice.

Caelan took over the questioning now. "What have you heard?"

"That is all," the Thyzarene said.

Caelan frowned, not believing him. "Do these Madruns come from over the border? Or are they leaving Imperia?"

"The new emperor has driven them from Imperia. They flee into Gialta—"

Elandra clenched her fists. "New emperor be damned! *That traitor*! I would like to see him gutted and left hanging for the vultures to peck!"

Enraged, she paced away. Both Thyzarenes stared after her with new respect.

"Truly a lady of warrior blood," Bwend said cautiously to Caelan.

He nodded. "Her father is Gihaud Albain of Gialta."

Fotel looked blank, but Bwend obviously recognized the name. "A ferocious warrior. Very rich."

"Yes. A man generous to those who help his daughter."

"I will fly her there," Fotel said, his eyes gleaming with avarice.

Bwend's elbow rammed into his ribs. "Nay, dog. My Nia will have the honor. She knows the softest wind currents, how to be gentle in the clouds. Your Basha is but half-trained and bad-tempered besides."

Basha roared and grumbled as though understanding every word. Across the clearing, Nia raised her head and trumpeted with a proud beating of her wings.

"Basha is hurt," Fotel said. "Let me tend him."

Caelan sheathed his sword and stepped back. As Fotel climbed to his feet, however, Caelan gripped him by the front of his tunic and lifted him onto his toes.

"Remember how I struck you without touch and laid you on the ground," he said through his teeth, glaring at the man. "Remember I can do it again. There will be no tricks from you. Do you understand?"

Bwend also rose to his feet to intercede. "I gave my blood-oath to her Majesty, Traulander."

"Fotel gave no oath."

"He is in my service. My oath binds him."

Caelan met Bwend's eyes and wondered just how far he could trust the man's word, especially once they were high in the clouds.

"It had better," he said, and released Fotel with a shove.

Fotel frowned up at him. "Are you of Neika blood?"

Before Caelan could answer this astonishing question, Bwend elbowed Fotel aside.

"Fool!" he said sharply. "The Neika do not fight."

"Neither do Traulanders."

Caelan looked down at them, and felt suddenly foreign in this land that had once been his. "I am Choven," he said bleakly.

Both Thyzarenes blanched and backed up. Fotel stared with his mouth open, fear in his eyes. Bwend bowed with almost the respect he had shown Elandra.

"We ask forgiveness," he said humbly. "We have been much mistaken today."

Caelan did not unbend. The admission had cost him. He felt as though his identity was being torn away in strips, peeling him down to something he did not recognize.

Giving Bwend a nod, he asked, "Must the dragons feed before they can fly?"

"No," Bwend answered. He jerked his head at Fotel. "Tend Basha's burns quickly."

Fotel sidled cautiously past Caelan and ran to his dragon, who grumbled and butted his head at the man in greeting.

"I have a request, lord," Bwend said to Caelan.

Not once, in all his wildest imaginings, had Caelan ever expected to someday hear a savage Thyzarene raider humbly call him lord. It was bitter to think these men had instantly believed him Choven, even when he physically did not resemble those mysterious tribesmen. It only confirmed yet again the truth of what Moah had told him.

"What is your request?" Caelan asked.

Bwend pointed at the dead boy lying in the snow. "That we may bury him from the wolves and lurkers that will come."

Caelan did not hesitate. "I will help you."

Chapter Sixteen

As LONG AS she lived, Elandra would never forget the experience of flying over mountains, forests, and marshlands, the clouds melting against her face or lying beneath her like a thick carpet. Swathed in furs against the cold, she soared and plummeted, borne easily on the back of the powerful Nia. Her only regret was that she was not cradled in Caelan's arms. Instead, she rode with Bwend—carefully respectful, but stinking of too few baths, too much peat smoke, and the greasy lard-based salve that seemed to be the Thyzarene solution for everything from chapped lips to burn treatments.

Caelan rode with Fotel on the bad-tempered Basha. Perhaps the dragon was in pain, or perhaps he did not intend to forget that Caelan had caused his burns. But every morning Fotel had to clamp the dragon's head between his arm and ribs in order for Caelan to get near the beast, much less climb on. The beast would rear and try to fly without Fotel, snapping at everything within reach of his fangs. At night when they camped in uneasy alliance, Fotel and Basha would move away to be by themselves. Elandra would hear Fotel singing softly in his native tongue to the dragon, cradling the beast's head in his lap and stroking it gently.

It took three days of steady flying before the air began to feel warm and moist. The clouds were very tall, rising above them like pillars and sometimes massing into thunderheads. Elandra's woolen cloak was plenty of protection, and she no longer needed the heavy furs that Lea had given her just before they departed.

Thinking of the girl, Elandra smiled involuntarily. Lea was as beautiful as her brother was handsome. Gowned in dark blue that enhanced her eyes, she wore a long overtunic of scarlet cloth embroidered all over with dainty flowers, a fur cloak, and soft red boots. Her golden hair hung unbound down her back to her hips, and her dowry necklace was most impressive with nine large, matched emeralds.

Riding a white pony, Lea had appeared from the forest at the very moment Caelan and Bwend finished burying Kupel. Elandra had been the first person to notice the girl, who rode erect and gracefully like a princess. She drew rein at the edge of the clearing and ventured no closer despite Elandra's beckoning.

Whether Lea was shy or afraid of the dragons, Elandra did not know. When Caelan did not immediately notice the new arrival, Elandra walked over to speak to her.

"You must be Lea," Elandra said with a smile, eager to meet her at last. "You look so much like your brother. I am Elandra."

Lea slid down from the saddle and curtsied to her. "Majesty."

"No, we are sisters now," Elandra said, taking her hand to put the girl at her ease. "Do not be formal."

"You are the empress," Lea said, keeping her eyes downcast.

"I love your brother very much," Elandra said. "Does that distress you?"

Lea did not answer, but finally she lifted her gaze to meet Elandra's. That's when Elandra realized the girl was not shy at all. Her blue eyes were as clear as a mountain lake, and as deep.

Elandra found herself falling into that gaze, and when she came back to herself a few moments later, she was oddly breathless and dizzy. She blinked, putting her hand to her temple.

"I am glad," Lea said. "You are worthy of his love."

It was a strange, presumptuous thing to say. Elandra could only stare at her, wondering what this girl had done to her mind. She felt as though her thoughts had been sifted and turned over the way someone might go through a box of deeds and papers.

"Do not be angry," Lea said. "I had to know if he would be well with you before I let the two of you go."

"Let us go?" Elandra said with a laugh. "But you cannot stop us."

"I brought you here," Lea said matter-of-factly. "I could make you stay. But Moah has shown Caelan his destiny, and he must go to it. As you must go to yours."

Elandra felt slightly chilled. Her hand went to her throat, and she couldn't stop staring at Lea, who looked like an innocent child, but who was obviously both a wisdom and a seer.

"You know of my destiny?" Elandra asked.

Lea smiled, showing a dimple. "Oh, yes."

"Are you of the sisterhood?"

Now Lea laughed, and the sound made Caelan look in their direction. He brushed soil from his hands and headed their way.

"No, I am not," Lea said merrily, her blue eyes dancing. "How angry the Magria would be if she knew you thought so. She would not approve of me."

Although the question was rude, impulse made Elandra ask, "And what exactly are you?"

Lea only threw her a smile and went skipping away to meet Caelan. He swept her up in his strong arms and kissed her on both cheeks.

"Am I forgiven?" he asked.

Lea flung her arms around his neck and hugged him tightly. "Always."

Watching them, Elandra felt like an outsider, then Caelan's eyes met hers over Lea's shoulder. He smiled only for her, and she felt warm and secure again in his love. There was no need to be jealous. She and Lea were not competitors in any sense.

"Are you ready?" he asked his sister, looking at the laden pony. "We must travel light—"

"Silly, I am not going," Lea said. She broke away from him and pulled out furs from the pack tied behind her saddle. "I brought you these to keep you warm while you are so high in the air."

Caelan scowled, and tactfully Elandra busied herself examining the beautiful furs, leaving brother and sister to argue in privacy.

"What do you mean, you're not going?" Caelan asked.

It was what Elandra privately called his barking voice. He could sound very clipped and stern when he was close to losing his temper. Seeing a stubborn light enter Lea's blue eyes, Elandra thought he should use a different tone with the girl, but it was not her place to interfere.

"Of course you are going," Caelan said. "I will not leave you behind."

"But the third dragon is dead," Lea pointed out. "And I have much to do here."

"I'll talk to Bwend. We'll get another dragon—"

"No," Lea said firmly, meeting his angry gaze without flinching. "It is not time for me to leave Trau. Not yet."

"I won't abandon you again."

Lea took her brother's clenched fist between her slender hands and kissed his knuckles. "I am not abandoned. But this is not my path of life, brother."

"Lea—"

"Hush," she said, trying to soothe him. "Accept what is. Save your fight for what is to come."

"I need you with me. You are my conscience."

Lea smiled and gave him a hug. "I will come later. I promise."

"When? How will you find me when I do not know where I'll be?"

"You will go back to Imperia and face Tirhin the Usurper," she said, her voice so calm and ordinary it took Elandra a second to realize she was speaking prophecy.

Startled, Elandra dropped the pretense that she was not listening and turned to stare at the girl.

Lea did not seem to mind. She gave Elandra a gentle smile, then returned her attention to Caelan. Her expression grew earnest, and she gripped his sleeve. "Tirhin was your friend once."

"No," Caelan bit off the word. "Never. He was my owner."

"Put away the bitterness," Lea urged him. "The past is gone. All that remains is the present . . . and the future. You need him, Caelan. You need to make peace with him."

"For what he has done, he cannot be forgiven."

Lea frowned. "Caelan, you must learn to forgive! Did today teach you nothing?"

"Stop pushing!" Caelan snapped at her. "Why are you never satisfied?"

"Because you have so much to learn."

Elandra was amazed to hear a grown man corrected by such a young girl, but she also knew that wisdoms seldom looked their true age. Lea was a very old spirit indeed inhabiting that lithe, youthful body.

Caelan hesitated, still scowling at her, then abruptly caught her hands in his. "Come with us."

She shook her head. "Not yet."

"When?"

"When it is time."

Frustration filled his face. "But how am I to know if you are well? How am I to be responsible for you? How am I to take care of you?"

Lea reached up to caress his cheek. "Look within your heart to know that I am well. But you have much else to tend now, my brother. I am not your task."

Then she turned and held out her hand to Elandra. "And you, dear lady who loves my brother, you also have much before you. Receive the blessing of the spirits to guide you on your way."

Surprised by the benediction, Elandra inclined her head. "Thank you."

"Good journey," Lea said. She drew a leather pouch from her saddlebag and handed it to Caelan. "This is food so you will not have to hunt on the way."

He took it in silence, everything he could not say knotted in his face. Wordlessly he swept her close and hugged her hard. "I cannot lose you again," he whispered.

Lea closed her eyes and hugged him back. "You never will," she promised. "I will come. If the gods are kind, I promise you I will come."

Then she pulled away from him, tears shimmering in her eyes. She curtsied to Elandra and climbed back on her pony. With one last silent wave, she rode away.

Since then, Caelan had been quiet and preoccupied. At night in camp, sitting together by the flickering campfire and listening to the strange sounds of unfamiliar plains and marshlands, he had little to say. Perhaps he did not want to speak of his plans while he could be overheard by the Thyzarenes. Perhaps something else troubled him. Elandra kept her own counsel and let him be. As long as his arms held her through the night, she knew all would be well.

And now, with the wind whipping her cheeks and sending

locks of her hair streaming out behind her, she looked down and saw the thick jungles of home.

Her heart lifted with joy. Suddenly she felt invincible, incapable of doubt or failure.

She pointed. "Look! There is the river."

Bwend nodded and nudged Nia with his left foot. The dragon wheeled lazily and turned toward the river. It was overflowing its banks this time of year, fat with monsoon rains, flooding the paddies and sweeping away humble villages. In places it spread all the way into the edge of the jungle, and lay there among the trees, stagnant and stinking with great clouds of flies rising off its surface.

The dragons did not drop altitude, and soon Elandra understood why as they came to mountains. Clouds mounded over the peaks, pouring rain on the near slopes. The water pelted Elandra hard, making her draw up her hood and shiver.

She didn't really care, however. The ripe, earthy scent of the jungle lifted to her nostrils, and she gloried in its untamable savagery.

Now they did drop lower, coming close enough in places for her to see the colorful birds and wild parrots that lived in the treetops. Screaming monkeys fled before them, surely fearing the great predator dragons that flew overhead.

Part of the mountain slope stood bare where trees had long ago been hacked down. Ancient stone ruins revealed themselves, bizarre faces carved on an immense scale and worn by time. Vines twisted over them, and from the darkness of a cave mouth there appeared to be a group of wild *jinjas* huddled together. They vanished before Elandra could be sure, but she found her heart beating fast with excitement just the same.

So this was where *jinjas* came from. These old temples of the ancient ways. The traders who brought young *jinjas* to the sorcery markets guarded their secrets jealously, telling no one where they captured their wares. Elandra smiled to herself. She must have a *jinja* of her own, one bonded to her. Perhaps Caelan would accept one for his own protection too.

"That way!" she shouted at Bwend, pointing.

He nodded, looking insulted by her directions. Elandra was

too excited to care. When she left her father's palace over a year ago, she thought she would never return. Her memories had not all been good ones, but how she missed the sights and smells, the heat, the lazy afternoons when nothing moved but the fans to stir the air; yes, she even missed the dreadful muxa bugs.

Laughing aloud, she glanced over at Caelan and saw him watching her. She waved at him, and he smiled.

Ahead, the jungle thinned out and ended. Lush fields of flax, rice, and aotta beans stood in water. The rain ended, and Elandra threw back her hood. How moist and heavy the air felt. She could feel her skin absorbing it. Her hair began to curl and riot about her face.

A break in the clouds allowed a luminescent shaft of sunlight to spear down to earth. And there stood the gleaming white limestone walls of Albain palace, as solid and safe as ever. Eagerly Elandra leaned low over Nia's neck, hoping she would fly faster.

Instead the dragon slowed and began to circle.

Disappointed, Elandra snapped her head around to look into Bwend's impassive face. "Why don't we keep going? Why do you circle here?"

He met her eyes, but said nothing. Catching up, Basha also began to circle. The Thyzarenes exchanged looks and hand signals.

Suspicion grew inside Elandra. Had they come this far, only to be tricked at the last moment? Caelan was peering down at the ground, and she could not catch his attention. She fingered her knife, vowing she would not be held for ransom like some helpless captive.

"Bwend," she said sharply, "remember I am your empress."

Nia bugled, and Basha echoed the sound. The dragons flew closer, then circled again, staying high.

Elandra gripped the harness so hard her knuckles turned white. She was furious at this delay. What was Bwend doing? Tormenting her? She could see her father's sentries gesturing. More troops came running. Some were archers. When they lifted their drawn bows, aiming at the dragons, she sat up straight on Nia's back and glanced again at Bwend.

"Yes, Majesty," he said, his voice dry. "If we come in too fast, they shoot us like birds for eating. You would not like to hit the ground that hard, eh?"

Elandra swallowed and felt ashamed of her previous suspicions.

They circled the palace again, staying out of arrow range. She could see the famous steps reaching from the broad courtyard up to the portico of the palace itself. Her father's banners of yellow and white flew proudly. She saw no imperial coat of arms, however, and wondered why her father had struck her banner.

The people of the household crowded onto the balconies, pointing upward. Soldiers poured from the barracks. More archers appeared.

Elandra frowned at them, wanting to shout a reprimand. After all she had gone through to get here, were they even going to let her land?

Bwend pulled a dirty white rag from his pouch and let it stream out for the soldiers to see.

The men changed formation, clearing a large space in the courtyard.

"This dangerous," Bwend said in her ear. "No flag to show imperial business. No reason to come."

She held her breath and gripped the harness strap more tightly. "I am ready."

Nia dropped in a plummet that left Elandra's stomach floating somewhere among the clouds. The watery sunlight vanished as the clouds closed again. Grimly, she realized she must look like a wild woman, arriving windblown in this bizarre fashion. She had no veil, no suitable gowns, no entourage. If her father was not at home, would anyone even recognize her?

Just as this doubt occurred to her, Nia bumped down and staggered forward a few steps on her awkward legs. Beating her wings, the dragon stretched her neck and roared loudly enough to make the troops back up. Then Basha landed, snapping his jaws and shaking the singed remnants of his beard. He roared and lashed his tail, and Caelan slid off his back hastily.

At once, Fotel spoke a command and Basha lifted back into the air, smoking and grumbling as he went.

Caelan took a moment to adjust his sword belt, then he

straightened himself to military posture and swept the silent Gial-tan soldiers with a single, appraising glance. The sight of them did not appear to daunt him at all.

Elandra's heart swelled with pride in him. Not a single man in this compound was Caelan's physical equal. He stood head and shoulders above them all. This morning he wore his long blond hair braided back warrior style, and his bronzed, chiseled face looked stern and handsome. His blue eyes were hard and obser-vant. He would miss nothing, she knew. He was evaluating their silent reception, gauging the possible dangers.

Wisely, Elandra curbed her own impulse to jump off the dragon and go running up the steps. She recalled the day she had left this palace in Bixia's wake. The soldiers had cheered her that day. But they stood silent and hostile now.

She turned to Bwend, whose eyes shifted constantly as though he expected to be attacked at any moment. "I owe you my thanks," she said. "Never again will I doubt the loyalty of a man of Thyzarene."

Bwend's gaze met hers. For an instant he smiled. "Never be-fore have I met an empress," he replied. "But my service is yours to command whenever there is need."

She smiled, and his eyes softened.

"If you will wait while I make greetings to my father, I will see that you are rewarded—"

"No, Majesty," he said firmly. "No reward."

She frowned in dismay. "But I promised—"

"No, Majesty. I have my reward."

She couldn't believe a Thyzarene was actually turning down money. "But—"

He gave her a shy little bow of his head. "This empress has smiled to me as a friend. This empress has spoken to me kindly as an equal. This empress has ridden the winds without fear. Surely this empress is worthy, and I serve her as a citizen of the empire."

She smiled and touched his gnarled hand briefly. "You are a good man, Bwend. When the empire is once again secure, will you and Nia come to Imperia? I would see a better relationship estab-lished with your people."

He looked startled. "Perhaps."

"Majesty," Caelan said, breaking in.

She glanced around to see him standing at her knee. He held out his hand to assist her down. His touch was formal and impersonal. He was wearing his most remote expression.

It was to help her, she knew, for as yet the men staring at her had no idea of who she was. Yet she refused to take what he offered.

Staring up at him, she said softly for his ears alone, "You stubborn, impossible man. All those times when I tried to get you to act as my official protector, you would not. Now, when I want you to enter my father's house as my equal, you retreat to my heels."

Caelan's blue eyes met hers. "Will it not help?"

"It might, but my father always said a person should begin in the manner he intended to continue. Kostimon's empire is ended. Let us begin the way we shall go on."

A very thin smile touched Caelan's lips and spread up into his eyes. He inclined his head to her, and when she extended her hand to him, he lifted it to his lips, then held it fast.

From their left, an officer in a turban and a long yellow and white surcoat worn over mail came striding up, spurs jingling, one hand gripping the hilt of his scimitar.

The dragon lifted her head and bugled at Basha, who was circling safely overhead.

Elandra turned back to Bwend. "I wish to thank Nia too," she said. "Will she let me pet her?"

Bwend frowned but gave her a curt nod. He spoke a sharp command to the dragon, who lowered her head and turned her iridescent eyes warily on Elandra.

Elandra held out her hand, palm up, and felt the hot, smoky breath of the dragon blow across her skin. "Thank you for carrying me so far and so swiftly," she said to the beast. "You are a good dragon."

Nia grumbled, clearly not having forgotten that Elandra had mesmerized her. Carefully Elandra reached up and scratched under the dragon's chin as she had seen Bwend do.

The dragon snorted in surprise, then stretched out her chin for more, half closing her eyes.

Bwend, looking jealous, spoke sharply, and the dragon drew back her head. She roared, sending men stumbling back, and beat her wings in a strong flurry. Her body lifted until her wings found the wind currents. Then she soared. She and Basha circled overhead once more, then flew away.

Elandra watched them go until Caelan's tug on her hand brought her attention back to earth.

She found herself facing the stern visage of General Alud Handar. There was no recognition in his eyes. His gaze swept over Caelan's imperial armor and sword, then returned to Elandra.

He had never seen her unveiled. And while the money-loving Thyzarenes recognized her from her coinage portrait, Handar clearly did not. She realized her hair was unbound and wild. Her gown was creased and stained from travel. Moreover, she was roasting in her wool cloak and probably stank like dragon.

But to be taken for a lady meant one had to act like a lady. To show doubt and hesitation was to awaken it in others.

"Greetings, General Handar," she said regally, as though dropping unexpectedly from the sky on the back of a barbarian looter's dragon was an ordinary occurrence. "It is good to see you again."

He bowed slightly, his frown deepening. "My lady."

"You will forgive my haste," she said. "I will present you formally to Lord Caelan later. We must speak to Lord Albain without delay."

"That is not possible."

She tightened her lips with frustration. She should have known her father would be away. "This is most disconcerting."

"I'm sure it is," Handar said. His tone was ironic.

She knew she had to curb that immediately.

Before she could speak, however, he was gesturing to his right. "If you will accompany me this way—"

"I shall not," she snapped. "If you do not recognize the daughter of your own lord and master, then I am sure one of the courtiers who witnessed my coronation will."

Handar's mouth fell open. Comprehension filled his eyes, and he turned pale. "Majesty!"

She lifted her chin. "Will I be kept in the courtyard forever, General, or may I enter my father's house?"

"Of course." He glared at an officer, who whirled around and barked out a series of commands.

The soldiers suddenly cleared a path toward the steps, facing it on either side and standing at attention.

Handar bowed low, humiliation written plainly across his face. "My deepest apologies, Majesty. I—"

He had been kind to her once, when she was only a frightened, baseborn daughter of the household, on her way to a new life. She had not forgotten, but the lesson had to be taught. She had learned that from Kostimon.

"Why is the imperial banner not flying?" she asked, cutting across his apologies. "Where is my father? When will he return? Has he gone to hold a war council?"

"No, Majesty," Handar replied, and there was a stricken note in his voice that caught her attention. "I am afraid there is no war council being held."

"What do you mean? What are you saying? Explain." But already she guessed something was very wrong. She stared at the man, and her head suddenly felt as though it were being crushed. She could not breathe. "Do not tell me he is dead," she said, horrified by her own words.

Caelan's arm went around her, steadying her as she swayed, but she barely noticed. Her eyes were focused only on Handar's face.

Her lips felt frozen. "Is Albain dead?"

Handar lowered his gaze from hers. "No, Majesty, not yet. But he is dying."

Chapter Seventeen

THE STEPS STRETCHED upward in endless progression, as though to the sky itself. Halfway up, Elandra began to tremble, and she thought her legs would fail her.

"No," she whispered, unable to believe it. "No!"

Caelan looked down at her in sympathy, and frowned a warning.

She understood at once and knew she could not submit publicly to her grief, but inside she felt as though she were being torn apart. She had not grieved for Kostimon, who in many ways had been more a father figure to her than her own. But Albain had been the first man she had ever loved. All her life she had looked up to him, admired him, craved his affection. She would have done anything for him. Just a glance or a quick pat on her head when she was a child had sustained her for weeks.

And now . . . now, when she needed him more than ever before, to hear he was dying seemed like a bad dream. She could not believe it, refused to believe it.

Handar escorted them into the palace, murmuring about accidents and bad portents. There had been lightning and earthquakes, he said. The river had flooded its banks, and one of the stable walls had fallen. Lord Albain had been crushed by a panicking elephant while he tried to help his men restore order.

Caelan never loosened his grip on Elandra's hand. She could feel the reassurance he sent her even as he pinned his gaze on the general.

"And are there no healers to attend him?" he asked.

"Indeed, yes," Handar replied. "Our physicians say he is injured inside."

Caelan frowned. "The slow bleeding?"

"It is as they say."

Elandra looked up at Caelan in hope. He was a healer's son. He understood what this meant.

His blue eyes darkened with compassion, and he gave her a small shake of his head.

Her mouth opened, but she didn't cry out. She had no breath to do so. The world swam before her eyes, but Caelan would not let her faint.

"Keep walking," he said softly. "Hold your head high."

She obeyed him, her eyes stinging with tears she would not shed. They found the vast entry hall full of courtiers and the curious, most of whom had gathered to watch her arrival. The women were veiled and gowned elegantly. The men wore gilded mail and silk surcoats heavily embroidered in gold and silver. She recognized coats of arms from across the entire province. *Jinjas* flitted here and there, peeking out from behind their owners, sharp teeth bared in curiosity, pointed ears twitching in response to the general air of suppressed excitement.

A part of her understood that her strange arrival, without guards, without her ladies in waiting, without evidence of her wealth and power, all served to diminish her in these people's eyes. These were the nobles and warlords, men she needed to impress, men who commanded armies she needed to call on. Yet she walked before them in mended clothes and unbound hair, lacking jewels, her face pale and ravaged.

The rest of her did not care if every opportunity was lost. She wanted only to break away from Caelan and the general and go running to her father's apartments. She wanted privacy, not these staring eyes. She wanted freedom to weep and call on the gods for mercy.

She began to tremble again. Her eyes were burning. She could not do this. She could not walk with cold composure into her father's chamber and gaze at him in a performance while everyone watched her. She could not.

"General," Caelan said.

Handar paused in the center of a long gallery. Tall windows on one side overlooked the fields beyond the walls. People stood in bunches, pretending to chat among themselves, while in reality they watched like judges. At the far end of the gallery rose a stair-case carpeted in scarlet and dark green. The rosewood banisters were carved into the twisted, sinuous shapes of scaled serpents and lotus flowers. High above the staircase hung Albain's banner with the family coat of arms. Guards stood at the foot of the stairs, as though to bar the curious from the private region of the palace.

"Can someone be sent to attend her Majesty?" Caelan asked. "She has traveled far. She needs to prepare herself suitably so that she may honor her father."

Gratitude spread through Elandra, but with it came worry. "Is there time?" she asked.

Handar bowed. "Of course, Majesty. He lingers long."

"That means he is strong," Caelan said to her. "There is time for what is necessary."

She gave him a wan smile so that he would think he com-forted her. Inside, however, she remained like a clenched fist, too tense and worried to be reassured.

Handar snapped his fingers, and the major domo came run-ning to bow low.

"May I offer the most humble greetings and welcome of this house, formerly thy home, Majesty?" he said, never once looking directly at her.

"Thank you," Elandra replied in a hollow voice. Now was not the time to remember her childhood spent far from grand public rooms such as this. She had been treated like a servant. She had scrubbed floors for punishment, and she had mended and fetched like many of the other maids when her step-aunt ordered her to.

While the major domo issued discreet orders for a chamber to be cleared for her use, Handar spoke to a man in a long tunic trimmed in monkey fur. This man in turn summoned a lady who approached in a beautiful gown and curtsied perfunctorily to Elandra.

"May I assist you, Majesty?" she asked. "May I offer you the service of my own maids? My seamstress will be honored to alter some of my gowns for your use."

Elandra did not recognize her, but it hardly mattered. "Thank you," she said.

Caelan released her hand so that she could be led away in the care of the noblewoman and servants. Elandra started up the staircase, then glanced back at him, missing him already. But the lady was urging her on gently, and she kept walking, feeling numb.

Left behind with General Handar, Caelan watched Elandra walk out of sight with graceful dignity. Only he guessed how frightened she was, how shocked.

This latest blow of fate was surely one cruelty too many. Elandra had endured enough. To now lose her father, the man whose support she had never for one second doubted, on the heels of so many other tragedies was too much. If Caelan could have yelled at the gods and shamed them for their capriciousness, he would have.

As it was, he had to stand here, helpless and unable to comfort her.

But if he could not assuage her grief, at least he could change the hostility he sensed in this room. How quickly people could turn on each other. Petty, jealous, envious, and shortsighted, they forgot how much they needed to side together at this moment of crisis. Caelan swallowed his anger at the way Elandra had been received, and forced himself to pull his wits in line. There would be a change by the time she reappeared. He would make sure of it.

Setting his jaw, he turned on the general, who had been looking at him like he was some kind of encroacher. Caelan knew they had all witnessed the familiarity of his steadying arm around Elandra, the way she clung to his hand, the way she looked to him for guidance and comfort. He was no nobleman, by the state of his clothes or by his origins. And surely someone present had visited the arena in Imperia and would recognize him as a former gladiator.

For an instant Caelan felt the old shame of slavery like a ghost perched on his shoulder, then he shook it off. Kostimon had once been no one from nowhere, and he had made himself emperor. Without leadership, these fancy courtiers were doomed. It was time they knew it.

"We were not properly introduced," Caelan said to the general with a courteous nod. "I am Caelan of Trau."

Handar's eyes widened, but before he could respond, another voice rose from the crowd: "Caelan of the arena is more accurate."

Men broke into laughter, and the ladies nudged each other and smiled behind their hands.

Caelan's temper snapped. He whirled around in the direction the voice had come from. "Who said that?"

More laughter rose up, jeering and contemptuous. Caelan glared at them, refusing to be driven away, knowing that if his nerve broke here, he wasn't worthy to stand beside Elandra, much less face the coming shadows.

"Who spoke?" he demanded again.

"Really? A gladiator?" a rotund, red-faced man said, hooting as he held his sides. "Gault help us, a pretentious brute from the arena."

Caelan's face burned, but he didn't move. His gaze searched the crowd, while they laughed and pointed at him, insulting him openly.

Finally a tall, rawboned man with his black hair scraped back in a warrior's braid pushed to the forefront of the crowd. He wore old mail, and his surcoat was faded. His gauntlets were folded over his sword belt, and his spurs jingled as he walked. A long, white scar ran down one side of his neck, and he was missing his ear on that side. His thumbs were hooked casually in his belt, showing broad, callused hands scarred across the knuckles from fighting. His brown eyes held scorn, but they were wary, seasoned eyes that had looked on many battles. He was perhaps twenty years older than Caelan, and carried his age as a man in his full prime. Only the jewel in the hilt of his sword and the embroidered coat of arms on the breast of his surcoat proclaimed his high rank. Clearly this man had come for a war council.

He was exactly the ally Caelan needed. He was not someone to be made into an enemy.

"I am Pier," the warlord said, introducing himself in the stark way of the aristocracy. "I have seen you fight, and I have won money on you. You did once belong to Prince Tirhin. Now it seems you belong to the Empress Elandra."

Another murmur ran through the crowd.

Caelan glared at him. "I belong to no one," he said. "I was

born free. I walk free again. I have been a soldier in the Crimson Guard. Now I fight to save the empire from her enemies."

"Pretty speech for a gladiator," Pier said coolly. Snickers spread out behind him. "You wear the armor of an imperial guardsman. Some of it anyway, but you do not carry a guardsman's weapons. And you have no cloak to show your rank . . . or lack of it."

Caelan's head lifted proudly. "I have been told the men of Gialta are among the best warriors in the empire. I did not know this was a lie."

Angry voices rose up.

He lifted his own voice to carry over the buzz. "Or that the men of Gialta judge others by what they wear and how pretty they smell."

Several men now had their hands on their weapons. Caelan met glare for glare, not caring if he insulted all of them.

"Take care, stranger," General Handar warned him softly. "If the empress is all the protection you have, it will not be enough."

His warning only goaded Caelan's temper further. He let his contempt for them show plainly.

"The empress comes to you, having been attacked by demons and Madrun barbarians in the dead of night, within what should have been the safety of her own palace, her own apartments. She comes to you, having seen Imperia burn, having fled for her life from those trying to slaughter her. She comes to you, with the screams of dying men and women still ringing in her ears. She comes to you, with her husband dead, to find her father dying. Her own protector was slaughtered while saving her life. Her guardsmen were massacred in the palace. She has seen betrayal and evil from those whom she trusted. Yes, even from the son of the emperor, a man who drove her to her coronation in the processional and swore an oath of fealty to her that day."

The room stood silent now. Their eyes were all on him. They listened, despite themselves, to his scorn and condemnation.

"She has come to you, people of Gialta, for help against the darkness that would take this empire and crush it. For days she has spoken of little except the bravery of her native province, of the valiant warriors who live here, of the continued loyalty she expected to find."

Caelan paused, and a sneer curled his lip. "But because she did not come home riding on an elephant, dripping in jewels, and surrounded by an army of Imperia's finest, you have looked at her as though she were an oddity. Those filthy, half-savage Thyzarenes who made it possible for her to get here swiftly, *without walking* the entire distance, have shown her more deference and respect than any finely garbed courtier in this room.

"Was there one bow given to her, your crowned sovereign? Yes, a single bow from a servant. Was there one curtsy? Yes, from a lady forced to speak to her. But what of the rest of you? Because the empress has come here in the manner of a refugee, does that absolve you from courtesy? I have now seen the people of Gialta, and I am most certainly *not* impressed."

A furious babble of voices rose up. Several surged toward him, but Pier still stood in the way, thumbs hooked in his belt, his dark head slightly tilted while he listened and studied Caelan.

"Pretty speech," he said, and the others quieted reluctantly. "But what was she doing consorting with you while her husband lay dying?"

The jeers rose again, and Caelan's face heated. At that moment he hated and despised them even more than before. They were so stupid, so petty, so small. But most of all, he was furious at himself for having put her in this position.

"Aye!" shouted another voice from the back of the crowd. "Where has she been? There's a reward for her return. Did you carry her off, or did she go willingly to pinch those fine muscles?"

Enraged, Caelan stepped forward, but Pier blocked his path.

Caelan glared at him. "Step aside, that I may choke—"

"You'll make no move," Pier said.

The man's eyes were light brown, steady, dangerous. Caelan tried to beat down that gaze, without success.

"To insult me is one thing," Caelan said hotly, "but to insult her is another!"

"You have no right to defend the lady," Pier said in sharp rebuke. "You are a slave and an army deserter. The empress will be judged by her own people, but you—"

"Judge me by this!" Caelan snarled. He drew his sword, and even as Pier reached for his own weapon Caelan was already bending low to place Exoner on the polished stone floor. He sent it sliding over to Pier's feet. "Do you know what it is?"

Frowning, Pier stared at the sword, then at him, as though at a loss. Slowly he allowed his own weapon to drop back in its scabbard. "It is a very fine-looking sword," he said after a moment.

Caelan was boiling, but he managed to control his voice. He gestured. "Pick it up. Handle it. Test its balance."

"Why should I?" Pier asked. His eyes raked Caelan up and down. "When a rich city falls to invaders, any man may steal a good weapon."

Caelan jerked slightly, finding it all he could do to control himself. Pier smiled in thin satisfaction, and Caelan understood the man was trying to goad him into making a mistake that would get him killed.

"The sword is mine. I did not steal it. If you doubt that," Caelan said quickly as Pier opened his mouth, "pick it up."

Frowning, Pier stared at the sword, then bent to grab it. Before he could touch it, however, a child-sized creature with green translucent skin and pointed ears came whirling up to cling to the warlord's arm.

"Touch not, master!" it said in urgent warning.

Pier drew back. "Why? Is it enspelled?"

"Perhaps it's poisoned," another man said. "It's a trick to kill you."

Caelan was staring at the creature. He had never seen anything like it before. "What is this thing?"

"Have you never seen a *jinja* before?" Pier asked. The creature bared its pointed little teeth and sent its master an adoring gaze. Pier patted its head, and the *jinja* sneezed and scratched its ear.

"The sword is not poisoned," Caelan said. "If you're afraid to touch it, let the *jinja* tell you what it is."

Another *jinja,* this one garbed in silk pants and a short, sleeveless vest, sped up to them, zigzagged around Caelan almost too fast to see, then retreated to a safe distance. A third joined them, bright-eyed and plainly fascinated by the sword.

"Choven made," Pier's *jinja* said, scratching its ear again as though it had fleas. "Choven make for one only. Others no touch."

A strange expression crossed Pier's face. He bent and tried to pick up the sword, but dropped it immediately.

Several women cried out.

"I am not hurt," he said to the inquiries around him.

A courtier beside him gave one of the *jinjas* a shove. "What evil magic does he bring into this court?"

The three creatures raced around Caelan, darting close, then speeding out of reach. One ran at him and touched his arm, then fled, shrieking, "No magic! No magic!"

Pier snapped his fingers, and his own *jinja* ran over to jump onto the broad sill of a window. It perched there and started cleaning its ears with its fingers.

Pier studied Caelan a long while. "Your sword would not let me hold it," he said at last. "When my fingers tried to close around the hilt, some force pushed my hand away."

"It is magic," another man said.

"The *jinjas* say not," Pier said sharply.

"*Jinjas* can be wrong."

One of the creatures howled angrily at this comment, but was ordered to be silent.

Pier went on studying Caelan, and finally nudged Exoner back to him with his foot.

Caelan picked up the weapon, feeling it nestle in his hand the way a dog might thrust its head into its master's palm to be stroked. Caelan slid the sword into its scabbard, and let his hand rest there, drawing strength and confidence from the weapon.

"Only kings can carry Choven swords," Pier said finally.

"That's the legend," Caelan replied.

The round-faced courtier gasped and nudged his neighbor. "He claims to be a king."

"Outrageous!"

The murmurs rose again, but suspicion was darkening Pier's face like a cloud.

His eyes bored into Caelan's. "What are you up to?"

Caelan said nothing.

"You abducted the empress—"

"I saved her life," Caelan corrected him. He had Pier thinking now. He felt that was progress toward turning the man into an ally.

"Clearly she feels herself in your debt."

"No."

"Would you prefer I called it something offensive?"

Caelan's face burned again. He realized he had been optimistic too quickly. Pier was far from being on his side.

"You think that because you have the empress in your power, and you have paid the Choven to make you a sword worthy of a king, that *you* can take over the empire and set yourself on Kostimon's throne? *You?*"

Caelan said nothing. Pier's contempt was like a hot brand, burning him.

"Well, well," Pier said in mock appreciation. "How interesting to see what high ambitions arena trash aspires to these days."

Humiliation rolled over Caelan. It was exactly as he had feared it would be. He stood there, forgetting all that Moah had said to him about destiny and ability, while these highborn men jeered in his face.

Pier's face creased with disgust. He gestured at Handar. "General, see that this fool is thrown out."

Handar, a man almost half Caelan's size, drew in a resolute breath and started his way, but Caelan was not finished with Pier yet.

"And whom will you give your new oath of fealty to, Lord Pier?" he asked in a ringing voice that carried clearly over the noise in the gallery. "Will it be Tirhin the Usurper, who turned the Madrun invaders loose on his own people? Who was so anxious to have the throne that he could not wait a few days more for his father to die naturally?"

Pier's face darkened. "We know of Prince Tirhin's actions. We know he has proclaimed himself emperor. We also know he has driven the Madruns from Imperia, and now they rape and pillage the countryside, a problem for each province to cope with as they march homeward."

"Who named Kostimon emperor?" Caelan asked them. "Who can remember the legends? His father did not give him the throne.

No, he took it for himself. If you do not want Tirhin, whom will you name instead?"

Shouting broke out, but Pier held up his hand for quiet. "That cannot be decided now."

"When will it be decided? When Tirhin is finished dividing the empire into weak halves? When the treasuries are completely looted and the army revolts? When the darkness that is coming decides there is nothing to stop it? When will there be a council?"

Pier said nothing. Tight-lipped, he glared at Caelan, then looked at Handar. "I told you to put this man outside."

"Put me outside yourself," Caelan said, too furious to care what he said now.

Anger leaped in Pier's eyes. "Are you challenging me?" he asked in astonishment.

"Does that insult you?" Caelan taunted him. "I am so low, and your lineage is so pure. I am arena trash, as you have said, and therefore I have not even the right to look at you, much less talk to you, least of all challenge you."

Pier shook his head in disgust. "I will not fight you."

"Afraid?" Caelan said softly.

Pier's face darkened. A muscle worked in his jaw for a moment before he finally answered. "The master of this house is dying. In my respect for that man, I do not brawl while his soul departs his body."

The chastisement stung as though he had actually struck Caelan across the face. Caelan frowned and said nothing. In his anger, he had forgotten the circumstances. He was ashamed of himself, and yet he also knew Pier had goaded him to this point, deliberately pushing him too far. Now he had lost whatever chance he had to win respect from these onlookers. Like an idiot, he had fallen into Pier's trap.

It had been his goal to win these men, to improve things for Elandra. Instead, he had only made matters worse. If the faces had been hostile and judgmental before, now they were contemptuous.

He could apologize, and make himself look more like a weak fool than ever. He could leave, and have them despise him for running. He could stand here among them and bathe in their scorn. No matter what he did, it wasn't going to help Elandra.

Granite-faced, he wheeled around and walked down that long, long gallery to the portico beyond. Rain poured down in drenching sheets of water. Sighing, Caelan leaned his shoulder against a pillar.

Footsteps caught his attention, and he straightened up, looking around just as two burly men pounced on him without warning. Caelan's anger surged hot. He swung at one, but the other came at him from behind and slipped a thin noose around his neck. A deft yank of the man's wrist, and the cord bit into Caelan's throat, nearly strangling him.

"Don't struggle," the man said.

Caelan froze there, his neck stretched high as he tried to breathe. He might be able to kick the man behind him, but he would be choked to death before he could free himself.

The other one unbuckled his sword belt and relieved him of his weapons. Caelan stood there, helpless and steaming.

"Now," said the man who held the cord around his neck. "You will go down the steps, quietly. You will cause no more trouble. We will teach you better manners."

Furious, Caelan hooked his fingers around the cord to pull it, but the man jerked and twisted the noose so hard that blackness swam in front of Caelan's eyes.

When he came to, a few moments later, he was on his knees. The noose had slackened enough to allow him air. He sucked it in, his lungs burning, his throat on fire.

"You will not try that again," he was told. "Get on your feet and move."

There were times to fight, and times simply to stay alive. Caelan did as he was commanded.

Chapter Eighteen

ELANDRA WAS GIVEN the state apartments, reserved for visits of the very highest rank. The tall windows were hastily thrown open, letting in rain-dampened air that did little to dispel the mustiness of the rooms. As Elandra entered, she could hear the scurrying footsteps and muffled giggles of fleeing maidservants. The room was in order, but barely so. It had that hasty, put-together look of crooked cushions, a coverlet not quite smooth, flowers imperfectly arranged, and the suspicion of dust in the corners.

The lack of a woman in charge of this household was evident. Whatever her faults had been, at least when Hecati lived here there had been no dust, and no staff ever caught by surprise.

Scented bathwater was carried in to fill a tub of marble lined with copper. While Elandra soaked, fighting the urge to cry, the seamstress arrived with three gowns over her arm and a mouthful of pins. Food and drink were brought in on a tray, but Elandra gestured everyone away.

"Leave me," she said.

The noblewoman herself closed the doors on the bathing room and shooed out all the servants.

It was several minutes before she returned, knocking discreetly on the door before she eased it open. "Majesty?" she called.

Elandra was sitting on a stool at the dressing table adorned with fresh flowers and a row of alabaster jars. Swathed in a robe, she was rubbing scented lotion into her hands. Her wet hair hung down her back, still dripping a little onto the floor. Her reflection in the mirror showed her to be pale but composed again.

"Majesty?" the woman called a second time.

The short span of privacy had been enough. Elandra was still worried, but she had regained control of her emotions. She glanced over her shoulder and gestured for the woman to enter.

Curtsying, the woman said, "I am Lyticia, wife of the imperial governor of Gialta."

Elandra's brows rose. After her reception today, she had not expected the woman to be of such rank. "Then your husband is Lord Onar Demahaud," she said.

A surprised and gratified smile spread across Lady Lyticia's narrow face. She was handsome rather than beautiful, tall and almost thin. Her gown was splendid, and she wore tasteful bracelets and earrings. "Yes," she said. "Your Majesty's memory is most kind."

Oh, yes, Elandra's memory could not forget the name of the governor. Since Albain had no male heir, his land would be returned by law to the emperor's ownership, to be either redispensed or sold. Until either eventuality happened, the governor would be the overseer of the vast properties. He could rake whatever wealth he wanted into his pockets. At present, with the empire in chaos, it was likely that Lord Demahaud would be able to keep the vast estates for his own.

But Elandra said nothing of this, and her recognition seemed to gratify the woman.

With detente established, they got busy. Lady Lyticia had brought her seamstress, her maid, and her hairdresser. These individuals went to work, and in short order Elandra was dry, gowned, and coiffed magnificently. She felt regal again, and the increased respect in the women's eyes made her realize ruefully exactly how much importance Gialtans placed on appearances.

"May I have the honor of loaning your Majesty my jewels?" Lady Lyticia asked with tact.

"You are very kind, but no, thank you," Elandra replied firmly.

"But truly, I do not mind—"

"No," Elandra said.

Color spread across Lady Lyticia's cheeks, and Elandra felt impatient. Why couldn't the woman understand?

She didn't want to explain, but she sighed and took the trouble. "An empress may only wear jewels made specifically for her by the Choven," she said. "I am sure your jewels are splendid, but protocol forbids my acceptance of your generous offer."

Lady Lyticia smiled, pacified again.

Someone knocked on the door, and a servant entered to whisper in Lady Lyticia's ear.

She nodded and turned to Elandra, who steeled herself, certain she had primped too long and her father had died without her being at his side.

"The physicians have finished their ministrations, Majesty. If you feel ready to visit your father, this would be an excellent time."

Relief made Elandra shoot to her feet. Belatedly she remembered to walk gracefully and without haste. She had lost much ground here; she had much to restore. However foolish and of little consequence it might seem to her, these subjects considered their customs important. If she wanted them to treat her as an empress, then she must act like one, no matter how limiting or chafing it was.

She walked down long corridors furnished with fine Ulinian carpets, rows of chairs upholstered in leather, and walnut tables. Maids peeped from doorways, withdrawing at her approach and whispering behind her. *Jinjas* scampered here and there, leaping onto windowsills and staring at her with bright eyes. Outside, the rain drummed steadily, and the tall windows stood open to catch any hint of coolness to counteract the cloying heat and humidity. Curtains of sheer silk gauze billowed and blew in the damp breeze.

Elandra's own fear and rising anxiety constantly quickened her feet, although she tried to slow down. Despite her inner strain she managed to keep her face calm and composed, but she could not stop her fingers from knotting together.

Finally she reached tall doors at the end of a corridor. Bowing lackeys opened them at her approach. Guards in turbans saluted her, but Elandra barely noticed them. She hurried into the antechamber beyond and found it crowded with physicians in monkey-fur hats and long beards, chatting among themselves.

Silence fell over them, and they bowed to her in startlement. She passed them without stopping, heading for Albain's chamber.

Guards opened these final doors, and she walked inside, halting just across the threshold. She found herself suddenly without breath, her heart pounding too fast.

Tall-ceilinged and spacious, the chamber's walls were hung in silk that was sun-faded and out of style. Her father's bed was enormous, both broad and tall, with netting looped back out of the way. He lay on his back, his head propped up on a single pillow. His large hands were folded.

She had never seen him look so still, so thin, so pale. She stood there, afraid to walk closer to this stranger.

The room smelled of medicines and blood. A valet stood in a shadowy corner of the room, hastily bundling up stained sheets and sleeping shirt. A lackey with his sleeves rolled up held a basin of dirty water that he carried out through the servant's door. Her father's *jinja* lay curled up on a plump silk cushion at the foot of the bed, whimpering softly in its grief.

Elandra realized she was standing frozen in place while the physicians stared at her back. Frowning, she forced herself to walk forward, only barely aware of the doors closing quietly behind her.

The valet glanced at her, bowed, and departed. She was alone with her father, a man who had sired her and given her a home, yet little of his time and still less of his affection. She was only one of his many bastards, but unlike the others who worked as overseers and stable hands and gardeners, Elandra had a mother who was highborn. Albain had sired only one legitimate child: the vain, spoiled Bixia, who had thought she would marry Kostimon and who had joined the terrible Maelite order in anger when Elandra robbed her of that glory.

Where were his children now? Who of his family stood near to mourn him?

Elandra swallowed and walked to his bedside. His eyes were closed. She could hear the quick rasp of his breathing. His face was an ashen color that frightened her.

Slowly, she placed her hand atop his. She did not want to disturb him, yet it was important that he know she had come.

"Father," she said softly.

He did not stir.

"Father." She spoke more loudly. "It's Elandra. I've come."

He groaned, frowning and turning his head. Watching his

pain, she bit her lip and dared say nothing else. He had always been so large, so strong. She remembered him striding through the palace, bellowing orders and slapping his gauntlets in his palm. He always made noise wherever he went, whether it was his mail creaking or his spurs jingling, or his satisfied belches following dinner, or his fist thudding against his chair arm. He was life and movement, blunt and coarse and ferocious. Through his days, he had worked and fought with equal vigor. To see him now so thin and frail, fading before her very eyes, seemed impossible.

Her fingers tightened on his hand, as though by their pressure she could impart her strength to him.

A tear spilled down her cheek and splashed on the coverlet. She rubbed at the spot with her thumb, feeling helpless and afraid.

"Elandra?"

She looked up to find him gazing at her. His single sighted eye was bleary with pain and medicine, but he knew her. Her tears fell freely now, and she couldn't hold them back. Leaning over, she kissed his cheek.

It felt hot and clammy beneath her lips.

Finding a shaky smile for him, she said, "Hello, Father."

He let out his breath. "Thank the gods you are found. This madness in the—"

"Hush," she said, trying to calm him, certain he must not talk too much. "Be still. I am safe. You must not worry."

"Murdeth and Fury, but I do worry," he said, refusing to be quiet. "Kostimon dead. You gone to Gault knows where. That puppy Tirhin proclaiming himself. Madruns running wild. I—"

He broke off, coughing up blood. His face lost even more color.

Alarmed, Elandra took a cloth from the bedside table and pressed it to his lips. When the coughing fit finally ended, he lay back exhausted on his pillow.

Elandra drew in several breaths, trying to calm her pounding heart. "Now," she said at last when she could command her voice. "Let us have no more excitement. You must rest—"

His hand moved, and he shook his head. "The dead can rest," he whispered. "I have too much to do."

"Everything can wait until you are better."

His eye opened to glare at her. "Let us have honesty, not these damned lies," he said, wheezing. "I am dying, damn it. You know that."

Her lips trembled, but when she answered her voice was miraculously steady. "Yes. I have been told."

"Aye. Then act sensible. Will you fight for the throne?"

His anger had steadied her. With more calm, she said, "Yes. Caelan and I want the empire."

Albain frowned, and she hastily explained, "Caelan is the man I love. A woman may choose her second husband, and I have chosen him. His destiny is very great. He is the only man who can possibly defeat the darkness that is coming."

Albain's expression did not change. She could not tell whether he accepted what she'd said or was angered by it.

"You move quickly," he said.

She bit her lip, wanting his blessing. If she had that, she could ignore everyone else. "I met him first in my dreams when I went to be trained in the Penestrican House of Women. I did not know his name then or where to find him. We are destined, that is all I know. He has saved my life too many times to mention. He brought me safely from the palace when the Madruns would have killed me. He rescued me from the realm of shadows, where Lord Sien sought to trap me. Now he has brought me here, to you, Father."

Pain shadowed Albain's face. "You knew this man in the palace of your husband?"

Embarrassment filled her. "I was faithful to Kostimon," she said sharply. "Though he was not faithful to me."

Albain swallowed a cough. "Not required."

"Of him?" she said bitterly. "No, the man is always free, though the woman lives under rules like chains."

"Don't whine of your life. You are empress."

"Yes, I am. I would ask you to meet Caelan, Father. Later, for a moment, to judge him for yourself."

Albain closed his eyes and said nothing. She waited, wondering if her defiance had been too much for his scant strength.

But it seemed he was only resting. A few moments later, he opened his eyes again. "Who are his people?"

She wanted to laugh with relief. Albain might think he was still withholding judgment, but such a question gave him away. "He is a warrior, Father. He—"

"Who are his people?"

She stopped and frowned. A dozen convoluted explanations ran through her mind, but when she looked into her father's pain-riddled face she knew she must give him only the truth. "He comes from Trau," she said.

"That one!" Albain whispered. "I have heard of that one."

Elandra hesitated, then continued. "His father was a healer, the most renowned in the empire at one time. But Caelan has been touched by the Choven. They have given him his own destiny, and he is to—"

"Later," Albain whispered, his voice fading.

She picked up his rough hand and kissed it. "I'm sorry. I've stayed too long and tired you. I'll let you sleep now."

"Elandra."

His voice stopped her. She hurried back to his side. "Yes, Father?"

"Your plans."

"Oh, not now. You're too tired—"

He silenced her protest with a glare, then let his eyelids fall shut again.

She stood beside his bed like a schoolgirl and said quickly, "I plan to return to Imperia and confront Tirhin. Caelan and I need the army you promised me. With your men, it's possible we can persuade the imperial troops to join us, if they have not already scattered. I want the full support of the Gialtan warlords as well as the benefit of your secret alliances with warlords of the adjacent provinces."

He blinked, and she smiled. "Yes, I know about those. Kostimon's informant network was thorough. As long as you were loyal to him through the bindings of our marriage contract, he felt your private alliances only served to strengthen his base of power."

"Hell's damnation," Albain said, looking disconcerted. "What else?"

Elandra drew a deep breath. "I ask for your treasury, the contents of your armory, and supplies."

He scowled at her. "Want everything."

"Everything is at stake. Did you know the governor is here, ready to confiscate your lands?"

Albain's single eye grew fierce. "Scavenging dog."

"Yes. We must act quickly. I intend to hold a war council while all the warlords are here and convince them to support us—"

"Enough," he whispered.

She fell silent at once, watching him, worrying about him. On impulse, she put her arm across him and kissed his cheek again. "Please recover, Father," she said, weeping again. "Please don't die. I need you—"

His hand lifted and feebly patted her arm. "Come later," he said, his voice a rasp. "Bring him with you."

She straightened up, feeling hope. If Caelan passed her father's approval, then Albain would likely give her what she asked for. And how could he not be impressed by Caelan?

But her father's time was swiftly running out. He might die before his agreement was given.

Elandra watched him fall asleep and felt ashamed of herself. How could she worry about the empire when it was her father she should be concerned about? Must she be so selfish? What did it matter if Tirhin kept his ill-gotten throne? She and Caelan could go anywhere they wished, create a life together, find happiness.

Yet even as these sensible thoughts crossed her mind, she felt a sense of urgency drawing her onward to Imperia.

She wiped tears from her face, then tiptoed from the room.

Outside in the antechamber, she paused a moment to draw in deep breaths, trying to clear her lungs of the sickroom smell. While she was questioning the physicians, Lady Lyticia returned.

The woman curtsied, looking eager. "Majesty—"

Annoyed by the interruption, Elandra ignored her. "Can nothing else be tried?" she asked the chief physician.

He frowned, clearly put out by having his methods questioned. "It is not a matter of—"

"Majesty—"

In the palace, such impertinence would have been dealt with summarily on her behalf, but now Elandra had to personally put this provincial nobody in her place.

"Excuse me," she said to the physician, who bowed.

She turned on Lady Lyticia with a glacial look that did not seem to deter the woman at all.

"Majesty," she said, "there is a lady who wishes to—"

"You have not been acknowledged," Elandra broke in, and her tone sent color surging into the woman's cheeks. "How dare you approach me without leave? How dare you interrupt my conversation?"

Lady Lyticia's eyes grew very bright, and her mouth trembled a moment. She cast a swift glance around at the watching physicians and guards and tossed her head.

"Forgive me, Majesty," she said in a tight little voice. "I thought my position as the wife of—"

"Your husband does not own my father's estates yet," Elandra snapped.

"In the emperor's absence, *we* represent—"

Everything inside Elandra froze. She stared at the woman and had never been so angry before. Rage thundered in her ears, and her hands curled into fists. But at her core, she was brutally, ruthlessly cold. She realized that this woman was treating her as an empress consort, nothing more. Everyone was. She should have determined that from the first moment of her arrival, except the news of her father had been too much of a shock.

In that moment, Elandra finished growing up. She knew she could not be soft-edged and compliant, and accomplish her goals. She had always wanted to please others, to have others like her.

Now, none of that mattered. Her world was in chaos. Her father was dying. She had lost every material possession she owned. She had nothing to lose, no one to please, and only one direction to go.

Her gaze impaled Lady Lyticia's. She said, "You have forgotten that your sovereign is present."

Lady Lyticia turned pale. "But—but—"

"Furthermore, that means my father's estates will revert to me. You may tell your governor husband now to stop evaluating the contents of this household, for he will never put his hands on any of it."

"But—"

"You are dismissed."

Lady Lyticia stood rooted in place, livid and wide-eyed, her mouth open and gasping.

Elandra turned her back on the woman and looked at the physicians, who hastily assumed respectful poses.

"You were saying?" Elandra prompted the chief physician.

Holding his beard in one hand, he bowed low to her. "It is our concerted opinion," he said, his gaze flickering slightly as the guards put a sobbing Lady Lyticia outside the room, "that nothing can be done. When a man is crushed inside, he may live for several days in terrible pain, but his life force cannot be contained."

Grief stabbed through Elandra. "This is unacceptable."

The man bowed again. "Sometimes, Majesty, our desires are not sufficient to change the way things are."

She whirled away from him and swept from the room, barely aware of the guards saluting her. There had to be a way to save her father, some means other than feeding him opium for the pain and saying nothing else could be done. She knew only one person who might know what to do.

An empress did not run, but Elandra was past caring what anyone thought of her actions. Holding up her skirts, she strode through the corridors and down a series of steps.

When she passed a pair of guards standing at attention before a passageway that led to the kitchens, she paused.

"You and you," she said crisply. "I require your attendance."

Looking startled, the men approached her. They were much alike in appearance, both wiry and dark-skinned. Both wore sleeveless jerkins with dagger belts crisscrossed over their chests. They carried ceremonial pikes. They looked like brothers.

"Do you know who I am?" she asked.

Her tone was abrupt and harsh, not at all womanly. She had no idea as she stood there, fuming with anger and impatience, how much she sounded like her father at that moment, how her jaw was clenched just like his, and how fiercely her eyes were snapping.

The men bowed low. "Aye, verily," one replied. "Thou art the daughter of our lord. Thou art the wife of our dead emperor, a woman of full rights and property, unveiled."

Her chin lifted in satisfaction. "Protect me as you would Lord

Albain. I will endure no more insults beneath this roof. I will have no one stand in my way."

The men straightened. Their dark eyes gleamed with understanding, and before they spoke, she knew she had their absolute loyalty.

"Give me your names."

"I am Alti."

"I am Sumal."

"We are twins," Alti said.

"You are now my men," Elandra said. "Let replacements be found for your post. Let the word be passed through the barracks that I need a personal guard from any who will volunteer. When the hour of danger struck in Imperia, the elite Imperial Guard could not protect me from harm. Never again will I go forth without Gialtan fighters at my back."

Alti and Sumal grinned and looked as though their chests would burst. She knew their type, plantation-born, brought up to hard work, fearless, and incredibly loyal.

"The word shall be given, Majesty," Alti said.

She nodded. "Let the word also be passed that I want a *jinja* of my own. A real one, young and unbonded, from the wild. Not one retrained in the sorcerer's market. I trust my father's soldiers to find this for me. I will not ask a nobleman to perform this service."

Alti and Sumal exchanged glances, and their grins faded away. Somberly they nodded, understanding her meaning, respect increasing in their eyes. After all, she was Albain's daughter before anything else, and like Albain she understood that the true strength of Gialta lay in the hearts of its common fighting men.

"It shall be done, Majesty," Alti said.

Elandra smiled briefly. "Come, then. I wish to find Lord Caelan, the tall man who came here with me."

They frowned and again exchanged glances. "That is a difficulty, Majesty."

Impatience surged through her. "Why?"

"No one said he was a lord. There was trouble in the gallery, and now he has been taken to the whipping post."

Chapter Nineteen

FORGETTING DIGNITY, SHE whirled around and ran down the steps all the way to the gallery.

But the long room stood empty except for a trio of women gossiping in one corner and a pair of elderly men. The crowd of warlords and courtiers had vanished. She did not have to ask where they had gone.

Sickening anger at their caprice and cruelty filled her, but she wasted no time indulging her emotions. She could be disgusted with them later; it was more important now to stop them.

How?

If she ran outside to the courtyard, she might be able to shame them into stopping the flogging. But she might not. Dear Gault, if her own father perceived Caelan as no more than a lover tagging along in her wake, these dolts of his court must think exactly the same.

She could wait, gather allies from within the troops, and reprimand them later.

That would be very dignified, but it would not save Caelan's back. She needed Caelan to go to her father now. She hoped he might even know how to heal Albain. Caelan's father had been a healer. Caelan himself had studied the arts for a time. He must know *something*.

Beyond that, she could not bear to think what a public flogging would do to Caelan's spirit. He was just now beginning to believe in himself, just now beginning to reach out to all the possibilities before him. Being whipped would knock him back to his days as a slave, would bring back all the shame and humiliation he had endured before.

She would rather they whipped her than have Caelan go through something like that again.

Her hesitation lasted no more than a few seconds. Faintly from outside, she could hear people shouting and cheering in the mindless way of a mob.

"Fools," she said angrily, and headed for the portico.

Before she reached it, however, a woman stepped into the doorway to block her path.

She was a tall, fierce-eyed woman, slender despite her middle years. Her henna-streaked hair was expertly plaited and coiffed. Expensive rings glittered on her long fingers. Her gown was of straw-colored silk, full-skirted with a sheer green gauze overlay. She smelled of costly ambergris perfume.

Elandra stopped in her tracks, jolted by a sense of recognition although this woman was unknown to her. "Let me pass," she said with scant courtesy.

The woman did not step aside. "We will talk, you and I." Her gaze flickered past Elandra to Alti and Sumal. "Dismiss your dogs, and let us go the balcony gardens where we can be private."

Another, more boisterous roar rose from the crowd. Elandra glanced at her guards. "Move this woman out of my way."

They stepped forward, and alarm flickered briefly in the woman's face.

"Elandra!" she said. "I am your mother."

It was yet another shock, coming on top of too many. Elandra refused to deal with it. She couldn't. Caelan needed her more.

"Stand aside," Elandra said. "This isn't the time."

The guards gently moved the woman out of her path, and Elandra hastened on, fearing already from the jeering laughs and catcalls from the crowd that she was too late.

For Caelan, struggling with all his might to keep himself from being strangled, humiliation warred with his pride. All his tremendous strength and fighting skills availed him nothing as long as the air kept being shut off from his lungs. One quick twist of the noose, and his vision would fade. Then he would be helpless, gasping on his knees, sweat pouring off him, his strength gone from his limbs.

Each time he was allowed to draw in air until he could stand again. Then they would propel him forward in a halting, awkward progress down the innumerable steps. Whenever he felt stronger and started to think about what he might try, the man controlling the noose about his throat would jerk it hard, and the world would go black on him again.

The courtiers followed them in a stream, calling out merrily and laughing at the entertainment he provided. They seemed oblivious to the rain soaking their finery.

Caelan despised them, and wondered how Gialta had ever gotten its reputation for powerful armies when it had an aristocracy such as this.

But then, he would have despised anyone who came to laugh at his shame.

The noose around his neck reminded him of the slave chain he had worn for so many years. The public humiliation was like being marched to the auction block all over again. He would never forget the first time he was sold. But it had burned him no worse than what was happening now.

His ambitions and Moah had made him believe he could reach for the throne. But it was a delusion, one fed by Elandra's love and acceptance. Reality lay in the merciless faces surrounding him.

The rain poured into his eyes, drenching him and pounding on his breastplate.

When he reached the bottom of the steps, they took him across a courtyard to the edge of a parade ground. Near the barracks stood a whipping post, stout and scarred, heavy iron rings bolted to it where he would be bound.

The rain slackened, and men surrounded him to unbuckle his armor. For a moment the air felt cool against his sweat-soaked tunic, then he felt a tug at his collar and heard the ripping of cloth.

A cheer rose from the crowd, and Caelan closed his eyes against a raw surge of anger. He had no fear of the lash. Rage continued to build in him until it was an explosive force. Gritting his teeth, he held it back, knowing it would do him no good to struggle and yell curses. It would only make the crowd laugh more.

But he did not deserve this. He had done nothing worthy of this. He had taken no action against these people.

Gazing around at their excited, jeering faces, Caelan saw them caught up in the madness of the moment. He remembered the screaming spectators in the arena, how blood-crazed and wild they were, the frenzy of their cheering, their joy at witnessing death. Surely darkness ate the souls of such people. Worst of all, they were Elandra's people. He could not unleash *severance* on them.

Lord Pier stepped forward. He held a coiled whip in his hands. "Bind him to the post."

Caelan had planted his feet well, and it took four men to man-handle him over to the post. They bound his wrists securely, and only then did the noose come off his throat. He winced, feeling a warm trickle of blood slide down his neck.

Pier handed the whip to one of his minions and gestured. The men ripped Caelan's tunic away, and an appreciative gasp rose from the crowd.

"Gault above! Look at those muscles."

"He's bigger than I thought."

"He's a giant."

"He's very handsome."

"No wonder she brought him with her."

The comments ran on, growing freer and more ribald. Caelan closed his ears, feeling his rage pulse against his throat. He jerked against the iron rings, ready to yank them out by the roots if he could. He budged them not at all, but the violence in him and the loud rattle of the rings startled everyone. Even the man with the whip stepped back.

Caelan looked over his shoulder and met Pier's gaze. "This is not worthy of you," he said.

"You are an arena champion," Pier replied. "You fight well in the ring. You should have stayed there. Challenging your betters is not worthy of *you*."

Caelan stared at him in disbelief. Was that all this was? A reprimand to a man Pier thought was a slave? Did he think he could insult Elandra by publicly whipping her companion?

The rage boiled hotter, until Caelan felt his bones would melt. His fists clenched with the violence he could not unleash.

"You will regret this," he said to Pier.

The warlord turned away with a little shrug, unimpressed. "Forty lashes for his impertinence. Begin."

At that moment, the clouds parted overhead. Sunlight slanted down upon Caelan alone, isolating him from the crowd, which murmured and shifted back in wonder.

"Look at his back!" someone shouted.

"Look at the imperial mark!"

"His brand is glowing."

"It's glowing!"

Some fought their way clear, running and shouting for their *jinjas* to come. The rest stood there and stared, open-mouthed.

Caelan could not see what they were pointing at, but he could feel the place on his shoulder blade where his slavery mark had been canceled. It burned like fire, as hot as the moment the hissing brand had been pressed to his skin. His rage boiled inside him, burning him from the inside out.

They had no right to do this. No right to commit this act.

And he would not submit to it.

He strained against the ring bolts until the muscles in his arms and shoulders bulged and the cords in his neck snapped taut. A shudder went through him as he poured all his rage into this effort. The sunlight seemed to feed him its heat and strength.

The wood groaned, splintered, and cracked. The bolts pulled free suddenly, sending pieces of wood flying. Shouting aloud, Caelan dropped his arms and whirled around. He broke the ropes that fastened his wrists to the rings and slung them away. He was free and savage, his pulse pounding in his ears, his vision a blur.

Men cried out and fled from him, pushing and shoving each other in panic. Pier and his men stood fast, looking wary and frightened, but holding their ground.

The sunlight broadened as the clouds parted more, and Pier now stood illuminated also. For a moment his light brown eyes changed to black, and he stood revealed as a skeleton. Black tentacles curled about his bones, thrusting out through the empty eye sockets in his skull. Then Caelan's vision faded, and Pier was a man again—intelligent and dangerous. His hand was on his sword hilt, but he had not yet drawn his weapon.

He glanced at the man holding the whip. "Hit him. Drive him back."

The man shook out the whip expertly. Seconds later, the braided leather came whistling at Caelan. Caelan's gaze was locked on Pier. He didn't even bother to duck.

But when the lash struck him, it charred instantly to ashes that blew away in the wind.

More people screamed, calling on their gods for mercy. They trampled away, and even Pier's men backed up.

"Lord, come away. This is surely a demon."

But Pier apparently did not listen. He drew his sword and charged Caelan.

A quick glance to the side showed Caelan his sword belt lying on the ground. He reached for it, and Exoner almost seemed to leap into his hand. Caelan turned and barely managed to parry Pier's sword.

Metal clanged loudly, echoing off the stone buildings and silencing the cries of those fleeing. Many ran all the way across the courtyard to the base of the steps, but went no farther. Silence gradually fell over everyone. Even the soldiers kept their distance.

Caelan and Pier circled each other in the strange circle of sunlight. Pier's eyes were still black and unworldly, as though something unnameable had taken possession of him. Caelan felt only heat and fury. The sunlight burned his skin and seemed to fill his thoughts until he knew nothing else.

He attacked, swinging Exoner with both hands. Pier met the blow, and they were at it, swords flashing rhythmically back and forth to the grunts of the fighters. Sweat flew in droplets illuminated in the sunlight. The air felt heavy and thick, like trying to breathe water. Magic crawled through it. Caelan could smell it like a scorched scent overlaying the fragrance of recent rain upon the pavement.

Someone was calling frantically, "Bring the *jinjas*! Bring the *jinjas*! Hurry!"

He did not understand why those peculiar little creatures were wanted, but he could spare no thought for it now. Normally he judged a man's intention by the shift in his eyes, but Pier's black eyes were like opaque holes, impossible to judge. Caelan frowned and barely evaded the man's quick lunge. What possessed him? Either darkness lurked in this palace, or else Pier had brought it with him. Yet his first impression of the man had been favorable.

Caelan attacked in a furious flurry of strength and complex maneuvers that drove Pier back. Spectators fled before them, and Pier stumbled, barely parried as Caelan drove him harder, then mistakenly left himself open.

Caelan leaped at the opportunity, his sword thrusting deep, but at the last second Pier shifted his weight. Exoner did no more than slice along his ribs. Black blood spurted forth, and where it touched the Choven-forged metal, flames burst up.

Pier screamed and staggered back, clutching his side. For a second his anguished eyes met Caelan's, and they were their normal color again. Then the blackness engulfed them once more.

In a second Caelan realized what he had to do. Even as Pier slowly straightened and lifted his weapon to fight again, Caelan was charging.

He took advantage of his greater reach and heavier weight to tackle the man, heedless of Pier's sword, which raked across his ribs. Caelan gripped Pier by the front of his tunic, twisting it hard at the man's throat, and slammed him into the wall of the stables, pinning his sword arm beneath him.

Pier swore and struggled, but Caelan braced his feet and held him bodily. Then he pressed the flat of his sword against Pier's wounded side.

Arching his back, Pier screamed a shrill, piercing cry as though his soul was being torn from him.

Flames and steam rose between them as Exoner burned away the poison inside Pier. A terrible stench filled the air—not from burned flesh but from something much worse, something inhuman.

A man wearing Pier's colors dared grab at Caelan's arm. "In the name of Gault, desist! Take me, demon, and let my master go!"

Caelan glanced at him, and bared his teeth. "Get back," he said, spitting out the words.

The man turned pale and backed away.

But by then someone else was shoving a group of *jinjas* forward. "Stop the magic! Stop it!"

The small green creatures stared at Caelan and did nothing.

Relieved, he turned his attention back to Pier. The screams stopped. When Pier sagged against the wall, Caelan took his sword away. Pier was as white as the limestone wall behind him. He looked at Caelan as though he would speak, then swooned.

Gently Caelan lowered him to the ground.

Men rushed closer, but Caelan glared at them. "Stay back!"

"Monster!" one shouted back.

"Demon!" another cried.

"Will you eat him?"

"Lord Pier is dead!"

"He isn't dead," Caelan said grimly, touching the rapid pulse in Pier's wrist. "Not yet. Just stay back!"

But now the *jinjas* approached him. They bared their small pointed teeth and stared at him with bright eyes.

"No fear, master," one of them said. "We protect."

And they formed a ring around Caelan and Pier, keeping the others away.

Consternation seemed to flow through the crowd, but Caelan ignored it. He was grateful to have the creatures on his side.

Gingerly he tugged at the burned edges of Pier's tunic, parting the cloth to look at the wound. It was well cauterized, the bleeding stopped. Although burned and raw, the skin looked human. Caelan saw no more black blood.

Hardly daring to hope, he peeled back one of Pier's eyelids. Although the eye was rolled back, it looked a normal color.

One of the *jinjas* crouched beside Caelan and put its narrow hand on Pier's chest. "My master," it said.

Caelan frowned. "Is the darkness in him gone?"

"Mostly. I will take the rest." With that, the *jinja* stretched itself across Pier's chest and began to utter an eerie whine that made Caelan wince.

Hastily he backed away from whatever spell the *jinja* was weaving, for its magic was not compatible with his own.

Wiping off Exoner, Caelan slid the sword into its scabbard. The clouds closed over him again with a muted rumble of thunder, and it began to sprinkle.

Silence stretched over the courtyard. The crowd stared at

Caelan in wonder and fear. He frowned back at them, not certain what they had seen. There should be something he could say, to re-assure everyone and dissipate the tension that was like a wall against him. But no words came to his tongue.

Looking over their heads at the steps rising up to the palace, he saw a woman standing near the top, her full skirts billowing in the wind. His heart lightened at the sight of her; then he frowned again.

What would Elandra say about this debacle? He had not meant to alienate her people. Now they feared him, and soon that would turn them against her also. He had let her down, and he was sorry.

His gaze swept across the faces staring at him. "Lord Pier is not dead. Let me pass."

They parted for him and he walked alone, his head held high, his shoulders tense in expectation of an attack.

But no one dared move against him this time. He walked up the endless steps as the rain strengthened to a light patter, cleansing him of sweat and blood. The cut across his ribs stung, but it was hardly more than a scrape, and he ignored the discomfort.

A few steps short of the top, he stopped and stood there so that she could look down at him. A strange expression lay on her face. She seemed unaware of the rain pelting her, and her eyes held pain. He bowed his head to her, ashamed.

"I am sorry," he said.

"Surely thou art a god," she whispered.

His head snapped up. "No! Elandra, do not blaspheme."

"I saw everything. You were a column of light. He was a pool of darkness." Her eyes shifted away, then met his again. "It was a prophecy, Caelan. A prophecy of what comes."

"Whatever possessed Lord Pier," Caelan said thoughtfully, trying to pretend he felt no shiver of fear down his spine, "I think perhaps it possesses Prince Tirhin as well. My sister is right. I must confront him without delay."

She nodded, her frown deepening. "We will go. But you must meet my father first."

Only then did he remember the old man was dying. "Beloved—"

"He has asked for you," she said. Pleading filled her eyes. "Please . . . the physicians are such fools. Can you heal him?"

"No."

Her breath caught audibly, and he realized she was fighting not to cry. "You know more than they," she said. "You know many of the arts of healing. You do! At least try."

He took her hand in his. "Let us go in out of the rain. You're getting soaked."

She shook her head, but he escorted her back under the portico.

"Try, Caelan," she pleaded. "At least try. We need him."

"I cannot heal others, Elandra. That is not my gift."

"Are you sure?" she asked him. "Oh, please, please try. Have mercy and go to him. Please."

He frowned, ready to protest further, but she was not listening to him. He remembered how he had grieved for his own father, whom he had not even loved as Elandra loved hers, and he could not refuse again.

"Let me clean up."

She gripped his hand and drew him along. "No delays. Come now."

"But, Elandra, if you want his blessing, I would look better clean and clothed."

She wasn't listening. "I will have you go to him while the light still shines a little on your skin. If you could save me within the realm of shadow, and if you have released Lord Pier from the grasp of darkness, then surely you can also save my father."

He sighed. A physical injury was not the same as an injury to the soul. But Elandra's stubbornness was a wall around her.

Together they walked through the immense palace that rivaled Kostimon's in splendor and size. Two Gialtan guards trailed after them, although no one sought to stop them. Caelan did not think he would impress anyone with rain, sweat, and blood drying on him, his tunic torn off his back, and his hair hanging in his eyes.

In the antechamber, the physicians looked startled to see them. One of the men held open an ancient book with a crumbling leather binding and a lock and chain that swung freely. He paused with his long index finger still resting on one of the vellum pages.

Caelan glimpsed strange, arcane writings, and a sense of magic hovered in the air above the man's head.

Caelan frowned, focusing on the mortar and pestle the second man held and the bottle of liquid in the hands of the third.

They stared like guilty men caught in some act.

"Learned men," Elandra said with a courteous inclination of her head. "I return with a visitor—"

"Your pardon, Majesty." Caelan broke in with a sense of deepening unease. "Who are these men?"

She looked surprised. "The physicians—"

"Are they? What are you concocting?" Caelan asked the men.

The three exchanged glances, and he saw lies enter their faces.

"Only a potion to help soothe Lord Albain's discomfort," one replied. "The pain grows worse."

Caelan looked around. He felt a strange charge in the air, something unseen and unwanted.

The hair on his scalp prickled, and he would have set Choven warding keys on the doors and windows as protection if he'd had any.

"What's wrong?" Elandra asked him, her eyes wide. "What do you see?"

Caelan glanced at her two guards. "Do you serve her Majesty or have you been set to follow her like watchdogs?"

They bristled at his question, but Elandra answered for them. "They are my men."

"If you would save Lord Albain," Caelan said to them, and his glance moved to encompass the men guarding the door as well, "then get these physicians out of here and do not let them return. That is not opium they are mixing."

"I protest!" the tallest physician said. Holding the bottle, he stepped forward. "Majesty, this is an outrage. What manner of barbarian have you brought here? How dare he accuse and slander us?"

The guards stepped forward, but not fast enough. Caelan glimpsed a movement from one of the physicians and drew Exoner. As swift as thought, he sprang across the room and speared the ancient book on the end of his sword.

Flames burst forth, engulfing the book. With a scream, the physician dropped it. The fire blazed up, hot and hungry. Within seconds the book had been devoured, and all that remained was a small pile of ashes. The air stank most foully despite the open windows.

"Exoner is truth," Caelan said, glaring at the physicians, who watched him fearfully. "You are lies. Get out!"

The guards hustled them out, and Elandra ran to the door of her father's chamber. Flinging it open, she snapped her fingers.

"*Jinja!* Come forth and serve your master," she said imperiously.

She had to call a second time before a sniffing, woebegone *jinja* appeared. Its green skin was tinged an unhealthy gray. Its pointed ears drooped. It could barely drag itself along. When it came to the doorway, its eyes held only misery.

"There is magic here," Elandra said sharply to it. "Bad magic. Did you know? Why are you not protecting my father?"

The *jinja* did not appear to hear her at first; then it sniffed the air and blinked. Lifting its head, it sniffed again. A glower darkened its small face, and it straightened erect. Like a dog following a trail, it began to slowly zigzag back and forth across the room.

One of the guards returned, looking slightly breathless. Shame burned in his face. "Majesty, we beg—"

"Let no one enter," she commanded in a voice like iron. "*No one.*"

"Yes, Majesty."

Elandra stood in the doorway to her father's chamber and beckoned to Caelan. "Come," she said.

He could smell sickness and death ahead of him in the room, which was thick with gloom. If she expected a miracle, he could not give it to her, but at least Lord Albain could now die in peace, in his own time, not helped along by his enemies.

Sighing, Caelan squared his shoulders and reluctantly stepped inside.

Chapter Twenty

IT WAS A warrior's room. Besides the large bed, it contained a vast table weighted down by scrolls, scraps of parchment, broken pens, ink cases, books, deed boxes, strongboxes, lamps, a stirrup iron, dog collars, and a pair of daggers. The opposite wall held a beautiful collection of swords mounted in crisscrossed patterns. Starbursts of daggers adorned another wall. Albain's banner was flung over the tall back of a tapestried chair, and his boots lay forgotten in one corner. If the man had a valet, the servant must be forbidden to touch anything.

Still, Caelan could not help but smile a little at the disorder. This was a man's room. He liked it.

But Elandra did not want him to stand and gawk. She was already at her father's bedside, beckoning him to join her.

Throughout Caelan's boyhood, the sick and injured had come constantly to the house. If the infirmary was full, Caelan was forbidden to make noise in the courtyard lest he disturb the patients' rest. His father had worked tirelessly, calmly soothing fevers and talking away fears. How often had Caelan crept from his bedchamber in the middle of the night, following the glow of lamplight and the faint sounds to peer into his father's workroom? There Beva would sit, hunched at his table in the glow of the lamp, grinding herbs for his potions and making neat notations in his books of study.

The smell of sickness and herbs in the infirmary often crept into the rest of the house. Caelan had always hated that smell. While he felt sorry for the sufferers who came to his father for cures, he could not bring himself to be a willing assistant. He fled the moment his father released him from his chores. Never had he wanted to be a healer. Never had he felt comfortable around those in misery.

Now, in Lord Albain's chamber, he longed to turn and run. This was not the time to meet Elandra's father. Albain's reputation as a fierce old warlord was well deserved, from all accounts. He should be left alone with dignity and peace. He did not need quackery, or sorcery, or Caelan's unskilled fumbling.

But Elandra's eyes were on Caelan—trusting him, believing in him—and he could not refuse her anything.

Reluctantly he walked up to the bed and stood behind her, looking down over her shoulder at the battle-scarred old man. Albain lay there unconscious, moaning a little.

Caelan could hear the rattle in his lungs, could see the bloody froth on Albain's lips.

He frowned.

"What is it?" Elandra asked, watching him anxiously.

"He needs more pillows, to prop him higher. He can't breathe, lying down like that."

Hope flashed through her face. She rushed away, opening a servant's door and calling for the valet.

In a few minutes Caelan was carefully lifting the old man while Elandra and the valet piled pillows on the bed.

"I thought so," the valet kept muttering. "I wanted to do that, but the physicians said he should lie flat. I knew better. I am sorry, my lady. I—I mean, your Majesty."

"Yes," Elandra said, holding her father's hand and seeming to barely hear the man's excuses. "What else?" she asked Caelan, then glanced at the valet with a frown of suspicion. "Has he eaten? Has he had any water?"

"No, Majesty. They said—"

"Never mind what they said," she broke in sharply. "Bring broth, just a little. And cool drinking water flavored with the juice of lemons."

"Yes, Majesty."

She glanced at Caelan, who knew he could hesitate no longer. Carefully he unlaced Albain's sleeping shirt and gently probed along the man's ribs. They were spongy, and dark bruising discolored his sides. He groaned and coughed up blood, which Elandra wiped away.

"At least five broken ribs, maybe a cracked hipbone," Caelan said at last. He frowned to himself, trying to remember his old lessons. "One of the ribs has punctured his lung. That is why he coughs blood. There is more damage, but I have not the knowledge to tell you what it is." He met her eyes and told her the truth. "He bleeds inside."

"Can anything be done?"

"Yes, if we had a proper healer. My father could have mended him easily. Agel could do it." Caelan heard the futility of his own words and shook his head. "But we have no one of that—"

"We have you."

He sighed. "Elandra, I am not a healer."

"Your father taught you something. I know he did."

Caelan held out his hands. "I could not learn the healing arts. Yes, I learned *severance,* which I have explained to you, but I—"

"I know," she said eagerly. "That is why I am so certain you can do it. You must believe in yourself. You must reach deep and find the knowledge that you have. There is a way. There must be a way. I don't know why I feel so sure, but I do. You can do this, if you will but try."

He turned away from her, unwilling to face the pleading in her eyes. Elandra had never begged before, but she was begging him now. The worst thing, however, was that she was right.

He did not want to admit it.

He did not want to pay the price.

"Am I wrong?" she asked, her voice suddenly sounding dull. "Am I mistaken?"

He sighed. "We must all lose our parents at some time. It is part of life."

"Is this his time?" she asked fiercely. "Is it? Or has the darkness reached out to strike him down? When I lived here, the palace was not riddled with shadows and forbidden magic the way it is now. I can feel it crawling everywhere, seeking prey, ready to strike anyone who is unwary. The *jinjas* are supposed to sense it, keep it away, but they are clearly failing against what has come here. Everything is breaking down, Caelan. The closer we go to

Imperia, the more I think we will find much evil turned loose on our world. The darkness is overtaking us, one by one."

"All right," Caelan said, breathing deep against his own fear. She did not know what she asked of him. She did not know what this would cost.

"We need him," Elandra said passionately. "Not because he's my father. But because he is a fighter, like you. To his very blood and bone, he is a warrior. His joy is combat. His skills and his goodness come in battle. And he is true to the core. We need men like that to help us. Otherwise, we are lost. And the empire is lost. Everything and everyone we know will be taken."

"I know," Caelan said. For a moment Elandra's voice seemed to blur and become Lea's. He remembered saying that Lea was his conscience. Now it seemed Elandra was too. He was ashamed of his own fear, of his own instinct to save himself at the expense of others.

He gazed down at Albain's pain-wracked face, and felt a wave of compassion.

Reaching out, he took the man's slack hand from Elandra. It was callused like his, from long hours of wielding a sword. It was big-knuckled and freckled on the back, hairy and weather-chapped. He felt a touch of involuntary *sevaisin* that brought him the man's agony and the squeeze of a lung that would not fill, the heaviness of blood that was drowning him bit by bit.

Caelan gasped and flinched.

Elandra touched his shoulder. "Caelan—"

"Step back," he said grimly, pushing *sevaisin* away long enough to catch his breath. "You must leave us."

"But you might need my help."

He glared at her, fearing that if she protested too much he would lose his nerve and run from here.

She seemed to read his thoughts. Her own face drained of color. "Am I asking too much?" she whispered.

He dared not answer her. "Just go."

Consternation filled her face, but she stood on tiptoe to kiss his cheek. "I love you," she said and walked away.

"Let no one enter," Caelan called after her. "No matter what you hear, let no one in until I come out."

She cast him one last look over her shoulder, looking afraid, and nodded before she shut the door.

Caelan drew in a deep breath, trying to find his courage while the man beside him sank closer to death with every struggling breath.

There was a way to heal Albain. There was a way to summon the skills that Caelan himself did not possess. But it meant opening himself to that which he most dreaded. It meant becoming that which his father had always wanted him to be.

Had he been alone, Caelan would have put off the moment of decision, but Albain groaned and coughed. There was death in the sound. Caelan could feel his life force seeping away as he held the man's hand.

Bowing his head, Caelan sought *sevaisin,* and flowed into Albain's agony until it was his own. In turn, he shared his strength with the old man; then he *severed* the pain, sending it far away.

It seemed, in his vision, that he stood in a grove of short oak trees, the stunted kind that survived without enough water, unable to grow tall, unwilling to die off. Such groves were common in Imperia, but Caelan did not believe he was near the city.

Instead, it seemed to be a different kind of place altogether. The wind blew softly, a cold dry wind, and around Caelan there was only silence. He held Albain in his arms, and the old man's body was heavy, slack, and unbalanced—the most awkward kind of burden to carry.

For now, he had done all he could. Albain could not die while he was here, but neither could he go forth and live. They could stay here for eternity, trapped together.

Caelan gazed around him, but there was only emptiness among the trees as they rattled and lost leaves in the wind.

"Beva E'non!" he called, feeling himself choke as he spoke the name. "Beva E'non, I call you! I alone have the right to summon you. Come forth!"

For a long moment nothing happened. Caelan had always been too impatient, and now he tried to make himself still and calm. He must wait, no matter how little he wanted to.

Then a face appeared among the trees, distant from Caelan,

lacking any form to go with it. The face was blurred. It wavered, faded away, then returned and became more distinct.

It was Beva's face, stern and unloving. The cold gray eyes gradually grew more animated, more alive, more aware. They focused on Caelan, and recognition filled them.

"My son," Beva's voice said.

I am not your son! Caelan wanted to shout. Instead, he forced back the quarrelsome words.

"Father," he said.

"You have come, seeking knowledge."

"I have come, to save a life."

"I do not live," Beva said, wavering for a moment. "I do not heal."

"Give me the knowledge," Caelan asked.

Beva stared at him a long, long while. "My knowledge was offered to you when I lived. You refused it."

"I know."

"I gave you many chances, my son. You were my only son, my one hope of living on, of seeing my skills continue. You refused me."

"Yes."

"I am spirit now. I am *severed.*"

"I—I need you." Caelan had to struggle over a lump in his throat to say the words. Since the Choven had told him the truth, he had felt nothing for Beva. Now he had to beg, and it came hard. "I need the knowledge to save this man."

"You refused all knowledge. You were disrobed. You would not be taught."

"Not by the masters of Rieschelhold, no," Caelan said through his teeth.

"Not by me. You refused the purging after the wind spirits mauled you. Would you refuse it again?"

Caelan sank to his knees, unable to hold Albain any longer. The man was growing so heavy. Caelan's arms were trembling from fatigue, or perhaps from fear.

His mouth was too dry. He had to swallow twice before he could answer Beva's question. "I—I will not refuse."

To be purged was to have his mind ripped from him, sifted

through by a master healer such as Beva, and replaced. Many who were purged never regained their sanity. Those who survived were forever changed. They became slower of wit, duller of spirit. Beva's intention to purge his own son had been the final straw that drove Caelan to run away from home. He had never forgiven his father for wanting to do such a thing to him, and now Beva's spirit still clung to that same horrifying goal.

"Come closer, Caelan," Beva's spirit said to him.

Caelan tried, but he could not lift Albain from the ground. The old man lay ashen and limp in his arms.

"I can't come to you," Caelan said. "You must come to me."

Beva's face wavered and vanished, only to reappear much closer. Caelan found himself breathing too hard and fast. He could barely maintain *severance,* yet he knew without control he would be lost.

"Help this man," Caelan said desperately. "Give me the knowledge to heal him."

"What did I tell you once about *severance*?" Beva asked.

Caelan struggled to think. His wits wanted to flee like rats from water. "You said it is the taking away. You take away disease or injury. You bring the void, and wellness fills it."

"Yes. You remembered well."

"How do I bring wellness to this man?" Caelan asked. He prayed that Beva's spirit would become interested in Albain's injuries, that the old compassion would take over. Healing others was like an addiction for him. Never had he refused to help anyone. Even if he ultimately lost a patient, it was not for lack of trying.

"Look at this man, Father. Tell me what to do."

"Will you take the purging, my son?"

Caelan sighed. "I said that I would."

"Will you take it now?"

"No. The man must be healed first."

"If you will be purged, I will give you the knowledge you request."

It seemed they had made the bargain twice already, but Caelan nodded again. "Yes. I agree to your terms. We heal this man, and then I am yours."

Beva came even closer until his disembodied face hovered right over Caelan. "I must enter you. You will take my spirit. You will accept me. You will become me."

"Sevaisin," Caelan whispered, dry-mouthed.

"The way it was intended, not the idle sharing you have done."

Caelan felt the sting of Beva's criticism and sighed. Even his father's spirit had to lecture him about something.

"From birth you were difficult," Beva continued. "You always had to do things your way. I could show you nothing. You resisted training, resisted the ways of harmony. You were too much *their* creation, and not enough mine. They gave me my son, but you looked like me, nothing more. You were not me. You had not my abilities. You had not my qualities. You had none of my dreams, none of my direction. You were useless to me!

"I wanted a second child, a second son. But they tricked me again with Lea. What use was a daughter? She could not follow in my footsteps. Your mother never knew the truth, but it ate at me. It was a canker in me, which was rubbed raw every time you disobeyed me. I wanted to leave you in the woods to die, to be taken back to *them,* but I couldn't do it. I wanted you so much. You were my son, my straight-shouldered, beautiful son. I had so much hope for you. Why did you not feel anything for me?"

Caelan stared at Beva, feeling the spirit's anguish. His own torment rose in him. For the last time, he tried to make Beva understand. "If you had just let me be myself," he said softly, feeling his eyes sting. "I loved you, Father. I wanted to please you, but I couldn't be something I wasn't."

"But now you have come to me. You have changed," Beva said with satisfaction, as though he had won. "You will be what I want. You will become me, and I shall live on to continue my work."

Caelan bowed his head. That was the price. It had always been the price, even when he had not understood what truly lay beneath their animosity. Now he would pay it. Beva was finally going to win.

Caelan's arms slackened around Albain, and he closed his eyes. He felt a coldness upon his face, like a clammy mist. The coldness filled his body, making him shiver. He fought it a moment, not wanting this, fearing he would never be able to come back, and yet he had promised. It was for Albain. It was for Elandra. He forced away his fear, and let the presence enter, joining with him.

He shuddered once and felt cold and hollow inside. Opening his eyes, he found himself looking down at Albain as though from very far away. His mind grew very clear and detached. He recognized Albain, but the man's identity did not matter.

The injuries needed immediate attention. There was much blood pooled around the internal organs.

His hands reached down and down and down until at last they touched Albain. He let the healing pass through him, restoring the balance and harmony of the body's natural functions. The crushed bones mended. The damaged organs grew stronger. The bruising faded. The blood seeped forth from the tissues.

All the pain and damage left Albain and entered him. His body jerked back in agony, absorbing it, becoming it, conquering it. Then all became still and calm.

Caelan drew breath after a moment, daring to risk the return of that terrible pain. But the pain was gone, already fading as though it had never been. He looked down for Albain, but the man had vanished, and Caelan felt no more contact with him.

Instead, he felt his father entwined around and through him. Rebellion returned, and he wanted to fling his father's presence away. But Beva clung tightly.

"You promised," he whispered through Caelan's mind.

Caelan remembered what honor meant, and he forced his rebellion away. Shivering, he opened himself and let his father take over.

Beva's cold presence flowed down through his body, chilling him, then it seemed to vanish.

Caelan waited, but nothing else happened. Would he know when Beva took over his soul? Would he ever be aware of it?

Opening his eyes after a moment, Caelan blinked and once again found himself in the grove of trees. The wind had stopped blowing, and there was only silence. No life, no movement, no sound.

A trail stretched before him. Without knowing why, he followed it to the bank of a stream.

The water flowed swift and deep. If he crossed it, he would have to swim.

While he hesitated, he heard a sound behind him.

It was only one of the trees swaying.

Caelan relaxed, then frowned and looked at the tree again. It moved, its branches rustling and swaying, but no wind blew.

He turned around to face it, conscious of the water at his back, as though to corner him.

"You are not in danger," a voice said to him.

It sounded familiar, but he could not place it.

He looked around wildly, but saw no one.

More of the trees were moving now. They seemed to close in on him, yet they did not uproot themselves from the earth. He felt ripples and currents of energy in the air. The air shimmered as though with a rainbow.

"Your father's spirit is only memory, Caelan," the voice said. "Beva is no longer flesh. He cannot hurt you. He cannot possess you. Only his memories remain. Only his intentions. Only his knowledge. That is all. His spirit believes it has redeemed you into itself and is content. Beva will no longer haunt your dreams. Peace can be restored."

Caelan looked around again, unable to tell where the voice was coming from. "I don't understand," he said.

"In time, more wisdom will come to you. For now, we thank you for having made peace with your father. There can be harmony once more within the spirit world."

"Am I in the spirit world now?"

"No. You are between."

Caelan frowned, struggling to understand. "Have I much more to learn?"

"Much."

"How will I learn? What am I to do?"

"Live," the voice said. "Follow your path of life. Stay in the truth."

Caelan stared at the trees and felt like a child talking to someone very old and very wise. Was he in the presence of the gods of light?

"No, Caelan. Calm your thoughts. It is time for you to return."

"How?" he asked eagerly. "Don't I end *severance*?"

"You are beyond your own reach," the voice replied. "You cannot return from this grove by yourself. Even your gifts are not that powerful. Beva drew you here. Now we must send you back."

Caelan lifted his chin, trying to be accepting, although his mind was chaotic with thoughts and questions. "What must I do?"

"Enter the water," the voice said. "Do not fear it. It is warm and the current is gentle. Drink the water, then let yourself slip beneath the surface."

Caelan waited a moment, then frowned. "Is that all?"

"Be at peace," the voice replied. "You have done well. Trust in your return."

He looked at the stream flowing past him. The water was clear and clean. He could not see the bottom. It made no sense, but he did as he was told.

Sliding into the water, he found it warm and pleasant as the voice had said it would be. The current was strong, however, and he clung instinctively to the bank, resisting it.

But after a moment, he realized what he was doing was futile. There had been no explanation, but did he need one here where obviously nothing was as it seemed? Why did he care where the current took him, as long as it was back to where he belonged?

He lowered his face to the water and sipped it. The taste was pure. Realizing he was thirsty, he drank long and deeply, then released the bank and allowed the current to carry him along. He thought of trust. He thought of faith. Words he had sworn by all his life without ever having to really put them to the test. But no matter how strong he was, no matter how brave, he was still only a man. He could not do everything himself.

"Another lesson," he murmured wryly to himself.

After a moment, he drew in a deep breath and slid below the surface.

Elandra waited for two hours, while night closed around the palace and servants came on silent feet to light the lamps. The guards changed, and still she heard no sound from within her father's room. She paced slowly around the antechamber while the minutes dragged by. What could Caelan be doing? What was taking so long?

Again and again she was filled with the urge to rush inside, but she restrained herself. She had given her promise to Caelan. She would keep it.

Her father's *jinja* was as restless as she. It scratched incessantly at the doors, no matter how many times she shooed it away.

"You must be still," she told it. "Hush. No noise."

The *jinja* tilted its small green face up to hers and sighed. "I guard sleep. I watch."

"Yes, but you must do so out here."

The *jinja* shook its head fretfully. "Too far away. No good."

She knew better than to touch it. "You must be patient. Soon you can go back inside, but not now."

The *jinja* sighed heavily and sank down on its haunches by the door.

Satisfied, Elandra turned and went to gaze out the window. The rain had stopped, and the night lay heavy and still save for the sound of water running through the stone gutters. In the distance she could hear the hunting cough of panthers and the shrill death screams of their prey.

The sound of the opening door made her whirl around in relief.

But it was not Caelan who emerged. Instead, she saw the *jinja* darting inside.

"No!"

Exasperated, she ran after it, but the *jinja* was too quick. In a rapid blur of unnatural speed, it darted here and there around the room, finally coming to a halt at the foot of Albain's bed. The lamp had burned out. Elandra could see only by the light that shone inside from behind her.

She listened a moment, gazing about. Her father lay propped up on his tall pillows. His head had fallen over to one side. She did not see Caelan.

Hesitating, she opened the door wider, allowing more light inside. She even looked behind the door. Caelan was not there.

Her hand went to her throat in nameless fear. She looked at the *jinja*. "Is it safe?" she whispered.

The *jinja* shook itself the way a dog shakes water from its coat. "Safe. No magic. No bad."

She could not make herself believe it. Picking up a lamp from the antechamber, she went into the room and closed the door firmly after her. She went first to her father.

He lay so quiet and still she feared he had died. But when she touched his hand, it felt warm with life. Some color had returned to his cheeks, and she realized he was breathing normally, with none of the rasping struggle of before.

Hope made her draw in a sharp breath. She opened his sleeping shirt and ran her fingertips delicately across his side. Much of the bruising had faded. His ribs felt whole beneath her touch.

Albain stirred slightly, frowning, and she drew the covers higher, smoothing them and stroking his forehead. He no longer had fever. Clearly he lay in a healing sleep, already on the mend. The miracle she had asked for had been achieved.

Tears stung her eyes, welling up through her lashes. She blinked, and twin tears ran down her cheeks. Grateful, she sank to her knees beside him and clung to his hand.

"Oh, Father," she whispered through her tears of relief. "Oh, Father."

Chapter Twenty-One

CAELAN DID NOT return. No one had seen him. No one could explain how he had left Albain's chamber without being seen.

Frustrated and worried, Elandra retired to her apartments. By lamplight she undressed herself, wary of even the servants. She put her knife beneath her pillow and stretched out beneath the soft curtains of insect netting.

Her dreams were troubled and restless. She moaned and tossed in the humid darkness; then a sound close by awakened her. Opening her eyes, she found herself dazzled by lamplight shining over her. a shadowy silhouette stood by her bedside, holding the lamp aloft.

Elandra gasped and sat bolt upright with one hand on the knife under her pillow and the other gripping her jewel pouch.

"Begone from me," she said.

Her voice sounded quivery and afraid, not strong like she wanted it to be.

The figure lowered the lamp until her face was also illuminated. As she saw the features of the woman standing beside her, Elandra's fear was replaced by anger.

She flung aside the insect netting and scrambled out of bed. Dressed in shapeless linen that kept slipping off one shoulder, her hair flowing around her like a veil, she glared at her visitor.

"You pick a poor time to come calling," she said to the woman who had borne her. "Or do you always prowl in other people's rooms in the middle of the night?"

Her mother glared back, looking haughty and regal in robes of dark green. "Is that all the greeting you will give me? Is there no respect in you?"

"Do you deserve more?"

"Do you know who I am, Elandra?"

Elandra drew in a sharp, angry breath, but her mother raised her hand.

"I have the right to address you by your name, whether you wish it or not."

Slowly Elandra mastered her anger, controlled it. Her mother was correct, but she did not have to like it.

"Do you know who I am?" her mother repeated.

"Your name is Iaris," Elandra said coldly. "You gave me birth."

"I am your mother."

Elandra swallowed. As a child she had dreamed of her mother, longed for her mother. Now all she felt was rage and such pent-up resentment she thought she might explode. Again, using all that the Penestricans had taught her, she struggled to control herself.

"Yes," she said finally, "you are my mother."

Iaris waited a moment. "Is that all you have to say?"

"What should I add?"

"A word of greeting. A smile. Perhaps a remark expressing your feelings at our reunion."

"Is that what this is?" Elandra asked. "A reunion? The word implies that there was a previous relationship, does it not? I don't recall one."

Iaris's nostrils flared. Even in middle age, she was beautiful. Her cheekbones had a sharp, sculpted quality that would last all her life. Her eyes were tilted ever so slightly at the corners, like Elandra's. Their color was exotic, compelling. Her thick lashes swept down and up as her gaze locked again on Elandra.

"So it is to be like that," she said.

"Yes," Elandra said flatly. "It is to be like that."

Iaris frowned. "I tried to speak to you earlier. You refused me. Now we must talk."

"It can wait until morning."

"No, this privacy is better."

"I need my rest," Elandra said.

"You owe me this audience," Iaris told her.

Elandra shot her an angry look and raised her brows. She said nothing, but Iaris refused to be stared down.

"I am Lady Pier," she said harshly. "You owe me audience."

Surprised, Elandra studied her for a moment; then she gestured at the nearby chairs.

They sat in the gloom, facing each other like civilized ladies, but there was something unreal about the hour of night, the quiet in the room, the utter privacy. Elandra wondered if her guards at the door had gone to sleep, to allow Iaris her surreptitious entry. Could anyone come and go as they pleased in this palace? It did not used to be so.

She held her knife openly in her lap, and Iaris pretended not to notice it.

Silence stretched between them. Elandra was the one who broke it.

"You have my leave to speak," she said.

Iaris glared at her, obviously resenting Elandra's superior position, but she wasted no more time. Leaning forward with her hands clamped on the arms of her chair, she said, "What manner of man have you brought to Gialta? What is he?"

"He is the future of the empire," Elandra replied coolly. For a moment it was almost amusing. Being questioned separately by her parents about the man she had chosen. Did they expect her to grieve publicly for Kostimon? Did they expect her to drape herself in the veil of widowhood and hide for a year of official mourning?

She would not do it. Kostimon had been her husband in name only. Now she belonged body and soul to Caelan. She would make no pretense of it. She would not act the hypocrite.

"The future of the empire," Iaris repeated with a disdainful smile. "A very grand endorsement, but a vague one at best."

Elandra was tired. This had been a long day of shocks and worry. Her emotions had been pulled in all directions since her arrival, and she was very worried about Caelan's disappearance. She had no patience for games and verbal sparring. She wanted to end this interview quickly.

"Caelan is a king," she said, "from a land you do not know. A land where Choven—"

"Those creatures!" Iaris said scornfully.

Elandra met her eyes, understanding that Iaris used her pride to shield her ignorance. "Caelan is both man and Choven, his lineage both of this world and of the spirit. His destiny is that he will break the world. There is more, but I will not tell you all."

"These words are fanciful indeed," Iaris said. "Who could believe such stories?"

"You asked a question. I have answered it."

Iaris frowned. "Will you now state the truth?"

Elandra said nothing.

Iaris's frown deepened. "This is ridiculous. Pier says he is nothing but a gladiator, a former slave who was bought at auction by Prince Tirhin."

"Lord Pier should be grateful for what Caelan did for him today."

"Nonsense! That humiliation—"

"He saved Pier from the darkness."

Iaris gestured this away, plainly not believing anything Elandra said. "This Caelan is no one, an upstart with ambitions who has bewitched you. Oh, I am sure it is his excellent body which attracts you. He is handsome, in a brutish way. But why do you make yourself a spectacle by consorting openly with this barbarian? Can you not play with him in private and stop trying to proclaim him the next emperor?"

Elandra's hand tightened on her knife hilt. "I have not seen you since I was four. Prior to the day you cast me out, you were a stranger who came but occasionally to look at me and see if I thrived. You did not even suckle me at your breast, and I understand that at my birth you cried in relief that I was finally gone from your womb. Based on this, I do not accept advice from you. I do not hear your words. I grant you no right to offer them."

Iaris rose to her feet. "Stop playing the wounded heroine," she said scathingly. "You were not hurt. You grew up to become empress of the land. You have fulfilled your destiny. You have prospered. There are no complaints you can offer."

"I am not complaining," Elandra said through her teeth. "I know that your affair with my father came against your will, that the Penestricans forced your union so I could be born."

With widened eyes, Iaris stared at her.

"Yes," Elandra said, her tone flat and unyielding. "I also know that Albain loved you—"

"Men are such fools," Iaris said with a dismissive gesture. "He mistook a spell for his own emotions."

Anger crawled through Elandra's veins, but she concealed it. More than anything she would have liked to shout at her mother, to accuse her and shame her into even a slight amount of contrition or regret, but she restrained herself. She could not judge her mother. She had not stood in her mother's exact circumstances, but she had been married against her will to a man old enough to be her father, a man who was a stranger, a man who never loved her. To that extent, at least, she knew what it must be like to have others meddle with your emotions, meddle with your life. She could understand her mother's resentment and coldness. What humiliation had her mother faced in explaining her pregnancy to her returning husband?

Lord Pier, the man who had picked a fight with Caelan today, and lost.

Elandra gazed up at her mother, saw the tight clamp of her lips, saw old battles still raging in her eyes.

"Albain still loves you," Elandra said. "He will love you to the grave."

Iaris was pacing back and forth behind her chair. She thumped the back of it with her fist. "That won't be long."

Elandra shot to her feet. "You are wrong. He recovers."

"Impossible."

"When he calls this court to heel, you will see it is not impossible."

Iaris frowned at her. "Albain is finished. Everyone but you accepts that."

"My father will live. Already he—"

"Don't delude yourself! Gialta looks to new leadership even as the empire prepares to accept a new emperor. Albain has held back this province long enough, but that is over."

"My father will not support Tirhin on the throne," Elandra said furiously. "Nor do I."

Iaris laughed scornfully. "Do you expect the warlords to support your claim? They will not do it. Nor do you have Albain to make them do it."

Frustration filled Elandra. "Tirhin betrayed the empire. Can your husband not see that? Or doesn't he care?"

"Pier cares about avoiding a bloodbath," Iaris said through her teeth. "He plans to give his oath of fealty to the new emperor."

"Tirhin is a traitor!"

"Turn red in the face and make fists at me like a spoiled child if you wish," Iaris said scornfully. "Your throne and your privileges have been swept away. That is what you cannot forgive. But your time is over, daughter. Whatever the Penestricans meant to accomplish with you did not come to pass. We face a new age, and a new emperor who is bold enough to take what he wants. Pier respects that, as do I. As do others. Don't start a civil war, Elandra. You and your pet gladiator have no chance of winning."

Elandra met her mother's eyes, and it was like staring at a wall. She knew further argument was futile.

"Are you finished?" she asked through lips that felt like wood.

"Yes, I think I have said enough." Iaris drew up her robes and walked to the door. She paused and glanced back as though she meant to say something else, but then did not.

As soon as the door closed behind her, Elandra threw the knife. It thunked deep into the wood panel of the door and quivered there.

A guard peered inside, his gaze widening as he saw the knife sticking out of the door. "Is everything well, Majesty?"

"Why did you admit that woman without my permission?" Elandra asked him.

The man's eyes went blank. "Admit who, Majesty?"

Elandra frowned, and she knew then that the Gialtan balance of power was shifting into different hands. Even the guards' loyalties were going to Lord Pier, who as the second most powerful warlord in the province after Albain was poised to seize the reins of leadership. If Pier convinced the other warlords to accept Tirhin, then Elandra's reign would be over before it began.

She pulled her knife from the door and held it a moment,

thinking hard. There had been something strange about Iaris's visit, something almost triumphant.

If Albain recovered, he would not let Pier support the new emperor. There would be no shift of power, no redistribution of the Albain estates. That meant Albain's rivals could not allow him to get well.

Fear spiked through Elandra. She must have cried out, for the guard looked at her worriedly.

"Is something wrong, Majesty? Are you unwell?"

She sent him a wild look. "Am I permitted to leave my apartments?"

His frown deepened, and he exchanged a wary look with the other guard. Neither of them were known to her. Alti and Sumal were off duty, and she realized how truly alone she was right now.

"Answer me!" she said sharply. "Am I permitted to leave?"

"Of course, Majesty," the guard said with a bow. "But if you are unwell, perhaps it is better if you do not wander the corridors."

The answer hidden in his unctuous words was clear. She felt her face go smooth and blank.

"Thank you," she said. "I will retire now. See that there are no more disturbances. I may wish to sleep late into the morning."

"Yes, Majesty."

He bowed low, and she slammed the door. Whirling around, she felt frantic and unable to think for a moment.

It would be so easy to put a pillow over Albain's face and finish him.

Fear gripped her, making her gasp for breath. She donned clothing and slippers hastily, then took her knife and the lamp and slipped through the servant's door.

Here, in the cobwebbed passageways known only to those who scrubbed, fetched, and carried, Elandra sped on her way. She knew these passages as well as anyone in the palace. She had grown up in them, working hard to avoid whippings, wearing rags whenever her father was away. She knew all the shortcuts.

As she ran she berated herself for having left her father. Why had she not realized the danger? She was not thinking, not being sharp enough. Kostimon would have scolded her for her mistakes.

"Strategy," she seemed to hear his voice saying in her ears as she hurried faster. "Always know your enemy and where he will jump next. Always know where you will go after that. Be ready. Outsmart your opponent."

She climbed a tight spiral of stairs, hoping that Iaris's visit had been to gloat, to anticipate what was to come and not what had already happened. *Let me get there first,* Elandra prayed.

More stairs, another long passageway. She passed an alcove where servants on night duty dozed on stools beneath bells attached to various bedchambers. There was no time to be cautious, but her slippers made little sound, and no one woke up.

She hesitated at a fork, then took the right passage, climbing up an uneven series of steps to a short hallway. There was the valet's nook. He lay asleep on his cot, his tunic folded neatly on its stool. She slipped past and eased open the door into her father's bedchamber.

Her lamp sent a feeble ray of light into the room, pushing back the shadows that surrounded the bed. The *jinja* raised up on its silk cushion and stared at her, but did not protest.

Albain slept, undisturbed.

Elandra's relief was intense, rolling over her in a wave that nearly pushed her to her knees. She closed the narrow door behind her without a sound, breathing hard through her mouth, and felt herself tremble with delayed reaction.

Only now was she aware of how much her side ached from running. Her hands were shaking. She put down the lamp, afraid she might drop it.

All was well. Her fears had been groundless. How foolish she was, dreaming up night terrors.

Then the *jinja* glanced at the door. Elandra looked that way too, listening.

She heard the soft murmurs of hushed voices in the antechamber, furtive footsteps, and the incautious sound of a dagger drawn too hastily.

Fear clamped around her throat, and she longed intensely for Caelan. Why had he deserted her like this? What was the good of saving her father, if he was not going to stand and protect him?

She knew she was being harsh and irrational, but she needed

something to build up her courage. In a moment they would be coming through the door.

Crossing the room, she took down a sword. It was incredibly heavy, and she nearly dropped it. Lugging it with both hands, she carried it over to the bed and slid the hilt next to her father's hand.

She shook his shoulder, hating to wake him but knowing she had no choice. "Father," she said, her voice soft but insistent. "Father, wake up."

He frowned and snorted, his eyes dragging half open. "Wha—"

A rattle of the door latch brought the *jinja* off its cushion. Ears erect and spitting, it jumped onto Albain's bed. "Danger," it said. "Danger!"

Elandra ran back to the weapons display and dragged down another sword. It was of a different era from the first, not as heavy. She returned to her father's side and shook him again.

"Wake up!" she whispered. "Assassins come for you."

He coughed and rubbed his face, making groggy sounds. She gripped his shoulder hard in warning, and his good eye snapped open. He looked first at Elandra, standing at his side with a sword in her hand, then at his *jinja* crouched on the foot of his bed with teeth bared.

Sitting up with a wince, he gripped the sword lying beside him just as the door flew open and four men came rushing inside.

In a glance, Elandra saw that none were warlords. Their insignias had been torn from their surcoats to conceal the identity of their cowardly masters.

Rage swelled inside her. "Stop there!" she commanded.

The men faltered within two steps, for whatever they had expected, it obviously was not Elandra and her father side by side, armed with swords and ready for them.

The *jinja* squealed loudly and began to jump up and down on the bed. "Danger! Danger! Danger!"

Albain's face turned scarlet with rage. Brandishing his sword, he yelled, "What in Murdeth's name are you doing in my chamber? Bandits and thieves, the lot of you!"

His free hand swept past Elandra and seized one of the fist-sized stones rowed up on the bedside table. He hurled it up at the large bronze bell hanging over his bed. A mighty gong reverberated through the chamber.

Panic filled the men's faces. They turned as one and battled at the door, all of them trying to go through it at the same time.

"Damned assassins!" Puffing, Albain flung off the bedcovers and went staggering after them in his sleeping shirt.

"Father, wait!" Elandra said in alarm. "Don't chase them. Father!"

Albain ignored her, busy jabbing one of the men in the buttocks with the tip of his sword.

The valet came running in, his hair askew and his eyes bugging out. He set up a shout while the *jinja* went on shrieking at the top of its lungs. Elandra followed her father, terrified that the assassins might yet turn on him.

The guards lay slumped on the floor, drugged or dead. Albain stumbled over them and stood roaring in the corridor while more guards came running.

"Catch those men! Stop them!" he shouted.

The guards ran in pursuit, their feet pounding over the carpets. Courtiers in night clothes appeared, only to stare in astonishment. An alarm bell began ringing belatedly, rousing the entire palace.

Albain wheezed for breath and swayed.

Alarmed, Elandra threw down her sword and steadied him. "Careful, Father. No more shouting. Catch your breath first."

His arm went around her and he leaned hard against her, his weight making her stagger. "Damnation," he swore softly. "Don't squeeze me so hard. My ribs feel like they've been kicked by a mule."

She had the sudden urge to laugh. He was alive, as ill-tempered and loud as ever, and everyone was staring at him as though he were a ghost.

Albain seemed to finally notice the stares and frozen stances of the courtiers. He glared at them and hefted his sword with an angry growl in his throat. "What in blazes are you staring at?" he demanded. "Where's the officer on duty? Where's my own squire? Who the devil chose the guard roster tonight?"

Chaos broke out anew as everyone started talking to each

other and pointing. More guards came running up, along with a pale-faced young captain. A moment later General Handar himself appeared.

He stepped forward and saluted, his eyes round and astonished. "My lord!" he said, sounding out of breath.

"Handar, report! Were those men captured, or are they out setting fire to the stables by now?"

Albain's acerbic tone darkened Handar's cheeks. He stood stiffly at attention, looking like a subaltern getting his first dressing down. "Captured, my lord."

"Hmpf." Albain coughed and glared with his one eye. Without warning he turned on his squire. "Be useful! Bring me that chair."

"Yes, my lord."

The young man dragged over the chair, and Albain lowered himself heavily into it with a grunt. Only then did he seem to be aware of his thin linen sleeping shirt and bare feet.

His face turned scarlet, and he gestured with his sword. "Captain!"

"My lord?"

"Clear the hall of these women! I'm not a spectacle for them to gawk at!"

One of the women tittered loudly, and there was a sudden flurry as people retreated.

Albain's face stayed red. "What in blazes is the matter with this household, letting everything fall to ruin the moment my attention is elsewhere?"

Handar swallowed. He was still staring at Albain as though he couldn't believe his eyes. "My lord," he said respectfully, "you were dying."

"Yes, I was, damn it!" Albain shouted at him. He paused to catch his breath, then continued. "And someone came tonight to help me along, since I was obviously taking too long. Heads will roll for this, I promise you."

"Yes, my lord."

"Question those men. Use any torture you like, but get answers. I want to know who paid them, the blackguard."

"Yes, my lord."

"And get some order established. Who the devil are all these people? Am I housing the entire population of Gialta?"

"Mostly, my lord."

"Vultures," Albain muttered.

But at least two of the warlords were venturing closer now. Neither of them was Lord Pier, Elandra noticed with scorn.

"Albain," one of them said. "This is truly a miracle. You're alive."

"Eh? Of course I'm alive. Why shouldn't I be?" He scowled at the man. "What are you doing in my house, Humaul?"

The warlord opened his eyes very wide. "I came for a council of war. There was your successor to choose, and a decision has to be made about the new emperor."

"Emperor?" Albain barked, turning red again. "The emperor's dead, man."

"Prince Tirhin is ready to take his place."

"Father," Elandra said in quiet warning, observing the sheen of perspiration on her father's brow. He was doing too much, growing too tired.

Albain shifted in his chair, grunting at her without looking around. "Tirhin is a fop, a puppy," he said, then grimaced. "All right, a council of war. But not tonight. A man should be able to sleep in his own bed without fear of cutthroats bursting in. Handar, I want this place in order come morning. Is that clear?"

"Yes, my lord."

"And I'm going back to bed. I'm too old for such excitement in the middle of the night. I need my rest. My ribs hurt like the very hell. You, help me get up."

The captain of the guard obliged, and supported Albain back down the hall into his apartments. As Albain sank onto his bed, wheezing and grunting, the captain saluted smartly, wheeled around, and marched out.

Elandra heard the man issuing a string of orders before he reached the outer doors, and footsteps thundered up and down the corridor.

There was the *jinja* to be soothed, the swords to be put away, the bedclothes smoothed, pillows plumped, the valet to be reassured, her father to be quieted.

"I'm hungry," Albain complained as Elandra pulled the coverlet over him and tucked in the edges. "My stomach's flapping against my backbone. Have the kitchen send up a haunch of roasted gazelle. Cold meat will do."

"Hush," Elandra said, mopping perspiration from his face. She nodded at the valet, who left to fetch some food. "You must lie quiet and rest now. You've done enough."

Albain grunted, clearly enjoying the fuss.

Servants kept peeking in at him, only to whisk out of sight the moment he or Elandra looked their way.

"Will they stop doing that?" Albain complained. "Throw my boot at the next one who—"

A fit of coughing interrupted him. When it was over, he lay spent on his pillows.

Worriedly, Elandra listened to his lungs. They sounded clear, but he needed to conserve his strength.

"Be still," she said in growing exasperation. "I'll get you some broth—"

"Broth! Gault's breath, I don't want broth!"

"Then you won't have anything," she shot back at him while the valet nervously brought in a tray containing soft bread, a bowl of steaming soup, and boiled eggs. "Be reasonable, sir, and let me take proper care of you."

He scowled. "I won't be coddled and unmanned by a bunch of women and servants. I want meat, not broth. Do you hear?"

"I imagine the whole palace can hear," she said dryly. "When you're done shouting, perhaps you'll remember that a few hours ago you were trying to breathe your last. You might also realize that your ribs wouldn't hurt so much if you'd just calm down."

He snapped his mouth shut and glared at her so ferociously she was tempted to kiss his cheek. Instead, however, she gestured for the valet to put the food tray on the table. She began cutting up one of the eggs.

It wasn't until she popped a piece into her mouth that Albain blinked.

"Elandra!" he said in consternation. "You aren't going to eat my dinner right in front of me, are you?"

"You don't want it."

His scowl came back. "Unnatural girl—"

"I learned from you." Smiling, she held out a piece of the egg.

After a moment, his expression softened, and he took it. He ate everything on the tray, and drank two goblets of water, complaining all the time that he wanted wine.

"No wine so soon after a fever," Elandra said firmly as the tray was removed.

She smoothed the coverlet again, whisking away a few crumbs, and Albain caught her hand.

"Daughter," he said gruffly.

She paused, meeting his gaze.

"How did you know to wake me? How did you know about the assassins?"

She frowned, not wanting to hurt him. "We'll discuss it in the morning."

"No, we'll discuss it now."

"Father, you're tired."

"Don't evade me, Elandra!" he said sharply. "What do you know about this?"

"I have only suspicions, no proof."

"You had something, enough to come and save my life."

Elandra bit her lip, but his eye was relentless. It bored into her, refusing to let her escape an explanation.

"Speak up. No lies!"

"Very well. Lady Iaris came to my rooms tonight."

His expression grew blank. He dropped her hand. "Iaris."

Elandra nodded. "She had questions about Caelan, who he was, where he came from. But I sensed another purpose in her."

"What else did she ask?"

Albain's voice was quiet now, perhaps too calm. His face gave nothing away.

"She and Lord Pier intend to sway the council in Tirhin's favor. They don't want me or Caelan upsetting the new balance of power. Lord Demahaud is counting on inheriting your estates, and Lord Pier wants your rank and influence."

"Go on."

"You stand in their way if you oppose Tirhin and support me. They despise Caelan completely because of his past."

Albain said nothing, but simply scowled in the distance, deep in thought.

Elandra rubbed her face wearily. Most of the night was gone. She felt wrung out and restless, too tired to sleep now.

Albain sighed at last. "Politics are a damned nuisance. I'd rather have a simple war any day."

Despite herself, she gave him a wan smile and kissed his cheek.

"I'll dig into the rest of it later," Albain said, yawning. "Don't look so worried, child. Your mother can't hurt me. The only thing between us is you, and that we dealt with a long time ago."

"The Penestricans told me the truth," Elandra said softly. "About you and her."

Startled, he met her gaze, and sadness filled his eye. "I'm sorry," he said after a moment. "I never meant you to know that."

"Thank you," she said. "I wish I did not know it either. But in a way it prepared me for this meeting with her. She would have hurt me had I not known. Truth is better than one's dreams and imaginings."

Albain gripped her hand hard. "I wish to Gault you were a boy. I would set you on the throne myself."

That, unlike everything else, did hurt her. It hurt her deeply.

She stared at him a moment, then bent her head and rose swiftly to her feet.

"Elandra," he said.

"I must go."

"Elandra, wait."

He said it as a command.

She stopped unwillingly, her back to him to hide the tears swimming in her eyes.

"It was a stupid thing to say. I retract it," he said to her earnestly. "I'm sorry. I owe you better than an old man's outdated way of thinking."

"Everyone else thinks the same way," she said, struggling to keep her voice light. "It doesn't matter."

"It does matter. It should matter. Kostimon could see farther than that. He gave you a chance. And I promised you my army."

She turned on him, not caring now if he saw her tears. "But can you hold your own warlords?" she asked. "They scheme and intrigue and throw spells the *jinjas* do not sense. We are slipping from the light into darkness, and every man is running to grab what he can."

"The man you brought with you," Albain said wearily. "Where is he? Why did he not help you tonight?"

Her fears came boiling up, uncontrollable. She gripped her hands together and tried to keep her lips from trembling. "I don't know where he is."

"What?"

"I don't know! He is gone. Vanished without a trace. And I fear for him. I—"

"But you must explain this. He came to me, did he not?" Albain hesitated, looking unsure. "He healed me."

She nodded, crying openly now, unable to stop herself.

"I saw him," Albain said slowly, "as though in a dream. He was tall and well muscled. Manly. Tanned as dark as a laborer, with hair like gold."

"Yes."

"He held me, and the pain left. He spoke to spirits, who came and gave me strength again."

She pressed her hands to her face. "His father was a healer, Beva E'non of Trau."

"Traulanders have a gift that way."

"His father died several years ago. It was his spirit Caelan sought to help you."

Albain stared at her, looking awed. "He can enter the spirit world? Death was carrying me there, but do you mean this Caelan can enter of his own will? Can he return?"

There it was, her fear articulated now and brought into the open. She raised brimming eyes to her father and shrugged. "I do not know. I thought he could. From things he has told me, he has gone there before. He can do so much other men cannot. He—" She stopped and swallowed, trying to compose herself. "But he is gone. I fear he cannot return, and that he has given himself wholly to save you."

Albain held out his arms. "My poor child."

She ran to him, hugging him tight and weeping against his chest. "I made him do it," she confessed, sobbing bitterly. "He was afraid, and I begged him. I didn't listen. All I wanted was to save you. And now he is gone. He is lost. It is all my fault."

Chapter Twenty-Two

THE RAINS CONTINUED the following day. It was winter, the time of monsoons, when the laborers worked hour after hour to channel the river away from villages and planted fields. The river, swollen and threatening to rage out of control, coughed up Caelan from its muddy depths shortly after midday.

One of the laborers who was pulling logs from the water with grappling hooks and the help of an elephant found him floating unconscious in the water.

This man, streaked with mud and clad in nothing but a loin-cloth and turban, came running to the gates of the palace and shouted for admittance.

In the council room, Lord Albain, wearing mail and a face as grim as war itself, presided at the head of the table. Elandra, gowned regally, sat erect and silent at his side like the queen she was. She had said nothing all morning while the men argued, hurling accusations and denials. Now and then her gaze moved to the face of Lord Pier, looking pale and drawn after his adventures the day before.

Agreeing to speak under truth-light, Pier had explained his actions to Albain. He made no excuses, no justifications. His report spared neither himself nor the others. It was as though his encounter with dark magic had shaken him. But while he had sought to make trouble yesterday against Caelan, whom he still considered an upstart piece of arena trash, he was not behind the plot to kill Albain in his bed.

The four assassins had confessed at dawn and were already hanged. They were employed by the governor, Lord Demahaud, who was now sitting in the dungeons, an agent of the empire no longer.

Albain had scant interest in what he considered a minor attempt on his life. Once more he pulled the discussion back to the emperor's successor.

Lord Pier rose to his feet. "I support crowning Tirhin. Despite the initial chaos, he succeeded in pulling together a fighting force, and he has driven the Madruns from Imperia."

"Yes, to set them loose on the other provinces," a man piped up on Elandra's left. "My lands border Ulinia, you know. I am responsible for protecting half that province. And the Madruns will cross my personal estates before they get this far."

"They will not get here," Albain said with a growl. "My dispatches say that the Lord Commander has deployed three legions to cut them off."

Men pounded the table in approval, and several shouted in satisfaction.

Pier, however, was still standing. "All the more reason to send our delegation to Tirhin and proclaim him emperor quickly. The empire needs order restored. This will do it before we have more invaders on our hands."

"Don't forget who brought the Madruns here in the first place," the small man who had spoken before said. "He let them sack Imperia."

"Renar, hold your tongue," Pier said sharply. "You don't know that is true—"

"*I* know it is true," Elandra said.

Pier scowled fiercely at her, and several more men jumped to their feet.

"These interruptions cannot be permitted, Albain!" one roared. "The council room is no place for a woman."

"Silence!" Albain shouted, his voice louder than any of the others. "Whether you like it or not, she has the right to speak."

"A woman—"

"In her official capacity, she is *not* a woman. She is sovereign crowned, and she remains so until Tirhin's coronation. If that should even come to pass."

"It must!" Pier said.

"Why?" Albain retorted. "Because you have been promised new lands if you will join his cause?"

Red darkened Pier's cheeks. "Have you not annexed property since your daughter went to the imperial palace? It is to your personal advantage to keep her there."

Silence fell over the room. Elandra's face was burning. She gripped her hands together in her lap and forced herself not to move. It took all her strength to keep her face impassive.

Albain did not rise to his feet. From his chair he glared at Pier, who did not back down. The men watched intently to see what Albain might do. He had been known to issue a combat challenge on less provocation.

"Yes," Albain said at last, his voice heavy. "It is to my advantage that my daughter keep her throne. It is to the advantage of all Gialta. Is she not more likely to favor her home province than Tirhin? Blood ties are stronger than promises."

"We have seen no advantage thus far," Renar piped up.

"That was Kostimon's doing. When the empress fled Imperia, to whom did she come to raise an army? Us! Not the—"

A knock on the door interrupted him.

"Yes?" Albain called, glowering. He took advantage of the interruption, however, to press his hand to his side and lean forward carefully to pick up his wine cup.

Elandra watched him in concern and said nothing. She had promised him she would stay silent, and she was trying to keep her word despite that one slip. More than once her fists had clenched in her lap, and her anger had nearly driven her to reprimand those who were foolish, ignorant, or wrongly informed. She had been in Imperia. She was a direct witness to the events and the terror. She had been the last person present to see Kostimon alive. Yet these men would not question her. They ignored the information she could have provided.

She sat there, seething, and hated them all.

A guard entered the room and saluted smartly. "The man has been found, my lord."

"What?" Albain asked. "What man?"

But Elandra was already on her feet, her heart in her mouth. She rushed around the table and went out the door, leaving the guard to follow her.

Out in the corridor, she looked around wildly.

The guard bowed and pointed. "This way, Majesty."

She followed him, with Alti and Sumal trotting at her heels. They were not permitted in the council room, but after last night they had come to her with deep shame and apologies, vowing they would not leave her side again.

Outside, the rains had stopped. Puddles steamed in the humid courtyard. A laborer, muddy and practically naked, stood there ringed by soldiers. His elephant held an unconscious man in its mouth.

Elandra recognized Caelan at once. She stopped in her tracks with a gasp.

The captain of the guard took one look at her face and issued orders. The elephant slowly lowered Caelan to the ground.

"They pulled him from the river, Majesty," the captain said.

Elandra kept her distance. Her heart was pounding. She felt as though she might faint, but stiffened her knees and held on.

A voice, too strange and hollow to be her own, asked, "Is he dead or alive?"

Someone knelt and touched Caelan's throat. "Alive, Majesty."

Her ears were roaring. She felt as though ground and sky were trying to turn upside down. Somehow, however, she fought off her dizziness. She dared not move, dared not kneel beside him to wipe the mud and slimy weeds from his face. She feared if she did anything, the bands of her self-control would burst and she would fling herself, howling, across his chest.

She made a small gesture. "Take him inside quickly. See that he is cared for. And reward this man well."

The laborer bent double in his gratitude. Elandra turned away, following the men who struggled to carry Caelan up the steps into the palace. She felt as though she were floating, as though her head had sailed far above the rest of her body. With every step, a corner of her mind chanted, *He is alive. He is alive.*

What he had been doing in the river was something to determine later, if it mattered. He was alive. He had come back. The pain in her heart could leave her now, and she lived again.

Inside the palace, she summoned servants and issued orders. Her father's own valet, understanding exactly what his master owed Caelan, came and washed him personally, dressed him in a sleeping shirt, and tried to revive him with various remedies that Elandra inspected herself.

He seemed unharmed. No bruises or cuts marred his skin. His breathing was even. No fever raged in his body.

But he would not awaken, no matter what they did. Finally, Elandra sent everyone away and settled herself at his side. She held his strong hand in hers, tracing her fingertips over his knuckles and the taut veins in the back of his hand, needing the contact of her skin against his, her flesh to his.

"Please come back to me," she whispered to him. "I need you so. Please come back."

Eventually a soft argument outside the door caught her attention. She straightened just as the door eased open.

Alti looked inside. "Your pardon, Majesty. A visitor has come."

Expecting her father, she smiled. But when Iaris walked in, the smile dropped from Elandra's lips.

Her mother carried a small stone flask in her hands. Ignoring the hostility in Elandra's gaze, she walked up to the bedside and put the flask on the small table. Then she stood, gazing down at Caelan. Her eyes, as usual, were unreadable.

"So this is the man who replaces your husband."

Elandra's face grew hot. "This *is* my husband."

Iaris's brows shot up. "I see."

Her voice held censure and contempt, but Elandra met her gaze without shame. It was Iaris who looked away first.

"You make a scandal," she said.

"Kostimon is dead," Elandra replied. "Now I make my own choices."

"You want the throne. That binds you to the place of a widow."

"I *have* the throne," Elandra said angrily.

Iaris's eyes flashed. "Do not deceive yourself. In name only, if that. No matter how much your father yells and blusters, the men of Gialta are proud. They will not follow a woman to war."

Elandra rose to her feet and pointed at Caelan. "They will follow a warrior. They will follow him."

"A slave? My dear, hardly."

"I told you he is a king."

Iaris smiled, but it was not kindly. "You live in dreams."

"And you judge like one blind. Did Pier's men try to drown Caelan in the river?"

"No."

"I hope you speak the truth," Elandra said fiercely. "You do not want to become my enemy."

Her mother looked at her harshly, then turned on her heel and left the room.

Elandra frowned after her a moment, then picked up the flask and unstoppered it. She sniffed cautiously at the stopper, and wrinkled her nose. Suspicious, she closed the flask and threw it out the window.

A moment later, Caelan opened his eyes. They were deeply, intensely blue, and they looked at her without recognition.

She smiled at him, gripping his hand. "Hello, beloved."

He frowned, gazing around before his eyes returned to hers. "Hello." He sounded very tired.

"What were you doing in the river?" she asked with a little catch in her voice.

"River?" His frown deepened. "I had to swim."

"I see." She smiled, pretending that his incoherence didn't frighten her.

"I had to go under and not come up. I don't remember why."

"It's all right now. You're back. You're safe."

The puzzlement in his eyes faded. He smiled at her. "Elandra."

She smiled back. "Yes. You know me now. Are you hungry?"

He shook his head. "He can't hurt me."

"Who?"

"He can't. I was so afraid of him, but he is only memory."

"You're not making much sense, you know."

He smiled again. "It is strange to be here. You look tired. Has something happened? Your father?"

He tried to sit up, but she pressed him back. "Father is much better. Practically well, and he won't stay in bed. Everyone is afraid of him because he recovered so suddenly. They think he is enspelled." The lilt in her voice dropped, and she pressed her lips to Caelan's hand. "Thank you," she whispered brokenly. "I know it cost you too much. But thank you."

He stroked her hair and didn't answer. Whatever had worried him before seemed gone. There was something dreamy and far away in his eyes, an unconcern that worried her anew. He ate a little under her persuasion; then his eyes closed.

She watched him sleep, watched rest restore color to his face and take away the purple smudges beneath his eyes. She could never tire of looking at him. She wanted to memorize every line and feature of his face, for last night she had lain awake, unable to bring him into her mind. It had frightened her, not to be able to recall him with more clarity. She did not want that to happen to her again.

Alti knocked on the door. She went to it and looked out at the guard.

"Lord Albain, Majesty," he whispered. "He has sent for you."

"Is he still at council?" she whispered back.

"Yes, Majesty."

She glanced over her shoulder and saw that their voices had awakened Caelan. He sat up, running his hands through his long hair, and she sighed.

"Let my father know I will come shortly."

"Yes, Majesty."

She closed the door and faced Caelan. "I'm sorry."

He flexed his shoulders, stretching until his rib cage arched above the concave ribbing of his stomach. Her own body grew warm, wanting him. But not with her father waiting for her.

Fighting for breath, she said, "Do you feel well enough to face him?"

"Albain?"

"Yes."

An insolent grin slowly spread across his face. He knew what she had been thinking, and that knowledge in his eyes made her blush.

"Caelan, no," she said shyly. "Not now."

"Come here."

She went to him, loving the circle of his arms. If only they were free, if only they had just themselves, then she could stay in his arms all she wanted.

He kissed her long and deeply, robbing her of breath and thought, melting her to her very bones. When she finally came up for air, her mind was buzzing and foolish. She clung to him and barely managed to say, "Stop. My father is waiting."

"Your father," Caelan said with regret.

She pulled free of his grasp, and he sighed. "It's time we met, I suppose."

"Yes, it is."

He shrugged. "Send our regrets, and let us think only of ourselves."

"Certainly not," she said primly, although an inner spirit of rebellion longed to do exactly as Caelan urged. "Here is clothing. Please hurry."

He groaned and stood up. "The efficient woman."

"Hurry," she told him, refusing to relent.

When she bent over to pick up a garment, Caelan grabbed her from behind and spun her around. "You could say I have a raging fever."

Laughing, she had to fight her way free. She pushed the tunic into his hands to keep them occupied and backed out of reach. "I will not," she said, still battling to keep a smile off her face. "They are waiting—"

"Who is waiting?"

"The entire war council."

He pulled on the linen tunic and held up the mail shirt. "What is this?"

"Armor."

"Not likely."

"Now who is more closed-minded, the Gialtans or you?" she teased him. "You can wear protection without looking like a turtle."

He frowned. "A what?"

"A turtle. A creature that lives in a shell. This gives you more freedom of movement. It is more modern."

Caelan pulled it on and moved his arms experimentally. "It's too tight."

"On you, everything is too tight," she said, handing him a sur-coat of dark green. "It will do for today. You can discuss a better fit with the armorer later."

The leggings and boots fit him well enough. The surcoat hung to his knees, and made him look even taller and more imposing than before. He buckled on his sword belt, swept back his hair with both hands, and faced her.

"Will you do the inspection, Majesty?"

"You are beautiful."

Amusement lit his face. "Exactly the quality most likely to impress a room filled with hostile warlords."

Her eyes grew troubled. "Oh, they are very hostile indeed. You must take great care. I have told them you are a king, but—"

"A king!" he said in consternation. "No, Elandra, why?"

"So they will accept you."

"Do they?" There was a world of bitterness in his voice.

She gripped his hand. "But it's true. You wear the sword of a king. Your destiny—"

"No, Elandra," he said with more firmness than before. "These are not things to speak of."

"But—"

He lifted his hand to silence her. He was frowning now, all the fun erased from his face. "You must understand this," he said seri-ously. "I am not a king. The sword does not make me a king."

"But only kings can carry such—"

"Choven steel is the only metal that can fight darkness."

"That isn't true!" she protested. "I have seen you attack *shyrieas* with ordinary metal. You destroyed General Paz when he—"

"Demons and those who are possessed are one thing," he said, shaking his head. "But I am speaking of the darkness itself."

She spoke the syllable "Bel . . ." and Caelan held up his hand to silence her, then nodded. She drew back, drenched in fear. "No," she said. "No, Caelan!"

"Elandra—"

"No!" she shouted. "You're telling me that you went to the Choven for that sword, that you need it so you can fight— In the name of Gault, don't seek the dark god!"

"Please—"

"No, I refuse to listen to this. I won't allow it."

"You can't stop it."

"You said you wanted to rule. You said you wanted to be emperor, the two of us side by side."

"Yes, I said that," he agreed. "And I do. I have ever since I was joined with Kostimon and you in the ring of Choven fire. Kostimon's ambition touched me. It made me think there was a chance to rise from nothing."

"It *is* possible," she said. "Kostimon did it. I have done it. You can too."

He smiled at her ruefully. "My path of life leads elsewhere."

"Don't say that! You're tired, confused. You don't—"

"No, Elandra. Don't lie to yourself. I was created to fight. It's all I can do. It's all I know. Everything that has happened to me in my life was to shape me for what is to come."

"But you're mortal!" she cried. "You can't go in search of Beloth! You can't win. I have seen him. I know what he is—"

"Kostimon loosened his chains," Caelan said grimly. "He is breaking free."

She pressed her hand to her lips in an effort to hold back her sobs. "But what about us? Why have you let me think we were going back to Imperia to reclaim the throne? Why do you tell me now?"

"Because you must keep your throne," he said. "And I must fight what comes. We will both return to Imperia. I promise you that. But stop persuading these warlords to support me. Don't try to shape reality to your desires, Elandra. You will only get hurt."

Tears streamed down her face. She was losing him, losing him to death, and she could not bear that. Was there nothing she could say that would deflect him from this course?

"They will not follow me," she said.

"You will find a way."

"Caelan!"

He looked down at her, and his gaze was loving, sad, and implacable.

Suddenly she hated him. Sniffing, she said, "I wish you had

told me the truth before I gave my heart to you. Am I to have you, only to lose you?"

He stepped back, and something seemed to close in his face. "Do you think I will lose?"

"You think it," she said bitterly, refusing to let him shift blame onto her. "Why should I not believe as you do?"

He had no answer.

Angrily she wiped her face. "What will this self-sacrifice accomplish? Will it stop the dark god? Or will you be as a moth, flying toward the fire, burned to death before you can even strike a blow? It is glory, I suppose, but what else? What can you do?"

He shook his head, his expression bleak. "I shouldn't have told you. I meant to say nothing until it was time. I shouldn't have spoken of this now."

That hurt her more deeply than anything. She saw how little her words mattered, how little impact her feelings and opinions had. It had been the same with Kostimon and her father. Were all men like walls? Did they never consider the ones they left behind, the ones who had to cope with the aftermath?

She was not impressed. Caelan's death would not keep her warm at night. His death would not give her comfort during her days. She could not talk to a dead man. She could not love a dead man. He would have glory, and she would be alone. He would be gone, and she would go as spoils to the victor.

Silence filled the room. Wearing his granite face, Caelan went to stare out the window. Elandra poured a ewer of water into a basin and washed her face to remove all evidence of tears. Last night she had thought him lost to her forever. She had grieved and worried. Now he stood no farther away than across the room, and it was as though he had ceased to exist. She had lost him, would lose him. Whatever days or hours remained for them were already shadowed by the future.

She had never been so angry, or hurt.

"I am ready," she said in a small, cold voice. "Come."

Without waiting to see if he followed, she opened the door and stepped outside, walking away rapidly with her guards at her heels.

Chapter Twenty-Three

THE GUARDS OUTSIDE the council room threw open the double doors as she came striding up, her eyes snapping, her head high. She swept inside and found the men on their feet, chatting idly.

They had the air of having reached a decision. Their conversations faltered as they all turned to look at her.

Sunlight shone through the windows, rare at this time of year. She walked through it, and it struck fiery glints in her auburn hair and shimmered over the gown of gold silk that she wore. Her eyes were like fire, and when she met her father's gaze he frowned at her in inquiry.

Saying nothing, she went to stand beside him.

He bent his grizzled head to her. "Daughter?" he asked quietly.

"He's coming," she replied. Her voice was like glass, smooth and cool, giving nothing away.

Albain's frown deepened, but he did not press her further.

By then Caelan was coming in. He paused just inside the doorway and stood there in unconscious male magnificence. Dressed like a Gialtan warrior, he still looked foreign and exotic. His shoulders seemed to fill the doorway. His blue eyes were wary but assured.

The moment he appeared, the atmosphere changed. Every warlord present squared his shoulders, drew himself taller, let his hand fall with false idleness onto his sword hilt. No one had forgotten yesterday. The air felt male and violent.

Elandra sensed it, and her scorn grew. They might as well pound their chests and scream at each other. Or perhaps, like yesterday, they would go outside and fight. Men were such fools.

It was Albain who should have made the first move, but Pier

stepped forward to face Caelan. Almost of equal height, the two men eyed each other, their faces giving nothing away.

Elandra glanced at her father, curious to see how he tolerated Pier's actions. Albain was first warlord of Gialta; Pier was only second. Why must Pier constantly test Albain, constantly push?

"You enter this council room by permission, not by right," Pier said to Caelan. "Is that understood?"

"Yes."

Pier looked as though he would say something else; then he stepped aside.

Elandra glanced at her father again. His expression was as stony as Caelan's.

He stood where he was and let Caelan advance to him. Caelan's stride was like a panther's—graceful, lithe, hinting at explosive strength. In spite of herself, Elandra could feel her admiration returning. There was no welcome for him in this room, but he did not seem to care. She told herself that this was a man who had walked into arenas and been stared at by tens of thousands of people. This was a man who had impressed Emperor Kostimon. A few Gialtan warlords were no match for such experience.

They had all—except Albain—witnessed his tremendous strength and fighting prowess yesterday, although it was only a hint of what he could do. There was not a man present who did not envy him, who did not long to take him.

He stopped in front of Elandra and Albain. Not once did his gaze flicker to her.

Respectfully he bowed to the older man and waited for Albain to acknowledge him. He showed no impatience when Albain let the silence stretch out. Albain studied him openly, almost rudely. But if he thought to disconcert Caelan, he did not realize Caelan had learned to endure worse examinations on the auction block.

Caelan's indifference to the scrutiny was the best response he could have chosen, made better by the fact that it was natural and honest, not an attempt to impress Albain.

"So you are the man who saved my life," Albain said.

It was a public declaration of indebtedness. Elandra caught

her breath. Her father was moving quickly, showing his hand to them all.

"Thank you," Albain said.

"You are welcome," Caelan replied.

Albain grunted, still not looking impressed. "I understand you should also be thanked for saving the life of my daughter, the Empress Elandra."

"That was my duty," Caelan replied in the toneless way of a soldier. "I need no thanks for that."

A gasp went through the room, and even Elandra was startled. In that casual remark, Caelan had tossed away an incredible debt. Albain offered him everything in that admission—his wealth, his lands, his political support—and Caelan refused it.

Whether he wanted to be thought of as a king or not, he was acting like one. The gesture was a grand one, something most ordinary men would not have been able to make.

Albain's eyebrows shot up. He seemed nonplussed and glanced at Elandra with a shrug.

She said nothing. She was not going to help them.

"Very well," Albain said finally, clearing his throat. "Let us get to the point. The empress has asked me for an army and full support in overthrowing Tirhin's claim to the throne."

An angry buzz went through the room, but Albain ignored it. He went on, glaring at Caelan. "My warlords are opposed to civil war. They feel it is in the best interests of the empire as a whole to accept Tirhin's coup and allow him to be crowned. I will say that I think neither solution ideal."

Someone, probably Pier, snorted at that last remark.

Albain's scowl deepened. "The Madruns must be driven out and kept out. We may have to reduce our borders until the army is restructured. There are many problems in many areas. But what is most important is that we do not allow Kostimon's death to leave us in chaos much longer. Or we will have no empire to squabble about."

"We've been through that," Pier said impatiently. "We're all agreed on that point."

Albain ignored the interruption. His gaze never left Caelan's. "I have promised my army to the empress—"

"You have not promised mine!" Pier said furiously.

"Nor mine!" cried another man.

Albain held up his hand in an angry demand for silence; then his gaze returned to Caelan. "If you have any claims, make them now."

"Why should he?" Pier demanded, unable to keep quiet. "This Traulander is no—"

Caelan's head lifted. "I know Prince Tirhin well," he said to Albain. "I witnessed his plotting with the Madrun ambassador. I know he bribed and suborned officials and chancellors as well as army officers to look the other way as the barbarians were let across the border. He also—"

"Tirhin is not on trial here," Pier said.

Caelan turned on him so fiercely the warlord backed up a step. "If you will bend your knee to the man and call him your emperor, you had better try him!"

Silence fell over the room. Caelan scowled at each one of them in turn. "Try him to the depths of his soul before you give him your fealty oath and put him on the throne. Search out whether his allegiance is to the light or to the realm of shadow, for this world depends on the answer."

Several of the men frowned thoughtfully, but Pier's eyes had gone hot. "You accuse him of belonging to the shadows?"

Caelan never hesitated. "Yes. As you did, until yesterday."

Pier flushed scarlet, but his response was lost as the others started talking at once. Albain leaned over and pounded his fist on the table for quiet.

"Caelan," he said gruffly, "where do you place your allegiance?"

"I follow the empress."

His blue eyes were as clear and sure as an eagle's. Elandra looked at him and felt her own sting with tears. Hastily she restrained them. Her emotions clawed in her throat, and for the first time she was grateful for the customs that required her silence. At that moment she would not have trusted herself to speak. She still did not forgive him, but she realized she could not stop loving him either.

"Then enough of this yammering," Albain said. "You've all had your say. Now I will speak."

"You've already told us where your support lies," Pier interrupted. "That doesn't mean I—"

"Where is your oath?" Albain shouted. His face turned scarlet, and his single eye glared at the warlord. "Tell me! Where is your oath?"

Pier's mouth clamped so tight that the muscles bunched in his jaw. He glared back at Albain, resentment like flame in his eyes. "In your service," he said at last.

"Aye! Renar! Where is your oath?"

The smaller man's gaze fell. "In your service."

"And the rest of you?" Albain said, his voice hammering at them. "In my service. My decision stands for all of you. I would prefer you serve me willingly, but by the gods, I'll force each and every one of you if I must. Well? Will you now break your oaths of fealty to me? Do any of you dare?"

No one spoke; then Pier cleared his throat.

Beside her father, Elandra closed her eyes with dread. She did not want Pier to challenge her father for supremacy of the province. Not now, not when Albain was still not fully recovered.

"Well, Pier?" Albain said gruffly. He stood there like an aging bull, showing no fear. "Has the time come?"

An urgent knocking on the door interrupted them. The door opened without permission, in itself a grave breach of orders, and a captain appeared, saluting smartly.

Albain roared in fury and kicked over his chair. "What in blazes do you mean, coming in here like this? Get out! I'll have your rank for this, you fool!"

The captain turned white, but he didn't flinch. "My lord, I am sent by the general. You must come at once."

"The devil I will. Get out!"

"My lord." The captain swallowed hard. "My lord, the imperial army is outside our gates. You must come at once, or we fear they will break in."

"What?" Albain stared for a moment, then blinked and seemed to recover from his astonishment. "What the blazes are they doing here? They are supposed to be headed for Imperia!"

"The general says to tell you they are demanding the empress."

Silence gripped the room. Elandra felt as though she could not breathe. A smile spread across her face. "At last," she said in relief. "They have come to offer their support."

A fearsome scowl creased Albain's face. Ignoring Elandra, he went on glaring at the captain. "Is it true? Have they come to support her? Or arrest her?"

The captain's gaze darted to Elandra even as he shook his head. "I know not—"

"Bah!" Muttering curses, Albain headed for the door. Glancing at each other, the other warlords fell in behind him.

At the doorway, however, Albain paused and looked back at Caelan. "Protect her," he said. "Until we know where they stand, be prepared to get her out of sight."

Caelan nodded, but Elandra stepped forward. "What do you mean? What are you talking about?"

Albain swept on without answering, his expression very grim indeed.

Elandra turned on Caelan. "They would not dare arrest me!" she said indignantly, incensed by her father's assumption. "Father is too suspicious. The Lord Commander has come to give us his aid, and if Father angers him—"

"I have heard the talk," Caelan said, breaking in. "Remember what the Thyzarenes said about a reward for you?"

Elandra shook her head. "They would not dare!"

"No? And Kostimon thought that Tirhin would not dare betray him, either."

Elandra felt cold. Her hand stole to her throat. "Then we are finished," she whispered. "If the army has turned against us—"

"My guess is that Tirhin wants you—"

"You mean to kill me?"

"No, Elandra," Caelan said in gentle rebuke. "Kostimon himself gave you lessons in strategy. What do you think?"

She drew away from him, hating the suspicions rising within her. "You are saying that he wants me as a prize? Great Gault, not as a bride!"

Caelan nodded grimly.

"Damn him!" she said in sudden fury, clenching her fists.

"If Tirhin marries you, he will avoid the threat of civil war. It is the neatest solution, from his viewpoint."

"No!" she shouted, shoving a chair out of her way. "I won't be handed over like chattel. I won't!"

"Elandra—"

Blindly she rushed from the room and went running down the long gallery, up the stairs, and outside onto one of the balconies. The bright sunshine made her blink, and she clutched the stone parapet, gazing out at the imperial army surrounding the walls in silent menace.

Elandra stared in disbelief. She had never seen so many soldiers. Their armor and helmets glinted in the sun; their banners flew; they bristled with weapons. The officers on horseback with leopard skins behind their saddles rode back and forth, keeping order. The army stretched up the road as far as she could see, apparently endless, impossible to count. In row after row, they spread from the walls, back to the fields, nearly to the very edge of the jungle.

She could not begin to count them. How many legions? How many tens of thousands of soldiers? From her vantage point she could see a man in resplendent armor, long crimson plumes flowing from his helmet to his shoulders, his cloak glittering with rank stripes, a lion skin behind his saddle, a standard-bearer beside him with the imperial banner flying above the crossed-spears insignia of the Lord Commander.

Kostimon's greatest living general, the supreme leader of the entire imperial force, stood at Albain's gates. She could just glimpse her father standing before the Lord Commander, arguing with vehement gestures.

Her heart sank, and she knew that her hopes were indeed over.

While the walls of Albain's stronghold were immense and tall, impossible to scale, and a symbol of her father's considerable power, the infinity of the army diminished it, threatened it as nothing ever had.

The army had seige machines and catapults of fire. They could assault the stronghold, batter it and hold its inhabitants prisoner until starvation decimated every person within these walls. Worst of all, with all the warlords of Gialta trapped inside, the rest of the province was vulnerable.

Elandra wiped away tears of bitter defeat. How had they marched here without a warning being given? Had her father's sentries and scouts all failed in their duties? Or, if warnings had come while Albain had lain ill, who had received them in his stead? Lord Pier?

When she was finally able to drag her gaze away from the army, she looked up at the sky and saw a wall of black cloud stretching across the horizon—something she hadn't seen since she left Imperia.

Fresh fear swept through her. It suddenly seemed to her that this massive, silent force that had come from nowhere was in fact the army of Beloth, risen at last from the realm of shadow.

As she stared, their crimson uniforms changed to vestments of black. She stared down at the snorting, pawing horses and instead saw terrible steeds that snorted flame and reeked of destruction.

"It has come," she whispered, her voice raw with panic. "It has come at last!"

She pushed herself back from the balcony, her gaze still mesmerized by the vision. Her heart thundered inside her. She felt dizzy and cold as though she might faint.

"Elandra!" Caelan's hands gripped her shoulders from behind. Spinning her around to face him, he shook her until she regained her wits. Once again the soldiers looked like ordinary soldiers, mortal men in crimson and steel.

She shivered and pressed her face against Caelan's chest. For a moment he held her tight, murmuring reassurance into her hair, and she could pretend that all would yet be well, that they still had a chance, that they could get away and find refuge elsewhere.

But her fantasies were in vain. If she ran away, she would not be able to live with herself. She would carry with her the guilt and shame of her own cowardice. There could be no refuge from that. If she ran away, the imperial army would label her father a traitor and tear his palace down. He would die in disgrace, stripped of everything because of her. Gialta itself would be plundered and burned, the peasants dragged away into slavery, the land impounded under imperial ownership.

How well she knew the imperial wrath.

"Pier must have known they were coming," she said hollowly, shivering. "While Father lay unconscious, Pier—"

"It doesn't matter now," Caelan said. "They are here."

"Is no one loyal any more?" she asked. "Has all honor and courage vanished from the world?"

"Men are afraid," Caelan said. "Their minds are twisted and rendered confused by things that should be simple and are not. The darkness comes. Look at the jungle, Elandra. Look at the river."

Only now did she look past the army to see birds streaming out of the trees in huge flocks as though driven. Monkeys on the move chattered, teeming in the trees. Animals, even the large predator cats, fled to the river, swimming across to bound out on the other side into the paddies and fields.

The jungle was one of the most savage places she knew. The predators were fearless. Every creature in it was a master of survival. But animals fled their natural habitat only in times of great disaster, such as fire or annihilation.

She looked again at the cloud, awed and afraid of the menace it represented. "Does it stretch all the way from Imperia?" she whispered.

"Yes." Caelan lifted his head high, his eyes studying the cloud. "I feel its power. I hear the whispers within it. The darkness comes, Elandra. It is engulfing the light and all that lives in it. We are running out of time."

She clutched at his surcoat. "What are we to do?"

"Meet our destiny," he replied in a grim voice.

"To Imperia, then?" she asked quietly.

He nodded. "It is the quickest way. All of this is centered there."

"I must be their prisoner, but you can evade the soldiers," she said. "You must stay free. Quick! Let me show you the hidden passages—"

"No." Caelan gazed down at her. His eyes were gentle upon her, loving her, already telling her farewell.

She clutched him, wanting to cry out. "You must not argue. You are the hope of—"

"I am to be arrested," he said. "I lingered behind you long enough to overhear some of the terms. The Lord Commander is here on Tirhin's direct orders. You are to be escorted back to the capital in your full sovereignty, and I—"

"You're his scapegoat," she finished, hating Tirhin to the depths of her soul. "That pathetic coward!"

"He has outmaneuvered us."

"No!" she said fiercely. "I won't submit to him. I won't! I don't care what the Lord Commander's orders are, you will not go back to Imperia in chains. You must escape."

"I will not run away."

"Then fight—"

Caelan touched her hair, stroking it. Resignation lay in his face. "And give them an excuse to destroy your father? Why should I sacrifice a piece of myself to heal him, only to bring about his execution now?"

She let out a sigh then, struggling not to cry. "I'm sorry," she said. "I keep saying the wrong things. I haven't even thanked you properly for what you did before—"

"Hush," he said softly into her hair, resting his chin on top of her head.

She slapped tears from her eyes, angry at herself for being so emotional. "I never used to cry like this. I used to have control."

"If you had no fears now, I would not trust you," he replied, kissing her forehead. "Do you still hate me?"

She shook her head and hugged him tightly, trying to become part of him, unwilling to let him go.

Finally he pulled away, loosening her fingers when she held onto him. "We must face this," he said. "We must be brave for the others' sake."

"I don't want to be brave!" she cried. "I don't want to lose you!"

Voices carried through the palace. Hearing them, she stiffened and tightened her grip on Caelan. Everything was ending. She could not bear this.

"Oh, my love," she whispered brokenly, sobbing freely now. "I cannot give you up. I love you so much—"

He kissed her, deeply, possessively, until her thoughts were spinning and she was drowning in the emotions he wrought in her.

"We are one," he said, cupping her chin between his hands. His eyes held hers, although her tears caused her view of his face to blur. "We shall always be one. Believe that, my dearest, no matter what befalls us."

"Empress!" called a voice from the room within.

Elandra turned that way, then glanced over the railing of the balcony. They were trapped. She still could not accept this defeat. Her heart raged at the injustice of it. She did not know how Caelan could be so calm.

"Compose yourself," Caelan urged her softly. "Let them see an empress."

"I am a woman," she protested, sniffing and trying to dry her eyes, "and I am losing all I hold dear."

"We are not defeated yet," Caelan said.

"And when I am married at spear point to that traitor?" she retorted in fresh fury. "When I am forced to his bed? Will you be so calm and able to speak of strategy and—"

"Majesty." A soldier appeared, one of her father's men. "Compliments of Lord Albain, and will you please go to your apartments? I am to escort you there personally."

Elandra opened her mouth, but Caelan took her hand.

"Come," he said. "I will walk with you there. Your father wants you to wait for them with dignity."

His voice and gaze were filled with warning. Elandra did not want to go, but he was right. All that she had left now was her pride, and if even it was failing her, then she must pretend to have it.

Alti and Sumal were waiting for her at her apartments, looking big-eyed and worried. Caelan opened the door for her and led her inside.

"Make your preparations," he said. "Be ready for whatever comes."

She felt her lips tremble anew. "Can't we—"

"Remember that I love you. As long as the gods give me breath and the strength of my arm, I swear I will not fail you."

He kissed her, grave and unhappy, and went out.

As the door shut behind him, she buried her face in her hands. She wept long and bitterly, feeling the sourness of defeat. Everything she had hoped for, everything she had planned for, was ending. She could feel the hand of Fate on her, and she hated it. What was the good of wearing a crown and having people call you Majesty, if in the end you were only a pawn in a larger political game, to be pushed here and pushed there? She would have been better off to have spent her days still doing the mending and scrubbing floors.

A faint noise brought her out of her misery. She looked up, frowning, and turned around.

She saw a large sack of coarse homespun lying on the floor. Its bulging contents shifted and moved. Another faint noise, almost like a whimper, came from within.

Elandra held her breath a moment, then approached it cautiously. Drawing her knife, she wondered if it was a trap placed here by her enemies. There had been attempts made on her life before. This sack could hold anything from a bundle of cobras to a demon.

But she thought—she hoped—it held something else. She decided to take the chance.

With her knife, she slashed across the sack, slitting the cloth, then jumped back.

Nothing happened at first; then an eye peered cautiously out. She caught a glimpse of golden skin and knew swift disappointment.

It wasn't the *jinja* she'd hoped for.

She stepped back and put away her knife, intending to call Alti to take it away.

But a small hand reached through the slit and ripped it wider. A head emerged, swiveling around to reveal a triangular face, dainty pointed teeth, large defiant eyes, and pointed ears.

It was a *jinja*, after all, but she had never seen one that wasn't green. This one climbed out of the sack and crouched there, clearly

wild and terrified. Its gaze darted in all directions, and nothing reassured it.

There should have been handlers. There should have been
some preparations, a bit of initial training to the creature to gentle
it prior to the bonding. She did not know where or how Alti had
managed to get one captured from the wild on such short notice,
but he had.

Now that it was out in the sunlight that streamed in through
her windows, she could see that its golden skin had a greenish undertone. It was much smaller than the usual *jinja,* not even reaching to her waist. She wondered if it was fully grown.

"Little one," she said softly, reaching out her hand.

The *jinja* panicked. Screaming, it zigzagged about the room,
darting madly, knocking over furniture and objects, leaping at the
windows like something crazed, only to fall back into the room as
the screens held.

Panting, it lay on the floor and moaned to itself.

Elandra dared not approach it, fearing it would go into another frenzy and do itself serious harm. Not knowing what else to
do, she drew out her topaz and held it up so that the light could
shine on it.

"*Jinja,*" she said softly, crooning to it, "golden like this
jewel, golden in my chosen colors. Good *jinja,* rare and valued
jinja, brought to me as an omen in this day of trial and sore need."

The creature rose up on its haunches, its gaze fastened on the
jewel, which had begun to shine. The topaz seemed to gentle it,
mesmerize it, exactly as it had done to the dragon.

"I will not hurt you," Elandra said to the creature. "I will keep
you fed. I will give you pretty things. You will sense the magic for
me. You will keep it from doing me harm."

The *jinja* swayed, its large eyes glowing. It reached out one
hand. "Give rock."

"The topaz is mine," Elandra said with gentle firmness. "And
you will be mine. My possessions are together, close, but I am mis-
tress of them. Come and bond with me, pretty *jinja.*"

She put away the topaz, and the *jinja* hissed in disappointment. Angrily it bounded away. Elandra sighed and settled herself
in a chair, forcing herself to pretend patience she did not feel.

Finally, after tearing apart a pillow and scattering the stuffing everywhere, it came back to her and crouched just out of reach.

It stared at her long and hard. She stared back. She could feel magic crawling about the room, but whether it came from the *jinja* or from another source she did not know.

"Hurt me," the *jinja* said, eyes flashing.

"The trapper? I am sorry. You have been frightened too. You are far from your jungle temple and the caves which should have kept you safe."

The *jinja* drew back and rocked itself, looking awed.

"Yes, I know of your home," Elandra said. "I am very great among the humans. I have much consequence. You will have consequence too. Everyone will see how pretty you are, because you are mine. Will you bond with me?"

"Bonding mean serve."

"Yes."

"Trapper make do. Trapper hurt."

"If you will not bond, I will not force you," Elandra promised. "If you will not bond, I will have you released back into the jungle."

"No!" the *jinja* said in alarm. "Not safe. Danger!"

Elandra thought of the fleeing animals and birds. "Are you safer with me?" she asked, and again held out her hand.

The *jinja* tilted its head to one side and studied her a long time. Then it glided closer, its tiny feet not even touching the ground.

"You bond with wild *jinja*? No tame. No sorcerer touch."

"I need help," Elandra said. "I need a good *jinja* to serve me and protect me."

The creature bared its pointed teeth conceitedly. "I best *jinja*. Best!"

"Then we are together?" Elandra asked it.

The creature took her hand and lifted her fingers to its face. It began to hum, a sweet eerie sound that vibrated through Elandra's bones. She shut her eyes, trying not to fear the sound. A peculiar feeling washed in and out of her, and the humming stopped.

She opened her eyes and found the *jinja* crouched at her feet, its face against the floor. It was trembling. Concerned, Elandra bent over and stroked its bare back gently.

"Are you still afraid?" she asked it. "I'm sorry." This wasn't going to work. The creature would have to be set free, discreetly so no one else would catch it. "I'll tell Alti to let you go."

The *jinja* jumped up fiercely, eyes flashing. "No go! No go! You promise good eats, pretty eats! You promise."

Elandra laughed. "All right. If you're going to stay with me—"

"Bonded now. No leave."

"Oh," Elandra said in surprise. "I didn't know it was that easy."

The *jinja* scampered away and kicked at the torn bits of cushion. "I punished?"

"Not this time. Only if it happens again."

The *jinja* shook itself rapidly and scratched its ears. "Maybe."

Laughing again, Elandra rose to her feet. But before she took two steps, the *jinja* darted over to her and clung to her hard.

"What is it?" Elandra asked, stroking its head.

"Danger," the *jinja* whispered. "Much danger."

"Here?" Elandra asked in alarm, glancing around.

"Soon. You go to it. You take *jinja* there?"

"I'm afraid I have no choice."

The *jinja* shook its head and scowled. "Much sad to come. Much sad."

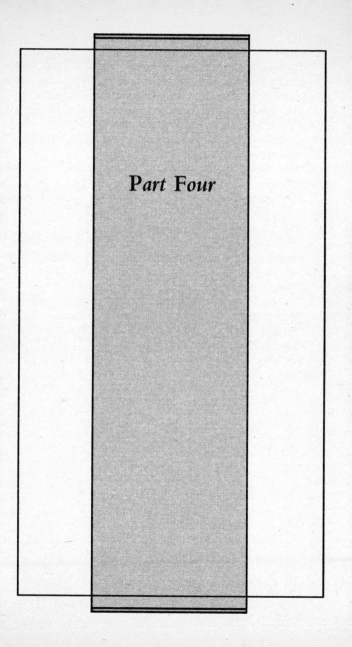

Part Four

Chapter Twenty-Four

THE SUN WAS setting over the bay when Elandra and her escorts rode into Imperia. She could see the huge, ruddy orb of the sun dropping to the horizon despite the veil of gloom that shrouded the city. The black cloud covered the city completely, keeping it in perpetual twilight. The air smelled of smoke and ashes, and the cold wind of winter seemed especially sharp as her horse picked its way over the rubble and debris filling the streets.

She rode with her father, Lord Pier, Iaris, and a handful of frightened servants, surrounded on all sides by calvary. The soldiers had their hands on their weapons and were alert for trouble, their eyes shifting constantly, aware of every noise and movement.

Elandra said nothing, nor did her companions. The sight that stretched before her horrified her. Imperia, a city once so magnificent, now lay in ruins. Charred beams and timbers poked up here and there; sometimes a wall still stood, as though by accident.

She was reminded of the destroyed city *Vyrmai-hon* in the realm of shadow, and hastily shoved that comparison away.

"Don't ride too close to any walls," the officer in charge said. "Sometimes they fall."

There had been fire everywhere, decimating every house, every temple, every shop. There had been earthquakes, leveling what remained. Nothing looked recognizable. She searched for landmarks and could not find them. Even the hills stretching up from the bay looked different, and she saw there had been a landslide that scarred the slope and altered the curve of the bay itself. Crude tents and makeshift shelters housed what few citizens remained. Scavengers poked through the rubble, clutching shawls over their heads against the cinders and ash that still blew in the air.

The air reeked of death. She saw picked bones here and there in the rubble, although an effort had clearly been made to clear the streets of corpses. Vultures perched on walls, fat and unafraid even of the living. In the distance she thought she saw something inhuman and swift leap a pile of rubble and disappear around a corner, but she was not sure.

It was as though Beloth had already risen, destroying Imperia with one flaming breath. Elandra looked at the devastation numbly, too exhausted to weep for the grandeur of this once-proud city. It had been beautiful and corrupt. It had been magnificent. Now there was nothing.

If Tirhin expected to remain here, he must be insane. She could not imagine living in this place, beneath the cloud, breathing the evil miasma of death and decay.

A gang of men darted out to block their path, bringing even the soldiers to a halt. The ambush spot was well chosen. Half-fallen walls hemmed them in on both sides. Little torchlight reached here.

Brandishing clubs and crudely made spears, the men seemed unafraid of the soldiers, who were already drawing their weapons.

"Give us your horses!" the spokesman shouted. "Give us—"

"Shut up!" the officer replied. "Get out of our way."

"Just one horse. We have to eat. Please, we need to eat!"

Elandra could not bear their pleading. She glanced at the servants. "Throw them one of the food bags—"

"No, Majesty!" the officer said, turning in his saddle. "They'll be on us like demons, hordes of them. Give them nothing."

It was narrow here, and dark. Elandra could feel eyes watching her from all sides.

The brigands spoke to each other with quick whispers. "Who is she?" the spokesman called.

"Damn," the officer said.

"Who is she?"

"Tell them," Elandra commanded.

Albain reached over from his horse to grab her wrist in warning, but she pulled free.

"Tell them," she said again.

This had been her city. These had been her people. She had escaped, but they had not. She could not bear to witness this now, yet she forced herself not to flinch. She felt responsible for all of them. She must find a way to help.

The officer rose slightly in his stirrups. "You are blocking the path of her Majesty, the Empress Elandra," he said sternly. "Let her Majesty pass!"

The men fell back. "The empress," they said to each other, elbowing and pointing. "It's the empress."

Someone appeared at the top of the wall, holding a torch. It shone full on Elandra as they kicked their horses forward, and more people appeared as if by magic.

"The empress!"

"It's the empress!"

"Thank the gods, she has returned to us safely."

Their feeble cheers broke her heart. She waved to them, trotting past as the soldiers took advantage of the chance to get free. Again she glanced back at the servants.

"Give them the food," she commanded. "All of it."

"Majesty!" the officer protested in horror. "No—"

But the servants were already tossing out the food pouches. Five of them landed among the townspeople, who leaped on them in sudden kicking, screaming, flailing savagery, fighting like starving animals for scant reward.

"Move!" the officer bellowed.

They galloped away, bunched so tightly together that Elandra's leg was crushed against her father's stirrup. Then at last they broke clear. The streets widened in a place where fewer buildings were standing. Much of the rubble had been cleared away.

The horses slowed down, their shod hooves clattering loud on the paving stones. Up ahead, Elandra again saw something lurking in the shadows. Something that looked almost human, yet was grotesquely bent at the shoulders. It did not run, but watched them from the darkness as they hurried by.

"Blessed Gault," Albain breathed aloud. "We are surely at the end of the world."

Shortly thereafter, they arrived at a villa, its three stories miraculously intact within its garden walls. The gardens were trampled and ruined, but only a jagged diagonal crack across the front wall of the house showed any damage. Welcoming squares of gold light shone from the windows. Torches burned at the entrance. Elandra could hear sounds of music and laughter from inside.

She frowned. How could anyone feast and make merry when the city was like this? She was so appalled she could not comment on it.

A soldier's strong hands lifted her from the saddle and supported her a moment when her weary, cramping legs could not quite hold her.

Albain came and put his arm around her. "Can you walk, my dear?" he asked gently. "Try a few steps and see if your muscles don't loosen."

The journey had been long and brutal. They had spent hours in the saddle, riding at a hard pace that spared neither horse nor rider. In camp at night, she had wept with weariness, unable to eat, too frightened to care. Iaris had tried to care for her, but Elandra did not want her mother. She wanted only Caelan, but he was shackled and kept elsewhere where she could not see him. Every day she struggled for a glimpse of him, if only to know he was still alive, but they kept him hidden. He had been brought into the city by a different route from hers. Now his whereabouts were a secret. She grieved for him already, knowing Tirhin would grant him no mercy.

Elandra burned with resentment. She had tried to enlist the aid of the Lord Commander, but he refused to even grant her an audience.

Now she was here, being delivered against her will and her prayers, and there wasn't much she could do about it.

Her *jinja* came darting over to cling to her skirts. Albain pushed it away and it snapped at him, barely missing his fingers.

He swore, and Elandra pulled the *jinja* around to her other side, away from him.

"Stop that," she scolded. "You must behave."

"Danger," the *jinja* insisted, tugging at her cloak. "Danger!"

"I know," she said wearily, and walked into the villa.

The hall was cramped by Gialtan standards. Albain glanced

around, his one eye bloodshot and glaring, but Elandra had no curiosity for her surroundings.

Minions in Tirhin's blue livery scurried and bowed, offering them wine, taking dusty cloaks and gloves.

The servants were courteous and well trained. The furnishings were beautiful. A fire burned nearby, providing warmth against the chill of the night.

Elandra was oblivious to all of it. She stood in a fog, and cared not where she was.

"Welcome!" a baritone voice rang out.

Tirhin stood at the landing on the staircase, his arms outstretched in greeting. "My dear friends, I give thanks for your safe arrival."

He came down the stairs slowly, favoring one leg, then limped over to them. His handsome face beneath its jaunty velvet cap was beaming with delight. He made it seem as though they hadn't been brought here by force.

Pier bowed, but Tirhin came straight to Elandra. Taking her cold hands in his, he kissed her knuckles.

"My dear Elandra, the sight of you fills my heart with joy. I am relieved at your safe return. Welcome."

Elandra focused on his face. He looked flushed and sweaty, a little tipsy from wine. She saw nothing but deceit and treachery in his eyes. Her own hardened with contempt. Drawing her hand from his grasp, she said nothing at all.

Tirhin flushed, frowning in quick anger. He glanced around self-consciously.

Albain cleared his throat. "About the conditions in the city—"

"Terrible, are they not?" Tirhin said, looking glad to change the subject. "That is why I had you brought here to my residence. For safety—"

"Where is Lord Sien?" Albain asked. "Where are the Vindicants? Why haven't the temple fires been lit and something attempted to lift this cloud?"

Tirhin glared at him. "Is that a criticism, Lord Albain?"

Albain glared right back. "When I see chaos in all directions, people starving, hardly any organization or security to the place, and demons running amok as freely as they please, I feel I may comment, sir."

"We're all very tired," Lord Pier interjected, trying to smooth over the sudden tension. "Perhaps in the morning, everyone will be in better temper."

"Yes, yes, of course," Tirhin said, turning to him with a smile. He snapped his fingers to summon a servant. "We are cramped here, you understand. If the ladies will consent to share her Majesty's chamber, then I am sure we will be able to find accommodations for these men."

The servant bowed low.

Albain and Pier exchanged hostile glances.

Elandra turned her gaze upon Tirhin, noticing as she did so that some of his guests had ventured out onto the stairs and were gawking at her. She raised her chin very high.

"Your highness," she said loudly, using his old title to annoy him, "your men have dragged me here against my will. Now I am to be kept your prisoner in our once proud city, which you have ruined. I hold you to blame for everything which has befallen Imperia, and I state now that I shall never marry you to preserve the throne which you have seized by deceit. I love another man, and he alone shall possess me, body and soul. As long as he lives, I am his. As for you, I would rather die first. Good night."

Without another glance at Tirhin, who looked livid, she picked up her skirts and walked toward the stairs, forcing the servant to run after her.

"Show me to the quarters where I shall be imprisoned," she said, and swept past the gawking courtiers, who had heard every defiant word. In silence they bowed to her, although she did not acknowledge their presence with even a glance.

Looking vexed, Iaris hastened after her. Elandra smiled to herself. Tirhin was a drunkard and a fool. He would make her pay for tonight's humiliation, but right now she did not care.

Her chamber was luxurious and more spacious than she had expected. The opulent furnishings were not to her taste, but she had to admit the bed looked comfortable. Food and drink were waiting on a table, filling the air with their aromas. Flowers—if scraggly and none too fresh—stood in a small vase.

The gesture brought tears to her eyes. How pathetic to offer her flowers—and where had they possibly been gleaned from?—as though that was all it took to soften her heart. She sighed and stretched out her hands to the fire.

All she wanted now was a dab of water to wash her face, and the oblivion of sleep. Every part of her ached.

Iaris moved around briskly, peering behind drawn curtains at windows shuttered and barred, then coming back to rearrange the flowers and peek under the food covers.

"The food is hot," she said. "Come and eat."

"I'm not hungry."

"Don't be a fool. Do you expect to starve yourself to death? I warn you, it is easier to be defiant on a full stomach."

Elandra turned slightly to glance at her. The fragrance of food made her feel ill. "No, please go ahead. I don't want it."

"You've barely eaten in days," Iaris said. "Pining for your lost lover is one thing, but you must—"

"I don't need a lecture from you," Elandra broke in rudely. She crossed the room and sat down on the bed.

The lamps were too bright. Her eyes hurt, and her vision was blurred. She felt dizzy from the hot room and let herself sink down. The bed felt as though it were spinning. She closed her eyes.

The touch of Iaris's hand on her brow made her open them again. She frowned, wishing Iaris would leave her alone. Her mother had been hovering near her through the entire journey, watching and criticizing, providing little comfort.

"No fever," Iaris said. "You've been looking ill. Tonight you're very pale. Did the city upset you that much?"

"Why shouldn't I be upset?" Elandra retorted, draping her hand across her eyes to shield them from the light. "There's nothing left."

"Cities can be rebuilt," Iaris said.

Elandra pushed herself up on one elbow and glared at her mother. "Stop it," she said angrily. "Stop trying to meddle."

"You must think positively. The empire will go on—"

"We are being swallowed by darkness, the darkness that Kostimon and Tirhin have unleashed on us," Elandra cried. "We face our doom, and ignoring the problem does not solve it."

"You are fretting for a man who is condemned. You are being excessively dramatic and exaggerating everything."

"Didn't you hear the soldiers?" Elandra asked her. "It's dark even when the sun rises. The dark god is coming—"

"Stop it!" Iaris said, jumping up from the edge of the bed. "I will not hear such blasphemy."

"Then stay away from me!"

"It is my duty to help you."

"No," Elandra said curtly. "You hope Tirhin will reward you if you persuade me to marry him. Dear Gault, the man's arrogance knows no bounds. He acts like a bridegroom already."

"But, Elandra, is that so awful? Yes, you're infatuated with this Caelan. But that must end. Your rank, your lineage all forbid anything more than a mere dalliance. It's time you thought about your future, and the future of your family."

"Meaning you," Elandra said in a tight voice.

"Albain and Pier will both profit from this alliance, if they negotiate carefully."

"There will be no alliance," Elandra said through her teeth. "I will not consent."

"Your actions tonight were foolish. Tirhin is clearly besotted with you—"

"No!" Elandra stared at her in amazement. "He is not."

"I saw him, child. He was beaming until you were rude to him. That is unwise, no matter what your feelings."

"You forget that I know him all too well," Elandra said. "He could barely tolerate me while Kostimon lived. This is nothing more than an act, part of his hypocrisy."

"More drama. More exaggeration," Iaris said with a sigh. "Look at this room which he has given you. The best in the villa, obviously. Food, flowers, and a good fire have all been provided for your comfort. He is—"

"What else could he offer me?" Elandra asked coldly. "I am the empress, and he is only my stepson. At the moment, most of his consequence lies in his imagination. Without me, he has nothing."

"Then take care how you deal with him," Iaris said in exasperation. "You are in an excellent position to negotiate. Few women are given this opportunity. Make the most of it."

"I do not want to hear anything more from you," Elandra said, averting her face. She was too tired and ill to go on arguing. The whole discussion was futile.

"You are putting all of us at risk!" Iaris told her. "If you care nothing about yourself, then think of your father at least."

"I am. But I am not for sale."

Iaris glared at her. "You have no choice."

"No. I had no choice the first time my father arranged a marriage for me. This time is different. He cannot force me. You cannot force me."

"As your mother—"

"You forfeited that status when you sent me away!" Elandra said. "Besides, I have given my vows to Caelan. I will not take them back."

Rage spread through Iaris's face. She slapped Elandra hard across the face. "You fool!"

The crack of her hand stung mercilessly. Elandra lifted her fingers to her cheek. Enraged and shocked, she stared at her mother.

Iaris glared right back. Her eyes were wide and furious. "Do you carry his child?"

Rising from the bed, Elandra said nothing.

"Do you?"

Elandra still did not speak. Inside, however, her mind was spinning at the thought of it. Perhaps that was why she was so prone to crying of late. Perhaps that was why she wanted no food, why she felt so tired. She suddenly wanted to clutch her stomach in fierce joy and triumph. Caelan's child. Oh, blessed goddess mother, let it be true. Let her have some hope in this.

But she refused to show anything to Iaris. Nor would she answer.

"You will not tell me," Iaris said, pacing back and forth in front of her. "Insolent, stupid girl. If you are breeding, then you will ruin everything. Tell me the truth!"

"I will tell you nothing," Elandra said.

"You look green enough to be quickening," Iaris said. "And by Gault, if you are, then you have put all of us in jeopardy."

"No more than we already are."

Iaris uttered a sharp, short laugh and tossed her head. "Really? Then think on this, my girl. If Tirhin entertains even the most remote suspicion that you have lain with that gladiator—"

"And what if it were Kostimon's child?" Elandra said.

Iaris stopped in mid-stride and stared at her. Conflicting emotions chased themselves across her face. "The Penestricans ordered you to bear his child, did they not? They taught you how to seduce him. They gave you exact instructions as to—"

"If I bear Kostimon's child," Elandra said coolly as though she did not see the naked ambition in her mother's face, "then the empire is his. The child would outrank Tirhin, whose mother was only a consort, and Tirhin's claim would be futile."

"Take care with your lies, my girl," Iaris said suspiciously. "Everyone in your father's palace saw how you looked at that gladiator. No mourning for Kostimon. No veil of widowhood. This wanton behavior—"

"I know exactly which man is the father," Elandra said wickedly, "for I have lain with only one of them. But the rest of the world will have to wait until the child is born to know."

Iaris glared at her, too angry to find a retort.

Elandra turned her back. "Leave me. I wish to be alone."

She stood there, exhausted by the scene, but glad that for once she had left her mother speechless.

Iaris's footsteps crossed the room, then returned. "Forgive me, Majesty," she said with mock courtesy, "but I cannot obey you. The door is locked. It seems we are prisoners together."

Sighing, Elandra started to speak, but just then the floor trembled beneath her feet.

The bed hangings swayed, and a crack ran up the wall from the corner of the fireplace.

Iaris cried out in fear. "Merciful gods, what is happening?"

Elandra glanced up, saw the ceiling cracking, and dodged a piece of falling plaster. She grabbed a bedpost to keep her balance, and the motion stopped. The room was silent, except for the hiss of the fire.

Iaris stood white-faced with terror. "What was it?" she asked. "Where is your *jinja*?"

The tiny creature popped out from beneath the bed and began to explore. Elandra brushed plaster dust from her hair.

"Stop shrieking, Iaris," she said. "It was only an earthquake."

"It is the return of the gods," Iaris said. "The world is ending. We are all going to die, consumed in—"

Elandra poured a cupful of water and threw it in her mother's face.

Sputtering, Iaris stared at her.

"Now be quiet," Elandra said. "I want my rest."

Chapter Twenty-Five

THE PUBLIC DUNGEONS lay beneath the ruins of the old arena, converted from its underground warren of training rooms and quarters. Torches burned at the rubble-strewn entrance, and gaunt-faced soldiers in tattered cloaks huddled around a roaring bonfire for warmth.

Beyond the firelight, furtive glowing eyes watched from nearly every nook and cranny. The soldiers talked loudly and nervously, pretending to ignore the watchers. Now and then there came the abortive scream of a hapless victim out in the darkness.

Riding through the terrible streets, Caelan held himself tightly *severed,* fearing any contact with the darkness that now ruled Imperia. The smell of death sickened the air, along with the scorched, fetid stench of forbidden magic.

Tightly guarded by men who rode with drawn swords in their hands, Caelan soon gave up any attempt to keep his bearings. With the city destroyed, nothing looked as it should. But when they reined up at the dungeons, Caelan gasped in surprise.

How well he recognized the public square and entrance to the arena, with its stone pillars and a massive lintel carved to show a stylized border of swords laid end to end. The arena itself towered there no more. Only a single section of seats remained, the top half broken away. The rest lay in rubble that filled the ring.

"Get off," ordered a weary voice.

Caelan dismounted, the shackles on his wrists clanking softly. He still wore the mail shirt Elandra had given him, and during the past few days he had been grateful for it. The long sleeves had protected his wrists from being rubbed sore by his chains. As his mount was led away, he stretched himself carefully, taking care to make no sudden moves that would get himself beaten. It felt good to stand on the ground again.

The soldiers exchanged information. Caelan learned he was a special prisoner of the emperor-elect, to be kept in a solitary cell until he was sent for. No visitors. No one was to talk to him, on pain of death.

The irony of it made Caelan smile without amusement. Some men walked a path of life that progressed in a straight line from birth to death. Others meandered, finding what accomplishments they could. Still others walked in a circle, ending up where they had started. Thus it was for him. He had begun life in Imperia as a slave, chained and beaten, imprisoned beneath the arena with his only future seeming to be a quick death in the ring. Now he had returned, once again in chains, once again under the dominion of Tirhin.

His head lifted, and he gazed out into the darkness. Tirhin would not own him long this time, for indeed the world was ending. Time was running out for all of them.

The tip of a spear prodded him in the back. "Get moving."

"Watch him!" another said in warning. "He's a big brute."

"Aye, Giant was always dangerous."

Their fear made them nervous and sweaty. Caelan had fears of his own. Imperia was no place to be shackled and weaponless. If anything attacked, the guards would protect themselves, not him.

Nervously, he flexed against his chains, but they were well forged and held him.

Something that sounded suspiciously like a *shyriea* shrieked nearby. One of the soldiers flinched, and nearly ran his spear through Caelan's side. The rings of his mail protected him, but Caelan turned on the man.

"Have a care, you fool!" he said angrily.

Another soldier stepped between them and rammed Caelan in the chest with the butt of his spear. "Quiet!"

Caelan drew in a painful breath, his temper hot, but he restrained himself, knowing that to argue would only bring on another beating. He'd had enough of those.

"I want to see Prince Tirhin," he said hoarsely. "I am a member of the Crimson Guard. I demand—"

The spear shaft swung again, cracking him across the jaw and knocking him down.

Caelan lay there, stunned, his head ringing.

They kicked him. "You're a deserter. Now get up! Get moving!"

They stripped off his mail, then kicked and pummeled him, thudding into the sore places. He pulled himself to his hands and knees, swaying as his head spun. Blackness dipped and swooped at him. By the time he drove it away, they had yanked him forward by his arms and were shoving him down a ramp into a torchlit maze of passageways. He walked past beat-up wooden doors banded with iron. The smell was even the same—musty and damp, sour with old sweat and blood.

He was shoved into a dark cell, hard enough to make him stumble into the back wall. The door slammed, and he heard the bolts shoot home. Caelan clung to the wall, fighting off his dizziness. Pain was still exploding in his jaw. He felt it gingerly, decided it wasn't broken, and spat out a bloody tooth.

He stumbled over an object that went skidding across the dirt-packed floor. A stool, he thought. The door had a narrow opening set with bars. Meager illumination from the torchlight in the passageway barely reached into his cell. Exploration told him he had a stool and a pile of dirty straw, but nothing else, not even a pail of water.

Ignoring his thirst, he sat down on the stool and bent over with his elbows on his knees. The bruises were nothing. He would mend . . . if he lived long enough.

No one brought him food or water. He listened as the guard was changed about sunset. Shortly thereafter someone came through with a barrel of pitch. The man replenished the torches, keeping them burning brightly, as though light alone could hold the demons at bay. Caelan remembered his boyhood conviction that warding keys could drive away any attacker, even Thyzarene raiders. He had learned that day that evil came in many guises, and often it laughed at the protection mustered against it.

Still, it would do no good to tell this worker that his efforts were in vain. If the shadows decided to come creeping into these dungeons, they would do so whether the torches burned or not.

Needing something to do, Caelan watched the man work. There was something familiar about the man, something in the set of his shoulders, the way he moved. He wore a long leather apron to protect his clothes from the pitch. His head was concealed by a hood, worn presumably for warmth. Caelan could not catch a glimpse of his face. Yet his hands were powerful and broad. He swirled a torch in the barrel of pitch, then lifted it and lit it.

As he set it in a sconce near Caelan's door, his uplifted face was partially illuminated for a second.

"Orlo!" Caelan said eagerly. "Orlo, it's you!"

The man looked around as though startled, then backed away hastily into the shadows.

"Come here, you old donkey," Caelan said, glad to see his former trainer. "It has been too long."

Orlo glanced up and down the passageway, as though making sure no one overheard them.

"No talking!" he said sternly. "You're under a rule of silence."

Caelan obediently lowered his voice to the merest whisper. "Come and let me look on your face. I am glad to see you."

Orlo, however, hunched his shoulders and pulled his barrel and cart down the passageway. He set to work busily with the next torch, ignoring Caelan completely.

Hurt, Caelan stared after him. "It's me, Orlo. Caelan. Don't you have—"

Cold water came splashing through the window, hitting him in the face and driving him back. Sputtering, Caelan wiped his eyes and found a bearded face glaring in at him.

"Shut up!" the guard said. "Or the next bucketful will be dung. We'll put a muzzle on you if we must."

Caelan stepped all the way back to the far wall, saying nothing. He knew what a muzzle was, a terrible torture device that was fitted over a man's head and slowly tore out his tongue by the roots.

Not daring to move, he waited until the guard walked on. There was a brief murmur of conversation between the guard and

Orlo; then the guard's footsteps gradually faded. Only then did Caelan venture back to the window and peer out.

Orlo had gone around the corner and was no longer in sight. Caelan waited a long time, hoping, but Orlo did not return.

Someone moaned in a cell farther down the row. Another man coughed constantly, as though he had a rotted lung. Those were the only sounds.

Orlo had been his trainer, gruff and brutal at times, relentless as he drove Caelan through his drills. But he had taught Caelan how to fight and how to survive the ring. He had made Caelan a champion, and eventually the two men had become friends. But that had all ended the night that Caelan was wrongly accused of attacking and injuring Prince Tirhin. Orlo had believed the accusations, and until now Caelan had never seen him again.

It seemed Orlo had not softened. Caelan waited, but his former trainer did not come back.

Hours went by, enlivened only by occasional light earthquakes that shook the walls but did not bury Caelan alive. With nothing else to do, Caelan paced and bleakly looked into his own future. So much for destiny, he thought. So much for carrying Exoner against the dark god.

A commotion in the passageway sent him to the rear of his cell, out of reach and out of trouble. A face peered inside.

"You! Stay back!"

It was an unnecessary command. Caelan knew they were about to open the door. He could smell food, and his stomach growled urgently. This wasn't the time to make a break for freedom. He could hear the other guards grunting and clanking their weapons restlessly. They were just hoping for a prisoner to try something stupid. A dead prisoner was a prisoner who did not have to be fed.

A scrawny boy came stumbling inside. He set down a pail of water, sloshing half the contents over the sides, and slammed down a bowl of food beside it. Then he backed out, and the door was bolted shut.

A face watched Caelan from the window, but he did not venture forth to get his food until the guards gave up and moved on to the next cell. Then Caelan rushed forward, picked up his food and

the water pail, and retreated with them. He knew about prison life
and the cruelty of the guards.

The occupant of the next cell was not as lucky. Caelan heard
the sloppy splash and a cry of anguish. The guards laughed. Caelan knew they had just emptied a dung bucket over the hapless in-
mate when he tried to get his food.

Angrily Caelan picked over his own food. He drank his water
after sniffing it. Then he tapped his stale bread against the wall to
drive out the weevils and ate with all the control he could muster,
chewing thoroughly, giving his stomach a chance to accept the un-
palatable food. The rest of it was greasy and cold. He ate it anyway, knowing the rats would steal it if he didn't.

A faint scraping noise from behind him made him turn
around. Instantly alert, he listened a moment, watching as a block
of stone in the wall was carefully removed by someone on the
other side.

Caelan crouched by the hole and said nothing.

Another block was removed, then a third. He squinted
through the gloom, trying to see who it was.

"Giant?" the voice whispered softly.

"Orlo!" Caelan whispered back. Joyfully he gripped another
block of stone and found it loose. He pulled it away and grinned
through the opening. "I thought you had abandoned me for certain—"

Orlo's fist smashed into his face, catching him right under the
eye. Grunting with pain, Caelan reeled back. As soon as he could
see again, he found Orlo glaring at him.

"What—"

"That is for almost getting me killed," Orlo whispered furiously. "You're under an order of silence, on pain of death. What in
hell's own flames were you doing yelling at me like that?"

Contrite, Caelan probed the swelling knot under his eye and
grimaced. "Sorry. I was glad to see you. I didn't think—"

"You have never thought. That's why you're in jail."

Caelan didn't mind the tongue-lashing. Orlo had always criticized him. "What are you doing in the dungeons?"

"This *was* the arena, remember?" Orlo replied scathingly.
"My responsibility."

"So you came back here after leaving Tirhin's service?"

Orlo snorted. "Murdeth and Fury, do you think I'd serve that prancing fop and traitor one moment longer than I had to? I only went to his household for you."

"I know." Caelan reached through and gripped Orlo's arm. "I never did thank you."

"Bah. Swallow that nonsense. It made me richer than before. I cared for nothing else."

"You tried to warn me about Tirhin, and I didn't listen."

"No, you have a head like a block of wood and about as much sense."

Caelan grinned. "You should have fled the city."

Orlo snorted. "And go where? This damned blight that is upon us, it spreads everywhere."

"Can you get me out?"

"Of your cell? Aye. If you can get those big shoulders through this hole."

Caelan reached out, but Orlo suddenly hissed a warning.

"Not now," he said and started stacking the stones back up.

Caelan listened but heard nothing. "What?"

"This isn't the time."

"But what is it? I don't—"

"Shut up!" Orlo stuck his hand through. "Hand me that last stone on your side. Quick!"

"Orlo, I have to get out—"

"Later."

Orlo put the last stone in place and was gone, as though he had never been, with no explanation.

Only then did Caelan hear the steady tramp of booted feet in the passageway. There were more than usual. He could sense a change, a quickness in the way they walked. He heard the crashing fists of salutes, along with low, respectful voices.

Then one voice lifted above the others, a sleek baritone full of arrogance.

Recognizing Tirhin's voice, Caelan rose to his feet. Grim satisfaction filled him. So the prince had come to him at last. He was going to have his chance after all.

But then the footsteps walked on. Tirhin did not even look

through the window at him, did not bother to even speak a word to him.

Caelan rushed to his door and peered out, but all he saw were the backs of the soldiers, marching down the passage. Swearing in frustration, he slammed his fist against the door, making it rattle.

In the next moment, it was being unlocked. Caelan backed up just in time to avoid the door as it was slammed open. Guards filled the doorway, shining torches in his face and nearly blinding him.

"You! Come with us!"

They grabbed Caelan and dragged him forth, herding him down the passageway and around a corner. Several daggers were held against him. Had he tried to break free, he would have been spitted instantly.

Down they went, going lower into the older regions. Many of the bracing timbers showed signs of rot and neglect. The stone mortar was crumbling, allowing some of the walls to bulge from the press of the earth. Caelan saw some ramps and passageways choked with fallen debris, probably from the frequent earthquakes. He swallowed hard, thinking about being crushed to death down here.

"Where am I going?" he asked.

One of the guards struck him hard on the ear, making his head ring. "To die."

They all laughed, but Caelan could not share the joke.

Lifting his head, he gazed around, taking note as they descended another ramp. A series of doors along the passageway told him they were in the old gladiator quarters. Men stayed down here for entire seasons, never seeing the sunlight until they went into the ring. Most of them died minutes later, to be returned forever into the darkness.

Ghost voices . . . the faint ring of swords . . . the roar of the crowd. Caelan shook off the memories. When they went down a short flight of worn steps, he recognized another scent, faint and fading now but unforgettable.

It was the smell of Haggai. Those loathsome creatures, part woman and part monster. It had been a long tradition in the arena that gladiators could sport freely with the witches the night before their combat. And if the Haggai had lived deep below the complex under the arena, did that not mean there was a physical passageway into the realm of shadows itself? Just as there had been a portal beneath the Temple of Gault in the palace compound?

Caelan studied the men around him. He had an escort of five guards, well armed and alert. Their weapons were drawn, which made seizing a spare dagger from someone's belt almost impossible. He narrowed his eyes, thinking about odds and possibilities.

The passageway ended at a closed door. One of the guards knocked perfunctorily, then swung it open. Caelan was shoved inside.

The room was circular and empty of furnishings other than a brazier supported by a tripod. A small fire burned in it, smoking heavily as though it had just been started. Torches blazed in sconces. On the wall opposite the door, a demonic face was carved into the stone. Its snarling visage caused two of Caelan's guards to make furtive warding signs with their fingers.

Caelan barely noticed the carving, however. His attention was locked on the occupants of the chamber.

Besides Tirhin, two bodyguards stood by the wall. Agel, wearing a white healer's robe beneath his dark blue cloak, hovered near the prince.

Caelan saw his cousin and frowned. He had thought Agel had died during the Madrun invasion. It seemed he was wrong.

Agel gazed at him with an equal lack of affection and handed a wine cup to Tirhin, who gulped the contents.

"Secure him well," Tirhin commanded between swallows.

One of Caelan's guards ran a length of stout chain through a massive ring bolt set into the stone floor, then looped the other end through Caelan's shackles. He secured the chain and gave it a strong yank.

"He is secure, Majesty."

Tirhin gulped down more wine and grunted. "Get out."

The guards bowed and shuffled outside, shutting the door.

Tirhin gestured at Agel. "You. I wish you to go."

"That is unwise," Agel said. His voice was the same as ever, slightly grave, holding a note of warning and counsel.

Hearing him, Caelan shut his eyes a moment. As boys, he and

Agel had been as close as brothers. He had had no better friend, but somehow it had all turned wrong. Now there was no going back, no way to regain what had once been.

"Go!" Tirhin shouted. He looked angry and flushed; whatever he was drinking only seemed to agitate him more. "I will speak to him alone."

Agel frowned at him, looking exasperated. "Even chained, he could attack you before the guards—"

"You're an old woman. I'm not afraid of him!" Tirhin said rudely. He finished the contents of his cup and flung it Agel, who ducked just in time. "Do you think he has the power to snap stone and steel? Go!"

Without further protest, Agel tucked his hands inside his wide sleeves and left. As he passed Caelan, his gaze flicked sideways to meet Caelan's eyes. He said nothing, however. His expression remained unreadable.

Caelan turned his head to watch Agel go. There was nothing left for either of them to say. They had chosen their sides. They would not change.

The prince swayed. A sheen of unhealthy sweat coated his face, which was far paler than usual. He had lost his handsome looks. His features were haggard, almost gaunt, with deep lines carved on either side of his mouth. His blue eyes seemed paler than Caelan remembered, and as the firelight reflected in them they appeared almost yellow.

Caelan thought of Kostimon's yellow eyes, so cold and strange. He remembered that Sien had also had yellow eyes, like a serpent's. Was this, then, a mark of the shadows?

Tirhin limped closer to Caelan, a sneer on his face, and Caelan tugged at his bonds, testing them with a strong bulging of his muscles. But unlike the bolt set into the pillar of wood in Albain's courtyard, this one was immovable. Nor could the chains be broken. They were strong enough to have held many a prisoner, many a gladiator, in the past. They were holding now.

Tirhin chuckled. "Oh, you would like to get at me, wouldn't you? I can see the heated desire in your eyes."

Tirhin stopped just out of Caelan's reach. The prince wore his usual blue clothing, sumptuous velvet trimmed with fur. His sword was too long and heavy for him. An emerald winked from the hilt, and Caelan recognized Exoner. He caught his breath sharply.

"Yes," Tirhin said, noticing where his gaze went. "This exceptionally fine sword is not suitable for a former slave to carry. I have taken it for my own."

As he spoke. he drew it from the scabbard and swung it aloft. He held it overhead a moment, long enough for his thin arms to tremble; then he brought it down in a vicious swing at Caelan's head.

Caelan met Tirhin's eyes, and never moved. At the last second Tirhin bent his elbows, and the blade missed Caelan by a whisper.

"Whack!" Tirhin said, with a hollow laugh. "There goes your head, rolling away like a ball."

He sheathed the sword and glared at Caelan, looking disappointed that he had failed to frighten his prisoner. "You always had ideas above your station. I gave you everything, showered you with gifts and wealth, and you have repaid me most ill."

"You brought the evil to Imperia," Caelan said. "You bargained with the Madruns. You unleashed the darkness—"

"Shut up!" Tirhin broke in hotly. His eyes opened wide, and he shook his head. "Damn you, how dare you accuse me! You are dung beneath my boots. This darkness was Kostimon's doing. Blame him, not me."

"Kostimon is dead."

"Is he?" Tirhin asked with an angry gesture. "Why do I hear his name at every turn? Why do I hear his voice in my dreams at night? It is said his ghost stalks the city. He is the man who bargained for immortality and paid the price by bringing this destruction down on all of us."

Caelan did not answer. Blame could be thrown in any direction. It did not change the circumstances.

"But you," Tirhin said, coming closer. "I have brought you back to revive the games, to give the people some entertainment."

"Haven't they seen enough death lately?" Caelan asked with scorn.

Tirhin flushed. "What spell have you cast over her?" he asked in a sudden change of subject. His voice was hoarse with fury. "What have you done to her mind?"

"Who?"

"Elandra! Don't play games with me. You are this close to death." Tirhin held his thumb and forefinger together. "This close! You could have had your freedom. Did I care? You could have gone back to your precious backwater province and rotted there. But why did you abduct her?"

"There was no abduction. Kostimon placed her in my protection," Caelan said coldly. As he spoke, he cast a glance at the two guards. They were still alert, watching him closely.

Tirhin moved away, and Caelan was not able to seize him. He could sense Exoner calling to him. The sword was practically glowing in its scabbard from their proximity to the realm of shadow.

Grim determination reawakened in him. He had to get that sword.

Tirhin kicked aside the wine cup and went to stand near the fire. He shivered, then moved restlessly back toward Caelan.

"Well?" he demanded. "You've had time to think up a lie. What is your hold on the lady?"

Caelan frowned, not sure what he wanted. Feeling the conversation was pointless, Caelan answered with the simple truth. "Love."

"Love?" Tirhin said the word as though it were foul. "She loves *you*? How could she?"

Caelan said nothing.

But Tirhin seemed to read everything in his face. He scowled. "This is absurd. You have enspelled her."

"I am only an ex-gladiator," Caelan replied satirically. "What powers do I possess?"

"Plenty of them, from all accounts. Your speed, your prowess, your ability to heal, your way of reading a man's mind. Agel has told me of the Traulander religion, of the special gifts and spells that can be performed."

"There are no spells," Caelan said, wondering what lies Agel had fed into this man's mind.

"How earnestly you say that," Tirhin said with a skeptical

laugh. "You were always such a literal fool, so honest, so upright, so faithful. But now you think you can take everything from me, just because of Elandra. You think her favor will make you a great man. But you are wrong!"

"The men are already calling you Majesty," Caelan said, trying to provoke him. "Did you crown yourself today?"

"Damn you!" Tirhin glared at him with clenched fists. "Taunt me again, and I'll cut out your tongue."

"Before or after you cut off my head?"

One of the guards growled a warning and reached for his sword.

Tirhin waved him back. "I don't need you. Keep away."

"But, Majesty, he is dangerous—"

"Get out, both of you! If you won't obey me, I won't have you with me."

"Better let them stay," Caelan said softly.

Tirhin jerked around to stare at him. Whatever he read in Caelan's eyes made him blink. He stepped back and glanced at his guards. "Very well," he said. "But keep quiet."

Caelan started over. Tirhin was a man on the edge. Whether pain or fear drove him hardly mattered. He was half-mad, fevered, far from being in control of himself or his men.

"Elandra will not marry you of her own free will," Caelan said, still speaking softly. "Has she told you that yet?"

Tirhin's face turned bright crimson. Hatred gleamed in his eyes. He was breathing hard, but he did not answer.

"Is an alliance with her the only way your chancellors will let you be crowned?" Caelan asked. "Imperia politics are so complicated. How much easier it all seemed when you thought the Madruns would slaughter both Kostimon and Elandra in their beds, leaving your succession a clear and simple matter. Did Kostimon accuse you of treason before he died? Is that why the Lord Commander of the army still hesitates to give you his allegiance?"

"The Lord Commander is here, damn you," Tirhin breathed, staring at him in fascination. "He came to me. He brought the army to me."

"But has he sworn fealty to you?"

Tirhin's mouth trembled, but he said nothing.

"Has Lord Albain?"

"That old fool! His head will roll after yours!"

"And will that make Elandra smile at you with more favor?"

Tirhin lifted a shaking fist. "She'll come to fear me. I don't want her love. I want her cooperation."

"You want her crown, and you'll do anything to get it. The problem is, you're about to be emperor of nothing. Imperia is doomed, and you can't put the monsters back. Do you think they will spare you when they've eaten everyone else?"

All the color drained from Tirhin's face. His eyes snapped open wide, and they were utterly mad. He gripped Caelan's sword. "I will not be their creature!" he shouted. "I will not surrender to it, nor to you!"

Caelan held his breath, praying Tirhin would draw the sword and swing at him. There was a chance that he could seize the weapon and take it from the prince. If only Tirhin would get close enough.

But instead, the prince ran the back of his hand across his mouth. He was shaking visibly; his eyes rolled from side to side. He staggered back, too far away for Caelan to reach him.

"No," he said raggedly, as though talking to himself. "No, not on my hands. An emperor does not stoop to . . . you are nothing." His gaze swung back to Caelan and focused. "Do you hear? You are *nothing*!"

"Tirhin," Caelan said desperately, "wait—"

Tirhin made a chopping gesture to silence him. "For the good service you once showed me, I had hoped to spare you, but you are no longer of any use to me. As long as you are alive, she will hope. If she has hope, she will resist me."

Caelan frowned, his wits scrambling for a way to reach Tirhin. "If I die, she will hate you more—"

"Guards!" Tirhin shouted.

The two men came forward. The others walked in.

"Execute him," Tirhin said. "I want him dead. Now. Tonight."

"At once, Majesty."

Saluting, the sergeant turned around and gestured at his men. One of them yanked at Caelan's chains, pulling him down to his knees. The others drew their daggers, blades ringing out the song of death.

Exoner called to Caelan, its voice an ache in his veins. If he could only get Tirhin to come close, close enough for him to grasp the hilt, he would still have a chance.

The sergeant gripped Caelan's hair and tilted back his head to expose his throat. He placed the edge of his dagger under Caelan's jaw. The steel felt cold against Caelan's skin. He could tell how sharp and well honed it was. He hardly dared breathe against it.

"Will you give the order, Majesty?" the sergeant asked.

Caelan's gaze found Tirhin's. "Why not cut off my head yourself?" he taunted. The dagger nicked him as he spoke, and he felt a hot trickle of blood slide down his throat. "Do you fear me, emperor of nothing, or are you too little a man to dirty your hands?"

Rage darkened Tirhin's face at the insult, and the sergeant cursed Caelan.

Before he could slit Caelan's throat, however, Tirhin jerked up his hand.

Caelan knelt there, his whole existence poised on the edge of that trembling blade. He could feel the violence in the metal, feel the previous deaths coating the steel, feel the outrage in the sergeant who hungered to slash hard and cleanly.

Eyes blazing, Tirhin glared at Caelan. He looked more fevered and ill than ever. His thin body swayed as though he could barely stand. Breathing hard, he hesitated there, and his fists clenched and opened, clenched and opened.

Caelan never let his gaze falter from Tirhin's. *Draw the sword,* he commanded in his mind. *In Gault's name, draw the sword.*

Tirhin's gaze narrowed. His hatred seethed in him plainly, but after an eternal moment he stepped back.

A low rumble ran through the room, and dust sifted down on Caelan's shoulders. He frowned, glancing up involuntarily to see if the roof was going to fall on them.

The sergeant laughed deep in his throat. "Scared of a little shake?" he taunted. "We get them all the time down here. You'll be dead long before you're crushed."

"Stand down," Tirhin said.

His voice was choked, hoarse, almost unrecognizable.

The sergeant stared at him in consternation, then reluctantly moved the dagger away from Caelan's throat. He released his hold on Caelan's hair.

Gritting his teeth, Caelan lowered his head a moment to ease his neck muscles. Inside he was cursing with a mixture of relief and frustration.

Was Tirhin having second thoughts? What plot was being cooked up in the prince's devious mind now? But any delay was a chance, however slight.

"I thank you," Caelan said breathlessly, "for your imperial mercy."

Tirhin's dark brows knotted together. He swept a cold look at Caelan and said to the sergeant, "Wait until I am gone, then execute him. Don't just slit his throat," Tirhin added as a slow smile returned to the sergeant's face. "Cut him into quarters and throw him outside to whatever hunts the darkness."

"A pleasure, Majesty."

"And, Sergeant?"

"Yes, Majesty?"

Tirhin's gaze returned to Caelan's. "Cut out his heart and send it to me. Then I shall know for certain that he is well and truly dead."

The sergeant saluted.

A chill swept through Caelan. His plan had failed him. If he died here like a dog tonight, Elandra would truly be alone. His promises to her now seemed like idle boasting, deflated wineskins swinging in the wind.

"Your highness—" he said.

But the prince started laughing. It was a low sound without amusement, a sound of madness, a sound of bitter enmity. He paused only to spit in Caelan's face, then resumed his laughter as he limped out.

Chapter Twenty-Six

TIRHIN'S BODYGUARDS FOLLOWED him out of the room, leaving only the five prison guards surrounding Caelan.

He knelt on the gritty floor with his fingers tight on the chain, considering his odds, forcing himself to be calm and wait for the moment, however slim. There was always a moment, a slight second of inattention or carelessness, when a guard might glance away or move fractionally too close. If no moment came, Caelan intended to create one.

The links of the chain were stout and well forged. The only weakness lay where the chain had been fastened through the ring bolt. Caelan eyed it, flexing his muscles to keep them loose, aware that his heart was racing.

The sergeant took off his helmet with a grunt of relief and massaged the red marks on his temple where the helmet rubbed it. "Koloth, go watch for when he's reached the upper levels. That'll be long enough to wait."

One of the guards saluted and left. Caelan bowed his head to hide his satisfaction. Only four men now. His odds were improving. He drew in several deep breaths, gathering his strength.

A bestial howl rose in the distance.

The men froze in silence for a moment, then unconsciously drew closer together, holding their daggers. Only the sergeant did not seem concerned.

Tucking his helmet under his arm, he spat on the floor and grinned derisively at his men. "Relax," he said. "It won't come this far."

"We're very deep in the ground," one of the guards said nervously. He looked younger than the rest, a stout lad not quite fully grown into his big hands and feet, awkward and gangly in his armor and weapons.

The oldest of the bunch, bearing a puckered scar across his face, rolled his eyes and chuckled. "Maybe the sergeant will let us go lookin' fer Haggai after duty," he suggested with a leer.

The boy blanched.

"Shut up, Mox," the sergeant said. "You know the orders."

"Aye, but I got me a taste for some—"

Breaking off, he gestured suggestively with his hands and laughed.

Watching them, Caelan realized Mox was a gladiator, or had been. No one he'd fought personally. Strictly second rank, but it explained his lack of military discipline and the sloppy look of him. But even if his armor needed polishing, he would fight mean and he would fight dirty.

As for the sergeant, he was clearly a legion veteran. His ugly face was sunburned and coarse, weathered from long years on the march, his eyes empty of anything except his orders. A little nub of skin and scar tissue was all that remained of one of his ears, and his left cheek was tattooed with the symbol of Faure, the ancient war god. He might command conscripted dregs such as old gladiators and green boys, but he was an imperial soldier, and as such he was one of the toughest, most fearless fighters ever trained.

Caelan made his calculations. Half closing his eyes, he drew *severance* to him, testing it, knowing that of late his ability to use it had been erratic. The gladiator and the sergeant must be the first to die. The boy would panic and might run. The remaining man looked tough and competent, but Caelan could take him.

"Who's to do 'im?" Mox asked, pulling out a dice cup and rattling it suggestively.

The boy grinned, then glanced at the sergeant and wiped his expression blank.

"Know 'im?" Mox said. "Called 'im Giant in the arena."

The sergeant glanced up from honing his dagger and shot Caelan an appreciative look. "Gladiator, eh? You're big enough."

Mox laughed. "Why, yer lookin' at the champion! Weren't no fighter able to beat 'im, never. Not a single defeat in all the time—"

"Shut up, Mox," Caelan said, furious at the man's chatter. Now they would be more on their guard. He shouldn't have waited this long to strike.

The sergeant sighed and leaned over to put his helmet on the floor. Taking off his cloak, he folded it neatly and efficiently into a square and laid it atop the helmet. He tested the edge of his dagger with his thumb and eyed Caelan.

"Arena bait, or not, he's finished tonight," the sergeant said. "Hold him."

"You were told to wait until the prince left the dungeons," Caelan said.

The sergeant sneered. "What the hell's the difference? Me and my men can't go off duty till you're done."

Mox rattled his dice box. "Can we cast lots fer the heart?"

Caelan glared at the gladiator, and *severed* without waiting for the sergeant's answer. To his relief, the swift icy rush of detachment engulfed him, and he went deep into the coldness.

With every sense heightened, he gathered his feet beneath him, ready to spring. He watched the guards approach him and saw their threads of life. The sergeant's were gnarled and tough, streaked black from dark deeds. The boy's were spindly. Mox and the fourth man moved behind Caelan, and there was no more time to calculate.

As the unnamed guard gripped Caelan from behind, and the sergeant reached for his hair, Caelan spun on his knees, *severing* as many threads of life as he could reach.

Screams filled the air, but Caelan had no time to count who was down and who was still standing. Sensing a blow from the corner of his eye, he ducked aside, hampered by his chain.

Roaring curses, the sergeant slashed at him with his long dagger, nicking Caelan's shoulder as he dodged again. It was a shallow cut that stung fiercely. But Caelan ignored it. He gripped the chain with both hands and heaved against it with all his strength. His muscles bulged. The linking pin of the chain sheared in half with a shrill *ping* and went sailing across the room.

Links of chain slid through the bolt, and Caelan went staggering off balance just as the sergeant tackled him.

They went sprawling together in a tangle of arms and legs.

Caelan blocked the dagger thrust with his elbow, feeling another slice of the point along his arm, and looped the chain around the sergeant's throat.

Choking and struggling, the sergeant tried to knee Caelan, but Caelan was already hauling himself to his feet, pulling the chain tighter and tighter while the man shuddered and flailed. The dagger fell to the floor. The sergeant's face began to turn scarlet, then purple. Veins bulged in his temple, and his tongue protruded from his open mouth.

Something sharp plunged deep into Caelan's back, catching him just below the rim of his ribs and slamming upward.

He dropped *severance* and staggered to one side, his strength gone, his breath gone, the world dancing in shades of black that flickered in and out of his vision.

The chain slid from his hands, and the sergeant dropped to his knees, making gasping, guttural noises.

Glancing over his shoulder, Caelan saw the hilt of a dagger projecting from his low back, and Mox's fingers whitening on it as he twisted the blade.

Screaming against the agony, Caelan turned and swung both his shackled hands together. His forearm slammed across Mox's face, knocking him back. It was a foolish blow, a good way to break his arm against the hard bones of Mox's skull, but Mox went sprawling awkwardly. He seemed paralyzed on one side, his left arm and leg not working right. But he came crawling back, his scarred face contorted, death in his eyes.

On Caelan's other side, the sergeant was still coughing and gasping, but he had pulled the chain away from his throat and was trying to regain his feet.

Caelan bent, still reeling from shock and pain, and picked the sergeant's dagger off the floor. The world tilted without warning, and Caelan staggered into the wall. The jolt brought a fresh wave of agony from his back that spread up through his chest. He struggled to reach the dagger, but his shackles prevented him. If he strained and twisted with all his might, he could just touch the hilt with his fingertips. But he could not grip it, could not pull it out.

A sound warned him. He turned, his reflexes blunted by pain, and the sergeant hit him across the chest with the heavy chain. The blow crushed the breath from him, breath he couldn't afford to lose.

He had black dots dancing in his vision. He couldn't draw in more air, couldn't move. The weapon wobbled in his slack fingers, and he was barely aware of the sergeant wrenching it away from him.

The dagger felt like a log inside his back, brutal and invasive.

"Damn you!" the sergeant said hoarsely, his voice ruined.

Gripping Caelan by his shirt front, the sergeant slammed him against the wall.

Brutal pain exploded inside Caelan as the blow rammed the dagger a little deeper. He tasted blood in his mouth, and knew he was finished. He met the sergeant's eyes just as the sergeant's weapon flashed up.

Glaring with hatred, the sergeant held his dagger up where Caelan could see it. "Get your eyes off mine!" he said. "You'll use no spells on me, you bastard."

Pinned against the wall, Caelan could barely focus on what he was saying. Caelan's whole consciousness had centered on the dagger hilt, jammed between his back and the wall. Every breath, every movement, every bit of pressure exerted by the sergeant brought fresh torment.

"Mox! Get up and help me, damn you!" the sergeant ordered. "Cut open his shirt."

"Watch 'im," Mox said, dragging himself upright with difficulty and staggering over to them. He took the sergeant's dagger and cut open Caelan's linen shirt.

"Going to cut out your heart," the sergeant said, coughing again. He sneered, pushing Caelan harder into the wall until Caelan felt himself suspended on that single pinnacle of pain, unable to move or even cry out.

"Hurry, Mox! Damn you, be quick!"

Snarling, Mox raised the dagger. "Slit 'is throat," he growled.

"No!" the sergeant said, intervening. "I want him alive while we cut out his heart. I want him to feel it pumping in another man's hands. I want him to know when we rip it out of him."

Caelan rolled his head to one side, gasping for breath, feeling the blood bubbling up where it didn't belong. All he knew was that he had failed. This time, his strength and his gifts hadn't been enough. It didn't seem fair that he should die like this down in the grubby depths of a dungeon room, stabbed in the back, chained like an animal, outnumbered. As a destiny, it was sordid and pathetic. And the prophecies he'd been told were lies.

He thought of Elandra, wondering if she would ever know his fate. He longed for her, wished he could tell her once more how much he loved her.

His only prayer was that she would be safe.

"Make it quick," he said to the sergeant.

The sergeant put his ugly face close to Caelan's. "Do you hurt now? Eh? Does that knife in your back make you want to beg and puke? Well, see how this feels." He grinned. "All right, Mox. Make it clean, and make it slow."

A furious pounding on the door awakened Elandra. Disoriented and groggy, she pulled herself upright on the bed while the *jinja* hissed and sniffed the air.

She looked at the small, golden creature. Its big, luminous eyes met hers. "Safe."

Iaris, who had been asleep in a chair, rose and walked over to the door. Her unpinned hair streamed down her back, making her look younger and more vulnerable. Holding a lamp in her hand, she spoke to whoever was knocking, then glanced at Elandra.

"It is the guard," she said. "He is to escort you to the emp— the prince."

Elandra's eyes widened. "Now?"

"Yes."

Elandra glanced involuntarily at the window, seeing her wan reflection shimmering in the darkness beyond the glass. "What is the hour?"

Iaris yawned. "It does not matter. Your presence is requested. You will go."

Defiance tightened the skin around Elandra's eyes, but before she could speak, Iaris was striding toward her.

"Don't be a fool!" she snapped. "You are his prisoner, as are we all. Thus far, he has treated you with the greatest courtesy, but that could change in one snap of his fingers." Drawing a gown from Elandra's journey chest, Iaris flung it at her. "Get dressed."

Within the hour, Elandra was beautifully gowned and her auburn hair was sleeked back in a heavy coil at the base of her neck. Her topaz hung in its pouch between her breasts, and she kept her hand on it for comfort as she walked through the corridors of Tirhin's villa with her head held high.

Guards were stationed throughout the house. They snapped to attention as she passed them. She glanced at their weathered faces, seeing experience and long years of service in every crease and scar. Crimson cloaks hung from their shoulders, proclaiming them as the elite Imperial Guard, but most of them had the rough look of common foot soldiers, as though they had been pulled from the ranks for Tirhin's service.

None of them met her eyes. Elandra kept her expression confident and assured, as though she was accustomed to being summoned by her sworn enemy in the middle of the night. But her heart was pounding in short, hard jerks. It was one thing to belittle Tirhin and defy him in public. It was another to face him alone, without protectors or allies. She felt as though she were marching to battle, and she went armed with nothing but her wits and a sleeve knife. If she still possessed any courage, it seemed to be in tatters at this moment.

"If you have no bravery, at least pretend to the enemy that you do," her father used to instruct his troops.

Elandra clung to that advice now, wishing her father were walking at her side. But this she must face alone.

She was escorted downstairs to the ground floor. The house was all shadows and golden pools of lamplight, filled with hushed quiet.

Her escort paused at a pair of carved doors and knocked quietly. The doors were opened a crack.

"The empress," her escort said.

The doors swung inward, and Elandra's guards stepped aside. In unison they saluted as she walked alone into the room beyond. Then the doors were closed behind her.

Elandra found herself in a study. The room was square and small, with a vaulted ceiling. Animal skins lay upon the polished marble floor. A heavy wooden desk had a map spread across its surface. A burning lamp cast soft light. Shelves filled with scroll cases flanked a tall window. Busts of learned philosophers were displayed on pedestals according to an old-fashioned notion that the likenesses of great thinkers could impart wisdom. The room smelled of leather and old parchment.

She drew a deep, steadying breath. This civilized room reassured her. Although she knew herself to be foolish in thinking so, she felt marginally safer here.

The individual who had admitted her now bowed. It was Agel, the healer.

Recognizing his thin, handsome face and cold eyes, Elandra lost her assurance. She stared at him, feeling suddenly afraid, and did not trust her voice enough to speak.

Agel gave her a perfunctory smile, as though he could read her thoughts. "Please wait here. Sit if you wish."

Elandra glared at him. "How kind of you to give me permission," she said regally.

He flushed, frowning, and left the room through another door behind a tapestry.

As soon as he was gone, Elandra paced over to the window. She stared out into the hostile darkness, sensing the evil that lay within it, feeling the evil here around her. Her fingers rubbed the cold glass, tracing the tiny bubbles and imperfections within its surface. With every passing moment, her agitation grew.

A sound behind her startled her. She whirled around, gasping for breath, her heart like thunder within her breast.

Tirhin came limping into the room, using a carved ebony cane for support. Unlike her, he was attired informally in a linen undertunic with a long robe of midnight blue silk belted around him. He moved slowly, with great difficulty, making no attempt to mask his pain.

"Elandra," he said, his voice soft and velvety despite an underlying note of strain. "Thank you for coming. I thought we might begin anew in private, where we have no need to act as our rank demands in public."

His face was as white as his undertunic, throwing his black brows and hair into dramatic contrast. His eyes caught the firelight and shimmered for a moment, paler in color than she remembered, almost yellow.

Despite herself, she shivered.

"Come," he said, reaching out his hand to her with a smile. "Let us sit and talk."

Elandra did not move. Her fear was unreasonable, for she could see no threat in his face or manner. Yet she remained afraid.

"Please," he said.

She heard fatigue and pain in his voice and realized he was waiting for her to sit down before he did the same. His knuckles were white where they gripped the top of the cane.

Compassion touched her then, and she took one of the chairs, sitting erect with her long skirts belled around her, her hands folded in her lap.

Tirhin dropped heavily into his with a grunt of relief and stretched out his bad leg before him.

This close, she could see how much he had changed. Deep lines had been carved around his mouth. A permanent crease between his brows marred his forehead. He looked older by years, and his eyes seemed haunted. Tension radiated from him.

She looked at him, and was glad he suffered. She hoped his guilt consumed him, for no punishment could be more appropriate. Had he sat before her sleek, contented, and fat with his ill-gained riches, she would have thrown her knife at his throat. But this pain-wracked shell of a man, this prince who had lost his youth, vitality, and laughing good looks was someone she could tolerate. Barely.

He met her eyes and gave her a tentative smile, then lifted his forefinger at Agel, who hovered discreetly in the background. "Some wine for the lady, healer. Oh, and bring the box."

In silence Agel brought a tray containing a flagon of amber-colored wine, two goblets of hammered gold, and a small wooden box with an ornate lid.

Elandra watched scornfully as the healer filled the goblets. "And when did this skilled healer become your servant?" she asked.

Agel did not glance up as he finished pouring the wine, but his nostrils flared.

Tirhin chuckled. "The slaves have all been sent to bed. Our conversation is private, not for idle ears. Thank you, Agel. That will suffice."

The healer bowed and left the room. Elandra breathed easier after he was gone. "I thought Lord Sien would be at your side."

"Sien died when Kostimon died," Tirhin said. "Agel has saved my life." He drank thirstily from his goblet, then handed the second goblet to her.

Elandra lifted her hand in refusal. "I am not thirsty."

"At least let us share a toast, Elandra."

She stared at him coldly and made no move to take the goblet, which he still extended to her. "We have nothing to celebrate."

"Not even a mending of a broken friendship?"

Elandra did not relent. "You are premature."

His smile faded, and a shadow crossed his eyes. He set down the goblet with enough force to slosh its contents. "Will you not meet me halfway?"

"Why should I?"

He struggled a moment with himself, as though to keep his patience and his temper. "This hostility from you is most unbecoming. It does nothing to show the people that we are united in—"

"We are not united," Elandra said sharply.

"Let me finish," he said. "I was going to say united in friendship. Why do you fear me? We are family. I mean you no harm."

"Do you not," she said softly beneath her breath.

He overheard and frowned. "I am not your enemy, whatever you may think."

"Then why am I your prisoner?"

Tirhin leaned back in his chair. "Leave if you wish. Go. I will not stop you."

"My chamber door was locked tonight."

"For your protection."

She sniffed. "I was brought to this room by an armed escort."

"For your protection. In Gault's name, Elandra, you have seen the city. You must surely realize the danger that surrounds us. These walls offer some protection, but not enough. Twice the guards have killed things which crept inside somehow, things you do not wish to meet."

"You brought them here."

Anger flashed in Tirhin's face. He slammed his fist down on the arm of his chair. "Kostimon brought them! Do not lay that blame on me!"

Her gaze dropped a moment; then she looked up again. "And what blame will you accept?"

His mouth tightened. "I let the Madruns sack the city. I regret that now, but at least they have finally been driven out. At the time it seemed my only chance of seizing the throne from the old devil."

"Couldn't you have waited?"

"For how long?" he retorted.

"A few weeks. A few days. Your father had little time left."

Tirhin snorted and drained the contents of his goblet. "Do you think he would not have found a way to thwart death again? I tell you, he was planning something—"

"How could he—"

"Why not?" Tirhin broke in. "He made his bargain before with the dark god to evade death."

"Yes, but that was over."

"Was it? I'm not so sure." Tirhin poured himself more wine with an unsteady hand, spilling some of it. "He and Sien were plotting some scheme with the darkness."

"But—"

"I tell you, he would have succeeded!" Tirhin said sharply. "You knew him only a short time, but even so, do you truly believe that he would not have tried again to keep his life and his throne, if there were any way to do it? No matter what the cost?"

Elandra sat in silence a moment, but finally she replied with honesty. "Yes, I believe he would have taken any chance offered to him."

"Yes." Tirhin shifted in his chair and grimaced.

Elandra rose to her feet. "You are unwell. The hour is very late. We can talk later—"

"We will talk now!" he said forcefully, glaring up at her. "This is our only chance for privacy. There is little time, and I will not be put off."

Pain gripped his face again, and he rubbed his leg fretfully.

Watching him, Elandra frowned. "You are exhausted, and

your wound pains you. Can this not wait until morning when you are more rested?"

He bared his teeth in a bitter version of a smile and shook his head. "There is never a moment when the wound does not pain me," he admitted. "I do not sleep at night. While the rest of the world lies quiet, I have nothing to do but fill the hours with activity."

Elandra stared at him in consternation. "You do not sleep at all?"

"No."

"But you must take rest."

"Oh, yes, I rest. But there is no sleep. Please, sit down."

She sank back into her chair, feeling more pity for him than she wanted to. "But how can you live if you do not sleep?"

He shrugged and ran the back of his hand across his forehead.

"Can the healer not cure you?"

His lips curved bitterly, and he would not meet her eyes. "Obviously not."

"I do not understand. For all his faults, Agel is a most skilled healer, trained in Trau's best school."

He stared into the bottom of his cup. "Some hurts are beyond all the skill and ability of this world."

Understanding came to her. Chilled, she shrank back in her chair and stared at him with new eyes. Memories of General Paz came to her, along with memories of her own poisoning.

"The darkness is within you," she whispered.

Still he would not meet her eyes.

She swallowed hard, not knowing what to say. She had escaped the trap, but could Tirhin? "Is it the poison?" she asked.

He shook his head.

"If we appealed to the Penestricans—"

"Those witches are not coming within a league of me," he said, and filled his goblet again.

"But if they could help you—"

"They will not," he said.

"Tirhin, it can be fought. It can be—"

"But I don't want to fight it," he said. He turned his pale yellow eyes on her, and she felt as though she had been physically shocked.

She opened her mouth, but no words came out.

"It is time to be frank, Elandra. I want no secrets between us," he said, leaning forward. "The throne will be mine, and once I have it, I shall not relinquish it. I have taken the darkness in exchange for the same life span as my father."

Horrified, Elandra stared at him. "Tirhin, no!"

"Yes. The wound will never heal. I can never sleep again, but I don't care. All is worth it."

"But your father did not—"

"No," he interrupted quietly. "Kostimon did not make the same bargain I have. Kostimon did not pay the same price. But you see, Kostimon had to pay when he died. I am paying now, in exchange for something far sweeter."

She frowned. "I don't understand."

"You don't have to. But I am nothing to fear, I assure you. I shan't turn into a monster when you least expect it. I am as I shall always be. Young and manly. In my prime."

Elandra blinked. Was he mad? Did he not see how thin and haggard he actually was? Was he unaware of how ill he looked? Did he still believe himself the strong, handsome young man he had been only a few months past? He was lying to her; most certainly he was lying to himself if he believed any of what he had just said.

"Now I have been open and honest with you," Tirhin said, putting his cup aside. "I have explained my reasons and shared my plans for the future with you."

"Future?" she said in astonishment, and gestured at the window. "What future do you expect? Darkness has swallowed Imperia. Soon it will engulf all the empire."

He nodded. "Things are changing, but we will rebuild the city. We—"

"Tirhin!" she said sharply, forgetting caution. "Are you mad? Do you not realize that we are ending? The demons will rule, not you."

"We will rule," he said, leaning forward to grasp her hand. She tried to pull free, but he held her fast.

"Listen to me," he said intently, gazing into her eyes. "I have nothing to fear, and once you are married to me you will have nothing to fear either. There are ways to survive, even in perpetual night."

"No," she whispered, trying again to pull free.

"You are a beautiful woman," he said. "Courageous, well-born, intelligent. The people love you. When my father chose you, he chose well. Together, we can mend what is broken in the empire. You are already crowned. Our alliance will be—"

"No!"

She jerked her hand from his and stood up, circling to stand behind her chair. She needed that physical barrier between them.

"Elandra, listen—"

"I will not hear you," she said in agitation. Dear Gault, she had even felt sorry for him. She had forgotten how charming the man could be, how persuasive.

"Elandra, it is imperative that we marry."

Her face grew hot. She glared at him defiantly. "Imperative for you, perhaps, but not for me."

"You cannot rule the empire alone. The people will not accept it."

"Then I shall not rule," she told him.

He laughed and levered himself painfully to his feet. "That is a lie. I can see ambition in your face, hear it in your voice. You were hoping to align yourself with Gialta and the imperial army, but as you have seen, neither of those factors belong to you. I made sure of that from the start."

"Then you do not need me."

"Our borders are weak. Our enemies think we can be taken while we are in this confusion. I don't have time to deal with internal problems and an unruly populace. The people accept you. Don't throw away your crown."

He stared at her a moment, then tilted his head to one side. "Am I so horrible, so repugnant, as a price to pay for your throne? After all, you were married to Kostimon in a political arrangement. This is no different."

"It is very different," she snapped.

Color darkened his cheeks, and his eyes narrowed. "In what way?" he asked.

The cold anger in his voice was a warning, but her own temper was flaring. "I was married to the *emperor*," she said. "You are only a usurper."

Her words were intended to hurt as much as possible. The widening of Tirhin's eyes told her she had succeeded.

Crimson surged into his face, then receded, leaving him paler than before. His eyes glittered with fury, and he lowered his head between his shoulders like a serpent about to strike.

"You fool," he said, his voice cutting. "You are not a peasant girl, able to pick from your offers. You are of the imperial house, and you have no choice. I tried to make this pleasant for you, but if you insist on being enemies, we can be, quite easily. The outcome does not change. We will marry in the morning."

She stepped back from the chair so fast she almost stumbled. Horror filled her, bringing with it a sweep of anger, defiance, and fear. "No."

"Yes," he said, limping slowly forward. "Protest all you want, but we will be wed."

Elandra lifted her chin, breathing hard, defiance giving her strength. "Not while I live," she said. "I will never enter your bed. Never!"

Amusement crossed his face, surprising and dismaying her. She had wanted to insult him, not make him laugh at her.

"Very spirited," he said appreciatively, in a way that made her blood run cold. "Very becoming. You must know that when you lose your temper, your beauty increases twofold."

Glaring at him, Elandra backed up again. "Get away from me."

He stopped, but the smile still lingered on his face. It was a cruel smile, one without mercy. "I remember when you first came to Imperia on one of your father's elephants. You were a shy, trembling maiden, hiding behind your veil, hardly daring to lift your eyes to anyone. And now you defy me like a warrior queen, proud and fearless, your eyes flashing like magnificent jewels. You have changed, Elandra."

"Yes, I have changed," she said, thinking of the past year in her life and its many hard lessons. "I had no choice."

"Oh, I think we can simplify this. You were a well-behaved, biddable maiden, incredibly modest while you were married to my father, very obedient and anxious to please."

Elandra glared at him, resenting his patronizing tone, hating the way he smirked as he said those things.

"But now you are stubborn and defiant. You refuse to be sensible. You are taking a dreadful risk by insulting me."

"I don't care."

"I know." He looked at her and nodded. "You are in love, are you not?"

Again heat flamed in her face. She bit her lip, knowing her expression had given her away.

"Yes," he said, and his eyes were like stones. "You are in love with that musclebound brute in my dungeons."

"It is no secret," Elandra said. She tossed her head. "Yes, I love him. I say it proudly and without shame."

"Oh, he is the type to catch a woman's eye," Tirhin said. "But you must learn to conduct your liaisons with more discretion."

"Caelan is not a liaison," she said furiously.

"But of course he is. I do not condemn you for your amusements, my dear, but the people are more old-fashioned than we. There will be other slaves, handsome ones, in a succession that never has to end, as long as you are sensible."

"Stop it!" she said, stamping her foot. She loathed what he was saying, what he was implying.

"Don't be a hypocrite, Elandra," Tirhin said, watching her with cat-cold eyes. "Your honesty has always been your most striking virtue."

"I am not playing some lascivious game with Caelan," she said. "I am wedded to him."

Tirhin blinked, looking stunned. For a moment he stood statue-still, staring at her, with all the ruin of his ambitions plain to see in his face. Then rage filled his eyes.

His cane whistled out without warning, and would have struck her if she had not dodged. It hit the chair instead with a vicious thud. Elandra retreated behind the desk, acutely conscious that he was between her and the door. Never taking her eyes off him, she reached for her sleeve knife.

But Tirhin stopped his advance. His eyes narrowed, and he studied her as though he had never seen her before. Calm seeped back into his face, and it became an unreadable mask.

"It is something easily said, this marriage you claim. Do you have proof?"

"Only my word," she replied.

He snorted. "Alas, that is insufficient. Who spoke the words of binding over you? The priest can be traced."

"There was no priest," she said. "We exchanged the vows for ourselves."

Tirhin threw back his head and laughed. "A common-consent marriage?" he asked, when at last he could speak again. He wiped his eyes and laughed again. "Gods, what need have I to hire entertainment when you are before me? Am I expected to believe this wide-eyed tale?"

Elandra glared at him, saying nothing.

Finally he grew quiet, and met her gaze. He frowned. "Tell me this is a jest."

"No."

"You have promised yourself without witnesses to a *slave?*"

"Caelan is not a slave. Kostimon freed him. He is wellborn."

Tirhin waved away these distinctions impatiently. "You know what I mean. He is not remotely of your rank."

She raised her eyebrows. "You have no right to advise me."

"Take care, Elandra," he said. "We are family."

She snorted. "Do I make you angry? I don't care," she shot back. "I love Caelan, and I have bound myself to him."

"I am prince of the realm, soon to be emperor," he said angrily. "I recognize no such marriage."

She lifted her chin, refusing to be cowed. "Whether you recognize it or not, the marriage exists. You cannot force me to the altar, and any truth-light will confirm my claim."

Tirhin looked furious, and she was satisfied. She had blocked him and his plans. Let him choke on his ire, if he wished.

"We seem to be at an impasse," she said coolly. "May I return to my chamber now?"

His eyes glittered, and he limped slowly to the desk to pour himself more wine. As he lifted the goblet, he tapped its base against the wooden box.

"Very well, Elandra," he said in a voice like velvet. "The contents of the box are for you. If you like, you may consider it a wedding gift."

She frowned in suspicion, unable to believe he would accept defeat this calmly. "What is it?"

With a smile, he placed his palm flat against the lid of the box. "Do not fear. Open it and see. You will find it an ornament above price."

Fearing a trick, fearing poison, she refused to touch it.

"Will you not open it?" he asked. "Shall I open it for you?"

Her frown deepened.

"Yes." He put down his goblet and picked up the box. Opening the hinged lid, he peered in at the contents and smiled to himself.

Watching him, Elandra thought that truly he was mad. What kind of terrible, bitter amusement twisted inside him?

"I will not wear your jewels," she said in warning. "Keep your gift."

"Oh, no," he said, turning the box around and holding it out to her. "I want you to see this. Look at it."

Still she would not.

"Damn you!" he shouted, his mask suddenly ripped away. Furiously he glared at her and dumped the contents of the box onto the desk. A fist-sized, bloody object rolled across the edge of the map and stopped beneath the glow of the lamp.

Elandra stared at it, not recognizing it at first. Then she caught its smell, a horrible smell of blood and raw meat. A memory flashed into her mind. Her father's hounds, being fed meat and scraps after a hunt, the dogs leaping and snapping at the chunks tossed to them by the butcher.

Feeling faint, she drew in her breath sharply.

"It's Caelan's heart, my dear," Tirhin said viciously. He picked it up and squeezed his fingers around it. Drops of blood landed on the map and spread into the parchment.

Elandra's stomach heaved. She swallowed hard as the room

spun around her. "No," she whispered, unable to take her eyes off Tirhin's bloody fist.

"Do you believe me incapable of ridding myself of any opponent, any rival?" Tirhin asked, smiling. "Nothing will stand between me and the throne. When my chancellors told me that unless you and I are wed, I cannot be immediately crowned, I set to work immediately to remove all obstacles."

Elandra started shaking. She was so cold, so terribly cold. Tears spilled from her eyes, and she sent him a beseeching look. "Tell me this is only a cruel joke," she pleaded. "He cannot be dead."

"He is. I hold the proof in my hand. You are a widow, Elandra."

She cried out, lifting her hands to her mouth, unable to deny her pain. "No. No, I will not believe it!"

Tirhin came around the desk, tossing away the heart, and gripped her wrist with his bloody hand. "Believe it," he said harshly. "He is dead. I gave the order myself."

She wept.

"You are mine," Tirhin said. "Now, go back to your chamber and prepare yourself for the ceremony. It is nearly dawn."

Elandra barely heard what he was saying. Grief welled up inside her, drowning her in its icy depths. "If he is dead, then I shall die too."

"As you wish," Tirhin said coldly. He pulled her close to him, and his eyes bored into hers. "As soon as we are wed, your usefulness to me is finished. You will be quite free to kill yourself then if you please."

He released her, shoving her back with enough force to make her stumble. She righted herself, mute and shivering, feeling as though she walked in a dream.

"Now you may wear his blood to bed," Tirhin said cruelly. "Sweet dreams, my dear."

He lifted his voice to call for the guards.

Elandra turned her back to him. The room was spinning worse than before. She felt as though pieces of her were floating apart from each other.

"Caelan," she murmured, and fainted.

Chapter Twenty-Seven

CAELAN CAME BACK to consciousness as the dagger was drawn from his back. He struggled up, fighting the hands that pressed him down, and was forced to lie on his stomach, sweating and battling the scream in his throat. A man's knee pushed against his back, bracing hard as the dagger withdrew slowly. It drew Caelan's life with it, and he heard the blade scrape against bone.

Shuddering, Caelan pressed his face against the floor, and endured the agony until fingers tapped his shoulder.

"Easy, there," said a gruff voice. "It's out."

The pain remained, throbbing and hot. Men spoke to each other in low voices over him. He felt himself being bandaged roughly but expertly.

"Sit him up where he can breathe."

Pulled upright, Caelan sagged against the man supporting him and felt something placed to his lips.

"Drink," he was told.

He parted his lips, still half swooning, unable to grab a thought for longer than a moment.

The liquid filled his mouth. He choked, and for a confused moment thought it was blood, drowning him.

"Damn! Tip his head back. Hold him before he spills the lot."

Then Caelan swallowed, and tasted wine. His panic faded, and he swallowed more, gulping it until he choked again, coughing. They let him go.

Bending over, he slumped against the arm supporting him and fought to breathe. But the wine had helped. His vision cleared, and so did his mind.

He tried to lift his head, trembling with the effort. Sweat

dripped off him, soaking his hair into strings, stinging his eyes. Squinting, he looked at his chest and found himself still whole.

A short distance away, the sergeant lay on the floor in a pool of blood, sightless eyes staring at Caelan. Mox's body sprawled across the sergeant's legs like a doll dropped and forgotten. Strangers with matted beards and ragged clothes stood around idly, talking to each other in low voices.

Caelan frowned at them, not understanding who they were, and looked up at the man holding him. Orlo, his bald head gleaming in the torchlight, met Caelan's eyes and smiled.

"So you're with us again," he said. "Harder to kill than a Madrun."

Caelan stared at him, soaking in the realization that he had been rescued. He remembered none of it. He must have lost consciousness before Mox started to cut him. Absently, he rubbed his chest, and Orlo frowned.

"That reminds me," he said. "Pob, cut out a heart and take it to the prince's villa."

A dark-haired man with keen, intelligent eyes came over and crouched beside Caelan and Orlo. "Now?"

"Yes, now! Why in blazes did I just give you an order?" Orlo said grouchily. "Do it."

Pob smiled lazily, taking no offense. "Sure," he said, and drew his dagger. In a fluid motion, he rose to his feet and kicked the corpse of the sergeant over on its back. "Someone help me get this breastplate unbuckled."

"See that you save the weapons and armor," Orlo told them. "Then clean out this room. We don't want to draw the demons this high into the catacombs."

Pob and his companions nodded and turned themselves to their grisly task.

"Don't worry," Orlo said quietly to Caelan, patting his shoulder. "Tirhin will be happy with his prize, and it will take him that much longer to discover you've survived."

Caelan wanted to speak, found the effort too hard, and twisted his lips into a wan smile of thanks.

Orlo's own gaze turned sober. "How bad is it?" he asked.

"Hurts."

Orlo grunted, peering at Caelan's back. "I'll wager it hurts like bloody hell. Can you breathe all right?"

"Don't know."

"You've been spitting a little blood. If you can't breathe right, it's likely you have blood in your lung."

"Hurts."

Orlo nodded and squeezed his shoulder gently. "All right. I figure it just reached your lung. Maybe tore it a little, but it's not a bad puncture. I tried to draw it straight out at the same angle it went in. Less damage that way, provided you don't bleed to death."

Caelan shut his eyes, feeling tired.

Orlo patted his cheek. "Stay with me, Giant. I'm going to put you on your feet. No, don't help me. I'll do the lifting. But it's time we got you out of here. The smell of blood will draw things you don't want to meet."

Caelan nodded, then grimaced as Orlo pulled him to his feet. A wave of clammy misery swept through him, and the room spun violently. Desperate not to faint again, Caelan struggled to find *severance*. Shakily he pulled it around him, closing off the pain, and slowly straightened.

Orlo watched him, looking a little awed, a little frightened, a little admiring. "You're a tough brute," he said. "Always were. Even if you haven't any sense."

Caelan looked over at Pob, who was wrapping a bloody object in a rag while his fellow ruffians watched. "Gladiators?"

"Aye," Orlo said proudly. "Trained every man of them. Did you really think you could take on five guards by yourself?"

Caelan grinned at him and nodded his thanks to the men. "Four," he said, still struggling to find enough breath to talk. "Just four, but thanks for coming in time."

A rumble passed through the room, and the walls shook ominously. Caelan glanced up in alarm. "Earthquake?"

"Aye. Men, clear out!"

Lifting Caelan's arm over his shoulders, Orlo guided Caelan out into the passageway. Another rumble came, longer than the first, and this tremor was stronger. Dust rained down on them. Someone called out a breathless prayer. Someone else cursed the world, the gods, and the shadows. Pob tucked the wrapped heart inside his jerkin and ran ahead of them out of sight.

"We're too far down," Orlo said, breathing hard. He pushed Caelan forward. "Too close to—"

An unearthly cry uttered by no mortal throat came rising from below them. Caelan looked back. In the torchlight, he could see another flight of steps leading down. He pulled free of Orlo's arm.

"What are you doing?" Orlo asked in alarm. "You can't go that way. There's Haggai and worse down there."

The shout rose again, uttering words this time that seemed almost understandable. Caelan listened, feeling his skin crawl. "I should know that voice," he said thoughtfully.

Orlo gripped his arm. "Are you mad? Don't listen to it. If hell spills its jaws tonight, I don't intend to be standing down here to meet what comes out."

More howls, louder than before, echoed through the passageways. A swarm of rats came boiling up the steps toward them. The men turned and ran. Orlo ran too, urging Caelan along with him.

"Run, you big fool!" he said hoarsely. "Forget how much you hurt, and let's get out of here!"

Fear coursed through Caelan in waves. He could smell a terrible dank, decayed stench like the fetid breath of a predator. A shrieking, skittering, squeaking noise came, swelling in volume as the rats caught up with them and fled on ahead of them, both angry and panicked, their red eyes glinting in the torchlight.

"We can't let it out," Caelan whispered, feeling himself choking up. He coughed blood, and his knees tried to buckle under him. "Have to stop it."

Orlo kept him moving. "Come on! This is no place to fight, you idiot. Mender, come back here and help me. If he swoons, I can't carry him by myself."

The gladiator turned back to shoulder Caelan's weight on the other side. Caught between Orlo and Mender, Caelan ran awkwardly, trying to hold *severance* and consciousness at the same time.

He looked back once to see four-footed beasts like wolves bounding at them. The creatures came closer, and they were not wolves at all but furred things with claws and heads like cobras.

Their yellow eyes glowed ferociously, and their jaws dripped death.

Caelan gasped out a warning.

Orlo glanced back and turned pale. "Holy goddess mother," he whispered, skidding to a halt. He shoved Caelan against the wall and met the charge of one of the beasts with a hard thrust of his sword. The creature screamed and fell, its deadly claws missing Orlo by mere inches. Shouting in panic, Mender stabbed at another one with his spear, but it seemed impervious to the wounds he dealt it. Orlo struck it from behind, severing its spine in one blow, and it fell dead at Caelan's feet.

Gasping for air, Orlo stared at it, then shuddered once and gathered Caelan to run again. Other creatures appeared, frenzied and wild, as though driven forth from the realm of shadow by something more terrible than all imagination. More than once the men had to stop and fight off attacks. A cross passageway teeming with demons cut them off. Orlo, Mender, and Caelan shrank back into the shadows, and the demons rushed on without noticing them, howling in their madness.

The earth quaked again, rending and cracking. Caelan thought at any moment everything would come crashing down on them, but the old passageway timbers held, groaning, long enough for them to duck through.

They ran until he couldn't breathe. They ran until his lungs were on fire, and every step jolted the pain back through *severance* like stitches from a long needle. Even with all his control he felt the agony more and more sharply. He was gasping and staggering by the time Orlo half dragged him up the last ramp into the cold air.

Demons and monsters streamed into the streets.

Then a sudden, very strange hush fell over the chaos. Caelan turned his head, sensing something stirring, awakening, coming, something unbearable in its horror.

He shuddered in Orlo's hold, knowing this was what he had been born to face, but knowing also he was not ready, not up for it. He had lost Exoner, now in Tirhin's hands, and without the spell-forged sword he might as well throw stones.

Without warning, weakness sagged through his knees. Orlo grunted with the struggle to hold him up.

"Quick," Orlo said, panting. "Let's get him to a hiding place. There's no safety out here."

They pushed Caelan behind a shaky wall and crept along cautiously, heading toward a collection of buildings on the other side of the city square.

"It's coming," Caelan whispered, swirling through a mist of darkness and raw, burning pain. *Severance* came and went, sustaining him for a blessed moment of relief only to fade again. "Coming."

"He's raving," Mender said worriedly.

"I know," Orlo replied. "Let's go to the tavern. We can hide there."

Caelan knew he must explain to them. They needed to understand that he was warning them, not babbling in delirium, but he couldn't gather the words. Stumbling over rubble and timbers, he lost his footing and fell, half dragging Orlo and Mender down with him. From a long distance he heard them pleading with him to climb back on his feet and keep going. Orlo sounded afraid, and that surprised Caelan. He didn't think Orlo knew what fear was.

But the earth was spinning beneath him. He reached up, but the black waters of Aithe, river of dead souls, swept him away.

He slept and dreamed and fought the creatures that tormented him in his feverish haze. Concealed in the underground cellar of a burned-out tavern, Caelan lay propped up on a crude pallet of straw and blankets. He dreamed of red-eyed demons and men who breathed smoke. He dreamed of the arena, hot in the merciless sun, the spectators screaming. He dreamed of Elandra. Her eyes were radiant, glowing only for him.

"I have a secret to tell you," she said.

He reached for her, only to have her turn to smoke in his fingers and vanish.

And there stood Kostimon, yellow-eyed and sly, cloaked in purple with a crown of gold on his head. Pointing at Caelan, he laughed scornfully. Beyond the emperor, a trio of Penestrican women robed in black lifted despairing hands to the sky, while they wailed cries of mourning. Darkness crawled across the earth like a vast serpent, swallowing the light, swallowing Caelan.

Lea's voice called his name. Holding up a lamp, she came searching and did not find him.

"I'm sorry," he said as she passed him by.

"I'm sorry," he said, unexpectedly finding himself kneeling to Moah, the leader of the Choven tribes.

"I'm sorry," he said.

And Exoner lay broken in the snow, while he dreamed and shivered and burned in fire.

The queer tolling of cracked bells awakened Elandra. She could hear them across the city, some near and some faint on the distant hills. One rang whole and pure, its beauty serving only to accentuate the dead, flat notes of the others.

She lay there in her bed, in the fine suite of apartments, and thought of another day when the bells of Imperia had rung for her. It seemed a lifetime ago.

She had been on her way to be married.

"No!"

Sitting bolt upright, she flung off the covers and swung her feet to the floor. Around her, servants were moving quietly, refilling the lamps with oil and lighting them. Pushing back her hair, she glanced at the window and could see the sun hanging halfway above the broken spires of the city, still veiled by the hazy gloom.

She remembered the horrible talk with Tirhin last night, and fresh grief rose inside her along with grim determination. She would not marry the man. No matter what he did, no matter what he plotted, he could not coerce her.

Iaris came toward her, veering around a maidservant carrying a tray of food. "It's about time you woke up," she said. "Your bath is being poured. I've been sewing since dawn, trying to alter the wedding gown your groom has provided. He says it belonged to his mother. It's charming, but very old-fashioned. Still, we do what we must. Hurry!"

Elandra ignored her as she would a buzzing fly.

Gripping her by the wrist, Iaris marched her into a small

bathing chamber warmed by a burning fire. Curls of steam rose off the surface of the water.

"This is the fate of women," Iaris said, stripping the sleeping robe off Elandra's back and pushing her into the deep marble tub. "The more you fight, the more miserable you will be. The result is still the same. Find obedience in your heart, and cease this struggle."

Elandra sat in the water, letting it lap around her shoulders. She could not cry now. She had cried all her tears for Caelan the night before. Now she felt hollow and empty inside, as empty as the city around her. She felt as though she had died, yet still was able to move about and talk. It seemed so strange.

"I am a ghost," she said, staring into the distance. "I am nothing."

Iaris slapped her hard. The blow rocked Elandra backward, and stung enough to get her attention.

Lifting her hand to her face, she turned her head and stared at her mother.

Iaris was glaring at her, looking both angry and afraid. She gripped the rim of the tub so hard her knuckles turned white. "Stop this!" she repeated sharply. "Our lives depend on you. Don't you understand? Your father, Pier, myself, the others. If you displease Tirhin, he will hurt us. Not you. Us."

Elandra's eyes widened. She looked at her mother, heard the truth in her mother's voice, and felt shame rise inside her.

"You are safe," Iaris said in a tight, hard voice. "But we are not. No one in Imperia is safe except you. He needs you, Elandra. The rest of us are expendable."

Elandra's lips were trembling. She felt cold despite the warmth of the water. "He is a monster," she said. "A madman. He killed Caelan."

"He will kill Albain next," Iaris said. "You know that. Stop being so selfish, girl, and think of someone besides yourself."

Bowing her head, Elandra began to cry.

"Stop it! Pull yourself together. Did you tell him about the child?"

Still weeping, Elandra shook her head.

"Thank Gault for that." Iaris sighed. "I am sorry about your lover," she said, making her voice more gentle. "He was not suit-able in birth or rank, but—"

"He was noble in his heart," Elandra said, aching for Caelan. She told herself she would never see him again, she would never hear his voice or feel his arms around her. It seemed unreal. How his eyes lit up when he smiled. His mouth had a funny way of quirking up at one corner when he teased her. Oh, her dear, gentle Caelan, a man who could be fierce, savage, and unbending. He was also a man with a heart as tender as a child's, a man who gave himself heart and soul to whatever and whomever he believed in.

She looked at her mother desperately, seeking solace that was not offered. "What makes one man better than another? Is it an ac-cident of birth, or is it what he proves himself to be?"

"I don't know," Iaris said. "But if he is dead, then he is dead. Your tears won't bring him back. And if Tirhin is mad, then you truly are the last hope Imperia has. Don't throw that away, Elandra."

Elandra wiped her face and nodded. She felt colder than ever inside, but her grimness had not lessened. Nor did her intentions waver. No matter what her mother said, or how much she pleaded, Elandra would not let herself be made Tirhin's wife.

She thought of the Magria's strange prophecy and how she had been given two destinies. If she locked herself in her chamber, refusing Tirhin, there would be civil war. She remained popular with the people, and they would support her. But Tirhin had killed the man she loved, and Elandra hated him for that. Her grief hard-ened inside her, becoming cold, implacable hatred. She would not sit in passive resistance. No, she meant to strike hard. She must avenge Caelan. The goal burned in her heart like fire. *Woman of fire,* the prophecy had called her. So be it.

When she was dressed and adorned with jewels and veiled, Elandra dismissed everyone.

"I am going to say my prayers," she said. "I will be alone."

Iaris looked at her suspiciously. "What are you up to now?"

"By tradition, a bride has the night before her wedding to fast, meditate, and purify herself. I have not had that privilege."

"They are waiting," Iaris said. "There is no time for this."

"I will have my prayers," Elandra said angrily. She glared at Iaris with all the stubbornness she possessed.

"What are you up to?"

"Nothing more than I have said. I shan't be long."

Iaris pointed across the room at the window, where the *jinja* sat pouting because it was not allowed to go. "Go stand in that corner, then, and say your prayers quickly. The gods will understand your haste. I will wait here by the door."

Anger flashed through Elandra. Through her teeth, she said, "You are a blasphemous woman. Get out."

Red surged up Iaris's throat into her cheeks. But she never flinched. "I do not trust you."

"I have given my word," Elandra said. "Take care. You are treading close to treason."

Alarm flickered in Iaris's eyes at that threat. She frowned as though she would protest further, but instead she said, "Very well. But for a few moments only. The escort is waiting."

Elandra waited until the door was closed; then she ran across the room to the window. "*Jinja,* give it to me."

The *jinja* sprang up at her command and jumped off the window sill. It had been sitting on her sheathed dagger, concealing it from the maids who had straightened the room.

Elandra strapped the thin sheath on her arm and pulled the sleeve of her dress down over it. A more sensible, safer course of action would be to go through the ceremony today and kill Tirhin tonight in the bridal chamber, but she had no interest in safety. She would give Tirhin a knife in the heart instead of her vows. It would be her vengeance for the man she had loved. She did not care what happened after that.

The *jinja* pressed close to her skirts, making a worried, mewing sound.

"Danger," it said. "Danger great. Hide is better."

She paused and stroked its small, golden head. "I know," she said sadly. "But I can't."

"I go," the *jinja* said. "Bad magic here."

"No."

The *jinja* hissed, but she gave it no chance to protest.

"You will stay here and hide yourself from what will happen. That's an order."

The *jinja* glared up at her, its pointed little teeth bared. "No orders give to *jinja*. Only love."

She bent over and kissed the top of its head. "You have served me well," she whispered.

"Danger," the *jinja* insisted. "Need *jinja*."

She sighed. "The laws of Imperia forbid you to go with me."

Growling, the *jinja* darted away and jumped back on the windowsill with its back to her.

She stared at it a moment, but she could not relent. In silence, she fastened her veil in place, grateful that it would conceal the defiance in her face, and went forth with murder in her heart.

Chapter Twenty-Eight

CAELAN HEARD THE whispered argument before he heard the bells ringing over the city.

Dragging open his eyes, he saw Orlo standing across the gloomy cellar next to a wall of wooden kegs, gesturing and arguing in a fierce undertone with someone Caelan could not see.

He struggled to lift his head. "Orlo?"

The trainer broke off and came hurrying to his side. "We woke you. I'm sorry."

Caelan frowned up at him in the feeble flicker of candlelight, seeing the anger still stamped on Orlo's features. He glanced back across the cellar, but could not see the individual who stood motionless in the shadows.

"Who?"

"Hush," Orlo said, wiping his brow with a wet cloth. "Save your strength."

Caelan could feel a strange energy in the room, a force tightly leashed yet powerful. It emanated from the person he could not see, and he was afraid. For a confused moment he was a boy again, bruised and battered after his attempt to run away from school and join the army.

"Elder Sobna?" he said defiantly. "I won't be punished!"

"Don't talk," Orlo said gruffly. "You can't afford to start coughing again."

The energy rippled around the room. It was something he had never encountered before, very ancient, yet no menace lay in it. His initial sense of alarm faded, and he sighed.

Orlo tried to give him water, but Caelan turned his head fretfully from the cup. He beckoned to the person in the shadows.

Orlo gripped his hand and forced it down to his side. "No. You don't know anything about it. Go back to sleep."

But a figure emerged, robed and hooded in black. "His invitation allows me to enter," a woman's voice said.

Orlo scowled, putting himself protectively between Caelan and the approaching stranger. "You aren't wanted here."

Ignoring him, the woman went to the other side of Caelan's pallet. Her face was smooth and unlined like a girl's, yet her dark eyes looked old and weary. When she knelt beside him with her hands resting calmly in her lap, he saw how age-gnarled they were.

He stared at her in astonishment. "Penestrican," he said, his voice a weak rasp.

She inclined her head gravely. "I have come to offer you a lesson."

Orlo snorted. "What nonsense is this, woman?"

She glared at him. "Until you learn respect, you will be silent!"

Orlo opened his mouth, but no words came out. His eyes widened in alarm, and he raised his hands to his throat.

Alarmed, Caelan tried to sit up and only managed to prop himself up on one elbow. The room spun around him, and he could not breathe. He fell back, dizzy and sweating. "Don't . . . hurt."

"I haven't hurt him," the Penestrican said grimly, still holding Orlo silent in her spell.

The trainer glared at her and reached for his knife.

"No," Caelan gasped out, trying to intervene.

"Command him to be still," the Penestrican said sternly. "Otherwise, I shall be forced to hurt him."

"Orlo, stop," Caelan said, and broke into a painful fit of coughing.

He felt himself bleeding, the bandage under his back sodden and warm. He seemed to be floating, buoyed up on the pain that was like fire in his chest and back. Then the woman's hand pressed against his forehead, and his mind cleared anew.

Much of the pain faded to a bearable level.

"Give him water now," she said.

Scowling ferociously at her, Orlo lifted Caelan as gently as he could and held the cup to his lips.

The water was tepid and tasted awful, but it soothed Caelan's throat. He swallowed more of it thirstily and felt refreshed by the time Orlo eased him down.

"Release him," Caelan whispered.

She compressed her lips tightly for a moment. "Very well. But he must learn respect."

"I vouch for his behavior," Caelan said.

The woman pointed her index finger at Orlo, who touched his throat and coughed. "What is this?" he demanded. "Who is she?"

Caelan frowned, tired of argument. "You waste . . . our time," he finally managed. "Respect her."

Defiance filled Orlo's craggy face, but before he could protest, the Penestrican glanced at him. "Serve Lord Caelan," she said. "Obey him."

"Lord Caelan?" Orlo repeated, his brows shooting up, then he frowned and gave Caelan a long, searching glance.

The Penestrican took Caelan's hand between her own. "I have come to offer you a lesson, if you will learn."

Her face was growing hazy, merging with the halo of candle-light. Caelan found himself floating again. His lids dropped half shut. "Cold," he murmured.

"He's losing blood again," Orlo said. "If you have come to cure him, then do—please do it."

"I have come to offer him wisdom," she replied.

"It's life he needs more than wisdom," Orlo argued.

She smiled. "Are the two not the same thing?" she asked gently. "Will you come with me, Lord Caelan?"

He watched her dreamily as though from far away. "Are you the Magria?" he asked.

"No. I am only a dream walker. Let us walk together."

"Walk?" Orlo interrupted with fresh alarm. "You come to a man who's half-dead and expect him to go for a stroll? He can't—"

"Hush," she said, her gaze not shifting from Caelan. "Our walk is well within his powers."

Caelan met her gaze, and felt himself float farther away, sinking slowly into a mist of sleep.

Immediately he dreamed, not the earlier feverish fragments of faces and emotions, but of something calm and soothing.

He found himself standing on a headland overlooking the sea. Sunlight glittered upon its endless gray-green expanse. A strong, salty wind blew Caelan's hair back from his face. The waves below surged and broke upon the rocks with a restless, potent beauty.

At his back grew a grove of trees, and a single boulder rested upon the grass. It might have been a favorite sit-down spot for a weary traveler, but an aura of serene power lay over the clearing. Caelan suspected the stone might be a natural altar of sorts.

The dream walker emerged from the trees, her stride graceful and ee, her long gray hair spilling unbound down her back in the way of a girl. She smiled as she came to him.

"Welcome to the place of the goddess mother," she said.

Caelan stood facing her, aware of the crashing sea, the swaying trees, the immovable stone. The power centered in this spot seemed to be growing stronger, as though forces were gathering here around him. He understood now why the power seemed so unfamiliar to him. It was the force of the natural earth, with all her mysteries woven through the cycles of birth, life, and death.

"What must I learn?" he asked humbly.

The Penestrican looked at him with open approval. "You are very respectful, for a man."

He sighed, knowing he must curb his inner impatience and sense of urgency. "That lesson, the Choven taught me. It was not easily learned."

She smiled and spread wide her hands. Her sleeves belled in the wind, and her hair streamed out behind her like a banner. "Look at the stone."

He obeyed her, and after a few moments he heard footsteps.

He glanced up and found himself facing a slim woman with long blonde hair and intense blue eyes. Power and wisdom shone in her face. Her features were beautiful, yet beauty was not the word to describe her. She was as stern as his father had ever been, perhaps more so. Her eyes were like the arch of sky over them, full of infinite mysteries.

"I am the Magria of the Penestrican orders," she said. "You are Caelan, the Light Bringer."

He bowed to her in silence, awed by the power radiating from her. Her youth and beauty were deceptive. This woman was both ancient and ageless. He had no words to describe her.

"There is little time," she said. "Your injury makes this meeting difficult."

He understood that she must be expending tremendous effort to create this beautiful spot where he might walk about in complete health. Were they really in his dreams or far away? The answer mattered less than the situation they confronted.

He did not ask questions.

Shrugging a little, he said, "The dream walker offered me a lesson. What must I learn?"

"You are quick, Lord Caelan."

"I am not a lord," he said, thinking of his humiliation among the Gialtans. He had learned he could not invent a rank for himself and expect other men to accept it.

Impatience crossed her face. "If the gods grant you a title, will you refuse it?"

His eyes widened in surprise. "The gods?"

She nodded.

He frowned and dropped his gaze, not sure what to think. "I believe such a reward should wait until it has been earned. I have not yet—"

"And will you tell the gods what they may or may not do?" she rebuked him with visible amusement.

His frown deepened. Embarrassed, he said nothing.

"You need our help," the Magria said, switching subjects swiftly. "The Choven unleashed you on the world, but they enjoy their secrets and mysteries. Now you are in trouble, and where are they? Off busy with forges and chisels, more concerned with creation itself than with what should be done afterward."

"I don't understand."

"No. Will you accept the help of the sisterhood?"

"Gladly. What—"

"Then pay heed. Tirhin is not the enemy you must defeat."

Caelan looked at her. "I know."

"Good. Then I need not explain."

"Will you tell me how to kill a god?"

Her eyes flashed. "Where is your faith?"

"I don't know," he said, refusing to be intimidated. "My faith has always been in my ability to fight. But this is not about physical strength, is it?"

She gestured, watching him closely. "Have you other questions?"

He sighed. "Exoner has been taken from me. It is a sword, forged by the Choven."

"You will need more than a sword to face the darkness," she said severely.

"But this is no ordinary—"

"So your faith lies in a metal blade and your own muscle," she said scornfully. "Little indeed with which to face a god."

Caelan's temper began to fray. They could circle, parrying words, forever and come to nothing. "Or perhaps the dark god hasn't broken free. Perhaps he isn't coming. Wouldn't he have come forth by now if he—"

"You have seen the darkness," she said sharply. "Do you doubt?"

"No," he said, seeing that slim hope sliced away.

"I say again to you that Tirhin is not your enemy. Remember my warning when you go back."

He frowned impatiently. "Why should I forget it?"

"Because Elandra is to marry Tirhin today."

Fury ignited in him with such heat and violence he felt as though he had been torched. At the thought of Tirhin daring to put his hands on Elandra, he wanted to break the prince in his hands, *sever* his threads of life, one by one, until Tirhin screamed for mercy.

"I warn you a third time," the Magria said. "Tirhin is not your enemy. Do you hear my words? Will you heed them?"

Caelan clenched his fists and with difficulty brought his rage under control. He could not fight unless he could think. And he could not think as long as his wrath consumed him. But by the gods, he would pick a hole in Tirhin's hide, and he would—

"Stop it!" the Magria said forcefully. Her blue eyes flashed at him, and it was almost like a physical blow. "Will you be a fool at the last hour?"

"She is mine," Caelan said.

"She is her own," the Magria said, and every word was sharp and punishing. "Elandra does what she must do, what she was meant to do. You must do the same."

He felt trapped and increasingly frantic. What kind of insane sacrifice was expected of him and Elandra? That they should be apart forever? That he should stand aside and let her pass into Tirhin's hands? That cowardly pig of a traitor was not worthy to lick Elandra's slippers, much less proclaim himself her husband.

The wind ceased to blow, and all grew still and hushed as though the world held its breath. Overhead, the sun went behind a cloud. Thunder rumbled out over the sea, like an omen.

"Will you submit?" the Magria asked him.

Caelan lifted his head. Despite his efforts, his heart still raged at the unfairness of this. "Let her be free from him," he said, pleading for her. "Whatever happens to me does not matter. But Elandra does not deserve—"

"She is an empress sovereign. She will meet her fate," the Magria said. "Will you meet yours?"

"You ask too much," Caelan said resentfully. "We didn't have to let ourselves be brought back to Imperia. We could have fled, made a life elsewhere."

"For how long?" the Magria said, unimpressed. "Does love prevail against guilt, against a sense of failure, against the suspicion that one has left an important task undone? Can love alone make two people happy when there is nothing else to hold them in place? Or will the initial infatuation fade and tarnish, until only bitterness remains?"

He frowned, and had no answer.

"Do you love Elandra?"

He did not hesitate. What he felt for Elandra was the most sure thing in his life. "Yes, I love her."

"Do you understand what love means?" the Magria asked him, her cold, severe voice very precise in the silence. "Do you understand that it is more than a union of bodies, that it is responsibility and kindness and sacrifice?"

"Yes."

She looked at him very hard, and he almost expected to have a truth-light thrown over him. But perhaps in this grove of the goddess mother, truth could be read in him through other ways.

"You have said what you believe," the Magria finally announced. "Your honesty was described to me, but I wished to examine you for myself."

Caelan shrugged. "You have tested me, but I am not sure I have passed."

"Not yet. I ask again if you love Elandra."

He knew what was coming. His heart seemed to shrink inside him until it was a cold, tight knot. Unable to trust his voice, he nodded to her.

"In the culture of the Traulanders, there is a saying . . . to walk one's path. You must walk your path, Lord Caelan. And the empress must walk hers. Will you let her go to the altar today, or will you interfere?"

"Has she no choice herself?" he asked in anguish. "Can she not determine whether she must accept that—"

"You question matters which are her concern, not yours."

"What concerns her, concerns me."

"Not at this time. I will not ask you again, Lord Caelan. What is your answer? Will you let her go to the altar, or will you stop her?"

Fuming, Caelan turned away from the Magria. He knew the answer she wanted, the answer she was trying to force from him. But was he some weakling who could stand by while his love went to another man? No, he would fight for her. He must fight for her. She was all that was worth having. She was . . .

He glanced up at the dark storm cloud obscuring the sky and thought of the unnatural darkness that concealed the sky of Imperia. He thought of how again and again in his life he had been hurled against the wall of obedience, of how he had fought and defied everyone until he met the Choven. He thought of when he had sought help for the ailing Lord Albain, and how he had been asked to surrender to a force beyond mystery.

He was being asked again, asked to put himself and his own needs and desires aside for a greater good. When he had thought he had only his own life to risk, it had not been a difficult decision. But to leave Elandra in Tirhin's possession was more than he could do. Jealousy rekindled in him like a flame. But the fire was not as hot as it had been a few moments before. He was thinking now of the empire, of how threatened and unstable it was. Elandra would be safe with Tirhin. No matter how much such an admission cost Caelan, he could not deny it.

The fire inside him snuffed out. He felt cold and drained inside. Grimly he turned back to the Magria and met her gaze.

It was like shoving aside a mountain to say the words, but he said them. "I will let her go to the altar."

The Magria's face reflected no triumph, no flicker of satisfaction. Her blue eyes bored into his as though she would weigh his very soul. "This is your promise, your vow?"

A muscle twitched in his clenched jaw. "My word has been given. I will keep it."

"Ah. The word of Caelan the Light Bringer," the Magria said. "It is sufficient. But you speak with no pride in your voice. You look on the battle to come with no joy in your heart."

His gaze met hers like steel crossing steel. "I stand here, a man in a place devoted to all that is feminine. The wisdom of the goddess mother you serve is foreign and strange to me. It is the source of all that is mysterious in a woman. But I answer you now as a man, with a man's wisdom. To enter combat with joy is to mock and cheapen death. You think because I spent years fighting in the arena for the entertainment of spectators that I view killing as a game. But it is not a game. Battle requires respect. To seek to kill is not a matter of pride. It should be a matter of necessity, nothing more and nothing less."

She bowed her head to him. "I stand rebuked."

He wanted only to flee, to find a place of privacy where he could mourn for Elandra. But that was only emotion talking. He shut it away, refusing to listen. This place of women was making him weak. He could not afford to look back at his choice, or to regret it. He must look ahead, or he might break his word after all.

"You may go," the Magria said.

"Are you to tell me nothing else?"

The Magria lifted her brows. "What else remains to be told?"

"How I am to kill the dark god," he said.

She smiled. "But I have answered you already."

"You said I was to have faith." He shook his head. "I have no sword, no knowledge, no armor capable of withstanding—"

"Walk your path, Lord Caelan," she interrupted coldly, looking disappointed with him. "Keep your word. That is practicing faith. You will know when the dark god comes."

"But—"

"This time has finished. You must go back." She beckoned to the dream walker, who came forward to stand beside Caelan. "May the goddess mother fill your heart with courage. May the god of war strengthen your arms. May the gods of light unite in you, that you may prevail."

She lifted her hands, and the wind blew in a gust that nearly knocked him off his feet. By the time he regained his balance and stood braced against its force, the Magria had vanished.

"Walk with me," said the gray-haired sister. She gave him a kindly smile and brushed her hand over his face.

He closed his eyes instinctively for a second, opening them to find himself back in the cellar in the gloom and candlelight. Orlo was sponging his face, and the dream walker was gone. He lay there on the straw pallet, and felt feverish and hot. Disappointment filled him. Had it been only a dream? Had they done nothing to take away his wounds?

His head jerked away from Orlo's touch.

"Easy," Orlo said to him. "I don't want you moving now that the bandage is changed."

"Where is the sister?" Caelan asked. His mouth felt furry and thick, as though he had been sleeping with it open. "Where did she go?"

"Hush yourself," Orlo said, trying to soothe him. "She left long ago while you were sleeping."

Caelan frowned, feeling betrayed. What were these games they played with him? "Didn't she heal me?"

Orlo sat back on his heels and scowled. "The bleeding has stopped. Your wound is closing. Now the witch is gone, and I have seen enough magic practiced to last me a lifetime. Why did you never tell me the truth?"

Caelan's frown deepened. Dream or reality? Had he talked with the Magria? Her words merged with the crash of the restless waves, the two blending into each other. It was a haze, unreal to him now.

The sound of pealing bells, so flat and discordant, distracted him. He heard the beating of drums, a throbbing sound that pulled at him. A crowd was cheering.

Puzzled, he looked up at the smoky beams of the ceiling. "What is that?"

"The assembly," Orlo said.

"What is the hour?" he asked wearily. "Dawn?"

"Why, no," Orlo replied, tossing his sponge in a wooden pail of water. "It's nearly noon. The square is filled with the pathetic few remnants of Tirhin's subjects, such as they are." He snorted. "The owner of this miserable hole and his whole family have ventured out to watch the ceremony. I'm not going."

Caelan rubbed his forehead restlessly. "Ceremony," he said in a dull voice.

"The proclamation has been sent out," Orlo said. "The wedding will be directly before the coronation—"

"Wedding!"

Memory flooded through Caelan. He flung off the tattered blanket and tried to sit up.

Orlo pushed him down. "Are you mad? What are you doing? You can't get up!"

"Why didn't you wake me sooner?" Caelan said furiously. "Damn you, let me up!"

Again he tried to sit up and managed to get himself propped on one elbow. Breathing hard, he ran his fingers over the bandage. He felt sore and stiff. Pain still ran deep through him, but it was no longer the mortal kind of agony that had incapacitated him. This he could manage.

Groaning, he pulled his feet under him and lifted his hand to Orlo. "Help me up."

"Caelan, you must lie down. You'll start bleeding again if you move. You can't afford to lose more. You're already as white as a bone."

"I'm fine. Help me up," Caelan said grimly, gritting his teeth.

"In Gault's name, you'll kill yourself!"

Caelan glared at Orlo, but the trainer had a strange, mutinous expression on his face. Too much time had already been wasted in arguing. Caelan rose unsteadily to his feet. His balance was shaky. He was so stiff he could barely move. He needed a massage and some drills to stretch his muscles, but there was no time. Elandra was out there, going to Tirhin like a prize captured in battle. Gritting his teeth, Caelan forced down his anger and panic, seeking a center of calm. He could not find it, could not achieve the *severance* he sought and so desperately needed.

Closing his eyes, he struggled to find his balance, to find the icy void. As always when he was worried or upset about Elandra, he could not do it.

But this time he had to. Without *severance* he could not even walk outside, much less help her.

Keep your word, Lord Caelan, said the voice of the Magria in his mind.

His eyes flew open, and he looked around. He had heard her so clearly, it was almost as though she stood in the room with him.

But she was not there.

Only her words echoed inside him. He remembered his promise. He remembered what was at stake.

Orlo gripped his shoulder. "Stop this, you fool!" he said angrily. "You can't go out there and show yourself. Soldiers are everywhere. Tirhin thinks you're dead. Leave it that way. You can sneak out of the city after the ceremony and—"

"No," Caelan said.

The cheering grew louder. He glanced at the ceiling again, feeling the pull. It occurred to him that if Tirhin thought he was dead, then so must Elandra.

Closing his eyes, he shut his emotions into a box. He had given his word to the Magria. And though it would destroy him to see Elandra go to another, he would stand in the crowd where she could not see him and witness the ceremony.

Calmness flowed over him, and he slipped into *severance,* detaching himself from pain and weakness, locking his box of emotions with chains of purpose and determination.

The stiffness in his body was forgotten. He swung his arms,

loosening them, and stretched carefully until he felt his wound
pull.

"The armor that was taken from the soldiers we killed last
night. Is any of it here?"

"You're not back in the arena," Orlo said, watching him with
a mixture of fear and exasperation. "That crowd is not cheering for
you, Giant. You're champion no longer. There is no combat."

"Get me a breastplate," Caelan said. "And a sword."

"None of the breastplates will fit you."

Caelan almost smiled. "I forgot. The sword then, and a dagger."

Orlo hesitated. "The army stands guard in the square to keep
order. They won't let you near Tirhin."

"Give me a sword."

Orlo unbuckled his own belt and handed it over, but when
Caelan reached for it, Orlo held it fast. "Why did you lie to me?"

"About what?"

"Groveling as a slave all that time, letting yourself be
whipped and degraded. Why? If you are a lord—"

Caelan stared at him, and remembered how the dream walker
had addressed him. He laughed bitterly and shook his head. "I am
no lord," he said. "For a few days I thought I might become one,
but—"

"The Penestricans don't lie," Orlo said suspiciously. "Whatever else they do, they don't lie. She said—"

"Forget what she said!" Caelan shouted. He wrested the
sword scabbard from Orlo's grasp and slapped the belt around his
bare waist. "I'm a fighter, nothing more."

"I don't believe that."

Caelan concentrated on the buckle. "Believe what you like."

"Tirhin will never fight you," Orlo said desperately. "Listen
to me, just this once. You'll never reach him before the soldiers cut
you down. This revenge is pointless."

Caelan ran his thumb inside the belt, frowning. The sword's
weight seemed wrong. He could not get it adjusted over his hip the
way he wanted. Orlo was completely mistaken about everything,
but Caelan did not intend to explain. That would take too long, and
he doubted Orlo would believe him.

"You're getting it wrong," Orlo said gruffly. He brushed Caelan's hands aside and rebuckled the belt for him. He took extra care to slide the leather belt below the bandage.

Bare-chested, Caelan gripped the hilt of the sword and half drew it, then let it slide into its scabbard. He felt cold and detached, yet awareness of the shifting stamp and noise of the crowd overhead ran constantly through his mind. A fanfare of trumpets made him jump, his heart suddenly racing.

"Why did I save you?" Orlo muttered angrily to himself. "Why did I fret and worry over your miserable hide? You're going to destroy yourself."

Not listening, Caelan picked up a cloak lying across a stool and started for the crude wooden steps leading out of the cellar.

"Caelan!" Orlo called after him.

Without stopping, Caelan glanced back.

Orlo threw him a gladiator's salute, his face twisted with grief. "Fight long and die well, Giant!"

Caelan smiled and raised his hand in farewell.

Chapter Twenty-Nine

OUTSIDE, THE MIDDAY sun hung high over the city, appearing as an orb veiled in gloom. It looked like twilight, the air murky and evil, infinitely depressing despite the torches burning like beacons. The square looked larger by day than it had last night. Much of the rubble had been removed from it, piled instead in tall heaps of stone and wood at the edges. The proud statue of Kostimon on a charger lay in broken pieces atop the rubble. On the east side of the square stood what was left of the arena, with its yawning entrance that led down into the dungeons. On the west side, the square opened into the Street of Triumph, a broad avenue that had once been used for civic parades. The center of the square had been cleared of spectators by the soldiers, who stood at attention in their ragged cloaks and unpolished armor, holding back the motley crowd that had assembled. More soldiers lined the avenue, their faces impassive, their hands on their weapons. People stood huddled in nervous groups, looking pinched with cold and hunger.

A wagon rolled along the street, and a pair of soldiers tossed loaves of bread into the crowd to elicit noise and cheers.

Picking his way over the rubble at the back of the crowd, Caelan wrapped his cloak close around him to conceal his sword and merged with the people. Being in *severance,* he could see their threads of life as well as follow the furtive movements of shadow creatures lurking in concealment. Despite the pervasive gloom, the demons did not quite venture forth openly at midday.

Caelan looked again at the sky, at the sun so cloaked and veiled, as though Beloth had put it in chains. Once again Caelan felt ashamed of his own selfishness and resentment. If he alone could stand as some kind of sentinel against the dark god's return, then who was he to shirk from such a task, or even to complain about it in his heart?

The trumpets sounded again, catching his attention. He saw the wedding party approaching on horseback. A tawdry little open-sided pavilion had been erected in the square, and a Vindicant priest waited there in his brown and saffron robes. Smoke from burning incense boiled into the air, adding to the murk. Beyond the pavilion stood a small contingent of Penestricans. Past them were more women, dark-skinned and exotic, in garments that shimmered with power. Caelan thought they might be Mahirans. The people of Gialta, Albain among them, stood guarded by soldiers. Albain looked old, pale, and grim, his shoulders slumped in defeat.

Tirhin rode into the square to the cheers of the people. Smiling and waving, he was richly attired in heavy velvet and a fur-trimmed cloak. The cuffs of his gauntlets sparkled with jewels. His eyes glowed with excitement.

Caelan stared at him, feeling the temptation to cut this man's threads of life. How black and snarled they were already. He could reach out like the hand of Mael herself, and snip them. Thus would the reign of Tirhin the Usurper end in a sudden, pathetic sprawl on the paving stones.

With a wrench, Caelan closed off the temptation, afraid of it, afraid of the darkness that rose inside himself. Instead he turned his gaze toward Elandra, while the man in front of him stepped on his toes, and someone to his left elbowed closer in an attempt to see her.

She rode a white horse with queenly grace, gowned in pale sky blue and adorned with jewels. Her veil had been pinned back to let the people see her face. They cheered for her lustily, waving and shouting her name, and she waved back with somber dignity.

Blue did not suit her. She looked pale and unwell. Shadows ringed her eyes, as though she had not slept. Caelan watched her ride past, ducking his head at the last moment so she could not see him. His heart twisted inside him, and it was all he could do not to push his way forward and pull her from the saddle into his arms.

This could not be allowed. She was his. He was hers. They belonged together. He wanted to yell her name. He wanted to draw his sword and smite everyone who stood against them. Most of all he wanted to wipe that evil smirk off Tirhin's face.

Tirhin is not your enemy, the Magria's voice whispered in his mind.

His heart burned, but Caelan held his *severance* and his oath. He must not lose his temper. He must wait, no matter what the cost. But the cost was so damned high.

The chancellors, not as fat and sleek as they used to be, not as many in number, ringed the pavilion as witnesses. A guard stood nearby, watching over a wooden box that must contain Tirhin's crown.

Waving once more to the crowd, Tirhin took Elandra's hand and led her into the pavilion. He barely limped at all, and Caelan could see the potions within his body, disguising the dark disease that riddled it. It was not the poison that had nearly claimed Elandra, but something different, something darker and far more foul.

Frowning, Caelan shifted his gaze to a still figure in the crowd, a man in white healer's robes. In *severance,* Caelan could see a thread stretching between Agel and Tirhin. Caelan realized that Tirhin was nothing more than a puppet for the forces of darkness, manipulated, and probably unaware of it. Moreover, Tirhin was dying. Caelan could see death within him, held at bay by Agel's potions.

Pity melted away the anger in Caelan's heart. Tirhin might be mad, might be twisted with ambition and selfish conceit, but he had once been someone decent, strong, and kind. He was not worthy of hatred for the mistakes he had made. He alone was not to blame for what had befallen Imperia.

The priest lifted his hands and began a droning chant over Tirhin and Elandra.

A low rumble came through the earth, growing in volume and intensity. The ground shook and cracked. The pavilion swayed dangerously. People cried out in fear, horses reared and shied, and some of the soldiers broke ranks. Toppled off his feet by the heaving ground, Caelan fought to keep himself from being stepped on. A youth fell on top of him, and Caelan rolled clear. Then the quake ended.

Stunned silence lay over the square. The bells had even stopped ringing.

He pushed his way clear, wincing and holding his side as he staggered to his feet. The air smelled of dust. Slowly people picked themselves up. Some were crying. Others prayed aloud. Sergeants bawled out orders, restoring the ranks of soldiers.

Elandra still stood inside the pavilion with Tirhin, but the prince was gripping the hilt of his sword and gesturing angrily as he spoke to the priest, who shook his head in answer. The chancellors picked themselves off the ground, slapping dust from their clothes. Fearfully, they looked at each other. One of them spoke to Tirhin, who argued with more vehemence than before.

The earthquake was a terrible omen for a wedding. People standing next to Caelan shook their heads at each other.

"We ought to go," a man said to his wife.

"And miss the food they've promised us for coming?" she retorted.

Tirhin emerged from the pavilion and lifted his hands to the crowd. "My people, be of good heart!" he called. His melodic baritone rang out over the square, quieting the uneasy crowd. "There is nothing to fear. The earth is at peace again, and all—"

A terrible screech interrupted him.

Two *shyrieas* came flying from the entrance to the dungeons. Their black wings beat the air. Their misty, half-seen faces bared fangs of death. Fleeing, stumbling, screaming, the crowd pushed and shoved in panic while the *shyrieas* sailed over the square, circling and shrieking.

"Close ranks!" bawled a sergeant, and the soldiers blocked the exit into the street.

Some people went scrambling over the piles of rubble, clawing their way out. Others milled and jostled where they were, calling on the gods for mercy.

Caelan pushed his way forward, trying to get through to Elandra. A boy careened into him, shoving him into the back of a soldier, who turned with a drawn dagger and a snarl.

Caelan struck the soldier's chin with the heel of his hand, snapping back the soldier's head and knocking him sprawling. Caelan tried to jump through the break in the line, but three other soldiers rushed him, thrusting him bodily back into the crowd. Caelan found himself pressed on all sides by people, hemmed in and shoved back and forth. Cursing to himself, he tried to get clear.

A dreadful, bellowing cry came from the dungeons. It rose over the general pandemonium, and people stopped shoving long enough to look at the entrance.

A figure appeared there, emerging from that yawning darkness to stand between the burning torches. "My people!" it bellowed again. "Welcome me, for I have risen!"

Uneasy silence fell across the crowd. The soldiers turned around and stared. One of the men dropped his dagger. Others reached for their amulets.

The soldiers nearest the dungeons shrank back, their eyes wide with fear. Then hesitantly one man slapped his fist against his shoulder in salute, followed by another, then another, then another. Suddenly half the army seemed to be shouting, their cries growing lusty and triumphant.

A ripple of sound passed through the crowd.

"Kostimon?"

"It's Kostimon!"

"The emperor lives!"

Disbelief and astonishment filled Caelan. Like so many others, he stared, forgetting everything but the apparition before them.

A smoky mist coiled out from the doorway, obscuring Kostimon's feet. He stood there, surveying them all. His face was the same as it had always been—ruthless and imperious. He wore his embossed breastplate, a cloak of rich purple hung from his shoulders, and a wreath of ivy leaves entwined through his white curls.

It seemed as though a miracle had appeared in their midst. The impossible had happened. Kostimon the Great had risen from the dead, to lead them once again.

More of the soldiers took up the cheer, many of them pounding their spear butts on the ground, or beating their swords against their shields, until the noise echoed off the ruins and swallowed up all other sound. Across the square, the Lord Commander sat upon his horse with a face like stone. He made no move, nor did the officers with him.

Caelan glanced across the sea of faces, seeing every expression from naked adoration to relief to astonishment to fear. Women were weeping into their shawls. Grown men stretched out their hands like suppliants.

"Kostimon!" they shouted. "Kostimon!"

The mist spread ahead of Kostimon, swirling around his sturdy legs and gliding among the kneeling soldiers. The *shyrieas* flew back to land on the carved lintel over the doorway. Folding their wings, the creatures glared at the transfixed crowd. More demons crept forth in Kostimon's wake, small and ratlike, looking like Legion. They peered out from behind Kostimon, blinking and hissing to each other.

And as though chains dropped from Caelan's mind, he looked at the emperor with deeper *severance* and saw that Kostimon's eyes were red, not yellow. The ivy crown upon his head was withered and black. Faint curls of smoke came from his nostrils with each breath.

Fear struck deep within Caelan. This was not the emperor. This was no man who stood before them. He saw no threads of life, but instead a terrible dark aura surrounding Kostimon's form, an aura that flashed and crawled with miniature streaks of lightning. At his side, Kostimon held a sword with a blade of black metal. Evil swirled across the blade in a constantly shifting pattern of death and destruction. Horror spread through Caelan, and he did not want to believe his own eyes.

"Kostimon!" he shouted with all his might.

The figure did not react. Kostimon's terrible eyes swept the crowd again, and a slow smile spread across his face. He lifted one hand to the crowd, and fresh cheering broke out.

Caelan could no longer doubt the truth. This creature might wear Kostimon's exterior form, but the emperor did not live behind those dreadful eyes. What had Kostimon done, in his last moments of life? Had he tried to bargain yet again with the shadow god? Had he given his body to Beloth, thinking he could yet achieve immortality? Instead, Kostimon had only provided Beloth with the final means of stepping into the world from the realm of shadow. The last chains had been broken, and Beloth stood free while these poor fools cheered.

"Beloth!" Caelan shouted, and this time the creature heard his voice among the others.

Turning his head, Beloth looked right at Caelan. His red eyes glowed, and the false smile faded from his face. Beloth started walking across the square, coming straight toward Caelan.

The people surrounding Caelan cried out. Some of them surged forward with outstretched hands. Others drew back, trying to flee.

"No!" Tirhin shouted. Unexpectedly he came rushing out from the pavilion. His face was contorted with rage. "You are dead, Kostimon!" he shouted at the thing that resembled his father. "You are dead! Foul thing, go back to the grave where you belong!"

Beloth's attention swung back to the prince, and he laughed. The sound boomed loudly enough to drown out the cheering, which faltered and died.

But when he spoke it was with Kostimon's familiar voice, sounding both amused and contemptuous. "My son, am I spoiling your day of triumph?"

"Damn you!" Limping now as he crossed the square, Tirhin struggled to draw his sword. But something seemed to be wrong with the scabbard, and he was unable to draw the weapon. "You are dead. You cannot live forever. You will *not* return. I forbid it."

"But I have returned."

"No! I'll see you driven back to hell where you belong!"

Kostimon/Beloth raised his black sword, but Tirhin still could not draw his sword.

Movement from the corner of his eye caught Caelan's attention. He saw Elandra emerging from the pavilion with a sleeve knife in her hand.

Alarm filled Caelan. He knocked people flying, clearing a path for himself, and shoved past the soldiers into the cleared space. "Elandra, stay back!" he called in warning. "It's not Kostimon."

Her eyes flashed to him, and she stopped in her tracks. She stared at him, her face disbelieving at first, then filling with fierce joy. "Caelan!" she cried out. "You're alive."

Tirhin whirled around so fast he almost lost his balance. He stared at Caelan with bulging eyes. "Impossible," he breathed.

"You're dead. My father is dead." Flinging his hands to the dark heavens, he shouted, "I deny this! Both of you, go back to your graves!"

Ignoring him, Elandra came running in Caelan's direction, her face aglow.

Beloth looked at her and shouted. His words were incomprehensible, but fire burst in the air and fell in a shower of sparks. People screamed and shoved backward. Even Tirhin cried out and cringed from the flying sparks.

"Agel!" he shouted. "Send the Vindicants over here. They must work a spell and stop this—"

Beloth strode past Tirhin, brushing him aside as though he did not exist. The god aimed straight for Elandra.

"Elandra!" he shouted. "Empress of mortals, bow to me in acclaim."

Caelan reached her first and stepped between her and the god. Elandra clutched Caelan's cloak, breathing hard, her eyes full of emotion. "Is it true?" she asked, drinking him in. "You live? You are not spirit?"

His hand closed over hers, and he brushed her lips swiftly with his. "I live," he said. "Tirhin lied to you."

Her eyes grew steely, and she glanced at Tirhin as though she meant to hurl her knife at his chest. But Beloth was almost upon them, and neither of them could afford to ignore him.

"Elandra!" he bellowed. "Bow to me now!"

Elandra's face turned white with fear. "The vision," she said fearfully. "It knows my name. I cannot resist—"

Caelan gripped her arm hard. "Don't bow to it. Don't bow!"

She twisted, arching back as though struck, and screamed. The knife dropped from her fingers.

"Leave her alone!" Tirhin shouted. He whirled and came running at Beloth's back, an upraised dagger in his hand, his useless sword swinging at his side.

Just as Tirhin reached him, Beloth turned and swung the black sword. It hit Tirhin at the base of his neck and cleaved him from shoulder to hip. Blood spurted in the air, and both halves of the prince crumpled to the ground.

People in the crowd screamed. On the other side of the

square, Albain roared terrible curses and drew his sword, as did the Gialtan warlords. The Lord Commander snapped out orders, but the soldiers were in disorder, breaking ranks, refusing to listen.

Beloth roared and blew flames in a circle around the square. Men and women turned into sudden blazing torches, spinning in their death agony as they screamed and fell.

Others tried to run for their lives. Many of the soldiers threw down their weapons and fled, knocking down men and thrusting women and children aside.

Twisting, Caelan grabbed Elandra and pulled her to the ground, rolling frantically as the flames roared over them. Regaining his feet, Caelan ripped off his cloak and ran straight at Beloth.

"Caelan, no!" Elandra screamed behind him.

He paid her no heed. There was one chance to strike Beloth from behind, while his back was turned and he was busy roasting people alive. Grimly Caelan raised his sword, sharing with the weapon, feeling the death poised in the steel, feeling the lingering touch of Orlo who had owned this blade since it was first forged. It was a worthy weapon, well made, well kept in its long years of service.

Caelan swung it with all his might, but at the last second Beloth whirled to face him and parried with the black sword. Steel clashed against steel, and Caelan's weapon shattered into a thousand pieces that came raining down.

Beloth bellowed a word, and Caelan was knocked sprawling by the force of it. He landed with bruising force across part of Tirhin's corpse and lay there, winded and stunned. Pain from his back broke through *severance,* and he felt his wound reopen. His courage faltered. The Penestricans had not healed him completely; perhaps they had not had sufficient time, or perhaps they had not understood the all-or-nothing roughness of combat.

"Mortal fool!" Beloth shouted at him, and raised the black sword to finish him.

Caelan had no time to think. He rolled over, trying to scramble to his feet, and saw the hilt jewel of Tirhin's sword flashing above the edge of the scabbard. It was a large, square-cut emerald.

Everything froze for the space of a heartbeat as Caelan recognized Exoner. Tirhin had taken it from him, yet Exoner had been forged for one hand alone. It would not let Tirhin draw it against darkness, and Tirhin had died.

Now, Caelan could hear the song of the sword, calling to him, and his own spirit sang in answer.

But Beloth was swinging at him. Caelan rolled directly under the path of the black sword, and heard it whistling down as he gripped Exoner's hilt.

Strength flowed into him like a jolt, and light seemed to flash around him as the sword slid from its scabbard.

Caelan had no time to parry, but Exoner seemed to turn in his hand of its own volition. Its shining blade met the black one, and lightning flashed around them.

The air popped and shimmered; then Beloth went staggering back and Caelan had time to gain his feet.

They faced each other in the square, no longer aware of the people or the confusion. Exoner was dancing in Caelan's hand, humming with energy, its blade radiant with white light.

Caelan thought of Moah's teaching on the glacier, thought of the lectures of his father, thought of the mastery of *severance* that had brought him to this point and that sustained him now. He thought of the waters closing over his head, and how he had learned surrender and trust.

The Magria had told him to have faith. Clinging to that, he surrendered now, releasing *severance* completely. The pain in his side engulfed him. But he flowed into *sevaisin,* merging fully with the spell-forged creation that was Exoner. The white light within the sword flowed up his arms and down the length of his body, until he shone with the light, was filled with the light, became the light.

Beloth frowned and lifted his arm to shield his eyes. "What spell do you summon, mortal?"

"I am Caelan M'an i Luciel," he said, and his voice boomed over the square with as much volume as Beloth's. "I am the Light Bringer. I have come to destroy you, Beloth, and the darkness you bring."

Eyes afire with fury, Beloth circled him. Flames belched from his nostrils, but Caelan used Exoner to deflect the fire back at Beloth. The god howled, and the air grew rank with the stench of singed flesh.

"Feel what it's like to wear a man's body," Caelan taunted him.

As he spoke, he sprang. White sword met black in a furious scrape and clang, back and forth too fast for the eye to follow. Caelan could feel Beloth's tremendous strength pressing against him as their hilt guards locked. Not daring to meet Beloth's eyes, Caelan gritted his teeth as intense heat singed him. He felt as though he were being roasted alive. Through the roaring in his ears he could hear Beloth saying words of power, terrible words that burned in Caelan's mind, but Caelan hung on, refusing to give way.

The light flowing through him drew on Beloth's power, imbuing Caelan with barely enough of his own to withstand the dark god.

Then Beloth broke apart, heaving for breath. As he backed away, it seemed that he drew strength out of Caelan. Staggering, Caelan dropped to one knee. His head was spinning. He wanted to retch.

Beloth laughed, and the sound was like fire in Caelan's head. "You don't know how to be a god, mortal! You fail to use what you have been given."

Flames burst from his fingertips, engulfing Caelan. His clothes were on fire. He could feel his flesh melting, burning on his bones. His hair was on fire. He screamed, and the fire was sucked into his lungs. Writhing, aware of nothing but the agony, Caelan screamed and struggled.

Deep in the recesses of his mind, he heard a voice calling to him, a voice like the crystal waters of the Cascade River—pure, clear, and cold. It was Lea's voice, calling to him.

Desperately he reached out to her. "Lea! Help me!"

"Don't fight it," she said. "Accept the flames."

"I'm dying. Lea!"

"Accept the fire. Accept the death. Take it into yourself. The more you fight, the more you will lose."

The flames were horrible. He could barely hear her. He didn't understand. He could see his own skin melted off his fingers now, could see his charred bones gripping the hilt of his sword.

Then the sword began to sing to him. It sang in the language of fire and cold metal. It sang in the language of ice and water. It sang in the language of trees and wind and the earth itself. It sang of purity and courage, of the strength of mountains and the strength of life. It sang of light, and as it sang Caelan ceased to fear and struggle.

He let the flames become a part of him, as the light was, as once he had absorbed the fire of the warding keys so long ago. He absorbed all that Beloth hurled against him, and felt himself grow stronger. Radiance shone from him, burning back the gloom and darkness that veiled the air. The mist upon the ground melted back from him. Light—dim and feeble at first—began to spread across the square, becoming brighter with every passing moment.

Beloth staggered back, and the flames ceased. The god no longer wore Kostimon's features. Instead his face was a blank visage, lacking any features except his glowing eyes. And they were growing dull and dim.

"You cannot defeat me!" he roared. "I am the destroyer!"

"Then destroy yourself," Caelan replied, and lifted his arms. He swung Exoner with all his might.

Beloth's sword met it, but this time the black sword shattered. Beloth went down, screaming hateful curses, and Caelan plunged Exoner deep.

There was a great explosion, and the sound of stone breaking. The earth cracked open, yawning wide in a gulf that spanned the square and sent people scrambling for safety. Beloth clawed at the edge of the chasm, clutching at Caelan's ankles as though to pull him over too. Caelan called upon everything he had left and drove the blade deeper, knocking Beloth over the edge.

As Beloth fell into the chasm, Caelan pulled Exoner free with a shout of triumph.

Not yet able to believe it, his blood still thrumming hard, Caelan glanced down at himself and saw that his skin was whole. Not even his clothes were charred. So this was victory, sweeter and more glorious than anything ever met in the arena.

He lifted the sword and started to turn around, but felt a terrible pain plunge through his chest. Buckling to his knees, he glanced down and saw a hand reaching up from the chasm. It was a woman's hand, black with soil and ashes, and it gripped the long shaft of a spinning distaff that had been thrust through him.

She twisted her weapon, this symbol of Fate, and Caelan arched back, crying out as the agony tore the breath from him. The woman came climbing out of the ground in triumph of her own.

She was emaciated to the point of being skin and bones. Her hair was tangled in a filthy mat, and she was crusted with dirt. Her eyes held only destruction.

Twisting the long distaff, she jerked it from Caelan, and he fell there at the edge of the chasm. Exoner was still clutched in his fingers, but he could not feel the weapon. Its song had been silenced. He felt light and strength flowing from his wound like blood.

The light that had begun to shine over the city dimmed now as she raised her bloody distaff. It was as though she sucked all the life from the very air. Everything she gazed upon withered and died. The ground she stood upon burned with flames. When she turned her head to look at the screaming people who tried to flee, many of them fell dead.

Caelan stared up at her, trying to find one last measure of strength, something in reserve not yet exhausted and driven from him. He knew her, and her very name was enough to freeze his bowels.

"Mael," he whispered, "bringer of destruction."

She laughed at him, and her gaze stole the breath from his lungs so that he gasped helplessly at her feet.

"Mortal, playing at godhood," she said. Her voice rasped out, hoarse and ugly. "Don't you know the ancient legends? Have you pathetic mortals forgotten everything? In defeating Beloth, you have set me free. How will you rid the world of pestilence and plague? I have only to blow my breath across you to flail the very skin from your bones."

As she spoke, she lifted the distaff over him, ready to plunge it through his heart. Caelan could feel his blood running beneath him, soaking into the ground. He couldn't move, much less meet her attack. Exoner lay under his hand, the blade no longer shining,

as though they were dying together. He gripped the hilt, straining
to lift the sword one last time.

In the distance he heard female voices lifted in a shrill chant.
"Chiara kula na," they said over and over. *"Chiara kula na!"*

A strange wind rose up, blowing across the square. The hem
of Mael's dirty rags fluttered against Caelan, and even their touch
was like a burning brand pressed into his skin.

He gritted his teeth and rolled onto his side, trying one last
time to raise himself and strike. One final blow could take her at
the knees and send her toppling back to whence she came. He
strained until his vision danced with black, and the sword scraped
across the ground.

With a laugh, Mael stamped her foot upon his neck, pinning
him. "Die, mortal," she said. "And so shall the land die with you!"

Elandra crouched next to the fallen ruins of the pavilion. She
was still dizzy from the lump on her head and stunned from the
spells and dreadful forces that had raged in the square as Caelan
and Beloth fought. Now Caelan lay pinned by the horrifying Mael
herself, and everywhere people were moaning and sinking down in
their tracks, dying already in the goddess's presence.

She saw Agel fall, and Iaris. She saw Pier go down, and her
father stagger. The Penestricans scattered like birds, separating to
stand next to certain individuals as though to shield them from
harm. The Magria came hurrying toward Elandra herself, but just
then Elandra heard a shrill, warbling, ferocious sound rise into
the air.

Goose bumps rose across her flesh. It was a war cry such as
she had never heard before. Who was making such a noise?
Women? But not the Penestricans.

Then the outcry stopped, and a chant low and fierce started up
in its place. Elandra frowned. She had heard those words before.
They were Mahiran words, spoken to her long ago.

Chiara kula na. Woman of fire.

She remembered the legend told to her. She remembered the
second destiny foretold to her by the Magria. Now, at long last, she
understood. Rising to her feet, she drew forth the embroidered
pouch that contained her topaz.

The Magria reached her, gripping her arm in an effort to pull her down. "Stay low," the Magria said to her. "I shall try to protect you."

A cry of agony wrenched from Caelan's throat. Elandra whirled and saw Mael plunging her distaff through him once again.

Mindless fury possessed Elandra, driving out all fear and caution. Shaking off the Magria's grasp, Elandra ran straight at the goddess of death.

"Mael!" she shouted. "Begone from us! We will not worship you! We will not fear you! We will not submit to the death you bring!"

The goddess paused in her torture of Caelan and lifted her deadly gaze to Elandra. Her lips skimmed back from stained, rotting teeth, and she shouted a curse that buffeted Elandra.

Staggering to a halt, Elandra felt her mind go numb. She nearly fell, but the jewel pouch in her fist was burning her palm even through the cloth. The pain of its heat restored her wits. Breathing raggedly, she dug the topaz from its pouch.

"Puny mortal!" Mael shouted. "You can't—"

Elandra hurled the topaz at her with all her strength. The jewel struck Mael in the chest. Explosive flames engulfed her. Screaming horribly, Mael writhed back. She drew the distaff from Caelan's body and swung it blindly through the air. The flames fed on her immortal flesh, so hot and intense that Elandra was forced back. Unable to breathe the hot, stinking air, Elandra lost her footing and dropped to her knees, shielding her face with her arms.

Mael's body burned to a skeleton, some of the bones shattering from the heat. She dropped the distaff into the chasm. With a final scream, the goddess toppled over and fell in also.

The earth shook and shifted, throwing Elandra flat. A terrible thunderous roar shook the world, toppling the few remaining walls and buildings into dust, finishing the last of the city.

Clinging to the ground that heaved and shifted beneath her, Elandra prayed for mercy. Terrified that Caelan might also fall into the chasm, she crawled in his direction and caught him by his sword belt just as he started to slide over.

A bald, burly man she did not know came running to her aid and helped her drag Caelan to safety just before the chasm closed.

Elandra clung to his arm, weeping, not sure whether he lived or died, while the world shook and thundered.

Demons came boiling out of hiding, driven forth by the destruction of their sanctuary. The gloomy veil over the sun dropped away, and sudden dazzling light splashed across the city. The demons and creatures of shadow screamed and thrashed, many of them hurling themselves across the square in an effort to reach the dungeons. But the doorway leading beneath the ground had collapsed, and the creatures were forced back, wailing as they died in the light.

Finally the quaking and thunder ceased, leaving only dust and bright sunshine that hurt Elandra's eyes. Squinting and slowly realizing that it was over, she dragged herself up to her knees and looked around.

There was a strange hush and calm now. The few survivors began to stir, their faces dazed as they rose and looked and found themselves miraculously alive.

But Caelan did not stir. He lay there, broken and bleeding upon the paving stones. His eyes were closed, and his face had no color at all.

The bald man, his face creased with grief, bowed low. "Caelan," he said hoarsely, "what have you done? We are saved."

Elandra gave a muffled cry and threw herself across Caelan's bloody chest, holding him tight, willing him not to die. Her tears flowed freely, giving vent to unbearable grief. Could Fate be this cruel, to give him back to her one last impossible time, only to take him at the very moment of victory? She wept harder, refusing to let him go.

Then she felt him draw a long, shuddering breath beneath her cheek. Half disbelieving, she sat up and stroked his dirty face, heedless of the tears that still streamed down her face.

"Stay with me," Elandra said, rocking back and forth in her grief. She gripped his slack hand in hers, trying to pour all her will and strength into him. "Please, please, stay with me now."

He breathed, but he did not open his eyes. Losing hope again, she bent low, sobbing anew for him.

Gentle hands touched her shoulders, trying to draw her away from him.

She found herself looking into the grave face of the Magria. The Magria's blue eyes were soft with compassion.

"Don't let him die!" Elandra pleaded fiercely. "Use your powers and save him. In the name of the gods, save him!"

But the Magria reached out and wiped the tears from Elandra's face with a pure white cloth, squeezing them into a small stone bowl. "And so shall she weep great tears," the Magria chanted, "healing the earth and giving it renewal. As the earth is furrowed, and new life planted within the womb of the goddess mother, so shall the rain of healing tears feed and nourish all life."

Anger burned across Elandra's breaking heart. She turned away from the Magria, furious that the Penestrican was concerned now only with her rituals and ceremonies. Would no one help Caelan? Were they all going to stand around and let him die?

"Elandra."

It was Caelan's voice that whispered to her, soft and almost inaudible.

She saw him looking at her. His eyes were no longer blue. Instead they had turned a pale silvery hue, the color of rain. Yet they held all the love of this brave man's heart for her, all his goodness, all the exhaustion to his very soul. He looked utterly spent, yet he was alive.

Elandra stared at his wounds and found them gone. Even the blood was dissolving where her tears had fallen in it. Gasping, she gripped his hand harder.

"Is it a miracle?" she asked.

He smiled at her.

The bald man gently pulled Caelan up to sit propped against him, holding him so that those who were beginning to gather around could see him.

"Orlo," Caelan said weakly. "My friend."

The bald man gripped Caelan's shoulders and wept awkwardly.

Elandra heard rustles around her, and as she glanced around she saw the onlookers kneeling, one by one, then in twos and threes, then all of them going down on their knees.

"Caelan, forever!" called a man.

More took up the shout. "Caelan! Caelan!"

A Gialtan voice that sounded suspiciously like Lord Albain's bellowed, "Elandra!"

More cheers rose up, and they all began to shout, "Caelan and Elandra! Caelan and Elandra!"

Strength was seeping back into Caelan's face. His smile widened as he met her eyes. He gripped her hand and drew her closer to him.

"Beloved," he said in a voice just for her.

She sighed, allowing herself at last to believe there could be happiness. "It is over," she said.

"No," he told her lovingly, as the cheers roared on and on and sunlight streamed down upon them, "it is just beginning."

Epilogue

AND IT CAME to pass that Caelan and Elandra gathered the survivors unto them like children, leading them forth to a hill above the sea. There, they established a new city of strong walls and shining towers, called New Imperia. Scarcely had the foundations been laid out than did the tribes of Choven come, more walking together than had ever been seen before. On their shoulders, they bore twin thrones—one carved from a single massive emerald and one carved from topaz. Singing in their strange, ancient language, the Choven came in a long processional to present these magnificent gifts to the new emperor and his empress.

Other gifts came with the thrones—gifts of stunning jewelry, armor, weapons, gold plates, goblets, and cutlery, mirrors that reflected the soul or told the future, warding keys, magical locks, and treasure in such abundance it took the breath away.

The Choven set to work building the city, working faster than mere men could dress and position stone. They designed a palace of stunning architecture, laid out streets, created parks that left nature undisturbed. No arena for gladiators was built within New Imperia. The empress established schools for all children. Guild halls were built to encourage the recovery of trade and economy. The city bureaucracy was reformed; even the imperial army was reorganized. Treaties with neighboring lands were examined and improved. The Madruns were hunted down ruthlessly until none remained within the empire.

To the Penestricans was given the task of tracking down the Vindicants and purging away the lovers of darkness within the priesthood. Maelites were condemned without trial. Word went forth across the empire that all temples built to the darkness would be pulled down. Cults and blasphemers were rooted out without mercy so that all lingering traces of shadow might be expunged.

Lea came to New Imperia as she had promised her brother, but she refused to live inside the city walls. Instead, a small stone chapel was built for her within the forest. People troubled in heart, mind, or soul went to her. Children brought her wounded animals for tending. She received all those in need with kind tenderness and compassion.

The provinces arose and sent forth their nobles and warlords, who examined the shunned ruins of Kostimon's destroyed city, who saw the rising grandeur of New Imperia, who heard the accountings, who met their new sovereigns and saw a man with eyes of silver and a woman with hair like fire, sitting on thrones more magnificent than imagination. The coronation ceremony was held. Every warlord knelt in fealty and gave his oath.

In the fullness of time, the Empress Elandra bore unto Caelan a son, sturdy and well formed, with red hair and blue eyes. They named him Jarel after a legendary warrior from antiquity. Elandra was to bear two more children, a boy and a girl, for her beloved husband.

Throughout his life, Caelan walked among men as a living legend. His defeat of Beloth was never forgotten. Tales of it echoed down through the ages, passed from father to son, and each year ceremonies reenacting the battle were held, to keep it clear in memory. Caelan the Light Bringer proved himself a worthy emperor who kept his promises, enforced justice, and stamped out corruption. When he rode at the head of his armies, no enemy of the empire would stand and fight.

Elandra, beloved empress, worked tirelessly to revise the laws of the land. Through her efforts, women were allowed to own property and to be educated. Her grace and fiery courage never deserted her, even until the end of her days.

Thus did the empire prosper within the realm of light.